FIREBOLT

Joe Buckley

WOLFHOUND PRESS

First published in 1998 by
Wolfhound Press Ltd
68 Mountjoy Square
Dublin 1, Ireland
Tel: (353-1) 874 0354
Fax: (353-1) 872 0207

The Arts Council
An Chomhairle Ealaíon

Wolfhound Press receives financial assistance from The Arts Council/An Chomhairle Ealaíon, Dublin, Ireland.

British Library Cataloguing in Publication Data
A catalogue record for this book is available from the British Library.

ISBN 0-86327-601-6

10 9 8 7 6 5 4 3 2 1

Cover illustration: Peter Haigh
Cover Design: Brenda Dermody
Maps: Peter Haigh
Typesetting: Wolfhound Press
Printed and bound in Great Britain by The Guernsey Press Co. Ltd, Guernsey, Channel Islands

For Dad,
who loved the water and the wild places

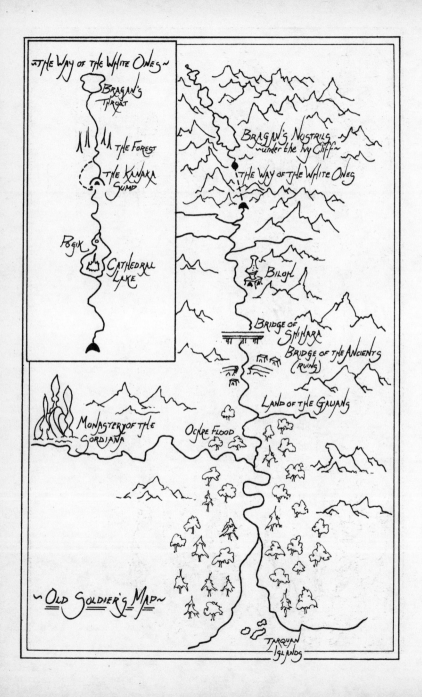

CHAPTER ONE

Branwald, son of Feowald the Protector, stepped lightly into his wattle-and-canvas canoe and pushed off from the pebbled shore. Black-haired and sallow-skinned, he was tall and well-muscled, though only sixteen. He settled himself comfortably on the stern seat of the open craft and dipped the single broad-bladed paddle into the rippling waters of Eagle Lake, the largest of the three lakes in the floor of the great bowl where the Island People lived.

When he had reached a point a hundred paces from shore, where the waves swept round the southern promontory of Redwood Island, he looked back. The low houses of Feyansdoon were sleepy in the early-morning sunlight. Branwald saw John the Scholar, his teacher, walking slowly away from him up Fisherway; on the tree-lined path above the houses, a group of workers was plodding to the Planting. Satisfied with his inspection, Branwald turned the prow of his canoe towards the Narrows at the northern end of the lake, and bent to his task. It was his Rest Day and, although he knew that some of the Elders disapproved of it, he was within his rights in going paddling on the lakes.

Branwald loved paddling above all other joys. He delighted in the fluid, frictionless glide of the canoe and the slicing thrust of the curved prow through the waves. He looked northwards, beyond the flat lakes ahead, towards the grey ramparts of the high Elvan Cliffs. The highest strata were yellow in the sunlight that was already streaming over the eastern peaks to his right. The wind was a cool breath from the south, with a promise of heat. The day was his to use.

When Branwald emerged from the Second Narrows into the northernmost lake, several hours later, the sun had already drawn a haze of moisture from the lake surface and the dewy

9

forest around. Unlike the large, oblong Eagle Lake and the meandering Woodfern Lake which Branwald had just left, Hazel Lake was almost circular. There was only one island on it, and it lay, ominous and threatening, in his path. It was a long, low, marshy piece of land, except for the sharp-faced hump at the eastern end, where the quarry was. It had once been called Hazel Island, Branwald knew, but the Elders had forbidden the people to use that name. Now it was simply the Island of the Banished, the forbidden place, where all those who had been found guilty of Deviation were sent.

Instinctively, Branwald turned the prow of his canoe to the left. Even to drift close to its reed-bound margins would be considered a serious fault in the Assembly; and, although he could not see any movement along the hazel-thronged shore, he knew that some of the Guardians would be watching.

Branwald did not falter in the rhythm of his paddling. To do that might betray curiosity or idle interest. But as he pushed towards the north-west, he stole occasional glances at the forbidden place. Above the tops of the hazels he could see the grey roof of a large building, too large for a dwelling-house. That would be the weaving-house, where the women and girls worked. Head bowed, he took another sideways glance at the face of the quarry, sharp and grey even in the shimmering air, but he couldn't discern any detail there, because of the movement of the canoe.

He turned away abruptly, as a wave of misery swept over him. No, he told himself, he would not let himself remember. He could not let that pain come back again.

He aimed for a deep gash in the wall of rock north of the lake, the first and lowest of the Elvan Cliffs; as he adjusted his stroke, he searched for the mouth of the Elvan along the brown reed-beds that formed a wall around the lake. A strange excitement was growing in him. He wished he was off the lake and out of sight of prying eyes.

CHAPTER TWO

For the last half-mile before it reached the lake, the wide River Elvan flowed between low forested banks. As Branwald forged upstream, however, and as the river narrowed, he found that the speed of the flow against him was increasing. He stroked long and smoothly, pushing outwards at the back of every stroke to counteract the swing of the prow. Ahead of him, the great cleft in the cliff out of which the river rushed crept closer and closer. This was the Karn Gorge, a cliff-lined corridor carved over centuries into the massive limestone by the Cataract itself.

Branwald had only once before come in sight of the entrance to the Karn Gorge. It had happened six years before. He and his father had been fishing on Hazel Lake in Feowald's big canoe. When the catch was safely stowed in the fish bags, Branwald found his father looking at him thoughtfully.

'We'll go as far as the Gorge,' Feowald said. Then, seeing his son's startled response, he added, 'Just so we can see the Cataract, that's all. Have no fear. We will not transgress.'

Branwald still remembered the flashing and glinting of the Cataract, several hundred yards into the spray-filled canyon. He recalled the distant muffled roar, and the rolling and dipping of the big canoe as his father fought to keep it steady in the swirling flood. Now, as his own light craft glided into the space between the confining walls and he saw the Cataract once again and felt the surge of the flood beneath him, his heart quailed momentarily. If only his father were there, with his quiet strength, it would be easier. But Branwald had not seen his father for two whole years.

The emptiness returned, making a void where his heart should have been. If only his father had not gone with that select band of men, over the high western ridge, to search for the mouth of the Great River! If only a message would come, even a message to say that he was dead, it would be easier. It was the silence, the not knowing, that tore at Branwald's heart whenever he remembered that quiet, kindly man. But as he faltered, and as the canoe began to drift backwards, he forced himself to believe that his father, Feowald the Protector, was alive and would come back; that even at that very moment he might be returning over the high pass, his mission complete, to see his wife and two children again.

Branwald's courage returned. He knew in his heart that his father would not have turned back at the mouth of the Gorge, on that autumn day years before, if it hadn't been for the frightened whimpering of his son seated alone in the prow of the canoe. When Branwald asked himself what his father would say if he were there, he knew the answer immediately.

Besides, somewhere in that part of him of which he was not wholly conscious, he had a sense that something was going to happen. Someone or something, he knew not what, lay beyond the Cataract, and it was calling to him. The image that had haunted his mind for days was there again, more defined than before: a low cavern, the silent swish of water in a dark cave, a deep grey-walled pit in the mountain, a mysterious presence that he could not picture .... The call was more insistent now, an urgent prompting that was hard to resist. Branwald grasped the paddle tighter, and pushed the canoe forward once more.

The Karn Cataract was a series of sloping rapids, dropping in four great steps until the frothing flood reached a level a little above that of Hazel Lake. When Branwald came within thirty yards of the seething lowest fall, he struggled to keep the canoe steady. All around him, great domes of frothing water boiled up from below, lifting and drifting the light craft across and back. His face, arms and clothes were covered with a fine wet spray, and the paddle felt slippery in his tight grip. Grimacing with effort, he studied the curved, thundering gush of the lowest cataract, and he knew that there was no way through for him. He would not be able to go on.

Just then, his eye fell on the layered limestone at the water's edge to his left. One band of rock, darker in colour than those above it, had resisted the higher floods of past ages more stoutly. It stood as a gradually sloping ledge that rose from the water's edge until it curved round a jutting outcrop and out of sight. A thinly worn track threaded its way through the grasses and mosses that grew there — a goat track. Maybe, Branwald thought, there is a way around the Cataract.

He allowed the canoe to drift to the left, till he was close to the looming cliff. He tried three times to run the prow up on the sloping ledge, but each time the force of the water shifted him away from it. On the fourth try, he dug deep and leaned back with the stroke, putting all his strength into the thrust. The nose of the canoe rasped on the rough limestone, and the pitch-painted canvas gripped. Branwald quickly stepped out onto the wet rock, dropped the paddle into the canoe and hauled the light craft up along the shelf until it was clear of the water. Then, on instinct, he looked back between the crowding walls of the Gorge, towards Hazel Lake, but he could not see clearly for the swirling mist.

He knew he should not go any further. Stern warnings from his mother only that morning, and from John the Scholar in the village school years before, came into his mind again.

'You must never take that canoe beyond the Cataract. Not even the grown-ups are allowed there,' his mother had said.

'But why, Mother? There's no danger,' he pleaded. 'I can manage the Cataract.'

Estel's eyes were severe. 'Branwald, you know that's not the reason. You know why no one's allowed there. How many times do I have to tell you?'

He sighed. 'All right. All right. I know. But the Forest People are never near there. And anyway —'

'You know that is not the only reason,' she persisted.

'Yes, but no one believes that old story any more. The Old Soldier hasn't been seen for years. He's probably dead, or if not, he's so old that he would hardly be able to walk. And as for the Firebolt —'

'Branwald, you know you must not speak of that!'

'But, Mother —'

She cut him off. 'The Elders have spoken. And as long as that is one of the Laws, you know there's no point in even discussing it.'

He had gone away from her, muttering, 'Well, then, the laws must be changed.'

Now, as he gazed at the path before him, his resolve hardened. There could be no harm in *looking* beyond the Cataract. And anyway, he convinced himself, there was no one around to see him and report him to the Assembly.

But another taboo reared its head in his mind, making him lift his eyes to the edges of the cliffs above. Ever since Branwald could remember, he had been warned never to set foot on the land around the Water Roads, the land of the Forest People. They were the inferior ones, uneducated and savage. What they would do to a young islander ...!

Yet in all his sixteen years, Branwald had never known the Forest People to harm an islander, apart from the time when Clem the Firemaker had persuaded the Elders to let him mount an ill-fated attack on the village of the Foresters on the Peninsula of Doodan. Clem had lost an eye in that débâcle, and had been lucky to escape with his life. Branwald had heard old Barmote joke that Clem and his small band of volunteers came back looking like porcupines, there were so many arrows sticking out of them. There were other islanders, however, who believed that when more land was needed to cater for the growing island population, they would have to make war on the Forest People in order to get it.

The cliff-tops were deserted. Branwald walked slowly upwards along the path, keeping his left hand in touch with the face of the cliff. Thirty feet below him, the first cataract rumbled and churned and spouted spray. Ahead, the ledge veered into a cleft in the cliff, which had been partially filled with a jumble of stones and smaller rocks. By careful climbing, he would be able to gain the top.

Warily, Branwald lifted his head out of the top of the cleft. Close at hand, the level limestone pavement was bare. Farther away it was covered by thin black soil, on which stood scattered pines between patches of yellowed grass. Still further away, the trees grew more densely, until the random corridors between their grey-brown trunks dwindled into dead ends. Branwald checked the cliff-top on the other side of the river. There were more trees, but the spaces between them were deserted. He stepped up onto the pavement and looked southwards, shading his eyes against the midday sun.

He had never before seen the lakes, or the forested mountains that encircled them, from such a height. Below him was Hazel Lake, hazy with heat; beyond that shimmered Woodfern Lake, long and narrow; and far off was the silver flatness of Eagle Lake, its two islands dark blobs against the reflected light. Branwald picked out the wide Rivelvan, winding away from the far end of Eagle Lake until he lost it in the deep haze and shadow of Bragan's Ramparts, where he knew the great sink-hole of Bragan's Throat lay. He had never seen it, but his father had told him about the cauldron that swallowed the waters of the great bowl back into the mountains; it was shrouded in a perpetual mist, which coated the leaves of the surrounding willows with a fine spray in summer and turned their smooth branches white with frost in the winter.

Looking northwards, Branwald saw that the next great cliff was over a mile away. His eyes dropped to the surface of the Elvan above the Cataract. He could not follow its course very far, however; the channel twisted and turned as it went away from him, and the encroaching pines formed a screen. He frowned. He could see no gap or chasm in the cliff, and no plunging waterfall. Branwald felt a tingle of excitement. Where did the river come from? Could there be a cave at the foot of the cliff?

His first impulse was to go forward on foot, but he decided against it. These were the lands of the Forest People, and the stories of their primitive savagery were too rooted in his memory to allow him to risk that. His canoe was light, though; he would portage it along the cliff-top until he was above the falls, then find a way down to the river and go as far as the next wall of cliff.

A short time later, Branwald was on the river again. This time he kept to the deep shadow of the right-hand wall,

15

where he would be less visible to a watcher. His paddling was more urgent now, yet the distant wall of rock seemed as far away as ever. The water below him was clear and honey-tinted, and it was good to see trout dart away from the canoe's squirming shadow on the sandy bottom.

At last he came to another slow curve and pushed round it. The sight that slid into view caused him to stop paddling. Low in the face of the cliff, not a hundred yards away, was a dark opening. A stab of excitement shot through Branwald, and he swung the canoe over so that he might see better. There was no doubt about it. The shadowy opening was a large cave, and the River Elvan flowed out of it.

Branwald hesitated. The cave mouth was very dark. He would not be able to go far into it; he had brought no candle or flint to light his way. Who could say what dangers lurked within? If he could approach the opening on foot, though ....

He scanned the rocky walls on either side of the river for a shelf where he might beach his canoe and step out. To his right he saw a narrow inlet enclosed by high walls. Further in, a small stream, tumbling from the cliff-top twenty feet above, had deposited a mound of rounded stones and gravel to make a small beach. Branwald swung the canoe into the shadowy grotto, pushed its nose onto the sandy pile, and stepped out. He bent down to touch the smooth grey stones of the beach, seeing the fine layering of the sediments and the patterns of the exposed fossils.

Suddenly he straightened. With a shock he became aware of another consciousness somewhere near. He glanced upwards, his body poised for flight, but the sharp edge of the cliff above him was clear.

And then, just below the top of the cliff, in a niche half hidden by the plunging stream, he saw the figure of a young man.

Branwald's first impulse was to leap into the canoe and push out into the river, but he resisted it. He felt such a strong sense of curiosity and amusement coming from the other boy that for a moment he was stunned. Surely it was not possible that one of the Forest People could speak to him without words, as his sister Eroona could!

He looked up at the other boy's face and saw no threat

there, only a half-amused expression. The youth, dressed in the typical green jerkin and tight leggings of the Forest People, stepped out of the shade of the sheeting water to the edge of the ledge. He pushed back the windblown brown hair from his face. His green eyes were bright.

'You are Branwald,' he said clearly.

Branwald stared at him, startled. 'How do you know this thing?' he asked.

The boy grinned at him. 'You do not remember me. I must have greatly changed.'

'How could I know you? I have never been ....' Branwald stopped, his eyes widening with realisation. 'You are not — you cannot be — Maloof?'

The other boy nodded. 'I am he,' he said.

'But you and your mother are on the Island of the Banished!'

'Not any more,' the boy replied. He searched for a foot-hold in the face of the cliff and lowered himself over the edge. In a moment, he dropped lightly onto the sand at Branwald's feet. Maloof was slightly shorter than Branwald's six feet, and lighter in the shoulders, but in his easy movements there was unmistakable strength.

Branwald stared at the other boy, unsure what to think or do. He had broken another Law of the Elders by speaking to one of the Banished. He was torn between the guilt of it and the bond — long weakened, but never completely severed — which he felt towards this boy who had been his childhood friend.

'You feel guilty about speaking with me. The Elders have you, too, under their control,' said Maloof. There was no reprimand in his voice, only sadness. 'But why have you come to this place, Branwald? Is it not still a forbidden place for all Islanders?'

'I ... I ....' stuttered Branwald, his feelings all awry. 'I cannot believe that it is you, Maloof. How ...?'

Maloof did not answer. His eyes searched Branwald's, as if he was unsure how to proceed. 'If I tell you how,' he said, 'will you not have to report this to the Assembly? And accuse yourself?'

'No,' Branwald exclaimed. 'I would never do so!'

'We escaped,' said Maloof. Branwald's eyes widened. 'It's true. We were there for several months after the decision of the Assembly. But my mother became ill. I could not stay and see her slowly dying in that place of toil. She had done no wrong. I had done no wrong. Yet they sent us there to labour in the foundry and the weaving house, just because she had followed the Law and confessed to the thought-speaking. It is a cruel, hard place. So' — he shrugged his shoulders — 'we escaped.'

'But how?'

'I made a raft, at night. And one day, when the Elders came to do the shriving rites, I waited until dark and poled us across to the forest shore. There we were found by the Forest People, and they have cared for us since that day. The Forest People are our people now.'

'And you *live* with them? You and your mother?'

Maloof nodded. 'Yes, Branwald. The Forest People are not as you have been taught. They are a gentle and kind people. And we have learned much from them.'

Branwald felt an old resentment growing within him again. 'I fear,' he said, 'that there are many things that I have been taught ....' He felt the need to explain something. 'I have often felt that someone should have done something, said something, when the Assembly gave their verdict. That even I should have spoken for you. But they told me that all the Elders were against you. And so I felt that what you had done must be wrong.'

'No, Branwald. There were some who spoke for us, but not enough. They were outvoted. And because they were afraid to speak of it outside the Assembly, there was nobody to contradict the version of the Elders.' Maloof paused. 'Branwald, has my father come home yet?'

Branwald shook his head. 'No, Maloof. They have not yet returned.'

'I knew it. When our fathers return, they will speak against this thing!' Maloof's voice was strong with emotion. 'They will change this!'

Branwald shifted the smooth stones of the beach with his

toe. 'They must come back soon,' he said.

The sun was sloping westwards, and Branwald remembered his mother waiting for him at home. Yet he did not want to simply turn and go. 'I know now that there is something wrong within my people, something which I cannot yet fully understand. Someday I hope to know what it is. For now, I am glad ....'

There was a silent exchange of thought and feeling.

'I am glad too, Branwald,' said Maloof. 'But you must tell me: what brings you to this place?'

The question forced Branwald to remember again the dark opening that lay upstream.

'It is difficult to explain,' he replied. 'I have been having a dream, about a certain place. And I think that it is here. There is something ....'

'In the deep cave? Calling you?'

'Yes. How did you know?'

'I, too, have heard — have felt something. But I cannot go in. I have no canoe.' Maloof glanced at the canoe by Branwald's side.

Branwald sensed the unspoken question. 'Will you come with me, in this canoe?'

'Could I?'

Branwald picked up the spare paddle which he always carried with him, and handed it to Maloof. 'Sit there,' he said, indicating the seat near the prow.

A little later the two boys guided the canoe out into the current, keeping the prow facing upstream. The cave, only twenty yards away, loomed over them.

'What do you think is here?' Branwald asked quietly, as if afraid of being overheard.

'Do you remember the story of the Old Soldier that John the Scholar used to tell us?'

'Yes. And the Firebolt?'

Maloof nodded. The mouth of the cave rose over them. 'The Forest People say that he still lives here, in the depths of the cave, and that he has the Firebolt with him.'

The shadow enveloped them. From somewhere ahead came the sound of water dripping from a height. Their eyes, accustomed to the light, saw only blackness.

'But how does he live?' Branwald asked, his voice almost a whisper, his paddle trailing.

Maloof turned to look over his shoulder. 'They say he eats the fishes, and that, at night, he has a way of coming up to the forest for nuts and other things. Others say that he needs no food. That he is not really human.'

'Has anyone ever seen him — any of the Forest People?' The canoe was almost at a standstill, drifting slowly among shadowy pillars.

'No. No one I have spoken to. But there are some who say that, on really dark nights, they have seen a light at the bottom of the old Kadach Pit; and that if you could climb down into that great hole, you would find this river at the bottom.'

Branwald was silent. He caught Maloof's feeling of reverence and dread. They stared into the black depths before them. The only sound was the dripping of water and the whispering swirl of the current round the columns and along the smooth flood-carved walls.

'We must go back,' whispered Branwald at last. 'I will come again soon, and bring a light.'

Maloof nodded. 'When you come, I will go with you.'

~

Back at the beach, the two boys stepped out of the canoe. Maloof regarded Branwald with serious eyes. 'You must be strong, when you go back to the islands,' he said quietly. 'Do not let a feeling of guilt make you go before the Assembly. You must do this for your mother's sake most of all. She does not deserve to be sent to that place.'

'I will do as you say,' Branwald replied. He dug his toes into the wet sand underfoot, struggling to find the words. 'When you and your mother went away, I — I felt .... It was like a death. It was as if you had died, and I would never see you again.' He glanced up at the other boy. Maloof's eyes had softened, and Branwald could see the pain in them. 'But I had friends to help me take the pain away. You had nobody.'

'Yes,' replied Maloof. 'At first it was like a death. But the people' — he smiled grimly — 'the Banished on the island, they have their pain too. They know what it is like. They helped us. And there are many of them who believe that it will not always be this way. So, as time went on, I thought that the day would come when we would meet again.' He shrugged his shoulders and smiled. 'And now it has come.'

There was a long moment of shared feeling. Then Maloof held up his hand in the old secret sign that they had used so often before. Branwald held up his hand too, and, as if they had never stopped, they went through the ritual: fingers clasped, then thumbs, then wrists, then fingertips hooked around fingertips, then hands upright, palms facing front, two fingers extended vertically. Then, awkwardly, they embraced — a strong grip, with strong arms. The distance of years was shrunk to almost nothing.

'What would you say to a swim before you go?' Maloof's eyes twinkled.

'I would say yes.'

In a flurry, they pulled off their clothes. There was a moment of embarrassment as they appraised each other's naked body.

'Race you to the far side,' said Maloof. They plunged into the water. The cold shock was momentary. Branwald surfaced and swam with easy overarm strokes out into the current, facing into the swirl so as not to be swept downstream. Maloof was on his right, his arms lifting and dipping. They were neck and neck halfway across the river. When Branwald touched the smooth rock on the other side, he turned his head to see that Maloof had touched too.

'Ha!' laughed Branwald. 'You still swim well.'

'At least I can keep up with you,' Maloof replied.

Branwald floated out into the stream again, confident and at home in the familiar element, as all the islanders were. He rolled onto his back, luxuriating in the sensual freedom of his body. The sky above him, broad and cloudless and pale blue, lay like a clear veil on the world. The meeting with Maloof had freed something inside Branwald that had been caged for a long time. He felt that the rigid doctrines of the Elders had no hold on him here. They could never hold him in their fearsome grip again.

And then, unaccountably, he thought of his father. A pang gripped his throat, and he turned face-down again. He dived down, down into the amber depths, seeing scuttling crayfish bury themselves in clouds of silt, surfacing only when the mottled gravel swam close to his face.

He rose, dripping, and danced a moment on the sand to shake off the clinging droplets. Maloof emerged in a cascade of water and swept back the long locks that clung to his face. In silence they dabbed themselves dry with their tunics and began to dress.

'Branwald,' said Maloof, 'be careful when you return to Feyansdoon.'

Branwald nodded. 'I will be careful.' He stepped back into the canoe and seated himself. 'I will come again on my next Rest Day. That is four days from now. Will you be here?'

'Yes. I come here often.' Maloof flung his hand back towards the top of the cliff. 'I am supposed to be guarding the goats,' he said, smiling. 'But the goats ... they look after themselves. I will watch for you.' He nodded towards the top of the cliff above him. 'From up there, I can see you coming from afar.'

'Look for me before noon,' Branwald called, as he pushed off.

CHAPTER THREE

Branwald had not travelled far along the river towards the Karn Gorge when he became uneasy. The sense of freedom which he had experienced while swimming with Maloof began to weaken, and in its place a feeling of guilt grew. He could not remember ever before breaking two of the Sacred Precepts on the same day. He had done wrong, he knew, and the thought that he might have to cleanse himself before the Assembly filled him with fear.

Yet what was so wicked about the Banished that one must never speak to them? Branwald could not bring himself to believe that Maloof was evil. And how could it be so wrong to go above the Cataract? Unless ... unless the cave was wrong, he thought; unless the potent force that was calling him into it was an evil one. If so, then he and Maloof, by responding to that call, were evil too. Branwald prayed to the Dread Spirit that he knew was watching him forever. 'Dread Spirit,' he intoned, in the Ritual manner, 'make me Your true follower. Bend me to Your Way.' Immersed in these sombre thoughts, he paddled towards the Karn Cataract.

Before Branwald even saw the swirling cloud of mist that drifted upwards from the churning waters, the speed of the river's flow told him he was near the Cataract. Then, above the suck and dip of his wide-bladed paddle, he heard a low rumbling ahead of him. He sat straighter on the narrow seat, and lifted his head to look for the first sign of a drop in the surface level of the Elvan. In the cliff to his right he saw the stepped place by which he had descended to the river. Yet he didn't pull over. He would go a little further and see. The danger filled him with apprehension and excitement.

The rumbling had become a roar. He stopped paddling. The water was carrying him along at a surprising speed, and

23

he knew that it was time to turn. He dug the paddle into the flow and back-paddled strongly, gritting his teeth. The craft came slowly round to face upstream. But the roaring behind him was growing closer.

Fear gave Branwald a desperate surge of strength. The veins on his forearms stood out like the snaky roots of an oak. He veered slightly towards the left wall of the Gorge, where the water would be slower. He was tiring. He grunted with the effort and veered out to avoid an overhanging bush. Twenty yards upstream he saw the sloping place where he had descended before.

He stroked powerfully, felt the canoe moving more easily through the water, and knew that he had won. Moments later, he jammed the blade of his paddle into a crack in the rock, steadied himself and stepped out. He was safe.

~

The sun was sloping towards the western rim of the valley when Branwald finally emerged onto Hazel Lake. Since he had left the high walls of the Gorge behind, some time before, he had kept his canoe in the centre of the river. Despite what Maloof had told him, the teaching of years still had a hold on him. He remembered Fetor the Boatwright saying at the last Assembly that the Forest People were becoming bolder, and were being seen on the lake shores more often. 'Next thing,' Fetor had said in that booming voice of his, 'we will see them poling rafts out to see if they can catch our fish on our waters.' The burst of laughter which had greeted this remark had puzzled Branwald. It was, however, only one of the many aspects of adult behaviour that he could not comprehend, so he did not dwell on it.

Branwald emerged from the twisting channel of the First Narrows onto Eagle Lake and headed for Redwood, the second and larger of the two islands, where his home village, Feyansdoon, lay. He knew his mother would be looking for him. Even though it was his Rest Day, he had been too long away, and he feared her incisive questioning.

He gathered his story in readiness for the approaching meeting. He had gone to the Cataract, he would say. Better to endure some measure of disapproval than to make her suspicious. He knew she would not ask him if he had gone above it, because for him to have done that would, in Estel's mind, have been unthinkable. He had been talking with Bern the Flymaker, on Woodfern Island, he would say. (It was true that he had called to Bern as he passed close to Woodfern, only a short time before, and Bern had called back in his raspy voice, 'Thou'lt be the best paddler of them all yet, my young Branwald.')

He hated having to deceive her. His father, before he had left, had made Branwald look him in the eye and promise that he would always be a Guardian of the Truth. But he dared not tell her the truth. His fear of the Assembly was too great. It had power over his mother, as it had power over all the mothers who had had to confess to their own and their children's Sins in the past. He had to protect her from that, and so he would lie.

The long stone jetty was in shadow when Branwald nosed his canoe in amongst the crowded craft drawn up on the silver beach. He strode up the gently sloping Fisherway, past the houses that stood at awkward angles along both sides, and turned into Watcher's Path. The house was set back near the pine trees, at the end of the stony path. The solid walls, made of limestone slabs stacked tightly together, made it look almost part of the landscape; the shingles on the roof were so grey and weathered that they merged with the rough bark of the pines behind.

In Branwald's memory, this house had always been here. It was permanent, like the rocks and the trees. It had once stood for everything in his life that was happy and secure, for love and closeness and comfort. It still meant those things to him, but now there was an empty space there too.

When Branwald reached the half-door, he saw his mother kneeling on the earthen floor of the Home Room, her head bowed low on her hands. She was praying. He wondered again why a woman so kind and good, so gentle and so full of life, should have to pray continually for cleansing and forgiveness. He stepped quietly towards his chamber, knowing that she had heard him but would not interrupt her prayers once they were started.

25

He hated to see her like this. It was as if a stone took the place of her heart when she prayed, making her hard and unyielding and fearful. If his father were with him, Branwald knew, he would explain the reasons for things, as he had so many times before. His mother could not. He would not ask her again. She had said, 'It is wrong to doubt, Branwald. You must accept the way things are, in faith. You will understand when you are older.'

Lying on the wool-filled mattress that was his bed, Branwald reflected that, on the contrary, his understanding grew more confused as he became older. He remembered the strange cave and his meeting with Maloof, and the uncomfortable feelings of guilt invaded him again. He relaxed his body and his mind and focused on the word that he so often came back to. Silently he repeated the word — *Firebolt* — until his mind let go of all discomfort and became a blank. It would have to remain blank when his mother next thought of him or spoke to him. Otherwise she would know.

'Branwald,' he heard her call. He rose and went into the Home Room. Estel was pouring water into a metal pot by the fire. She did not look up at him. 'Where have you been?'

'I went to see the Cataract,' Branwald replied boldly. Then, not too quickly, 'And I was speaking with Bern the Flymaker.' He tried to picture the bearded Bern in his mind.

His mother put the pot on the glowing embers of the fire and turned to look at him. Her eyes seemed to sweep around his body before they looked at his face. A slight frown creased her brow. He stared back at her, and the unease rose up in him again. For an instant he was aware of a faint green glow around her frame, but then he focused on her voice. 'Branwald, you know what can happen if you transgress.'

He found it almost unbearable to look into her eyes, but he steeled himself. 'Yes, Mother. I know,' he said.

Suddenly Estel turned away and went to the table, where three freshly-caught trout lay. 'Your meal will be ready soon. Go and find Eroona.'

Branwald stood there for a moment, his mind troubled by the fear that he felt in her heart. He wanted to go to her, to comfort her, to take away the heavy weight that he knew lay upon her. But he could not do it. Instead he turned and went out into the early-evening shade to look for his sister.

Eroona was in the house of her friend, Silvana, which lay at the top end of Fisherway. If Branwald had been asked how he knew she was there, he would have said, 'This is where she nearly always is.' But as he walked to Silvana's house, he was so certain of Eroona's presence that there was no doubt in his mind.

He found the girls sitting on the Home Room floor, play-ing with last autumn's chestnuts, a repetitious game that could continue for hours. Before Branwald spoke, he knew that his sister did not want to come home.

'The meal is nearly ready,' he said simply. Silvana looked up, startled, her hand to her heart.

'Branwald!' she scolded. 'You have given us a great fright.'

Eroona glanced up quickly from tumbling the chestnuts onto the patterned mat on the floor beside her. Her brown eyes were smiling when they caught her brother's. 'Yes,' she said. 'You have given us a fright. You must signal your coming more strongly when you come again.'

Branwald stifled a smile. 'I am sorry, Silvana. I hope I did not cause you to lose the game,' he said, although he knew that his sister was winning.

'Tell Mother that I shall be home in a short time, when we finish this game,' Eroona said, picking up her chestnuts.

In his mind, Branwald said, 'She is sorrowful again.'

Eroona swept back her black hair with a flick of her head and studied his face. Then she dropped the chestnuts on the mat. 'I will come now,' she said simply.

They left Silvana gazing after them with a thoughtful ex-pression on her face.

Branwald and Eroona walked side by side down the worn roadway. Four years younger than her brother, Eroona still carried the self-contained air of one who had not yet reached puberty. The woven woollen gown did not disguise the slim-ness of her frame. Branwald looked down at her. 'You must be careful always, little sister,' he said quietly. 'We do not know what Silvana would do if she found out.' He forestalled

27

her protest. 'I know she is your friend. But the Law of the Elders is very strict.'

Eroona regarded him seriously. 'I think Mother knows,' she said. 'She knows what I am thinking sometimes, I am sure. Mother would not say anything.'

Branwald stopped, catching Eroona by the shoulders and turning her. 'You must never say it to her, Eroona. As long as you never say it to her, or ask her about it, you will be all right, and she will be all right.' He shook her slightly to make her look into his eyes. 'Do you understand? It's very important. People can be banished for thought-speaking.' His fingers pressed into her shoulders till she squirmed.

'Branwald! You're hurting me!'

He relaxed his hold. 'I'm sorry. But I fear what might happen if the Elders find out about the thought-speaking. You do not understand now, but you will. Promise me you won't speak of it, to anyone!'

She massaged her shoulders, arms crossed. Across the lake, the great slope of Eagle Mountain was in deep gloom. 'It is silly to think that people would be banished for such a simple thing,' she pouted. 'And there's no need for you to squeeze so hard.' She turned back towards home. 'Anyway, why is Mother sorrowful?'

Branwald thought about that. After a moment he spoke. 'She does not know what is happening to Father. And she fears for us. She fears for herself.' He caught Eroona's arm again, stopping her. 'Eroona, you must promise.' She squirmed to escape, but he held her, forcing her to look into his eyes. 'Do you promise?'

She yielded to his will. 'Yes, Branwald, if you say so. I promise. But ....' She saw the anger in his eyes and stopped. Her eyes were serious now. 'I promise, if it's so important to you.'

'If you love Mother, and Father, and me, you will do so.'

'I will do so, Branwald,' she said simply.

He released her and she skipped away from him. Her eyes were mischievous. 'Race you to the door,' she called, and was gone like the wind.

～

As he and Eroona sat at the scrubbed pine table, waiting for the meal to be served, Branwald felt in his mind his mother's upset. He could see it in the pale yellow glow that surrounded her. And she refused to look him in the eye. Suddenly he felt that she could read his mind like a book, that she knew where he had been. He grappled with this new fear, glancing up at her when she turned aside from him, but he could not read her face, and her thoughts were gone from him.

His guilty feeling grew. He was causing his mother pain, and he hated that. There and then he resolved that he would never again go above the Cataract, that he would stop using the thought-speaking with Eroona and the others, so that his mother would have no further cause for anxiety.

Estel put the simple wooden platters of food before them and sat at the end of the table. All three bowed their heads, and Estel intoned the prayer. 'We who do not deserve it, we who are foul sinners, ask You, Dread Spirit, to grant us reprieve for another day.' She stopped, as she always did, and then added her own words: 'May Feowald come amongst us again soon. May he never offend You or bring destruction down upon his own head, as the Old People did in the Olden Days.'

Branwald was grateful for the unselfconscious chatter of his young sister during the meal. He was glad, too, when the meal was over. He diligently cleaned the platters in the earthenware basin and scrubbed the table. He brought in enough firewood to last for two days, and when his mother finally smiled sadly at him and ran her fingers gently through his hair, he put his arms around her waist and his head on her breast. After a moment he said, 'Be of good cheer, Mother. We must hope. And do not worry.' He looked into her eyes, trying to read her thoughts, but he felt only her fear and her sadness.

Estel held him to her again for a moment. Then she fixed him with a intense look. 'You are a strong one,' she whispered, 'like your father. But be very careful, my son.' Then she let him go.

CHAPTER FOUR

The next day was a work day, and Branwald was up early. The rocky peak of Eagle Mountain gleamed pink in the spring sunshine as he made his way down towards the beach, where the Fishers for the week were gathering. Vokt the Netmaker was already bent over some task in his great canoe. It was exactly like Branwald's own, except that it was more than twice the length, and there were six bench seats across its hold instead of the two in Branwald's light craft. Branwald picked up the wooden floats from the sand beside the great canoe and began to lay them carefully on its wet floor, beside the neatly piled nets.

'Good health to you, my young Branwald,' grunted Vokt, without straightening.

'And to you too, Master Vokt.'

There was a general bustle on the beach as the other two crews put their gear into their canoes. Although it was never spoken of directly, there was always a race to see which crew would be afloat first.

When Branwald had counted the floats, he looked for the paddles which he and the other three would use. There were none to be seen. He glanced at the canoe of Spen the Fishseer, and when he saw Spen's sly smile, he went to look into their canoe; but the missing paddles were not there. He caught Spen winking mischievously at his chubby son, Anspen, who was already positioned alongside the prow of his father's canoe, ready to push it off the soft sand. Branwald glared at the two in mock anger.

'Those two tricksters have buried our paddles again,' he said quietly to Vokt. He circled Vokt's canoe, searching for the tell-tale sign of freshly dug sand. Spen had just leaped out of his canoe, and he and his three crew members were preparing to heave it towards the water's edge. Branwald spied a mound of fresh sand. Dropping to his knees, he began to delve.

'Branwald,' called Vokt. He was chuckling. 'Watch this.'

Spen and his men bent their backs to their task. They gripped the sides of the canoe; at a word from Spen, they gave a great heave. The canoe started to slide. Then, just as it had begun to gain momentum, it came to a jerking stop. Vokt gave a great bellow of laughter when he saw the rope, which till then had been hidden in the sand, burst up from its hiding-place and tauten like a line struck by a fighting salmon. 'Come on, my lads,' he roared to his own crew.

Quickly, Branwald hauled the buried paddles out of the sand. Then he and the others grabbed their craft and slid it out into the shallows. From behind them they could hear the guttural tones of Spen calling the vengeance of the Gods down on foolish fishermen who had nothing better to do in the morning than to tie a great rock to the end of his anchor rope and bury it in the sand.

'Aha!' roared Vokt. 'If you had buried our paddles in the right place, you would have found that rock, you old rogue. We'll leave you a few tiddlers. Come on, lads!'

Branwald, Vokt and the others bent to their task, and in a moment, the great canoe was thrusting out into the still waters with hardly a sound.

~

High on the lifting currents above the great valley, the golden-headed eagles soared. They looked only momentarily at the slim canoes that crawled below them on the calm surface of the lake to which they had given their name. However, their piercing eyes may have rested longer on the small group of horsemen who were filtering slowly out of the high Pass of Feyan. It was unusual to see movement in the high, rock-strewn saddle that, though tortuous, was the only passable route through the jagged peaks that towered along the western rim of the valley.

A stocky, black-bearded man, dressed in a simple serge tunic and leather-thonged leggings beneath his bearskin cloak, was the leader of the group. As he came to a point above the tree-line from which he could look down on the lakes far below, he held up his hand and reined in his stocky, long-haired pony at the edge of a narrow trail. The man's face was grooved by years of struggle; it was the face of one who had seen life, and death. His eyes were a steely blue.

There were five others with him, all similarly bearded and long-haired, each mounted on a sturdy mountain pony. But these men carried weapons. Long scabbards and thick-handled daggers hung from their leather belts, and slung at their backs were strange long metal poles, with wider wooden stocks at one end. Behind them trailed six more ponies, laden with baggage.

The stocky man turned and spoke to the others. The words were harsh and guttural. He pointed towards a small patch of swaying meadow grasses nearby, and a stout man near him nodded. Then the stocky one uttered a brief word of farewell. He jerked his pack-pony's head roughly up from its grazing, pulled his mount's head to the left, and spurred it down the trail.

When he was out of sight among the first trees, the others trotted to the grassy patch, leading their pack-ponies. There they dismounted, and began to set up camp.

～

Branwald loved the work of the fisherman. He loved the forward surge of the canoe when the four of them pulled their blades through the water. He loved, too, being treated as an equal by the men. They knew he was a good paddler — he had won the Three Lakes race for the past two years against the other boys, some of whom were a year older than he.

Occasionally, however, he felt excluded. Vokt would break off, in the midst of telling a ribald story, as his eye fell on Branwald. At times like these, Branwald would crimson with embarrassment. He was not sure whether Vokt's inhibition came from the fact that many of his stories were about women, or whether he didn't trust Branwald not to go to the Elders and report the fault. Branwald felt guilty about listening to the stories, but it disturbed him much more to think that maybe Vokt didn't trust him. He wanted to say that there was no need for Vokt to fear him, but he didn't want it to seem that he wanted to hear Vokt's stories, either; so he never said anything. Such incidents, however, occurred so seldom that they did not tarnish Branwald's delight in the Fisher Task, which came round to his family every second full moon.

The fishing grounds were near the reed-fringed inlet where Otter's Brook flowed into Eagle Lake. The three men laid down their paddles and began to tease out the nets, hooking a float to the top edge every few yards. Branwald's task, at the stern, was to keep the craft moving slowly in a wide circle, a safe distance out from the reeds. When Branwald had brought the craft in a full circle, leaving a ring of bobbing floats in his wake, the men began to haul in the plaited rope that ran through the lower edge of the hanging net. Little by little the circle grew smaller, until at last it closed, trapping the fish inside. Then the hauling in began. The men heaved and strained at the nets, which, this morning, bulged with fish. Soon they began sorting the gawping catch on the floor of the canoe. Only fish of a certain length were kept; the others were flung back as quickly as possible. 'See you again next year, little tiddler!' Vokt would call as he tossed the fish back. 'Eat plenty and grow fat!'

When the remaining fish had been stored in smelly canvas sacks to keep the sun off them, Vokt turned to scan the expanse of water to the north-east. In the hazy distance Spen's canoe was circling slowly. 'Ha!' said Vokt, his eyes twinkling. 'Tomorrow morning we must be wary. That old one does not like to come second.'

The return journey was taken at a leisurely pace. Branwald, seated beside Vokt, didn't paddle, but used his wide blade as a rudder to keep the craft on course. He glanced at the weathered face of the Netmaker, trying to read his mood. He decided to risk the question that had been in his mind all morning.

'Master Vokt, did you ever see the Old Soldier after he returned from the Mouth of the Great River?'

There was a slight frown on Vokt's face when he looked down at Branwald. He stopped his slow paddling and stared long into the boy's eyes. 'That is not a question that young men are supposed to ask,' he said.

'I know,' Branwald replied. 'But can there be any harm in knowing about these things?'

Vokt glanced at the others. They were talking quietly at the front. 'If I tell you, you must never say it to anyone, you understand.' Branwald nodded earnestly. Vokt looked out across the lake towards the northern cliffs. 'Yes. I was a little older than you when he came back to the islands.'

Branwald waited, but Vokt was silent. 'What did he look like?' he asked.

'He was still straight and strong. Still like a soldier,' Vokt said quietly. 'But his face was ... was strange. I remember thinking, "What suffering this man has undergone!" There were great shadows under his eyes, and they stared out of their sockets like the eyes of a man who has seen a spirit or a ghoul.'

'Did you see the Firebolt?' Branwald felt himself becoming tense.

Vokt shook his head slowly. 'He would not allow any of us to see it, but we knew it was there, in a great scabbard thing. None of us wanted to see it, either, after we heard his story.' Another pause.

'Why did he go away with it?'

Vokt looked down at Branwald. His eyes were serious but kindly. 'How full of questions you are this morning, my fine Branwald! But you know the answer to that question. You have heard it often enough in the Assembly.'

Branwald tried not to let the older man see the compelling curiosity within him. He nodded. 'Yes, Master Vokt. I have heard many times.' He turned his eyes away towards Redwood Island, which was coming closer. He dared not let Vokt see his scepticism. He lifted his paddle and began to stroke in rhythm with the two in front.

It was not long before Vokt spoke again, even more quietly than before. 'Before he went, I heard the Old Soldier say that it was not because the Firebolt was evil that he had been punished, but because he himself had given in to his dark side and allowed his friend to use it to destroy his enemy. And the Firebolt destroyed them both. That was why he went away. He had to atone for the great evil that he had caused.'

Branwald looked northwards to where the Elvan Cliffs stood hazy in the yellow sunlight. He thought again of the deep cave out of which the river ran, and again he felt the call.

But another question rose to his mind. 'Master Vokt, do you think my father will come back soon?'

The older man stopped paddling again, and in his eyes this time there was a gentle sympathy.

'He will come back soon, my boy,' he said quietly. 'He is a strong and brave man, and those with him are stout lads too. They have been delayed for some reason, but I am sure they will return over the mountain soon.'

Ahead of him, Branwald could see the islanders beginning to filter down towards the Fish Tables by the beach, in preparation for the division of the catch. 'Do you think they have found any of the Old People at the mouth of the Great River?'

Vokt inclined his head to one side, as he always did when he was thinking. 'Who knows, lad?' he said. 'Some may have survived the Great Darkness, and kept the old ways going. Or they may have gone to seek another place. Or ....' He paused, and Branwald looked into his face expectantly. The Netmaker glanced at him, as if uncertain how to proceed.

Branwald finished the sentence for him. 'Or maybe they fell under the power of the Orelord.'

Vokt grimaced uncomfortably. 'You are a great reader of minds, Branwald. Who can say? Maybe the Orelord has been swept away into oblivion, many years past. There is none so strong that he can withstand the march of time.'

Branwald adjusted the angle of his paddle to bring the nose of the canoe into line with the stone wharf by the beach. 'What I do not understand, Master Vokt, is why my father had to go. Why did any of them have to go?'

Vokt dipped his paddle into the water and twirled it absent-mindedly in the dimpled surface. Again he glanced at the two men in front. 'You know very well why, Branwald,' he replied quietly. 'We are running out of metals on the islands, and we must find a source of fresh ores soon. It is believed that there is metal to be found near the mouth of the Great River, where the Old People lived.'

'But I have heard that there was great controversy in the Assembly before they went. There were many who did not want Father and the others to go. They said it would be easier to wage war on the Forest People and take the metals that they have.'

'You have been listening to too many empty voices, my fine young paddler. I only say these things to you because you are the son of Feowald the Protector, and I know that you feel the absence of your father greatly. But one last thing I say to you. Your father did not wish to fight with the Forest People, and I know he always believed that the Elders who fled to this place long ago had left some people behind at the mouth of the Great River. Often, while we were fishing, I heard him speak of going back there, if only to satisfy himself that they had survived. So, when you ask me why he went, I could say that he wanted to go. It was a point of honour with him. Another man may say that he went for a different reason.'

While Branwald was turning these thoughts over in his mind, the canoe slowed and the other paddlers began to stow their paddles under their seats. He, however, kept his paddle in the water and directed the prow onto the beach.

Several minutes later, when the sacks had been laid on the wooden benches near the beach, where the gathered people were waiting for their contents to be distributed, Branwald moved close to Vokt, who was overseeing the operation.

'Where do you think the Old Soldier went?' he whispered.

Vokt looked around warily, then down at his questioner. His face was almost stern. 'You have asked enough questions for one day, my fine fellow.' He raised a finger in warning. 'And remember what I told you.'

'I will remember.' It was clear to Branwald that he would get no further information from the crusty Netmaker.

CHAPTER FIVE

Branwald woke from his dream with a start. He was frightened. A pale beam of moonlight shining through the narrow window of his chamber made the shadows lurking in the corners seem all the more menacing. He gripped the edges of his woollen quilt. But there was nothing there.

Then, through the wooden partition, he heard his mother cry out. He leapt up from his couch, grabbed the polished paddle that hung on the wall beside him and rushed for the separating door. In the pale light, he saw Estel sitting upright in her bed, her eyes white and staring, her hand on her heart.

'What is the matter, Mother?' he cried, his darting eyes scanning the small compartment and the low window opening behind her. Her frightened eyes followed his, and she gave another low cry.

'Oh, Branwald!' she gasped. 'I had such a terrible dream!'

Branwald went to her. Only a dream! He put his arm around her. She was shivering. He took a gown from the seat by him and drew it around her shoulders, uttering soothing words, as she had so often uttered them to still his own childish fears. Eroona, white-faced and startled, came padding on silent feet, whispering 'What is the matter?' When she heard, she too knelt close beside her mother, her arms around Estel's neck. For a long time the three of them rocked gently from side to side, not speaking.

'What? What was your dream?' Branwald asked, when the shivering had stopped and they had lit a candle.

'You must not ask me that,' his mother said, with a shudder. 'It was too horrible.'

'Tell me, Mother,' he insisted. 'I must know.' He had a reason for asking.

Estel enfolded her two children in her arms and drew

them closer to her side. 'A monstrous black thing ... I could not see its face. It was pursuing me, a great dark shape like the figure of a man, only monstrously big, with a square head that had great burning eyes staring down at me.' She shuddered again at the recollection. 'And I was trying to escape from it. I, in this flimsy canoe, trying to paddle ....' She broke off when she saw Branwald's wide eyes staring at her. 'What? What is the matter, my son? It was only a dream.'

He knew what was in her mind. 'The Cataract, Mother,' he said. 'You were trying to scale —'

She gave a cry, and her hand went to stop his mouth. 'No, Branwald,' she pleaded. 'You mustn't say this.'

'But, Mother,' he whispered, his heart quailing with the returning fear, 'I had this dream too, just now.'

~

Morning came slowly. Branwald had returned late to his couch and had slept only for short, turbulent periods. Despite his mother's assurances that the coincidence of their shared dream had no significance, Branwald couldn't banish from his mind a strong sense of foreboding, a feeling that some evil thing was approaching. Something was happening, changing, and he could not tell what, except that he had a feeling close to certainty that it was going to affect him in some way.

~

Branwald was on Fisher Duty again that morning. He rose in the chill twilight and ate his bread with only water to wash it down. Sounds of deep breathing came from the other chambers.

A cool breeze was wafting off the lake when he reached the deserted beach. To the north, the upper Elvan Cliffs were enveloped in a light mist; the lower walls were grey and forbidding.

Vokt arrived, rubbing his hands together to warm them.

'Aha!' he called, when his eye fell on Branwald. 'We must make you labour a little harder today, my young Branwald. Then you will have less time for asking questions.'

The two of them busied themselves with their chores, and Branwald heard the older man chuckling to himself.

'That old badger drank too much ale last night,' said Vokt. 'He was in no condition to rise before the sun and interfere with honest fishermen's tackle.'

Spen and the others arrived soon, and the banter continued as it had on the previous day. Branwald was waiting for Vokt to give the word when he noticed that Vokt was staring at something near the bottom of Eagle Mountain. Branwald's eyes followed his gaze. At the near end of the low promontory known as Goron's Knoll, they could clearly see the flashing of a fire. The billowing smoke, drifting north with the wind, clouded the dark forest behind into a hazy blue.

'By the Spirit!' swore Vokt softly. 'The warriors have come back.'

Others had seen the fire. Spen called, pointing, and in a moment all the fishermen were staring at the distant, flickering light.

'They've come back,' rasped Spen in his cracked morning voice. 'We must go to them.' He turned to his crew. 'Come on, lads. Get this canoe onto the water.'

'We'll go with you,' shouted Vokt, gripping the gunwale of his craft. 'But wait! Someone must go and tell the Elders, and the families.'

His eye fell on Branwald, who was standing at the stern, ready to heave. 'Young Branwald —'

'No, Master Vokt. Please! Let someone else go. It is my father.'

Vokt hesitated. He looked at Garel and Tregor, his two crewmen, then back at Branwald. 'Run to the house of the Scholar, then. Tell him to tell the others. We will wait. Now *run*!'

John the Scholar's house was nearest to the wharf. Branwald raced over the grassy sward and hammered at the faded timbers of the door. After a few moments, he heard a cough within. Then the door rattled as a bar was taken down from behind it, and in a moment Branwald was looking into the peaked face and sunken eyes of the Scholar.

'Master Scholar,' he explained, 'please pardon the call so early; we have seen a great fire on Goron's Knoll. It is the signal. We think that my father has come back and we are going to go there. Can you tell the other Elders, and my mother?'

The grey-haired Elder squinted past Branwald, towards the bulk of the distant peninsula. The flames were leaping high into the air.

'I hope their journey was worth all this waiting,' he grumbled. 'Go. I will tell them.'

Branwald raced back to the water's edge and leaped into Vokt's canoe; Spen's craft was already pushing through the waves. Branwald paddled as he had never paddled in his life. As he laboured, he squinted his eyes against the wind and spray, trying to see if there were any figures close to the fire, but the movement of the canoe would not allow him to focus.

A traitor fear grew like a seed in his mind. What if only some of the band had returned? What if his father was not amongst them? Once again he peered at the fire, its flames not so high now, and he thought he could see a figure moving in front of the orange-red glow.

Vokt's craft had drawn level with Spen's, but there was no banter or comment from either crew. All were intent on their target. Branwald could clearly see a still figure silhouetted against the flames. There were no others to be seen. Could it be that there was only one? Please, Dread Spirit, let it be him ....

He stared at the figure, searching for any movement, any set of the head or shoulders that he might remember. As the canoe came closer, however, his hope faltered. This stocky figure, standing stolidly observing them, could not be his father. The long black hair and beard were too bushy, the girth of the waist too full.

The canoe slowed its pace as it came to the rocky shore. Branwald could see the face. It was hard and set; it was not the face of his father, nor of any of the men who had left in such high spirits on that sunny spring morning two years before. Desperately Branwald surveyed the open ground behind the stranger and the fire, but nothing moved there except two ponies, tethered by a long rein, which gazed in startled alertness at the arriving craft.

'Hail, stranger,' called Vokt, as the prow touched land. 'We have seen your fire and come, thinking it to be a signal from some of our own, who left here two years ago.'

The other raised his hand, palm facing front, in the customary greeting of the Island People. 'You were right to come,' he said in a guttural voice. 'I am one of the Ancient

People who have their home on the Tarquan Islands, at the mouth of the Great River. I have come with a message from those who left, which I must give to the ruler of your people.' The man bent to lift two bundles wrapped in the skin of some animal. His accent was strange to Branwald's ears. 'If you would ferry me across to your dwelling-place —'

'But what tidings?' interrupted Vokt. 'We have waited two years without any word. Tell us how they are, what has detained them from coming back to us.'

The stranger turned his cold blue eyes on his questioner. 'If you wish to know whether they still live, I can tell you that some of them do ....' He stopped, hearing the gasp from Branwald, who had stepped out onto the pavement. His eyes flickered over the youth.

Vokt explained, 'This is the son of Feowald the Protector, the leader of the men who left.'

The cold eyes lingered on Branwald's face for a second before the stranger spoke. 'The Protector still lives,' he said. 'It was he who sent the message which I must deliver in the presence of the Elders.'

The stranger glanced at the two ponies, who had trotted to the furthest length of their tethers and were prancing in a jittery fashion, ears erect. 'My ponies — is there any way of keeping them safe from the rude ones of the forest?'

'There is,' replied Spen quietly. 'The raft. But it'll take some time to prepare it and tow it across. If you want to keep them, we'll leave some men here to guard them until we return.'

'I want to keep them,' said the stranger, dropping his bundles with a thud into the bottom of Vokt's canoe. 'And now I must have sleep and food. I have come a great distance and have been travelling for many days.'

Branwald could not remain silent. 'But my father — why has he not come back? What has detained him?'

The stranger looked at him again, and Branwald felt a shiver run down his spine as the cold eyes met his. 'All these matters will be revealed when I speak to your leader.' Then the man turned away and prepared to step down into Vokt's canoe.

CHAPTER SIX

Tregor, one of Vokt's crewmen, volunteered to remain on Goron's Knoll with Kyle, from Spen's craft, until their fellow fishers returned with the raft which would ferry the stranger's ponies back to the island. As a precaution, the two men took the rough metal gaffs which were standard equipment on all the fishercraft. It was well known that the Forest People tried to avoid contact with the Islanders, as a general rule; but after the victory over Clem the Firemaker's impetuous band, some of the Elders believed that the Forest People could no longer be trusted. Branwald had once overheard old Kyran the Rulemaker observe that they were getting ideas above their station and might soon have to be taught a lesson.

The canoes started back for Redwood. In Tregor's place, in front of Branwald, sat the stranger. He had thrown off his unkempt bearskin, and muscles bulged beneath his sweat-stained tunic as he paddled with easy, powerful strokes. Behind him, Branwald worked mechanically, his mind filled with sadness. He wondered if his mother or Eroona had learnt of the fire and of the arrival of a traveller. Would they be waiting on the beach, their hearts on fire with expectation? He felt an intense pang of loneliness and grief when he thought of their disappointment. For himself, he could bear it. But he hated to see the pain in his mother's eyes.

He tried to push the dark thoughts away, but each time his eyes fell on the stranger's back, they returned. There was something wrong, and he could not tell what. It was something to do with the way the stranger looked at him, as if he were trying to close off his mind from any probing.

Then Branwald, watching the man's bulky frame against the dark side of the mountain, became aware of the glow which emanated from his body. Unlike the familiar radiant blue which had enveloped Eroona for as long as Branwald could remember, this man's aura was a dull brown.

Branwald shook his head to dispel these thoughts. The man was from a distant place where people were different, he told himself. Instead of being suspicious, he should be grateful. After all, the man had come with news of his father.

The canoe was some distance from the shore when Branwald noticed the crowd on the beach. People were streaming in ragged lines along the pathways that led down to the landing-place. The word had spread like wildfire. There was no doubt that his mother and sister had heard. They would be on the beach, beside themselves with excitement, and Branwald felt sick with pity for their coming pain.

The first moments after the canoe touched land were confused. People surged towards and around the craft, trying to get a glimpse of the stranger. They spilled into the water on both sides, and helping hands pushed the canoe far up on the beach. Those at the back, who could not see, were calling to those in front to report what they heard. Cries of 'What's the news, good Vokt?' and 'Who has come back?' came from all sides. Some questions were directed to the stranger himself, but he sat unmoved on the seat, his eyes impassively observing the crowd.

Vokt stood up on the bench beside Branwald and held out his hands for silence.

'Good people of Feyansdoon,' he called. There were calls from those near him for quiet, and gradually the silence filtered back to envelop even those just arriving. 'Good friends,' said Vokt, 'this is one of the Ancient People from the islands at the mouth of the Great River. He has news of Feowald and his band of men ....' An excited hum rose from the gathered crowd, and the ruddy-faced Netmaker raised his voice to be heard. 'And he says he will give this news to us at the Assembly.'

At the mention of the Assembly, the hum grew louder, and several voices were raised in protest. 'But what news, Master Vokt?' enquired Dame Aleena, whose husband, Glesh, had gone over the mountains. Her stout face glistened with perspiration, and she clutched the hand of a nine-year-old boy in hers. 'Can we not know of their fate now? This boy's father has been gone for nearly two years! We have heard nothing ....' Her voice almost seized up, but she forced down the feeling. 'Can you not tell us here and now,' she called to Urkor, 'what has befallen our men?' Her query was echoed by other voices in the crowd.

Urkor stood up on the next bench of the canoe and surveyed the crowd. There was an immediate silence.

'I am Urkor, of the Tarquan Island People. I have been sent here by the leader of your band, a man called Feowald, who is alive, as are most of the band who came among us many moons ago.'

There was a gasp from Dame Aleena, and a cry from someone in the crowd. 'Who among them is no longer alive?' an old man's voice called from the back.

Urkor ignored the question. 'Your leader, Feowald, asked me to speak only in the presence of your leaders, and there to deliver the words that he sent. If you consider that what I have to say is important to you, then you must call your Assembly. Then I will speak.' The stranger stepped off the bench and sat down.

There was a confused murmur of voices. Vokt held out his hands again and called, 'Well, then, we must have an Assembly. The Elders must call an Assembly for this very day.' His eye fell on an elderly, round-shouldered man who was standing alone at the back of the crowd. 'What say you, Elder Kyran?' called Vokt. 'You have heard what has passed. Many of the people feel that there should be an Assembly today.'

All eyes turned towards the back, and another murmur swept through the crowd. The Elder held up his hand as if to prevent Vokt from saying more. A frown creased his brow.

'These matters, as you all know,' he announced stiffly, 'cannot be decided by the common people, but must be discussed by a convention of the Elders. But ....' He raised his hand higher to still the rising sound. 'I will consult with the Elders of this island, and we will let you know our verdict.' With that he turned and began to make his way towards the village.

The crowd was not content. There were low mutterings in

several places, and Dame Aleena caused a frightened hush when she said aloud, 'They talk of Violations — *this* is a Violation! Why cannot a wife and child be told what has become of their husband and father?'

'Hush, good Dame,' said a neighbour. 'Be patient, and soon you will hear. Old Kyran will not let us down.'

'Bah!' retorted the woman, tugging her pale-faced son towards the edge of the crowd. 'I do not fear these dried-up old "wise men"!'

Branwald, who had been resting against the stern of the big canoe, had already located his mother and sister standing on the outer fringe of the crowd, near the fish tables. He had watched Estel's face as Urkor spoke, and the pain in her eyes cut him like a knife. But he was angry too. Why would this dour stranger not tell them about his father and the others, and ease the fears of many who stood there? What was he trying to hide from the people?

Branwald glared at the stranger from under his eyebrows, trying to read his thoughts. The man sat looking at the crowd with cold, unblinking eyes.

Branwald concentrated his powers. He became aware of an image forming — a grey, amorphous shape with strange and sinister patterns ....

Then, without warning, Urkor turned and fixed Branwald with his cold stare. Branwald, caught unawares, quickly looked away. The image faded, and in its place there remained only alarm. As Branwald began to move away towards his mother and sister, he knew that the man was watching him.

Vokt was again standing on the bench, calling for attention from the people, some of whom were already drifting away.

'Good friends,' he called, 'this man has come a great distance over the mountains to bring us some news. I am sure there are reasons why Feowald has asked that this news be given to us at the Assembly. In the meantime, it is surely not the practice of our people to leave this traveller, one of our own long-lost people, to sit here without food and refreshment while we make his arrival a source of dissent among ourselves.'

He turned to the seated Urkor, who returned his gaze.

'Friend Urkor, I invite you to come and dine with me and my family.' Then, to the crowd: 'And lest any of you should think that I wish to spirit our visitor away from the rest, I say now that the door of my house will be open to all who come.' A wry smile creased the Netmaker's face. 'But bring your own fish,' he told them.

Branwald went to his mother. She opened her arms wordlessly and gathered her two children to her. They stood together for a long moment.

After a time, Eroona sighed deeply. 'I thought Father had come,' she said.

Estel rubbed her cheek against the girl's hair. 'He will return,' she said. 'Come, let us go home.'

◆

A little later, after Eroona had gone sadly to Silvana's house, Branwald came into the Home Room, where his mother was sifting flour onto the wooden table. He had been pondering the events of the morning, and he could bear the burden no longer.

'Mother,' he said, 'do you think the stranger is speaking true?'

Estel looked up quickly from her work. 'Why do you ask, Branwald?'

He chose his words carefully. 'There is something strange about him — about his eyes. I do not like him.'

Estel looked down at her hands. With her finger she traced a shape in the powdery flour. 'He is strange,' she said, her voice so quiet as to be barely audible. 'But we must hear what he has to say before we can know for sure.'

'But will they tell us? You know how the Elders are, sometimes, when they come out of the Assembly. It is difficult to find out what goes on.'

'We may have to wait for a day or two,' she replied. 'But if they hold an Assembly, we will find out sooner or later.'

'We will know they are going to hold one,' Branwald said, 'if they send messengers to the other islands. I will watch and tell you.'

He kissed her on the cheek and went out into the late-morning sunlight, to climb the gnarled laurel that clung to

46

the scarp wall behind the house. From there he could see the lake shore, where the canoes lay beached. He lodged himself in a spreading fork, and settled down to wait.

~

Scarcely an hour had passed before Branwald saw movement near the beach. He recognised Vokt, Spen and several of their crewmen. When they began to make preparations for launching the two canoes, Branwald crouched forward, poised for action. Surely it would not require two full crews to take messages to the three other islands? He was on the point of leaping down and running towards the beach when he remembered the stranger's ponies. Of course: the two crews were going to collect the old raft from the mouth of Feyan's Stream and tow it off to the Peninsula, to collect Tregor and Kyle and the animals.

The two big canoes were hardly out of sight round the southern promontory, however, when Branwald heard the sound of voices from the higher ground behind him. Between the houses at the top of Fisherway he glimpsed a group of men, clad in white, moving down towards the lake shore. He knew immediately that they were Elders. They were coming from the Portal House, the Sanctuary of the Elders, on the top of the island, and they had come to some decision.

By the time Branwald had reached the junction of Watcher's Path and Fisherway, he knew that there was going to be an Assembly. Several of the Elders, dressed in their ceremonial white robes, were waiting outside the houses of Moot Sherewater and Limbur, son of Holeg. These two men were among the best and fastest paddlers on Redwood Island. They were going to be sent with a message to the other islands. There was to be an Assembly that very night.

CHAPTER SEVEN

It was late evening before the first canoes from the islands arrived. Branwald, who had spotted them from his vantage point behind the house, ran down and was waiting when the first wet prow scrunched the pebbles on the beach.

There were six Elders on board, each dressed in a long white hooded robe. Branwald recognised the white hair and whiter beard of old Ditric, the chief Elder of Woodfern Island. He and Breysheck the Sentencer were the last two left alive of those who had crossed the great mountains into the valley, when Feyan had led his straggling band to safety there after the Dark Time. People said that Ditric was nearly a hundred years old.

Branwald watched in silence as the four strong paddlers assembled a makeshift sedan chair, lifted the withered old man and placed him on it. He seemed very feeble, and his face, though partly hidden by the loose hood, had the pallor of death. When the second canoe arrived and the Elders from Raven Island had climbed out, the men lifted the chair and walked with measured steps up Fisherway, towards the Portal House, where the Assembly would be held.

In the distance, other canoes were moving purposefully towards the landing-place. One would bring the last of the Elders from the Island of the Banished; the others carried curious people who had heard the news. This event would be worth laying aside the day's work to witness. So the Island People were coming.

～

The Portal House, Sanctuary of the Elders, was located near the highest point of Redwood Island. Immediately to the north of it stood a great solitary outcrop of limestone, known as Feyan's Rock; it presented a steep wall on its southern side, which was riven and gouged by centuries of weathering. At the bottom of this cliff, Feyan, when he first arrived with the Island People, had found a cave. It was there that the weary wanderers had first sheltered; and there, even after they had built the first makeshift houses, the old man had remained, insisting on living alone amongst the frugal furnishings.

At last, fearing for Feyan's health and despite his protests, the people had built a dwelling outside and around the mouth of the cave. As the number of Elders had grown, so had the rambling structure. Now it extended outwards from the face of the cliff in a series of rectangular blocks, each one different in height from the next. The walls of each section were made of close-fitting pieces of limestone; set high in the blank walls were small square windows, which allowed light to filter in but which were too high for a man to look through. A wall enclosed the open space around three sides of the Sanctuary; the fourth side was the cliff itself.

This Sacred Place, this Sanctuary, was forbidden to all women — indeed, to all men except the chosen Elders, the overseers of the people's tasks, and those men and boys whom they employed to bring them the necessities of life.

∾

The evening sun had dropped behind Eagle Mountain when Vokt the Netmaker, accompanied by a crowd of curious people, led Urkor through the pine groves that led to the Portal House. Branwald, who had loitered near the Netmaker's house all afternoon, hurried back to inform his mother and then raced up the slope to join the crowd.

Speculation was rife among the adults. The stranger had sat in Vokt's house all afternoon, refusing to speak of the men who had gone over the mountains, rebuffing all attempts to engage him in the innocuous talk of everyday things that is the life-breath of a community.

When Urkor had entered the low doorway of the Portal House, old Kyran came to the enclosure gate and dragged it shut, pushing out the few brazen ones who had encroached too far. The Assembly was about to begin.

Amidst the murmur of talk, Branwald heard the strident tones of Dame Aleena near him. 'They can accuse me if they see fit,' she announced. 'But I'm not stirring a foot from this spot until I hear what has happened to my Glesh!' Somebody tried to hush her up, but she retorted, even more loudly, 'Hush up, you! You have not lost your husband, the father of your children.'

In the dwindling light Branwald drifted along the enclosure wall to the corner where it met the rock-face. He stood in the shadow of the cliff, thinking, watching the hundreds of people forming into huddled groups as they settled down to wait near the Portal Gates. He didn't want to talk to anyone.

In the east, the sky was purpling as the light faded. Within an hour, the night would be upon them. It was the first time that Branwald could remember an Assembly being held so late in the day.

Restless, Branwald turned to look up along the great rock. It was not completely vertical, and it was dotted by clinging bushes; he knew he would have no difficulty in climbing well above the height of the wall. From there it would be possible to look down into the enclosure, maybe even to see through one of the high window slits.

He thought about it for a few moments. Then, having glanced behind to check that no one was in sight, he began to climb.

Soon he could see one of the windows in the Portal wall. A dim light glowed within. He found a narrow ledge that took him across the enclosure wall and down towards the window. His need to know what was happening became like a fire inside him. It stifled and pushed out the knowledge that what he was doing was a serious Violation.

Branwald was almost level with the eaves of the Portal House, and the window was only six feet from him, when he first heard the voices. He listened, his heart pounding.

'... We have no force of men to send that great distance to fight against such a foe as the Orelord.' Branwald recognised the voice of Kyran the Rulemaker. 'We are not a warlike people; we are fishers and farmers. The men who left us were not instructed by this Assembly to engage in conflict with the Orelord. In this they have broken the covenant.'

Another voice spoke. Its quavering tone was that of an old

man whom Branwald did not recognise. 'What the venerable Kyran says may be true, but we must always remember that the people at the mouth of the Great River are our people, our own flesh and blood. They, like us, have survived the Dark Time and the years between. Now, when the danger has once again come out of the east to try and subdue them to its will, how can we blame Feowald and the others for trying to help them?' The speaker paused as a convulsion of coughing overtook him. 'Maybe it would have been better if these men had never gone from us at all,' he said. 'But once they had gone, who can blame them for helping their own?'

Another voice spoke. Branwald recognised the guttural tones of the stranger, Urkor. 'You must not forget the women and children of these men. They have waited long for news. Who here will go out from this meeting and say that these men have been abandoned to their fate? For unless help comes in some form, their fate is sealed as surely as I stand on this ground.'

Branwald's heart froze within him. His father was in great danger and needed help. Surely the Assembly would send it. How could there be any question about it?

But Branwald frowned. Why had Kyran the Rulemaker spoken so? Surely he had not meant that there was no one amongst them who could go across the Great Mountains and bring help! Branwald knew in his soul that he himself would be the first to go.

A different voice was raised, and Branwald strained to hear. The voice was unfamiliar to him. 'Let us be realistic, Urkor of our people. You say that our men — those who still live — are shut up in the great fortress of the Orelord, and that they cannot escape unless others come to release them. But how many soldiers would be needed to storm this place? Tell us truthfully.'

Another pause. Then Urkor spoke again. His tone seemed placatory. 'I cannot deny that the Bastion of the Orelord is mighty, built as it is on the mountain. Its walls are made of metal that is thicker than a man's wrist. In truth, it would take a great army to overpower it.'

Outside, clinging to the rock, Branwald was distraught.

The Orelord! His father and the others had been captured by the Orelord!

'But is there any chance that these men could escape?' Branwald thought it was the voice of Ditric, Chief Elder of Woodfern Island. 'If they work in a mine, can they not tunnel their way out?'

There was a harsh laugh. Then Urkor spoke again. 'The Orelord hates the Island People. When Feowald and his men drove the Orelord's first force away from the Islands, he swore a terrible revenge. Now that he has power over them, he has built a wall around the very mine itself. His men guard the great pit continually. No one knows how long he will stay there, or how long it will be before the mines are exhausted. It is said that when this happens, he will kill all those whom he has taken captive.'

There was another long pause. Branwald gripped the jagged rocks until his fingers were raw and sore. He looked upwards at the flickering stars appearing out of the smooth purple canopy of the sky. 'Oh, Father!' he whispered. 'Dear Father, let them not leave you to die ....'

John the Scholar was speaking in his hoarse voice. 'We all know that the Planting is just beginning, that there is need for fish to be caught until the lambs are big enough and the new crops are ready. If we send twenty — nay, even ten — men on this long and hazardous journey, then what will we do for toilers in the fields and at the fishing? What will the people do for food? I ask this, not because I want those men to die, but because I do not want this people to die also.'

Branwald groaned softly. 'But the women would do it,' he whispered desperately. 'Aleena and the others would do it, and gladly.' The stars blurred above him as his tears came.

There was a long pause. Then Urkor spoke again. 'There is one thing which Feowald told me before he was taken.' He spoke more slowly, and with emphasis. 'He said that if help could not be sent, I was to ask for one thing only.'

'What is that thing?' some Elder asked.

'He said that he did not know where it might be found, but that there were some among his people who did. He said that if he and the others were in mortal danger, these people would tell me where the Firebolt was hidden and let me bring it to him.'

Branwald heard the loud murmur that swept through the chamber: 'The Firebolt!' Then the mingled responses: 'No! Not the Firebolt!' 'The Firebolt must never be used again!' 'The Firebolt would only destroy them forever!'

'My people,' called Urkor, his voice raised above the hubbub, 'I know there are few who could be trusted with the Firebolt.' The noise quietened. 'It is not for me to use, but for the great Feowald, that wise and brave man. Think what he could do if he had it in his possession. Think what his wife and children — all the wives and children — would say if he were to free himself and the others from the bondage of the Orelord, and return to this valley. Then he could lay the Firebolt to rest forever. There would be no need ever to use it again. I only say this because Feowald and the others are my people, *your* people. We must not leave anything undone that could with safety be done.'

There was a surge of noise. It became an uproar, so loud that Branwald knew the watchers at the gate must hear it. 'The Firebolt!' he whispered to himself. 'Yes! The Firebolt can save my father!'

He started upright, ready to climb back outside the wall; but then the jangling of a bell from within caused the hubbub to lessen. Someone was calling for quiet. 'Peace! Let Breysheck the Sentencer speak! Hear ye! Hear ye!'

The bell jangled even louder, and slowly the noise subsided. There was silence.

The voice was cracked and piping. 'If Feowald said this, then he can no longer be called the Protector by this people. Everyone knows that the Firebolt is an evil thing. It therefore follows that he who sets his hand upon it is evil also.'

Urkor's voice, more strident now. 'The Firebolt saved your people — our people — from the power of the Oremen. Let us not forget this. And now —'

'Yes, but look at what it did to the bearer. It destroyed his soul. It condemned him to exile, to banishment forever!'

Urkor again, quieter, more controlled. 'The words of Breysheck have authority and wisdom, and must be respected.

But there are others here, I believe, who do not share his mistrust of the Firebolt. The Firebolt is a power. It can be used once again, to free your people, and then returned to its resting-place.'

Another Elder spoke, and Branwald recognised the stern tones of Kyran the Rulemaker.

'Even if what the man from the Great River says is true, there is no one here who knows where the Firebolt has been hidden away. It has always been a Violation for any of our people to seek it or have anything to do with it.'

'In a case like this, when the lives of our people are at stake, there can be no question of Violation,' Urkor retorted. 'It will be used in a good cause.'

Breysheck's quavering voice came again. 'People have said that the Old Soldier took it with him and cast it away, deep in the mountains above the Cataract. Nobody knows where it is. It is useless to speculate, anyway, because these places are forbidden to our people.'

There was another long pause. Then Urkor's voice was heard again. 'Is there nobody who knows where the Firebolt has gone?'

A low murmur grew within the chamber. 'My people!' Urkor broke in. 'How sad it is to me to know that this Assembly is about to abandon men of these islands, who went abroad on a mission from this very chamber! How can you say to the women and children who —'

Ditric's voice, shrill and petulant, cut him off. 'Feowald has been carried away by his own lust for power. His conflict with the Orelord can only bring sorrow to our people. Were he to have the Firebolt, who can foresee what evil he would let loose?'

'But —'

'This Assembly, which carries on the authority of Feyan, our venerable founder, has made its will known.' Branwald heard a murmur of approval. 'The Firebolt must remain where it is, buried far from human sight forever. There is no cause which would make it right to search for it. It is gone. Let it be.' Another surge of gruff sound. 'As for the unfortunate men from our islands, we feel their loss as much as all the others. But we cannot send a force strong enough to be of help. To do so would be to endanger the life of our people .....'

Branwald had heard enough. In his heart was a fierce and bitter anger. Scalding tears blinded his eyes as he groped his way back. The image of his father locked away in that distant fortress, waiting for the help that would never come, caused his breath to stop in his throat and his stomach to cramp in pain. And when he thought of his mother and sister, he had to stop his climbing and grip the craggy rock as a spasm of grief and distress swept over him.

At last he dropped to the ground outside. Above him, the stars flickered in the cold void of space. He stumbled towards the pine groves that grew on the west side of the outcrop, their tops silhouetted against the faint rose glow above Eagle Mountain.

He went amongst the pines, not caring about the prickly needles that brushed against his skin. When he came to the edge of the level area, where the land began to slope downwards towards the village, he stopped. Far away, on the lower slopes of the mountain, the lights from the Forest People's cabins twinkled here and there. Looking northwards, Branwald saw another flickering light, near where the Cataract should be, and he thought of Maloof. Little did *he* know of the drama that was unfolding on the islands. Little did he know that his hope and dream of his own father's return would never come true.

Involuntarily, Branwald's eyes were drawn back to the dark blocks of the Portal House. He knew that soon the Elders would have to make an announcement to the people waiting outside the gates. Maybe there would be a change of heart.

Clinging to this last straw of hope, Branwald turned back and jogged along the dim pathway. He would be there to hear.

CHAPTER EIGHT

When Branwald reached the open space where the light from the fires cast a lurid glow on the nearby trees and bushes, he skirted round in the shadows until he located the group where his mother and Eroona were huddled. Sick at heart, he withdrew into the gloom of the tree-trunks and settled himself to wait, seated on the bulging root of a tree. The people were quiet now, and many of them watched the blank gates of the enclosure. There was tension in the air.

A sudden rise in sound and movement roused Branwald from half-sleep. The crowd was coming to its feet. Something was happening. Standing up, Branwald saw that the high doors were still shut, but lights were moving behind the enclosure wall. In a moment, the head and shoulders of a man appeared inside the walls. It was Kyran the Rulemaker.

The crowd surged near, and Branwald followed. Ghost-like in his white cloak, Kyran raised his arms for silence. Immediately the crowd was hushed.

'People of the Islands,' he called, his voice cracked and rough as weathered limestone, 'it has fallen to my lot to speak to you. The stranger, Urkor of the People of the Great River, has told us about the band that left these islands two years ago. They have been captured and imprisoned by the Orelord.' A gasp from the crowd. 'He says that their leader, Feowald, has demanded —'

'Elder Kyran!' Dame Aleena's voice was louder than the others. 'What has the stranger said about the men? What is their condition? Which of them no longer live? These are things we must know!' A swell of approval followed her words, and the grizzled Elder raised his hands again.

'Be assured that the death of any man from these islands fills our hearts with sadness, as it does yours. The stranger says that five were killed in the first clash between the forces of the Orelord and the men from these islands, who should never have —'

'Well, *tell* us!' Dame Aleena called. 'Do not keep it from us!'

Even from where he stood, Branwald could see the anger in the Elder's face. 'Dame Aleena!' he retorted. 'Someday you will go too far ....'

But the voices of protest were many. They swelled, drowning the old man's voice. He glared at the crowd. 'I will tell you. He says that the ones who have died are Shaloss, Krifell, Chald, Frelt and Brador ....' His closing words were drowned by a heartrending shriek from somewhere on the right of the group. The cry was echoed by the voices of several other women and children, and the gathered crowd swayed and split as a wave of grief swept through it. But still there were voices raised and questions shouted at the old Elder, who stood stern and unmoved on his dais.

'What has the Assembly learnt about the rest of these men?' Branwald recognised the gruff voice of Vokt the Netmaker.

'He has told us that Feowald the Protector has asked that the Firebolt be found and sent ....' Kyran paused. An awed hush swept through the crowd. 'That the Firebolt be found and sent on the long journey to where he is, in order that he may extricate himself and his men from the danger that they have allowed themselves to become embroiled in.'

Kyran paused to draw breath. From somewhere down near the shore came the screech of a night-owl. The people were silent, their puzzlement showing in their faces. 'But, People of the Islands, this Assembly has decreed that the Firebolt would only unleash all the evil in the world, even if it could be found. The Elders are satisfied that Feowald and the others have gone far beyond their mandate in becoming involved in conflict with the forces of the Orelord ....'

Another, louder gasp from the crowd. Voices rose; questions stabbed the night air.

'Elder Kyran!' It was Aleena's voice again, more strident now. 'Surely you are not suggesting that we abandon our men and do nothing to help them?'

Kyran's face darkened. 'The Assembly of the Elders has

decided —' His voice was drowned by the uproar.

'Let us see the stranger!' a man's voice shouted. 'Let us speak to him!'

'Yes!' came another man's voice. 'The stranger must come before us!'

'Bring him out!' yelled a third. 'We will hear it from his very mouth!'

Kyran glared down at the speakers for a moment, his face hard and angry. Then he shouted something and began to descend from view.

Among the men at the front of the crowd, the call went up, more insistently. 'Let him come before us! Let him speak to us!' The old man ignored them and disappeared. But the clamour became louder and more insistent. Men, women and children took up the cry, 'Let us hear him!', and all surged forward towards the closed gates.

As the shouting grew in intensity, Branwald felt a strange alarm in his heart. He had never before seen such open anger expressed against the Elders. He had never before seen such Violation.

The grey head of Elder Kyran rose into view again. His face was livid. He waved his hands in an agitated manner, mouthing words that Branwald could not hear. The crowd quietened.

'The stranger, Urkor, will speak to you, as you have asked, but it is with the express permission of the Assembly that he does so. He will tell you that the men from these islands have offended a formidable foe, one who is beyond the power of this small people to defeat. And when he speaks of the Firebolt, I have to warn you' — Kyran's voice rose — 'that he is merely reporting the words of the leader, Feowald, who thinks, in his ....'

But the rising sound from the impatient crowd drowned Kyran's words. He looked down, beckoning to someone to mount beside him. In a moment the dark shape of Urkor stood there, gazing impassively down on the crowd. They were silent.

'I have been sent by Feowald,' he said evenly. A murmur. Branwald watched him, wide-eyed, needing to believe that in this dour stranger lay the main hope for his captive father. 'He and those who still live are imprisoned in the great Bastion of the Orelord.' A gasp from the crowd. 'He knows, as these your Elders know, that this is not a warlike people. He knows there is little hope that from here will come a force that will release him and the others.' Beside him, Kyran was becoming agitated. Urkor raised his voice. 'That is why he has asked for the Firebolt!'

Old Kyran was waving his hands as if to scatter to the wind the words just spoken.

'No! My people, the stranger does not know what he says! The Firebolt is gone! It has finished its evil work! Let it rest, wherever it is!'

But the crowd were loud in their response. The people turned to speak to one another. Then from the left came a woman's voice; Branwald recognised it as that of Meecha, the wife of Spen the Fishseer. 'That is what the Elders have always told us,' she called. She turned and spoke to the crowd, ignoring the two figures on the wall. 'But there are some among us who have another belief, which has often been spoken by those who have been banished. It is a belief that we have not been allowed to hold ....' Several voices tried to hush her up, but she responded with even greater passion. 'The husbands of many women who stand here tonight are in grievous peril. Yes, we know what has been said about the Firebolt. It has great power. We know it can be powerful for the work of darkness or for the work of the light. But it is also said that it all depends on the possessor! I say we must find the Firebolt and send it to our men. One of them, maybe Feowald, will use it well. It is the only way, the only hope!'

The voices swelled again, but now there was disagreement. Then, from the wall, Kyran's voice cut through the night air. 'People of the Islands! Remember our father, Feyan. Do not forget in your pride that it was he, speaking in the voice of the Dread Spirit, who gave this Assembly of the Elders the power to guide and curb the spirit of his people. This night the Assembly has spoken. Let those who stand against its word stand up before the people, so that all can see them in their wickedness and in their Violation. Let all those who fear the Dread Spirit go to their homes, so that they may not share the sin and condemnation of those who have Violated!'

The noise from the crowd faltered, became hushed. Kyran, his face black as thunder, glared down at them. Urkor seemed about to speak again, but when the old man flung his arms up imperiously, he turned abruptly and descended from sight.

There was a moment of uncertainty. Then several people on the edge of the crowd began to filter back towards the path that led to Fisherway. Some of the women cried out in protest, but those close at hand hushed them quickly and ushered them crying away. Soon most of the crowd was moving away from the Portal House.

But some were standing their ground. Dame Aleena glared defiantly upwards at the old Rulemaker. Vokt and his wife were there, and Spen with his wife and two children.

Vokt spoke, and his voice was shaking. 'Elder Kyran, I hope I may be wrong, but I fear that a great injustice has been done here tonight. There are many among the people who have thoughts to speak and wisdom to speak well. But their voices are not heard, and cannot be heard while —'

The Elder made a flinging gesture with his hands, turned and began to descend out of sight. Vokt broke off, shaking his head in anger. He looked down at his wife and at Spen's children. 'Come,' he said. He took his wife by the arm and gently turned her towards the path. She, however, pulled away; she went to Dame Aleena, touched her arm and spoke several words to her. The irate Dame turned and strode away, ahead of the small remaining group, towards Fisherway. As she passed him, Branwald saw that tears were streaming down her cheeks.

Branwald waited until Vokt was passing before he moved out onto the path. The Netmaker reached out his hand when he saw him; when Branwald came closer, Vokt put an arm around his shoulders. No one spoke until the small group had come to the top of Fisherway. Then Vokt stopped and turned to face Branwald.

'I do not know what words to say to you, my young hero,' he said gruffly, catching Branwald by the neck and shaking him gently. 'But these are matters which must be pondered upon.' His voice dropped so that even the others could not hear him. 'I promise you one thing. I will speak with Spen and the others. It seems very difficult, but we will see. You must keep your heart up. This is what your father would want of you.' With that, he turned to his wife, and together they went towards their house.

Branwald went home. His mother was waiting outside the door of the house. He steeled himself against her grief, and against her reading his thoughts.

'Were you there?' she asked. Her voice seemed calm. He nodded. Estel looked at him, and he read her thoughts as if they were his own: not sadness for herself, but a great flood of sympathy for him. He went to her.

'Something must be done,' he whispered hoarsely. 'They cannot let this happen.'

'Let us go to Eroona,' she said.

They found Eroona in her chamber, lying with her face turned towards the wall. She would not look at them when they entered. Branwald knew she was crying.

'Why can somebody not help him?' she whispered. 'They cannot leave him, and the others, there ....'

Branwald broke away from his mother and went out to the Home Room. His sorrow was turning into anger. He had always believed that the Elders were right, that in their authority lay the security and safety of the people. Now his belief was shattered, and the disillusionment was almost more than he could bear.

He went outside into the still, star-sprinkled night. The lights of the Forest People were fewer now, and there was no twinkle from the place near the Cataract. He stood by the friendly laurel, thinking, staring into the blackness where he knew the Elvan Cliffs lay.

Then it came to him again — the call he had heard before; but this time it was stronger and more insistent. It was not the sound of a voice, but something in his mind — a shape, an image hovering in a deep recess of his consciousness. And there was something else, nearer, more powerful, something he had not felt before. He experienced it as a deep desire, a lust for strength, for power, for vengeance, for striking with blind fury, for destruction, for his mother, for ....

The sound that came from Branwald's throat was a moan of disgust. He shuddered, aghast. How could he think in this way about his mother?

And then Branwald heard the soft rasp of a footfall behind him on Watcher's Path, and he turned his head to look.

At first he saw nothing except the black bulk of the trees and the houses on the upper slope. Then he made out a shape moving towards the door of his house. He stifled the impulse to call out. The lone figure, clearer now in the starlight, paused at the door. Branwald waited for the knock, but it did not come. He stood quite still, breathing through his mouth to quieten the hiss of air through his nostrils.

Less than twenty feet from him, the man stood unmoving for a moment. Then he slowly turned until he faced directly towards Branwald.

'Who is it?' Branwald asked in a low voice.

A pause. Then, 'It is I, Urkor.' Another pause. 'You are Branwald. I have come to speak with you, and with your mother.'

Branwald moved towards the door. 'My mother is in the house. I will tell her you are here.'

He reached for the door-latch, but Urkor's arm stretched out to block his way. 'Not yet,' he whispered. He caught Branwald's shoulder and moved him back towards the laurel tree. His fingers dug into Branwald's flesh.

Urkor turned Branwald to face him. 'You must listen to me. You are the only one who can help your father.' His breath was fetid on Branwald's face, and the boy involuntarily squirmed. 'But the others must not know what you tell me. That would be bad for you and for your mother. You have heard what the Elder Kyran said, yes?'

Branwald twisted his shoulder out of the man's grip. 'I have heard it.'

Urkor moved closer. 'Then you must tell me where the Firebolt is. It is the only way to bring back your father.'

Branwald looked towards the house. The oil lamp was burning in the Home Room. He needed his mother's presence. Yet it disturbed him that the lust which he had felt moments before was still there, stronger than ever. He thought about the Firebolt, and an image of deep amber water flowing from the mouth of the Elvan cave came into his mind. He lifted his eyes to search the dark face above him.

'I do not know where the Firebolt is,' he said, taking a step towards the house. Urkor moved to block his way.

'You know!' he growled, and there was menace in the tone. 'Don't be a fool! Your father's life depends on it, do you not realise that? No one need know what you tell me.'

Behind Urkor, the door of the house opened, and Branwald saw the figure of his mother silhouetted against the yellow light.

'Branwald?' There was alarm in her voice. 'Branwald! Where are you?'

He stepped around the stranger. 'I am here, Mother.'

'Who is with you? I heard talking.'

'I am with him.' Urkor's voice was like the growl of a bear. 'I have come to seek your help.'

Estel looked into the darkness of Watcher's Path. Then she stepped back towards the light. 'Come in,' she said quietly.

Urkor followed Branwald into the Home Room, and Estel shut the door. She indicated a chair for the stranger, but he remained standing, with his back to the entrance. Branwald saw the hard eyes looking at his mother's face, then at her body. The thought which came from the stranger made Branwald involuntarily step across in front of her.

'How can we help you?' she asked, placing her hands on Branwald's shoulders.

The eyes that looked at her were cold and hard. 'You are Estel?'

She nodded.

'Your husband asked for the Firebolt to be sent. Without it there is no hope that he will return to this place. I must know where it is, so that I can bring it to him.'

Branwald sensed his mother's hesitation. 'You cannot know how much we long for Feowald's safe return,' she said.

'But you have heard the words of the Elders. It is not through the Firebolt that he can be saved. There must be another way. There must be men in the Islands who are prepared to help him and the others.'

Urkor's upper lip curled in the beginning of a sneer. 'Yes, I have heard your Elders. But I have also heard them saying that it is not possible for anyone to go from here. In truth, they would achieve little. But there are those, as you know, who believe in the power of the Firebolt. If you were one of them, you would not hesitate to help your husband.' He half turned towards the door. 'I have come at his request. If there is no one here willing to help him, then so be it.'

'Wait.' Estel voiced the thought that was in Branwald's mind. 'If you were to find the Firebolt, how would you be able to get it to my husband?'

'We can — I can get it to him,' Urkor said. 'There are ways.'

'But surely he is guarded by the forces of the Orelord,' Branwald challenged.

The man's eyes rested on him, and there was anger and impatience in them. 'He who has the Firebolt can deal with a force many times greater than those.'

'But it is said that the Firebolt should not be —' The sudden sharp grip of his mother's hand on his shoulder made Branwald stop.

Estel spoke, and her voice was steady and strong. 'I do not want you to think that I am not grateful for what you are doing. But I do not know where the Firebolt is. They say it is beyond the great Cataract of the Karn Gorge. But it has been lost for many years, and the Island People do not frequent those regions. If we knew where it was to be found, and how it could be used to save my husband, then we could help you. But neither I nor my children know where it is.'

Urkor stood for a moment, staring at Estel's face. As Branwald stared back at the grim features, he became aware again of the glow around the man's body. At first he thought it came from the yellow light of the oil-lamp, but as he watched, it changed from orange to a dull brown. Then, with a searing glare at Branwald, Urkor suddenly turned on his heel, jerked open the door and strode out. As they watched his dark shape merge with the night, Eroona came from her chamber.

'I do not like that man,' she stated flatly. 'He does not speak truth. He is false and evil.'

Branwald closed the door and turned to face the others. 'I do not trust him either,' he said. 'But if what he says about Father is true, then it may also be true that only the Firebolt can help him.'

'But how —?' began Eroona.

'Branwald!' Estel's face was severe. 'You must not say these things.' She turned away abruptly, so that he could not read her face.

'Mother,' he said, 'I think I know where the Firebolt is hidden.'

She swung round, her eyes staring. 'Branwald,' she whispered, 'what are you saying? Why are you saying this?'

He took his courage in his hands. 'I have said it, Mother, because it is true. To say a true thing cannot be wrong. I think it is hidden in the depths of the cave from which the Elvan flows. I feel it. It seems to speak to me sometimes.'

Estel's hand went to her mouth to stifle the cry that leapt to her throat. It was as if something which she had always dreaded had happened.

'What do you mean, it speaks to you?'

'Do not be alarmed, Mother. It is just a picture in my mind, like a dream. I feel that I want to go to the place and see if it is there.'

She was distressed. 'No! No, Branwald! It cannot be you. You cannot be the one .... It is an illusion, a trick. You must pay no attention to this. It is for someone else, not for you.'

'But, Mother —'

'No. There must be another way.' There was a desperation in her that he had never seen before. 'Some of the other men must go to help your father ....'

Branwald shook his head. 'How can they, Mother? They have children and wives too. What could they do, a small force against the might of the Orelord?'

'Wait,' Estel pleaded. 'Wait till tomorrow. Something may

change. Some help may come ....' The tears overflowed her eyes. 'You are not old enough. You are not strong enough to know the Firebolt. It is not fair that you should be asked to do it.' She gathered him to her and reached for Eroona. Her grip was fierce and possessive, and her tears were wet on their faces. 'If you know where it is, then you must tell the stranger. He will bring it to Feowald and the others. He knows the way.'

Branwald pulled away to look at her face. 'Mother, he is not the one. You must know that. You must feel the strength and the power of the man. But it is not a power for good. Eroona feels it too. He is devious and dangerous, and there is something he is hiding. I know that you, too, can read his thoughts as I can.' He sensed the protest that was coming. 'Mother, there is no point in hiding the thought-speaking from me or from Eroona any longer. We can do it. You can do it. There are others who can do it. Even this stranger, I fear, can sometimes read my thoughts. Yet I cannot believe that it is a Violation.'

She looked into his eyes, and in hers he saw the old fear and sadness. 'It may not be, my son. It may not be. But I fear that the stranger has seen things in your mind that should not be there. You are not strong enough to know the Firebolt.'

But Branwald was shaking his head even as she spoke. 'This is something that I have to do. I am surer now than ever I was. If Father is to return to us, I must do it. There is no other way.'

This time Estel didn't protest. Instead she merely brushed back the dark locks from his forehead. 'Why did he have to go?' she whispered. 'Why couldn't he have accepted the way things were? Such a foolish notion he had — that somewhere there might be a better place, a better way ....'

Branwald squeezed her arm to emphasise his words. 'Maybe there is a better way, Mother. In this place. Maybe he should have stayed here and tried to change it. He and you and Vokt and Aleena and the others could change it.'

She seemed slightly dazed as she placed her finger on his lips. 'No, Branwald. Do not say this. I could not stand to see you on the Island of the Banished. For myself, I could endure it, but it would destroy me to see you ....'

'That is the first thing that must be changed,' Branwald said, his anger putting a gulf between them. 'It is wrong to shut people away like that.'

She shook her head slowly, her eyes troubled. 'If he were here, he would know what is best to do. But ... I cannot think.' She rubbed her forehead with long fingers.

'Mother, I have been speaking to Maloof.' He ignored the startled look and the sudden gasp from Eroona. 'He and Saneela have escaped. They live with the Forest People, above the Cataract. Maloof, too, has heard the call of the Firebolt. He and I together, we will search for it. I will not be alone. Together we will find it and take it to Father.'

'But how, even if you can find it?' Estel whispered, shaking her head. 'The way is ....'

'If we find the Firebolt, we will find a way. We must believe this. If we are meant to have it, then there will be a way.'

CHAPTER NINE

Dawn was only a faint pink glow beyond the top of Barren Peak when Branwald stole out of his bed. He dressed quietly in his linen shirt, calfskin breeches and woollen tunic, and looped his leather belt through the scabbard of his father's old hunting knife. Into a canvas satchel he stuffed his seamless red cloak and some spare clothes.

His mother was already in the Home Room, her face pale as she fanned the embers of the fire to flame. Without speaking, she set a platter of wheaten bread and a goblet of milk before him. On the table, beside two chubby beeswax candles and a box of flints, lay a wooden goblet and a bundle wrapped in a linen cloth — Branwald knew it was extra food. He put them carefully into his satchel. He took his bow and quiver of arrows from their wooden peg and slung them over his back.

Eroona came to stand beside the flickering flame, her face peaked with sleep, clutching herself to keep warm. The smoky glow of the oil-lamp threw shadows on the walls as Estel moved around Branwald. He wanted to be gone. He feared his mother might yet try to stop him.

When, a short while later, the time came for him to leave, she stood by the door, waiting for him to pass. Eroona came silently to him and held him for a moment.

'If you need help,' she whispered, 'no matter where you are, talk to me. I will tell Mother.'

Branwald nodded, and turned to his mother. Her face was calm. She held him tightly for a moment. 'May the Spirit go with you, and bring you safely back to us. Remember one thing, Branwald. It was once said that the one who wields the Firebolt must know his fair side and his dark side, else he may be destroyed. This is my fear for you. You are too young.

You cannot yet know yourself. Promise me, therefore, that if you find it, and when the flood of passion sweeps over you, as it surely will, you will leave the Firebolt from your hand before you act. If you find Maloof, and if he goes with you, say this to him: that he must take the Firebolt and fling it away before he can allow you to use it against the Force of Life. Promise me this, Branwald, and I will rest easier when you are gone from us.'

He gazed into her eyes. 'I promise, Mother. I will not forget.'

He left them standing at the door of the house and strode away into the half-light, his bundle slung over his shoulder. He did not look back until he came to the corner of Fisherway. His mother and sister were two dim silhouettes in the rectangle of light that was the doorway of their house. Branwald turned the corner and began his descent to the lake shore.

The lake was shrouded in a low white mist that lay still and eerie over the flat surface. Branwald readied his canoe, storing his bundle tightly in the prow. Then an image of amber water floated into his mind again, and he involuntarily looked northwards. Above the layer of mist, the bulk of the Elvan Cliffs loomed dark and forbidding. He slid the canoe out onto the water until only the tip of the stern sat on the dry sand. He stepped in, seated himself, and with one deft shove he was floating.

Before he dipped for the first stroke, however, he allowed the craft to drift round parallel to the shore, and he looked back at the village that he loved. His eyes took in the black shapes of the squat houses that flanked Fisherway. He followed the straggling line upwards into the gloom to where he knew his house stood, but under the black trees he could not discern its shape. 'Goodbye, Eroona,' he thought. 'Look after Mother and comfort her.'

Immediately the answering thought came, clear and strong. 'Goodbye, Branwald. Come back to us soon.'

He dipped the paddle into the still water, pointed the canoe into the mist and pulled back against the resisting water. When next he looked behind, he saw only the very tops of the high pines above the mist. The rest was a shroud of white.

Branwald was glad of the pale light that crept across the sky from the east. He needed to keep his course, and he found that by standing upright in the canoe at intervals, he could see the twin peaks which were beyond and in line with the First Narrows. Once he was through there, the narrowness of Woodfern Lake would keep him from going astray.

He thought of Maloof. There was little chance that he would be abroad with his goats so early in the morning. How would he know that Branwald was coming? Unless, somehow, Branwald might speak to him in thought .... He concentrated his mind on the area of the first Elvan Cliffs. 'Maloof,' he called silently. 'I am coming. Make ready.' He waited, trying to keep his mind clear and open, but there was no answering thought or image. Perhaps Maloof was still sleeping, he thought. He would try again when he was closer.

Woodfern Lake was silent when Branwald drifted onto it. High above, he heard the scream of an eagle, thin with distance. He looked up. High in the clear air, well above the great shadow thrown by Barren Peak, he saw the diminutive shape of the great bird, circling lazily on wings that were golden with sunlight. Unbidden, a prayer came to his mind. 'Oh noble one, give me your eyes to see, and your wings to carry me safely to where I have to go.'

~

When Branwald came to the mouth of the Elvan River, the peaks to the west were ablaze with gold and orange light. Soon he was hauling the canoe up along the sloping, shadowy ledge, all sound blotted out by the roaring and spitting of the great waterfall beside him. At the top, he laid the craft gently on several tufts of grass and turned to look southwards. He searched the white floor of the great basin for the flat place where Eagle Lake should be, and for the black mound of Redwood Island.

There it was, less dark because of the reflected light from the rocky walls to the west. The valley had never looked so beautiful. The scene was so still and quiet that it could have been one of Eroona's pictures. There was no movement except the dark figure of an early-morning stag or bear near the misty shore of Hazel Lake.

With a sigh, Branwald lifted the craft with both hands and made his way upstream along the cliff-top. When he came to the smooth flow of the river above the Cataract, he found the stepped descent in the cliff, eased the canoe onto the water and got in. In a moment he was paddling strongly upstream.

When Branwald came in sight of the entrance to the little inlet where he had met Maloof, he thought of his friend again. He focused his mind on a place he could not see, above the right-hand cliff, and called silently.

After a moment, he had a strong image of a stream falling onto a pebbled beach. With growing anticipation he watched the rift draw closer. He sensed a presence. Then, as the canoe drifted across the mouth of the inlet, he heard a call.

'Branwald!' Maloof was standing by the plashing water at the base of the cliff. 'Come in!' he called. Branwald drove the canoe in between the narrow walls, his heart suddenly light.

'How did you know I was coming?' he asked.

'I don't know. I just sensed it. What is happening?'

Branwald told him about the arrival of the stranger, and about the news which he had brought. Maloof's face brightened when he heard that his father was still alive, but grew serious at the news of his captivity. 'I do not trust this man from the far islands,' Branwald continued. 'He wants the Firebolt too much. I cannot believe that it is just so he can rescue our fathers. That is why I have come. I intend to seek the Firebolt myself and bring it to my father. He will know how to use it.' Maloof's eyes widened, but Branwald continued. 'I am going into the cave. You will come with me?'

Maloof bent to lift the spare paddle from the floor of the craft. 'If our fathers still live and are in need of help, I will go further than this cave with you, Branwald. Come on.'

At the mouth of the cave, Maloof steadied the drifting craft, while Branwald opened his bundle and took out a beeswax candle. He struck the flint until the tinder in the metal bowl caught fire, and lit the twisted wick. Setting the candle before him on the floor of the canoe, he began again to paddle. In the darkness ahead of them, the black water gurgled and plopped.

'Why did you come to the river?' Branwald asked.

'I had a dream that our house was being attacked by many bearded men on horses. They had firebrands in their hands. One of them was trying to break in through the window, and I was smiting him with my staff, but I could not keep him out. When I awoke I could not stop thinking that something fearful was coming. I got up and came to the river.'

In the darkness, the nose of the canoe bumped into something hard. Branwald back-paddled. 'Our eyes will grow accustomed to it,' he said.

'Did you know that the Forest People have seen a group of strangers on the high pass that leads towards the Great River?' Maloof asked.

'No. When were they seen?'

'Around the time that the stranger appeared. Our hunters say that they were camped just above the tree-line. They have many weapons. Our people kept well away from them.'

Branwald considered this. 'That is very strange,' he said.

The boys were silent. Slowly their eyes adjusted to the blackness. The weak candlelight showed pillars of glistening creamy-brown calcite on either side, while above them, great pointed stalactites hung ominously. Maloof's shadow was a huge wavering thing against the jagged roof and walls ahead. Branwald whispered, 'Here. You take the candle and hold it before you. Guide us while I paddle.'

Slowly they moved deeper into the cave. Maloof guided the prow, leaning forward at times to push away against the cold surface of a column or a cascade of calcite flowing down a wall. Once, Branwald looked behind him. The only sign that there was daylight in the upper world was the black silhouette of a forest of suspended stalactites and pillars like tree-trunks, against a faint small light far away. Beneath him the water, too, was black. He dipped his hand, cupped his fingers and scooped the cool liquid to his mouth. It tasted sweet. Reassured, he pushed ahead.

'The way is narrowing,' Maloof said quietly.

The walls crowded in and the passage wound to the right. Branwald felt a cool breeze on his face. The candle flickered, and Maloof twisted his body to protect the flame.

'Look! There is something!' Branwald whispered.

'Where?'

'Ahead. A little to the left.'

Maloof shaded the candle with his hand and stared into the darkness ahead. 'Yes! I see it!'

In the distance, suspended in blackness, a pale semicircle of grey was visible. Beneath it, quivering and moving, lay its faint reflection on the surface of the water.

The opening ahead grew larger. In the dim light, they could see the outline of curving walls and the fluted roof of the cave. Sounds were suddenly magnified. Now they could see bright daylight reflected on the layered left-hand wall in the distance. The water beneath them was regaining its honey colour. As they drew closer, it became clear that, though the roof and the left-hand wall of the cave remained intact, the daylight was flooding in through a long opening in the right-hand wall. It was as if the whole right side of the cave had been carved away for a distance of thirty yards. Straight ahead, beyond this wide gash, the cave continued into the depths of the mountain.

'Is this the place?' Maloof said quietly. There was wonder in his tone. They came to the opening and looked out. Beyond the riverside reeds, just a foot or two above the level of the river's surface, lay a flat open space, carpeted with grass and bushes. The area was small, enclosed on all sides by walls of limestone which rose vertically out of sight.

'Look,' said Maloof, pointing. Farther along the bank, partly sheltered by the overhanging roof, stood a wooden rack. It was festooned with the remains, in various stages of drying, of a number of fishes. A sudden movement behind a clump of bushes startled them. Next moment, they were looking into the placid eyes of a nanny-goat. She chewed impassively and regarded them with interested eyes.

Branwald drifted the canoe over to the shelving edge and grabbed at a tuft of grass. 'Come on,' he said. He stepped out, lifting his bow and quiver from the floor of the canoe. Nothing moved in the level area before him, except for the inquisitive ears of the goat. Together the boys lifted the canoe out onto the rocks. When they turned again, the nanny-goat was beside them, nuzzling at their hands as if expecting a tasty titbit.

'Who are you, my pretty one?' asked Maloof, stroking the animal behind the ears. Disappointed, she butted him gently on the thigh with her bare forehead, then ambled away towards the bushes again.

They came out from under the overhanging rock and looked up. Several hundred feet above them, a great round disk of sky was visible. Fluffy clouds drifted slowly past. The outline of the cliff-top all around was softened by clumps of shrubs and plants that hung like a tattered rug over the sides.

Maloof caught Branwald's arm. 'I know this place,' he said. 'It is the Kadach Pit. And we are at the bottom of it.' He looked around, wide-eyed. 'It is a place forbidden to the Forest People, because they fear it. They say that the ghost of the Old Soldier lives here.'

CHAPTER TEN

Branwald surveyed the clearing and the deep shadows in the layered rocks that encircled them. He was surprised that he did not feel any fear.

'Someone lives here,' he said. 'But I do not think it is a ghost.' For the past few moments he had begun to sense something: a presence, very close by. He scanned the walls all around, searching for a shape, a sign. He walked towards the centre of the open area. In the grass he found a brown path that snaked from the river towards a bulge on the wall. He followed it, his heart beating against his ribcage. Maloof padded softly behind.

'Hallo!' Branwald called. The sound echoed around them and drifted upwards. There was a raucous cry from above and a startled raven flapped up towards the rim, a hard black thing against the white clouds. Branwald continued along the path. To his right there was a stratum of rock in the face of the cliff, about four feet thick and about three feet up from ground level. Something on this surface caught his attention. Strange shapes, not natural; pictures, carved into the rock, standing out in relief from the fossil-speckled limestone.

'Look at this!' exclaimed Branwald. There was a series of scenes, each one several feet square and edged with a grooved border, stretching along the rock-face. On one he saw what appeared to be a great canoe, but such a canoe as he had never seen before. The vessel was short and squat, and its sides rose unusually high. Just below the upper edge, the artist had shown square openings, through which cylindrical shapes protruded.

'Look at this one!' said Maloof quietly, pointing at another picture. The relief showed a towering, helmeted male figure, standing on a platform or rampart of some kind. The well-proportioned body was suited in clothes that were made from many small overlapping pieces, as if of wood or metal. In his hand was raised an object like a sword, but shorter, with a cylindrical blade and no point.

Branwald's eye drifted to the next frame, but the square of rock was blank and untouched. The next one, however, was not a picture, but a map of some kind. The artist had carved range upon range of mountains, through which a deep valley had been cut. Along the valley floor ran a river, meandering in many loops until at last it reached the undulating surface of a great lake or sea. At the mouth of this river, a scattering of islands jutted from the frozen waves.

Branwald sucked in his breath. 'The Great River!' he whispered. He sought the source of the river and found it to be a semicircular hole near the base of a mountain. He searched for a lake-studded bowl among the ranges, but it was not there. There was no feature that he could recognise as the home of the Island People.

Branwald ran his fingers over the fresh grey limestone, and his eyes took in the scattered chippings on the ground at his feet. 'This has been done recently,' he said quietly. 'The one who did it may be nearby.'

The two friends stepped away from the wall, scanning to left and right, their voices and even their breathing stilled by expectation. The path which they had left continued towards the bulge in the cliff. They followed it.

As they rounded the curving rock, a low wall came into view, a three-foot-high barrier of fitted slabs of limestone forming a semicircle outwards from the cliff. A wicker gate, closed, blocked a narrow opening halfway along. And in the face of the cliff, at the centre of the semicircle, there was an opening.

The dark entrance was certainly a cave mouth, but of a shape that Branwald had never seen before. It was the width of the front doorway in his house, and it was crowned by a perfectly semicircular arch.

The two friends stared into the opening. A short distance in, there were steps leading upwards into the blackness.

'Hallo!' called Branwald again. 'Is anyone in this place?'

They listened. They heard only the breathing of the wind, high among the walls.

'Come on,' whispered Branwald. He was about to step over the low gate when Maloof caught his tunic from behind and held him. Branwald pulled away. 'Don't worry. There is no harm ....'

'Look,' Maloof whispered.

Branwald turned and followed Maloof's eyes upwards, along the grooved wall before them. About twenty feet up its face was a ledge. At one end of it was an opening, similar to the one at ground level, but narrower and lower. At the other shaded end, grey and unmoving as the rock-face, stood the figure of an old man. Though his body was erect and straight, his head was bent. His hair was grey and his head was encircled by a band of grey material, which matched the grey wool of his long hooded tunic. Only his face, deep bronze in colour, distinguished him from the rock behind. And although he could not see the old man's eyes, sunk as they were in cavernous sockets under white eyebrows, Branwald knew that this man was looking at him and Maloof.

Branwald felt his scalp tingle. He did not feel fear, however, for he was becoming aware of the faint blue haze that enveloped the man — a shimmering around his body, a halo of calm light. And being aware of it, Branwald knew that the old man was not his enemy.

'Who are you?' The voice was firm and deep. Only the lips moved. Branwald fancied that the deep-set eyes were fixed on him.

'I am Branwald, son of Feowald the Protector, of the Island People,' he said.

'And I am Maloof. My mother is Saneela and my father is Brugarh the Woodman.'

'Our fathers went away to the mouth of the Great River many moons ago,' Branwald explained, 'and they have not come back ....'

The old man nodded his head slowly, as if these things were known to him already. 'So you have finally come. I have been waiting. I have been expecting you for many moons.' The head moved slowly up and down. 'It is time. It is beyond time. It is ....' The voice became hoarse and faint. 'But you must come in. Come in.' The old man beckoned stiffly, indicating the entrance below. 'Come in. Do not fear.' Then he moved slowly along the ledge and, entering the low opening, disappeared from view.

Branwald looked at Maloof. 'Will you come?' he said.

Maloof nodded, his face softening into a smile. 'Having come this far, how can I not?'

The passageway was narrow and gloomy as it ascended. But the darkness was only momentary; then the walls fell away and they were in a low-roofed chamber. Branwald had time only to notice that light filtered into this chamber through circular shafts in the roof; then, from another opening in the wall before him, the grey figure emerged.

The pupils of the old man's eyes were distant black points in the caves under his brows. 'Sit,' he said, indicating a low bench hewn from the rock. 'You will have some refreshment.'

The man poured some liquid into two grey goblets, which he handed to his guests. The goblet felt to Branwald as if it had been cut from solid rock. 'Drink,' said their host.

The liquid was strange to the taste, but cool and sweet, and Branwald was grateful. When he handed back the goblet, he caught the intensity of the old man's eyes as he studied his two visitors. 'You must excuse me,' the man said. 'It has been so long since ....' He turned away to replace the empty goblets, then regarded them for a long moment.

'Your fathers are under the power of the Orelord. And you want to release them from his grip. This is why you have come, yes?'

Dumbfounded, Branwald could only nod. Maloof, too, was silent.

The creases round the old man's mouth stretched and deepened as he smiled. 'Do not forget that even an old man can speak in thought with those whose minds are free and unguarded.' But then his face became serious again, and he spoke to Branwald. 'You must tell me about the one who has come — the one who says he is from the Tarquan Islands.'

Branwald told the story of Urkor. The old man did not reply immediately, but turned his head and stared at the blank wall near the doorway for a long moment.

'This one wants the thing that is here, but we do not yet know his purpose.' He inclined his head once more, as if listening for something far away.

'Maloof has told me that there is a group of armed strangers camped on the Pass of Feyan,' Branwald said. 'They came around the time when the stranger appeared. I think the stranger may have come with them.'

A frown creased the old man's brow for a moment. 'It may be true,' he mused. 'The mind of the Orelord is a devious one. But it is good to know these things. To be forewarned is to be forearmed.'

He leaned forward towards the boys, his very posture demanding their attention. 'The journey to the mouth of the Great River will not be an easy one. This group of men is only one of the many dangers. Your hearts may fail you, and you may want to return rather than go on. Do not be afraid to listen to the words of the Spirit within you. Better that you should return unharmed and unharming, to wait for another time, than that the Firebolt should fall into the hands of the Orelord. Now, think well on this question before you answer.' The old man looked directly at Branwald. 'Will you accept the guardianship of the Firebolt?'

Branwald looked into the eyes before him. In their grey-black depths he sensed great suffering, but great wisdom too. And in that moment he felt his courage grow strong. He looked at the calm face of his friend Maloof. 'I will,' he said.

'Will you bear the Firebolt to the mouth of the Great River?'

Branwald did not hesitate. 'I will, if I am worthy.' Beside him, Maloof nodded his assent.

The old man stepped closer. 'No one is wholly worthy, my young hero. Remember this: to bear the Firebolt is a great privilege. It has great power, but he who would use it for good must also know his dark side. When the dark side is in the ascendant, the Firebolt must be laid aside. If necessary, you must cast it away from you, before you will use it or let it be used for the work of darkness.' The black pupils bored into Branwald's soul. 'Above all, do not ask another to wield the Firebolt in a struggle that is rightfully yours.

This can cause great, great sorrow.'

The old man's face was close to Branwald's. A sudden wave of grief and pain swept through Branwald's breast, so intense that he cried out and twisted away from the eyes that stared down at him. The weight was almost too much to bear. He had an urge to rise and fly to the daylight, but the old man gripped his shoulder.

'Do not go, Branwald. It is necessary for you to know something of my pain. But only something. It is enough.' The firm grip held. The pain eased and faded, and Branwald looked again into the piercing eyes. 'Your friend Maloof has many gifts. Listen to him. He will speak to you about the Earth Mother, who gives life to all things and who takes it away. She will be your guide, if you ask Her.'

He stepped back. 'Now, come with me.'

The old man led them down the winding steps by which they had come, out into the dazzling light of day, and towards the rock-face where the carvings were. He stopped before the first one. It showed several islands set in a sea of stone. On the shore of the largest of these, the artist had etched a collection of houses balanced on tall stilts. Beneath the houses were several long canoes similar to Branwald's.

'These are as I remember them,' the old man said. 'My recollection may be different from reality, or the reality may have changed. But this is the place where your ancestors came from, and where you are both going, if the Spirit so wishes. You will know you have arrived there when you see the houses standing thus above the tides.'

The old man moved to the picture of the squat, high-hulled canoe. 'This,' he said, 'is a ship of the Orelord. Those mouths which you see gaping from the side will spit iron and fire. They are capable of destroying another ship such as this, or a house set on stilts.' He looked at the two boys, and his eyes seemed to soften. 'These ships stay on the ocean. With luck, you will not need to encounter them.'

His eyes turned to the picture of the great iron-clad warrior. 'This one is as he was a little before I last saw him. There was a time when I thought him the bravest I ever knew.' The old man shook his head slowly. 'But wisdom passed him by. He thought that the Firebolt would give him power over all things. He thought that power was all. This was his great error. And that was why he died.' Branwald felt keenly the old man's sadness. 'But he is not the one you will have to contend with. Another man is the Orelord now. I know him, although I have never met him. I had thought that he might be different, but it does not appear so.'

The old man moved slowly on to the last representation, the map. He pointed with a long bony finger at the ribbon of river that wound through the mountains. 'This is your way from beyond these mountains to the mouth of the Great River. I have not shown how it leaves the bowl of the earth, your home valley. But I will give you a map, so that you may in safety take the first step of your journey, and at the same time avoid those strangers on the Pass.'

'What is this?' Maloof asked, indicating the blank space to the left of the map.

The old man looked for a long moment at the space, and Branwald felt a deep pang of sadness. 'Eleanora,' the old man half-whispered. 'Eleanora.' Then, as if suddenly remembering their presence, he said, 'This place is for someone very dear to me. I lost her many years ago. This picture must be the last, and I must begin it soon, before the memory of her face has faded in my mind.' The old man sighed and turned to look at the two boys. 'If I were stronger, I would essay the journey with you. But I cannot. It would be foolish.'

'But how have you made these?' Branwald asked.

'At the beginning, with the Firebolt. But later I fashioned other tools with it. With them the task is more difficult and slower, but it fills my days with honest labour, and my spirit with healing.' He saw the incomprehension in their faces, and the smile came again into his eyes. 'You do not understand this now. But you will, I hope, someday ....'

He broke off, and wheeled suddenly to look up at the high rim above him. He seemed to be listening again. The boys were silent, sensing something amiss.

The old man swung round, facing the river. 'Someone is coming,' he said. 'He is coming from above, not from the river.' He looked hard at Branwald. 'Branwald, son of Feowald,

81

did you tell the stranger from the far islands where you were coming this morning?'

'No. On my honour, I did not.'

'Then he has followed you. He is not far away.' The old man paused, listening again. 'There is anger and vengeance in his mind. But there is no danger yet. He would need to be a bird or a goat to reach here from the top. Come, it will soon be time for you to go.'

The old man led them back along the path till they came to the massive roof over the river. He passed upstream of the canoe and stopped at the water's edge, where the limestone dropped sheer into a deep pool. He knelt, pulling his right sleeve up until the white arm was exposed to above the elbow. Then, bending, he dipped his arm into the water, feeling underneath, as if under a ledge of rock.

His hand reappeared holding a long object wrapped in dripping animal skins. Carefully he laid it on the flat rock and began to unwrap the thong-bound skins.

'To keep its power,' he said, 'the Firebolt must see and feed off the sun every few days. You will know when it needs this nurture. Its beam, when you hold it by the handle, will weaken to nothing, and its blade will become dark blue.' He took off the last wrappings.

Branwald saw an object about three feet long. At one end there was a handle, similar to but thicker than that of a sword. The embossed metal of the handle had a silvery sheen, and there were elaborate curved markings or inscriptions on it. The blade, if blade it was, was about two feet long, a straight translucent tube of deep blue light. Its end was not pointed, like a sword's, but blunt, as if the maker had cut the tube square across.

The old man gripped the blade of the Firebolt with both hands and lifted it carefully. He stood up, holding it towards the bright cliff behind him. Branwald watched his face. The old man's eyes were riveted on the instrument in his hands; then they lifted to scan the cliff-top above. 'Do not forget that the Firebolt cannot be used against man or beast. If its use comes from anger or revenge, it will turn the user's own dark side against him. Whatever your needs are, if they tend to the good, it will help you to meet them.' The old man turned towards Branwald. He held out the Firebolt with trembling arms, one hand at either end of the blade. His voice became strident. 'Branwald, son of Feowald, take you this instrument! Be the protector of all that is true and opposed to the dark. It is your destiny from all time past. It is your destiny for all time to come. Use it truly, or cast it into the depths where no other may ever find it. Take it! Now!'

Branwald stepped forward and reached for the handle of the Firebolt. 'No, not by the handle!' the old man said. 'Not yet! Hold it by the blade!'

Branwald gripped the blade between the old man's hands, but a tingling shock ran up his arm and he recoiled. The old man shuddered violently, and his knuckles whitened as his hands gripped even harder. 'Take it!' he commanded. 'You must!' The voice was terrible in its intensity. Branwald jerked at the instrument, feeling again that tingling shock. The hands nearly lost their grip, but recovered.

Branwald felt anger rising in him. He had a strong urge to grab the handle. He pulled again, grunting with the effort — and again, harder. With a shuddering groan, the old man released the Firebolt.

He staggered backwards and sank down onto his knees on the rock, his breath rasping in his chest. The boys stared at him, seeing the old face slowly crumple and the tears begin to flow. The old man was speaking, but so low that they could scarcely hear: '... from the great burden. At last, after all the long years, I can have peace. Now the new warrior has come to release me ....' He wiped his eyes with his sleeve and composed himself, then rose unsteadily to his feet. 'You must forgive me,' he pleaded. 'It has been so long, and such a great responsibility.'

He looked at Branwald. 'One thing you must remember: when the sun has fed it and you hold the handle, the power will come out of the instrument — a beam of energy like nothing you can imagine. On your life, do not let the beam strike a living creature. If it does, it will destroy you both.'

He looked upwards, towards the silent cliff-top. 'The one is approaching. Take to the water now and you will outwit him. But do not return to your homes with the Firebolt. It would be too much for the people.' He bent and took from the rolled-up skins a single leather sheet. 'This will be your guide. It will tell you where to go and what to avoid.'

Branwald stirred himself out of his trancelike state. He saw markings — a map — on the wet skin. He took the dripping leather sheet and, wrapping it around the Firebolt, went to the canoe. Maloof threw the remaining skins on the floor and together they lifted the craft onto the water.

A question came to Branwald. 'When it is finished, will I bring the Firebolt back to you?'

'No. My work with the Firebolt is finished. I have handed it on to the Chosen One. If you do not cast it into the depths, as you may be forced to do, bring it, after all the strife, to the one place where it can be safe — the great Monastery of the Sordiana, beyond the mountains to the west. You will see its place on the map.'

The old man stepped closer to them. 'There is only one request that I make which pertains to me alone. If you — when you reach the Monastery, you must ask at the Sanctuary there for Eleanora. If she is not there, do not search for her. If you meet her, say only this: that Bradach has kept his word, and that he has never forgotten ... and that he asks for her forgiveness. She will know what it is I speak of.' He turned to look at the blank space of rock. 'When I know that you have finished your tasks, and that she has spoken words of forgiveness, then I will begin the last great work.'

'And if we do not find her there?' asked Maloof.

'If she is not there, then one of two things has happened. Either she is no longer living, or ... or she went back long ago to the place of him who was my ....'

He broke off to look out towards the cliff-top. His eyes focused on something, and he immediately stepped back into the shade. 'But hide yourselves. The one who is coming can be seen. He is searching for you.' Cautiously he peered out again. 'He is strong, with black hair and beard. He is —'

'It is Urkor,' Branwald said.

'Go. And may the Great Mother who gives life to all be your guide and comforter.'

The boys got into the canoe, paddles at the ready. 'But what about you?' asked Maloof.

The old man smiled. 'The stranger will not find me. I have prepared a place for a moment such as this. Unless this stranger can see through rock, he will not see me. And there is little he can do to my poor possessions, except for my gentle milk-giver.' He clapped his hands once. The nanny-goat, still nibbling in the bushes, lifted her head and looked at him. He lifted his hands, pointing the splayed fingers in her direction. A strange humming sound came from his throat. Immediately, the animal turned and made straight for the cliff. With several swift bounds, she reached a narrow ledge thirty feet above the ground. From there she looked down at them curiously. 'Meh-heh,' she said cheekily.

'My gentle one will be safe,' the old man said. 'One thing more. If your canoe can take you to the great sink-hole called Bragan's Throat, where the river plunges under the mountains, you will be able to avoid the men on the high places. They do not intend any good towards the one who has the Firebolt. But remember that they can see down into the valley. If they know where you are going, they may forestall you on the other side. When you are below the Cataract, find a place to shelter until night comes. The Firebolt will be your light, if you need it. But use it sparingly. It can be seen from a great distance.'

He crouched and gripped the gunwale of the canoe. 'There is so much that I would teach you, but there is no time. The dark one is descending. I can feel it.'

He pushed the canoe away from the rocky edge. The current caught it, and it began to move faster. 'Come back to me when it is over,' he called after them. 'And when they speak falsely of the Old Soldier, you must tell them what you know to be true. Say that you will!'

'We will,' they called back.

When Branwald last saw the old man, he was standing straight as an arrow by the water's edge, watching them go.

CHAPTER ELEVEN

The journey back through the Elvan cave was like a dream to Branwald. The blue glow from the Firebolt was stronger than many candles, and it bathed the first cavern in an eerie light. Every column and pillar glistened with a wet blue-tinted skin. And even though it had been barely an hour since he and Maloof had first traversed the winding cave, it seemed that many hours — nay, days — had elapsed; that great events had intervened since they had last been there. Time had become distorted, changed.

At last the white light of the entrance drew nearer. The boys could see the sunlight in the distance, and soon the brilliant arch where the cave ended.

Maloof broke the silence. 'Let us stay within the cave till we decide what to do,' he said.

Branwald started out of the reverie into which he had slipped. He slowed the canoe and shifted the stern close to the wall. They gripped the cold limestone and stopped.

For a long moment they gazed out along the smooth, reflecting skin of the river as it swept away into the gorge.

Maloof turned to look at Branwald, his eyes huge in the shadow. 'Can such things be?' he whispered. 'Or did we dream?'

Branwald carefully picked up the Firebolt, by the blade, from the floor of the canoe. Again the strange tingle ran up his arm. He caught the handle, pointing the blade towards the roof. A faint beam of white light, thin and perfectly straight, shot from the tip and played on the dark roof above.

'Be careful, Branwald!' Maloof warned.

Assailed by a sudden fear, Branwald dropped the instrument with a thud onto the floor. 'This is no dream,' he said. 'This is really the Firebolt ....' He swallowed hard and stared down at the thing on the floor.

'Branwald,' Maloof whispered, 'I know what you feel, but I will help you. We will help each other.' He reached out his hand and Branwald grasped it. The pressure was strong and firm. 'We have to do this thing,' Maloof went on. 'For our fathers' sake, we must go to the mouth of the Great River. You must be the bearer. You have been chosen. And I will help you.'

The insistent pressure of Maloof's grip forced Branwald to meet his friend's gaze.

'I know you are right,' Branwald said. 'But for a moment the task seemed too great. I fear that I may not be worthy ....'

'The old man said that if the task becomes too great, we can cast the Firebolt from us and return to our homes.'

'But where? Where can we ... where could we leave it? What if others were to find it? What if it were to fall into the hands of —'

Maloof's grip on Branwald's hand tightened until it was painful. 'Do not think about these things too much, Branwald. Do not be fearful. This fear is something the Elders have given you. But the Elders have lost their way. This is what my mother says. Their ways are not the true ways. Their ways will not last. My mother says that we must have courage and belief in a better way. And this' — he indicated the instrument on the floor of the canoe — 'the Firebolt may lead us to it. Branwald, we must believe this!'

For a long time they sat in the shadow of the opening, their hands clenched in a brotherly grasp. Branwald sat with his head down, his eyes closed, struggling with the fear in his breast.

At last he spoke. 'It should be you, Maloof. You are the one who should have the Firebolt. You are stronger than I.'

Maloof smiled, shaking his head. 'I know that this is not the case. I can't explain it, but I know it. What I do not know is where my strength comes from, because it is not from me. All I can say is that for this moment, I must be strong. There will come a time soon when you are the one who must be strong.' He squeezed Branwald's hand again. 'This is what I feel.'

Branwald took a deep breath. His fear had lessened. 'We will go,' he said. 'We will go to the mouth of the Great River.'

'There is just one thing,' Maloof said, releasing his grip. 'I must tell my mother what I am going to do. Our village is not far from here. I will not be long.'

'No, Maloof! She will surely stop you. Do not go to her!'

'But she knows!' Maloof argued. 'I have spoken of going to the mouth of the Great River many times. Only the moment of departure is waiting to be decided. She will not hold me. Indeed, she will let me go more willingly when I tell her that you are with me.'

'And what about the Firebolt? Will you tell her of this?'

Maloof thought for a moment. 'I do not know. I will tell her if I think she needs to know. But do not worry. Only she will know this.'

'But if she wants you to stay ....'

'I tell you, she won't. Remember, my father is with your father. That is why I, too, must go.'

Branwald remembered his own mother and sister. 'All right,' he agreed. 'I will wait by the stream.'

He guided the canoe out into the sunlight and down to the mouth of the cleft where he had met Maloof. When he looked into the shadowy place by the tumbling stream, however, there was another canoe drawn up on the pebbly beach.

Branwald recognised it instantly. 'That canoe belongs to young Sildon. Urkor must have taken it to follow me.' He turned to scan the rocky terraces high above them.

'He will not come for a long time,' said Maloof. 'There will be time for me to go and return.'

Branwald nodded, guiding the canoe into the inlet. 'If he comes over the high places, I will see him from afar. I will take the canoes out onto the water and wait there for you. He can do nothing to me if he has no canoe.'

Maloof stepped out onto the wet pebbles and pushed the other canoe into the water, where Branwald caught its trailing leather thong.

'I will be there and back before that cloud leaves the sky,' Maloof said, pointing at a billowing cumulus drifting slowly from the west. 'If you need me before, speak to me in thought. I will be listening.' Lithely he climbed up the layered face of the rock. At the top he turned and waved. Then he disappeared from view.

Branwald tied the thong from the other canoe to the thwart of his own, and reversed out into the main river once more. He needed to get away from the cascading stream that muffled all sounds, and also to keep the cliff-tops in sight. He drifted to the opposite wall and made his craft fast to the limb of a gnarled willow. Then, his eyes resting on the high places before him, he settled down to wait.

He was hungry. He reached behind him for the bundle which his mother had given him, and took from it two wheaten cakes. But he decided to wait till Maloof returned; he would be hungry too. Branwald licked the white flour from his finger, and the taste brought him back to the simple house where his mother was. A pang seized his heart at the thought that he might not see her again for a long time, perhaps never. It seemed to him that the life he had known was gone. He thought of Eroona, and the pang made him groan. Then he remembered. He could speak with her. She had told him to.

He focused his mind on her familiar form and called. Instantly there came an answering thought. 'Branwald!' He held the image in his mind and listened.

He felt a strong surge of affection and then of questioning, so he carefully recalled the events of the morning since he had left the house, trying to keep each image steady and clear, aware that with the images went also his feelings. Step by step he took Eroona through the journey, feeling her fear and wonder as he recalled the cave, the great pit where they had found the old man, his first sight of the Firebolt and the hasty departure with danger threatening from above. At last he came to the present place.

He wanted her to feel that he was calm and strong and unafraid. Impulsively he leaned forward and picked up the Firebolt. The translucent blade, having lain a few short minutes in the sun, glowed with a stronger light. Branwald felt a strength grow in him. 'With this weapon,' he thought,

'Maloof and I will journey over the mountains to the mouth of the Great River, and we will rescue our fathers from the grip of the Orelord. Nothing will stand in our way when we possess this weapon.'

A strange and terrible anger was growing inside him. He lifted the Firebolt and pointed it at the surface of the water, several yards ahead of him. He willed it to strike; he willed it to show its power, *his* power.

A brilliant beam of light, no wider than the blade itself, shot forth from the hollow tip. It struck the water's surface and penetrated it to the depths. There was a sizzling sound, and a long wisp of steam rose from the bubbling spot where the beam met the water.

Taken by surprise, Branwald released his grip on the handle and took the instrument by the blade. Instantly the beam vanished, and the surface of the river returned to smooth normality. Branwald dropped the Firebolt with a clatter onto the floor, and sat staring at it, disturbed both by its power and by his own passion.

'Branwald!' Eroona's thought came again. 'What is happening? What have you done?' She was concerned.

He reassured her. 'I am safe. It is the Firebolt. It has a great power which I must learn to use well. But do not fear. Maloof will help me.'

'Be careful, Branwald. Remember what Mother said about the Firebolt. We pray for your safe return.'

Branwald was about to respond when Maloof appeared on the top of the low cliff opposite. He was carrying some kind of satchel in one hand and a longbow in the other. On his back hung a quiver of arrows.

'Branwald,' he called, 'come over. I am ready!'

Relieved to see his friend, Branwald waved in acknowledgement of the call, but he did not move. He thought warmth and affection and deep love. 'I will come back. But Maloof is here and we must go. My love to Mother.'

He waited for the answering wave of love, which came like an orange-red glow in his mind. Then he cast off from the willow and aimed for the mouth of the cleft again.

Maloof was already waiting on the pebbles when the

canoes beached. He bent to lift the spare paddle from the prow of Branwald's craft. 'I will take this,' he said, indicating the other canoe. 'We must not leave it here.' He dropped the paddle, the longbow and the arrows onto the floor, and placed the satchel carefully in the bow. Branwald saw the bone handle of a dagger standing up from a sheath by Maloof's side, as he eased himself down onto the seat.

'I was thinking,' Maloof said. 'When we get back to Hazel, we can take to the forest on foot. The watchers will not be able to follow us there.'

'But the Forest People ....' It slipped out before Branwald had time to think.

'The Forest People will not hinder us,' Maloof said. 'And anyway, I am known to those who live on this side of Otter's Brook and even beyond. I have been there before.'

Branwald hesitated. 'But what about me? What will they think?'

Maloof smiled. 'The Forest People think that the Great Mother does not distinguish between boys from the islands and boys from the forest.' He pushed off against the grinding pebbles, and in a moment his canoe was floating. 'That is another thing that I have learned. The Forest People are not like the Island People in this. Anyone who comes in peace will be welcomed.'

Branwald thought for a moment. 'The Old Soldier said that we must not return to our homes with the Firebolt, because it might be too much for our people. I would not trust some of my own people with the knowledge. I think the Forest People should not know either.'

Maloof was silent for a moment. Then he nodded. 'Then we will keep apart from even the Forest People, if that is necessary. There are many quiet ways through the forest.'

CHAPTER TWELVE

Branwald was relieved to be paddling again. He and Maloof sped along the fast-flowing river till they came to the Cataract. They carried the two canoes around the seething falls and down the sloping goat-track to the water's edge. Before pushing off, Branwald checked the heights to the north again. There was no sign of Urkor.

'What did your mother say to you?' Branwald asked, when they were back on the water.

'She was not happy, and yet she was not completely sad. She knew that I would go at some time. She says only that it is a task too great for the strength of two boys. That is her fear. But I told her that if the obstacles become too great, we will return.'

When they reached the level land below the high walls of the Gorge, where only the riverside trees screened them from the high places to the west, they found a sandy place by the river's edge and beached the canoes. Under the drooping willows they sat and ate Branwald's cakes and some apples which Maloof had brought. They scooped up handfuls of water from the shallows to slake their thirst. The sun was beginning to slant towards the west.

When the meal was over, Branwald took out the water-stained map which the old man had given them. There were markings on both sides of it. He spread it out on the grass and he and Maloof crouched over it, examining it in silence. The marks and lines were a faded blue on the tanned leather. Across the surface were rows of zigzag lines, like the teeth of a saw. All of these, except those at the very top, were cut in half by a snaky line that ran vertically down the page.

'That is the river,' breathed Maloof.

'Yes, and those sawtooth lines must be the mountains,'

Branwald agreed. 'This is the mouth of the river.' He pointed to where the river widened until it opened out into an island-speckled sea, on which the words 'Tarquan Islands' were written in ancient script.

Their eyes sought the northern places, seeing only fleetingly the many strange words scattered along the valley. Near the top of the map, the sawtooth lines were no longer horizontal; they curved upwards, becoming more and more concentric until, near the upper left-hand corner, the innermost line formed a complete oval. Within this elongated circle were drawn what appeared to be three lakes, all connected by a winding river.

'Here is our home,' said Branwald, pointing.

They followed the course of what was clearly the Elvan and, south of the lakes, the Rivelvan, until it stopped at a blue-shaded circle, beside which were written the words 'Bragan's Nostrils — under the Ivy Cliff'.

'Bragan's Throat! It must be!' said Maloof. Leading southwards from this circle there was a jagged, broken line, cutting directly downwards across the mountains. Beside it was written 'The Way of the White Ones'. When it came to a blue-shaded semicircle, the broken line became solid again. Winding southwards, it became one of the many tributary streams that made up the headwaters of the Great River.

'This is the way under the mountains,' said Branwald, indicating the broken line. 'But how can we get to the bottom of Bragan's Throat? My father saw it once. It is a maelstrom, he said. No living thing can survive there.'

'"Bragan's Nostrils",' Maloof mused. 'Maybe this is a clue of some kind.'

Branwald did not reply. Another thought was demanding attention. 'Do you know why this way is called "the Way of the White Ones"?'

'The Forest People say that there is a race of people living in the darkness of the Way. They say that they have been there since the Dark Time, when they took refuge there from the spreading cloud. Their skin is supposed to be pure white.'

Branwald looked at his friend in disbelief. 'A race of people? But they could not live there. What would they have for

93

food? It is not possible.'

Maloof shrugged his shoulders. 'It is just a story they tell to their children,' he said. 'Some of the old ones say that they have seen these White Ones. But nobody believes them. What is on the other side?'

Branwald turned the sheet over. They spread it on the grass, holding down the edges. On the scuffed leather, faint blue markings depicted another map. Near the top were the words 'The Way of the White Ones'. Beneath, a rough circle had been drawn beside the words 'Bragan's Throat'; a winding line led downwards from this circle, ending two hand-widths away at a half-circle. Written at different places along this line were the words 'The Forest', 'The Kanaka Sump', 'Pogik' and 'Cathedral Lake'.

Branwald lifted his head to the hazy bulk of Eagle Mountain. He squinted his eyes and sought out the Pass of Feyan. At this distance, even the trees, which petered out several hundred feet below the summit, were indistinct; above them there was no sign of a trail leading to the Pass, and Branwald could make out no distinct shapes on the grey slope.

Maloof read his thoughts. 'The way through the high pass is a difficult one,' he said. 'They say that the climb itself takes two days, and that a man would need to be protected against the freezing winds that blow there.'

'It is not the climb or the cold that I would be wary of,' replied Branwald, 'but the men your people have seen. They are with Urkor, I feel certain. And if they are, they also want what he wants.' He began to fold the map.

Maloof stood up. 'I believe that if this is the way the old man told us to go, then we must try it.' He searched his friend's face for a response.

Branwald nodded. 'It can't be any worse than the mountain,' he conceded.

～

Soon they were on the river again. This time they were both in Branwald's canoe, with the other, tied to the stern, following in their wake. On the choppy waters of Hazel Lake they released the second canoe where the light wind from the west would catch it and sweep it towards the sombre island in the

94

distance. Then, searching the western shore, they found the reed-choked mouth of Sitkin Stream and welcomed the clear water. The heat of the afternoon was rising in waves from the land, and the distant cliff-tops were shrouded in shimmering haze. If Urkor was there, they could not have seen him.

'Do not fear,' said Maloof quietly. 'Without a canoe, he cannot be near this place till after nightfall, unless he can fly.'

Branwald was surprised that he felt no fear entering the land of the Forest People. The feeling he had was one of excitement and awe. Here was a place that he had always been forbidden to visit, a place that had haunted his childhood imagination. He was surprised to find that the stream looked quite like many that he knew on the islands.

There was only one difference. Even from the centre of an island, the lake was never very far away; the islands were contained and finite. Here, however, Branwald had the impression that he was moving into terrain that had no such boundaries. These forested slopes could go on forever, for all he knew. He could climb and climb until he came to the summit — and then, his father had once told him, there would be summit after summit, ranging in ranks away to the west and south until, after an aeon of distance, the sea would be there. His father had said that the sea was like the greatest lake one could imagine, stretching as far as the eye could see, and beyond.

They had paddled only a few hundred yards along the quiet stream when Maloof began to guide the prow towards the left-hand bank. 'If we go much further,' he said quietly, 'we will come upon the village.'

They found a grassy patch between the crowding shrubs and stepped out. The nearby trees were not densely packed, and the clearings between were deserted. They lifted out the canoe, settled their few possessions so that the weight was spread evenly and, with Maloof leading, set off southwards.

Because they wanted to avoid the open ground as much as possible, the route was much longer than it might have been. The canoe, hardly a burden at first, seemed to grow heavier with each passing minute. Their pauses to rest became more and more frequent.

They were passing a thicket of stunted juniper when Branwald stopped. 'Maloof,' he said quietly, scanning the parkland ahead, 'there are people not far away.'

Maloof did not respond, but he became quite still, his body tensed and listening. Some distance away, in the trees to their right, they heard the sound of dogs barking excitedly.

'The Forest People are my people now, Branwald,' Maloof said. 'There is no threat from them.'

'Yes, but the Firebolt,' Branwald argued. 'The Old Soldier said not to let it be seen.'

Maloof listened for a moment. The sounds seemed to be coming nearer. He turned towards the dense thicket beside them. Stealthily, he pointed the nose of the canoe at the prickly mass of needles; thrusting his shoulder forward, he advanced into the greenery. Branwald followed. In a few moments they were crouching in the deepest part of the thicket, the canoe resting at an awkward angle between them. They listened. Branwald reached into the canoe and began to extract the Firebolt from its wrappings.

'They are not after us,' Maloof whispered urgently. 'It is just a hunt. Listen.'

There were several dogs barking, and the sound was growing louder. Then came the sound of men shouting. As the tension rose within him, Branwald kept his hand on the Firebolt's blade. He tried to see through the tangle of branches but could not. Maloof turned to him again, with his finger on his lips.

Then they heard another, nearer sound. It was the thump of feet. Something heavy began to force its way into the thicket. Branwald twisted to face the sound, at the same time drawing the Firebolt by the handle clear of its wrappings and holding it in front of him, pointing it at the ground in the direction of the intruder. By the white glow of the Firebolt, he could see the shape. It was a stag. Its head was near the ground, and its breathing was laboured.

The animal came to a sudden halt. It had seen the light. Its eyes were white and staring. Behind it, the urgent baying of dogs was clear and close.

'It's been wounded,' whispered Maloof. In the light,

Branwald saw the shaft of an arrow protruding from the animal's neck, and a dark stain running downwards from it.

Torn between fear of being discovered and sympathy for the wounded animal before him, Branwald was uncertain what to do. He moved the Firebolt to one side to see the animal better. The light from it grew stronger. The movement, however, startled the stag, and it bolted away from them. But the sound of its crashing charge back towards the open ground was swallowed in the feverish baying of dogs and the urgent shouts of men. They were just outside the thicket.

Branwald dropped the Firebolt onto the ground beside him and remained still, listening. The baying turned to yelps of excitement; the dogs had seen their prey. A man shouted, 'Hold him, Elku! Hold him, Kisku!' The yelping was centred in one place. And then the crescendo of sound abruptly diminished. The dogs' clamour became muted. A man called, 'Heel, Elku! Heel, Kisku!' Another man's voice said, 'It is well. You have done well, young pups. You have done well.'

The boys exchanged glances. It was clear that the animal had been killed right outside the thicket. They would have to remain hidden until the men had dealt with the carcass.

Branwald was startled by a rustling in the bushes to his left. He heard a dog sniffing close at hand, and then a deep threatening growl as the animal saw them. He saw its bared teeth, its glaring eyes, as it advanced through the juniper stems. Branwald dropped his hand to feel for the Firebolt, but Maloof's whisper made him pause.

'No, Branwald. Do not use it!' Maloof held his hands out in front of him, fingers pointing towards the dog. He spoke in a low, soothing tone, staring into the animal's eyes.

From beyond the bushes, one of the men called the animal. But the dog was calmer now, its eyes riveted on Maloof's face. Slowly the bristling hairs of its mane relaxed. Then its tail began to wag.

'Come on, boy,' Maloof crooned. The young hound advanced; in a moment, it was sniffing at Maloof's hand.

But the voices were drawing closer on either side of the thicket. 'There's something else,' one of the men said. 'Kisku, go on! Flush him out!'

Barking furiously, the other dog entered the thicket behind the boys. Maloof looked at Branwald. 'We'll have to speak to them,' he said. 'Else they may shoot us, thinking we're game.'

Branwald made up his mind. He started to wrap the Firebolt in the leather covering. 'You speak to them,' he said. 'Tell them that we are from the islands, and that we do not mean them any harm.'

Maloof lifted his head and spoke in the direction from which the first voice had come. 'Hold your arrows! It is only I, Maloof, the Island Boy, and my friend, Branwald,' he called.

There was a pause. Then the man called back, 'Well, come on out, Maloof of the Islands. Let us see you.'

A moment later, when the two boys emerged from the thicket, they saw a tall, ginger-bearded Forester standing before them. Branwald thought he saw amusement in the freckled face. The man wore a leather jerkin and breeches over a long-sleeved green smock. On his feet were laced-up moccasins, and a leather band decorated with coloured beads encircled a mass of unruly flaxen curls on his head.

'Well, well,' said the hunter. 'It *is* the Island Boy.' He raised his head and called over the thicket. 'Mitko! Come here. See what I have found.'

The other man was sheathing an arrow as he came into view. He was stockier than his companion, and his round face was clean-shaven under a mop of black curly hair.

'Mitko,' said the first one, 'how would you like some island boys to roast on your spit tonight, eh?'

Branwald glanced at Maloof's face. He thought of rushing back into the thicket for the Firebolt. But the second man's reply dispelled his fear.

'Island boys!' he roared, his face creased with a grin. 'They don't taste very good. The last time we had one, he was bitter and hard. Give me a happy forest boy any day!' Mitko glanced with mild amusement at the boys as he walked past them, drawing a long-bladed hunting knife from a sheath on his belt. They saw that he was going to the fallen stag. Three feathered arrows protruded from the animal's side, but, even at that distance, the boys could see that its foreleg was moving weakly.

'We will talk with the Island Boy and his friend when we have set this fine stag at peace,' the first one said, as he too strode past them in the direction of the animal.

The two men knelt by the fallen animal. It made a last feeble attempt to rise, but the tall one held it down by the antlers. He too drew a long dagger. Holding it poised in his right hand, he spoke to the stricken animal. In his quiet voice there was pity and regret.

'Forgive us, swift one, that you must give your life so that we and ours may live. We thank the Great Mother that she has given us this gift. It is the way of all life.'

Then, with one swift thrust of his knife, the man sliced into the animal's throat. Blood pulsed out onto the matted grasses. The animal made one last movement of its legs, but the life was flowing from it. At last it was still.

The tall man wiped his knife on the grass and, sheathing it, stood up. 'Well, island boys. What brings you two stalwarts into the home of the Forest People?' he asked, stepping over the carcass and pulling the animal onto its back.

There was a moment of hesitation. Then Maloof spoke. 'We are on our way out of the valley, to search for our fathers,' he said boldly.

The man called Mitko, who was already cutting into the animal's stomach in a businesslike way, looked up at them, frowning. 'You mean over the mountains?' he asked.

'Yes, our fathers went —'

'We know,' grunted the tall one. 'And they have not come back.'

Branwald, uneasy with his friend's revelations, chose his moment. 'It is time for us to move on,' he said, glancing back at the thicket.

'Do your mothers know what you are about?' Mitko asked, pulling a mass of glistening entrails from the stag's belly.

'They know,' said Branwald.

Mitko spoke to Maloof. 'This one' — he indicated Branwald — 'has he escaped from the Island of the Banished also?'

Maloof hesitated. 'Yes,' lied Branwald. 'I have.'

The tall man gave him a searching look. 'You travel light for such a difficult journey.'

Maloof indicated the thicket. 'We have a canoe with us, and possessions.'

At the mention of the canoe, the two men stopped what they were doing. 'A canoe?' said the tall one. 'Where?'

Unable to change his story, Maloof went on. 'In the thicket. Here.'

'Let us see,' said the tall one.

The boys exchanged glances. They had no choice but to do as they were asked. They pushed their way into the thicket and dragged the craft out into the open, leaving the Firebolt where it lay.

The two men examined the canoe with great interest. They touched it in various places, lifted it off the ground, felt its weight and the texture of the pitch-painted canvas, and marvelled at the dexterous way in which it was morticed together.

At length, Mitko turned to the boys and spoke. 'This canoe will not avail you when you begin to scale the heights of the mountain. Why do you bring it with you?'

Branwald was reluctant to give further information, but before he could think of a response, Maloof said, 'We are going by way of Bragan's Throat — that is, by the Great Cauldron. We believe that there is a way through to the other side.'

The two men exchanged incredulous glances. 'No one has gone into the Great Cauldron for many years now,' said the tall one. 'You know it is a perilous way?'

'Yes, we know,' replied Branwald. 'But we can manage.' He did not feel as brave as he tried to sound.

'Why do you not go over the Pass?' Mitko asked. 'It is long, but it is safer.'

'We have received a message that our fathers are in danger,' said Branwald. 'We must go to the mouth of the Great River as quickly as possible.'

Mitko regarded him thoughtfully. 'Or is it that there is some danger on the Pass that you wish to avoid?' he asked.

Branwald saw no purpose in pretence. 'Yes,' he said.

The tall one spoke. 'The one who came down through the

100

forest with the two beasts — where is he now?'

Branwald felt his eyes drawn to the high cliffs in the north, but he resisted the urge.

'We do not know where he is,' he answered boldly.

'Hmm,' replied the man, smiling. 'You Island People, you do not easily trust those who would be your friends. You have much to learn.' He turned and strode back towards the half-dressed carcass.

Branwald struggled to find words. 'You must understand that we are two young boys. We do not yet know who are our friends or who are our enemies. We have to —'

'Aagh!' retorted Mitko, waving his hand dismissively. 'Do not worry. We understand the Island People. Maybe when you return to your homes, you can tell them that the Forest People have their own wisdom.' His face opened into a grin. 'And that they do not cook island boys over a spit for supper.'

'We will tell them,' Maloof said, smiling.

~

The sun was dropping towards the western mountain when the ruddy-faced Foresters took their leave of the boys. The men had shared a meal of roasted nuts and cold baked potatoes with them, after they had dressed and quartered the stag. The tall one, Chenk, cut several round red fillets from the loin of the animal, wrapped them in a strip of the hide and gave them to the boys.

'A short time over the fire will have them ready for eating,' he said.

'It will be nearly dark,' Mitko said, pointing southwards through a forest clearing, 'by the time you come to the stream which you Island People call "Otter's Brook". Beyond that, the lowland is boggy and treacherous. From there you must either go higher into the forest or take to the lake which, amongst your people, is "Eagle Lake".'

'Thank you,' said Branwald, as the two men prepared to leave. 'We will tell our people about the People of the Forest.'

'If you meet any more of our people,' Mitko said, 'tell them that you have supped with Mitko and Chenk from Salcha. Then they will know that you can be given free passage through our lands.'

When the men, laden down with the deer quarters, were gone, the two boys prepared to resume their journey. Branwald recovered the Firebolt and laid it, free of its wrappings, on the floor of the canoe, where it would be exposed to the afternoon sun. The unexpected friendliness and generosity of the Foresters had increased his confidence. Yet he was still anxious to put as much distance as possible between himself and the Elvan Cliffs while the daylight remained.

'If we can get to Otter's Brook,' he said to Maloof, 'it will be easy to get onto the lake.'

They continued their trek, still keeping to the fringes of the trees whenever possible. Only once did they halt and take cover. They heard the squeals and cries of a group of forest children long before they saw them. The children were foraging in a thicket of hazel trees that grew on a sandy knoll. From his position behind a fallen pine tree, Branwald watched with some interest. The children seemed happy and carefree in a way that he could not remember ever seeing the island children.

'This is a difficult time of year for the Forest People, when the store of nuts is growing small,' Maloof said quietly. 'Now they forage to see if there are any of last year's lying under the leaves, where the squirrel and the chipmunk could not find them.'

The boys evaded the noisy children by making a detour deeper into the woods. Several times they crossed well-trodden paths, but on none did they see any people.

The side of Eagle Mountain was in deep evening shadow when the boys finally saw the winding course of Otter's Brook in the low meadow ahead. Looking south-eastwards through the tree-tops below him, Branwald saw the distant shimmering that was the surface of Eagle Lake. He raised himself to his full height and searched through the branches for Redwood Island. His breath caught in his throat as he saw the dark spine of trees on the crest of the island, and the twinkle of early-evening lights. He wondered what his mother was doing, where Eroona was. A sudden longing to see them welled in his breast. If only they knew how close he was! It would be so easy to speak with Eroona again ....

Yet he hesitated. It was hard enough for him to look across that short stretch of water. He was afraid that if he once began to speak with his sister, his resolve would weaken ....

Maloof's quiet voice startled him. 'I have stood many times and gazed at that island as you are doing now. And I have wished that there might come a day when I would be back there as in former days. But now I know that that day will not come unless our fathers return.'

Branwald sighed. 'It will be a great day when we come back in the company of our fathers. That will be a day of joy.'

Maloof glanced upwards, towards the Pass of Feyan. 'If we go onto the lake now, they may still see us from above.'

'Yes. We will wait for the night to fall before we take that chance.'

They found a secluded nook on the higher ground, where a cluster of pines grew unusually close together. They dragged the canoe into the centre of these and found a soft bed of needles where they could stretch out their limbs.

'My arm is several times longer than it was this morning,' Maloof complained.

'This morning!' exclaimed Branwald. 'It seems as if a week has gone past since then.'

He threw his body onto the soft mattress of needles, grateful to be able to stretch his limbs. He closed his eyes. Somewhere in the forest behind him, a thrush was still singing his shrill notes. Still higher on the mountain, a fox barked. The only other sound was the quiet sighing of the breeze in the pines. Maloof said something, but his voice seemed far away. Branwald slept.

CHAPTER THIRTEEN

Branwald woke with a start. The daylight was gone, and in the gloom of early nightfall, the wind was breathing through the treetops above him. He turned to where Maloof lay, a dark lump, curled in sleep beside him.

'Maloof! It is time!' Branwald said, shaking him. Maloof sat up, his eyes staring. Branwald caught his shoulder. 'It is time for us to go onto the water.'

Crouching, they pushed their way out of the aspens into the cool night air. There was a light wind and hardly any cloud. Above them stretched a great vault in which twinkled millions of stars. A crescent moon, holding in its arms the faint shape of its shadowed face, hung low over the distant crest of Barren Peak. Down on the lake, the faraway sprinkle of lights on Redwood Island twinkled warm and inviting.

They plodded to the boggy edge of the river, where the cool mud oozed up over their moccasins and seeped down between their toes. When they finally pushed off and felt the flow carry them away, they took off their footwear and took turns dipping first one foot and then the other into the cold water. Then they dunked their sopping moccasins and sluiced out the sticky mud.

It was not long before the channel began to widen and a wall of reeds appeared along each bank. They were approaching the lake. Branwald guided the canoe close to the edge, where the reeds would provide shelter from the wind. As they hurried along in the gloom, the papery rustling of the reeds and the swish of wavelets through their close-packed stems drowned out all other sound.

The lake shore would soon swing southwards, Branwald knew. The distance from the mouth of Otter's Brook to Bragan's Throat was about five miles, he estimated, the last two occupied by the Rivelvan as it sped towards the great sink-hole.

It was almost two hours later, judging from the position of the moon, when the boys noticed the lake narrowing again. The reed walls on both sides were coming closer, and beyond them the forest seemed denser. The water, too, was flowing swiftly, and the canoe sped along.

'We will hear it long before we see it,' Branwald said in reassurance. 'They say that it is always raining round Bragan's Throat.'

Overhead, a scattering of puffy clouds had begun to drift from the west. The rustling of the reeds beside them was louder, and the boys saw that the flow of the water was leaning the long stems towards the south.

'Stay close to the reeds,' Maloof said.

Branwald had the impression that the black mountain ahead was rearing upwards into the night sky. He peered anxiously into the darkness at its base, but he could distinguish nothing there. He felt a coldness on his face; when he touched it, it was wet. He thought he could hear a new sound, a low rumbling, from ahead. Gaps began to appear in the wall of reeds, and the trees behind loomed closer and closer.

'Pull in!' shouted Branwald. 'Into the reeds!'

They came into a cluster of reeds, too fast. The canoe sliced in at an angle, the nose whacked against something solid under the trees, and the two boys were pitched forward from their seats. Branwald's shins cracked against the rear thwart, and he heard Maloof yell. As he came up he saw that the stars were slowly circling round, and he knew that the canoe's stern, still projecting into the speeding current, was being caught and swung downstream.

'Catch the reeds! Hold on!' he shouted. He lunged at the nearest reeds and felt the canoe tilt. At the prow, Maloof was leaning forward, grabbing handfuls of stalks.

The craft steadied, the stern drifted round against the reeds, and in a moment the canoe was secure. Relieved, they hauled it under the trees until they felt the canvas side scrape against rock.

Then they heard a new sound. It came from downstream — a dull, thundering roar, the sound of the Rivelvan dropping into Bragan's Throat.

It was not easy for the boys to get a foothold on solid ground. The bank under the trees, though not steep, was a jumble of boulders and tangled roots. When Branwald grabbed an overhanging branch and stepped carefully down, his foot slid along the angled face of a rock, down into the water. The water was cold, and when he found a knee-deep foothold, he felt its flow tugging at his leggings. He stretched his hand into the darkness under the nearest tree and grimaced with pain as a spiny briar stabbed him. He changed direction and tried again; again the stabbing briars.

'Wait,' he said. He reached into the canoe and took the Firebolt from its covers. He felt the tingle in his arm as he gripped the handle, and saw the blue glow of the blade whiten. A beam appeared from its tip.

Branwald held the handle aloft, with the blade pointing downwards. In the brilliant white light he saw a mass of tangled briars. They rose to a height of about five feet above the surface of the water, completely enveloping the lower trunks of the nearest trees. How far inland they stretched he could not see.

Branwald aimed the Firebolt's beam directly at the nearest briars. He focused his mind and will on the instrument, tightening his grip as he did so.

Immediately the ray of light became like a solid thing. There was a sizzling sound from the briars. The beam cut through them as a scythe shears through stems of grass.

Branwald cut from the top down to ground level; then he shifted his aim a few feet to the left and repeated the downward motion. There was a crackling and snapping as the block of vegetation between the two cuts sagged down and forward. But it was still too high. Branwald moved the beam from side to side through the mass, chopping the leaves and branches into pieces.

Suddenly, from the other side of the briars, there was a groaning sound. 'Look out!' yelled Maloof. A tall pine tree, directly behind the two initial cuts, began to tilt slowly to the left. The boys froze, watching its descent. There was the sound of splintering branches and colliding foliage as the tree fell slowly to the ground.

Branwald looked, aghast, at the Firebolt in his hand. The beam wandered aimlessly through the thicket and burned its way into the forest. Another tree, further back, began to tilt slowly forward.

'Put it down!' Maloof urged. 'Turn it away from the trees!'

Without thinking, Branwald lifted the point of the instrument upwards. The beam of light, straighter than any arrow's flight, shot towards the stars. Realising his mistake, he lowered it to aim at the briars at his feet. There was more sizzling and crackling, and the powdery smell of burning rock rose to his nostrils.

Panic began to rise in Branwald. He wanted to turn off this frightening power, but he did not know how.

'Drop it!' Maloof urged. 'Let it go from your hand!'

Branwald willed his fingers to release their hold, but they would not move. Something inside him resisted the command. A part of him wanted to hold on. From a spot near his feet came several loud cracking sounds.

'Drop it!' Maloof shouted.

Branwald stared at his hand and willed it to loosen its grip. Slowly his fingers straightened, and the Firebolt dropped with a clatter to the rocks. Immediately the light diminished, the beam vanished, and the blade became what it had been before — a dully luminous blue bar, its handle now submerged in water.

The boys were silent. Above the roaring of the falls, they heard a night-bird shriek close at hand, its cry echoing away to nothing. Branwald felt weak, his body drained of energy. He sat down on a rock, staring at the fallen Firebolt.

'By the Dread One!' he swore. 'It lopped that tree like a thistle!'

'You did too much,' chid Maloof. 'You must be more careful.'

'But I could not help it. It is so powerful!'

'You sent a light into the sky. Anyone could have seen it.'

'But it was only for a moment ....'

'Branwald, what if the stranger or those men on the Pass had seen it?'

A pause. 'Yes, Maloof. You are right. I should have been more careful.'

But Branwald's sense of having erred was mingled with exhilaration. There had been such a feeling of power, of control, while he was wielding the instrument, that he hadn't wanted to let go.

His cheeks were burning, and he felt faint, as if strength had gone out of him. He stared down at the Firebolt, wanting to have it in his hand again. He bent down to reach for it.

'No! Leave it!' Maloof told him, his voice harsh and urgent. 'I will get it!'

Branwald felt a stab of annoyance. He tried to grab the handle, but Maloof lunged across the canoe and gripped his arm, pulling him away. Branwald caught Maloof's wrist and tried to break free, but Maloof pulled him off balance. The canoe wobbled and scraped against the rocks beneath as they struggled across it.

'Branwald!' Maloof panted, his face only inches from Branwald's. 'Remember what the old man said! You must not abuse the Firebolt. If you do, it will destroy you!'

They stood their ground, glaring into each other's eyes, their breath coming hard and quick.

'If we fight here,' Branwald said after a long moment, 'the canoe will be damaged.'

'I do not want to fight, Branwald,' Maloof said. 'All I want to do is pick up the Firebolt and return it to the canoe.'

Branwald loosened his hold on Maloof's wrist. 'Then do it,' he said shortly. He watched sullenly as Maloof picked up the Firebolt by the blade and dropped it onto the floor of the canoe.

'Come on,' said Maloof quietly. 'Let us find a place to sleep.'

They dragged the canoe through the narrow corridor which the Firebolt had cut through the briars, manhandled it across the fallen pines and found themselves treading on a soft carpet of needles. Branwald took out his flint and tinder and ignited a cluster of dry twigs; from the nearby trunks,

Maloof lopped off low branches which no longer bore foliage, to feed the blaze.

Soon the tantalising smell of grilling venison steaks was heavy on the air. They ate the meat with some of Branwald's wheaten cakes, washed down with draughts of water from the river. They wrapped the remaining two venison steaks in fern fronds and put them in Maloof's satchel. They would use them later. Then, having added a rotten stump to the fire, they curled in their cloaks beside it and prepared for sleep.

'I did not think that we would quarrel,' Maloof said.

'We will not quarrel again,' Branwald replied. 'I was wrong. I wanted the power of the Firebolt too much. I know now what the old man meant when he spoke about the dark side. It frightens me to think how badly I wanted it.'

'You wanted it, yes. But you were able to let go of it. Remember that too.'

Branwald was silent for a while. 'If I must go through with this, Maloof — I do not think I could face it if you were not with me. I am sorry for —'

'Do not speak of it,' said Maloof with a laugh. 'Today it was you. Tomorrow, it may be me.'

～

Branwald lay on his back, watching a handful of flickering stars through a rent in the branches overhead. The thundering of the river into Bragan's Throat muffled even the sound of the wind in the treetops.

His body was weary, but sleep would not come. It had been the most incredible day of his life. Not only was he going to spend the night in the land of the Forest People, but, in order to get here, he had broken almost all the major precepts of his religion and of his society.

Branwald knew he should be feeling guilty. Yet, when he searched within himself, he could find no trace of that familiar feeling. Instead there was a kind of exhilaration, tinged with uncertainty. It came from his meeting with the Old Soldier, and from the Firebolt, he knew. He recalled the tingling when he had used the weapon on the briars, and the feelings it had evoked. It was as if the Firebolt had wanted to change him, to control him in some way .... He turned on his side to look at it lying on the ground beside him. A faint blue glow came from a point where it protruded from its coverings.

'Branwald,' Maloof said quietly. 'Do not be fearful. If we are meant to save our fathers, then we will be able to do it. The Earth Mother will protect us and we will protect each other. This is what you, too, must believe.'

Branwald felt better. His last thoughts, before sleep came, were of his mother and Eroona. He missed them greatly. He would speak with Eroona in the morning, when his mind was fresh and clear. He hoped they were not too sad. He hoped they were comforting each other.

CHAPTER FOURTEEN

When Branwald awoke, it was dawn. He felt cold and damp. He recognised the sound which he had been hearing in half-sleep for some time: it was the soft plashing of big drops of water onto the forest floor around him. The hollow rumbling of the falls seemed to have been in his ears ever since he had been born. He sat up, reached over and shook Maloof's shoulder.

Without a word, they rose and turned for the river's edge. Bragan's Throat lay less than thirty yards south of where they stood. They saw the water at the lip sheet into the beginnings of a curve and then disappear. Just beyond, where the great hole was, clouds of mist swirled and boiled up from below, obscuring the far wall and the steep slope above it. Looking towards the north, they saw the river rushing towards them, sweeping between walls of yellow reeds and lines of sentinel trees.

'We must search around the Throat,' Maloof said.

Breakfast was short and cold: wheaten cake and river water. Then they left the canoe where it lay, and began to make a passage through the trees to the edge of the sink-hole. Maloof carried his bow and quiver of arrows, while Branwald held the Firebolt, wrapped in its leather covering.

'If we stay in the trees and swing around towards the cliff yonder ....' Maloof said, indicating the precipitous wall that loomed behind the great sink-hole. In the thinning mist they could see joints and ledges on its face.

They bent to their task again. The slope became steeper. The trees, however, were less dense, and here and there lichen-encrusted rocks began to appear.

As they ascended, the great hole came into view on their left. They stopped on a mossy ledge and gazed down. The river sheeted clear and flat to the very edge. Then, as the water reached the lip and dropped into space, it became a brilliant white, frothing downwards into the pit. They could not see the bottom for the swirling spray, but the sound, to Branwald's ear, was deeper and more booming than the Karn Cataract. How could it be possible for anyone to venture even close to that place? he thought.

He looked upwards, at the stepped wall behind the sink-hole. His eyes picked out a track, running from a little beyond where he stood to a high ledge halfway along the back wall. The cliff above the ledge was curtained with hanging ivy. There were gaps in the ivy, but Branwald could see no rock there. The spaces seemed hollow and black in the grey light.

'Look. There,' he said, pointing.

It took them only a short time to scale the rocky steps that punctuated the path.

'There is a cave,' said Maloof, who gained the ledge first. He went to a gap in the ivy, widened it with both hands, and looked into the darkness within. There was a sudden startled shriek as a bird flapped out past his head and sped away over the falls. Maloof stepped into the gloom, and Branwald followed.

Inside, after the white daylight, there was total blackness. Branwald felt a warm breeze blowing against his face. He uncovered the Firebolt and grasped its handle.

Maloof stepped to one side as the beam became white. 'You must take care where you point it,' he said.

Dutifully, Branwald aimed the point at the floor before him. As its glow grew stronger, he began to discern shapes around and above him. The low roof was arched, jagged with hanging points; the walls, festooned with creamy flowstone, glistened with moisture. The floor ahead was encrusted with stalagmites and great, bulbous rocky shapes, and there were few level places. Branwald held the Firebolt low, to search for a way forward.

Then they saw what appeared to be a path. It was a smooth place that wound away from them through the distorted shapes. They bent to examine it. In the soft, wet clay before them was the clear imprint of a human foot, toes pointing in the direction they were facing. Around it there were older, fainter prints, facing in both directions.

'Someone has been here before us,' Branwald whispered.

Maloof did not respond. He was staring at the distorted landscape ahead. Then he shook his head. 'The Forest People do not come here. They respect the place of the White Ones and do not intrude. Anyway, it is not likely that the Forest People would be barefoot.'

Unwilling to accept what he did not want to believe, Branwald lifted the Firebolt and searched the shapes ahead. The cave sloped downwards and away to the right. His eyes darted from shape to shape, searching for movement in the shadows that swayed and changed as he moved the Firebolt. But there was nothing. He listened, but heard only the sound of his and Maloof's breathing against the faint rumbling of the falls.

Maloof stepped forward on the track. 'Come on,' he said.

Branwald followed, pointing the Firebolt to one side, no longer so fearful of its power. The light grew stronger.

The cave widened as they descended the twisting path. Around them the shadows became more contorted. Everywhere there were great stalks of creamy rock. In places the roof was covered so thickly with thin white stalagmites that there would have been no space between them for even a finger. They passed bulbous creamy-white columns that seemed to have dropped in a single mass from the roof to the floor. Their path wound past rounded mountains of calcite, from which stumpy stalagmites protruded in fantastic shapes.

Suddenly, from somewhere ahead came a piercing sound, a shrill wail that froze the boys in their tracks and made the hair rise on the napes of their necks. It rose and rose to a high pitch, held there a moment, then gradually descended and faded until only the echoes were left, drifting away into the depths of the cave.

Branwald's skin tingled, and his whole body shuddered. The light from the Firebolt grew brighter as his grip tightened. In front of him, Maloof slipped an arrow from his quiver, fitted it to his bow and moved forward again.

'No, Maloof. Wait.' Branwald caught Maloof's jerkin and held him. 'That was a warning.'

Maloof stood still. 'Yes, but maybe not for us. It could be a warning to one another that we are coming.' He lifted his head and called into the shadows ahead. 'Hallo-o-o! We come in peace. We mean you no harm.'

The echoes of his voice reverberated into the depths. They listened in the following silence, holding their breath, but there was nothing except a faint rumbling coming from ahead.

'Maybe we will see one of them. Maybe we will be able to talk to them,' Maloof said. 'But be careful with the Firebolt. The sight of it alone may be enough to frighten them, and you must not use it against them.' He lifted his bow. 'I have this, if need be.'

They moved on, more slowly, their eyes searching every shape and shadow. To Branwald it seemed as if there were a thousand sinister forms watching them from the darkness, but when he turned the Firebolt's glow towards them, they turned again into rock.

The way led down and down, sometimes rugged and stepped, sometimes winding between giant blobs of calcite. In several places the path split and branched away into smaller passages, but the soft damp breeze and the muffled rumbling were their guides, and they followed them.

Soon the rumbling grew louder. Then the floor began to level out and the cavern to widen. Branwald thought he saw a faint light far ahead. He put the Firebolt behind his back and looked again. Against a dim light in the distance, he saw a forest of shapes hanging from the roof.

At last they saw the frothy white surface of the river ahead. The noise of the falls was deafening. They came out into a high-roofed cavern on a sloping muddy bank. The tumbling water raced away into the blackness to their left. Fifty yards upstream of them, framed in the mouth of the cavern, they saw the maelstrom that was the bottom of Bragan's Throat. It was an assault on their eyes and their ears. They stood for a long moment watching the white fury of the plunging Rivelvan and hearing its thunderous clamour.

But Branwald was watchful, too, for other things. The noise of the falls would drown any other sound in the cavern. If there was to be an attack, this would be the time for it, when he and Maloof were trapped against the edge of the river.

'Keep watch behind us,' he shouted into Maloof's ear.

He turned to look downstream, lifting the Firebolt aloft and pointing it into the tunnel before him. The frothy river sped away from them into the gloom. Branwald was about to turn again to Maloof when his eye fell on several canoe-like crafts by the river's edge. Branwald reached out a hand to touch his friend, but Maloof was already moving towards the canoes.

Branwald swept the cavern with his eyes, but all he saw was rock and dark places. He moved closer to the craft. The canoes were of a similar design to their own, with supple hazel frames, except that their covering was made of skins, sewn together, with the hair on the inside. Beside the canoes, stretched on rough wooden frames, lay what appeared to be fishing nets.

Branwald felt that it was time to go. He indicated to Maloof the passage through which they had come. They started to move back.

Suddenly Maloof grabbed Branwald's arm. He was pointing at something in the passage ahead and mouthing soundless words. Alarmed, Branwald looked in that direction, turning the Firebolt defensively, but he saw nothing.

'What?' he shouted.

Maloof turned and shouted into his ear. 'Did you not see it? Something white?'

A cold shiver ran through Branwald's hair and down his back. He lifted the Firebolt, and the beam played on the dark walls ahead. Maloof caught Branwald's arm and forced it downwards.

'No, Branwald!' he shouted. 'The White Ones will not harm us! Put it down!' Maloof's eyes were intense. 'Branwald, remember the old man! You must not do this! It is dangerous — it is dangerous for *you!*'

Branwald started to struggle, but the fierce intensity of

Maloof's glare made him pause. 'Come on!' Maloof mouthed, turning into the passage by which they had come. They hurried back up the steep, twisting slope.

When they came to a point where a tributary passage joined the main one from the left, they stopped. The noise of the falls was quieter now.

'What did you see?' Branwald demanded.

'I saw a white shape, like a person. It was in the mouth of the passage, but then it moved up this way.'

Branwald stared at his friend. 'Are you sure?'

Maloof turned to look into Branwald's eyes. His voice was calm and without rancour. 'As I am Maloof of the Forest People,' he said, 'I am sure of this.'

Branwald glanced around. 'But where did it go?'

Maloof peered into the mouth of the adjoining passage, but nothing was visible in the darkness.

'There are so many ways it could have gone,' he said.

The cold chill crept up Branwald's neck again. 'Come on. Let us go up.'

They made the return in silence, their eyes watchful, their ears alert to any sound. Branwald was relieved when the ivy-shrouded opening appeared. He saw that there were actually two arched openings, side by side, separated by a narrow column of rock.

'Bragan's Nostrils,' said Maloof. 'This place is well named.'

Outside, they stood on the grassy ledge for a while, looking across and down at the Rivelvan's final plunge into the earth. The morning was still grey and sombre. Branwald glanced warily at the dark openings behind him. He could not put the fear of the White Ones out of his heart.

Maloof spoke first. 'We will get the canoe.' It was half question, half statement.

Branwald looked up along the flank of the mountain. He could not see the summit for the grey cloud roof above them.

'Branwald, this is the way. The Old Soldier said that we can follow this way. He would not deceive us.' Maloof's eyes searched Branwald's face.

Branwald would not look at him. He knew Maloof could sense his fear, and he resented it. 'The old man has not always done the right thing,' he grumbled. 'How do we know that what he says is true?'

Maloof sat down abruptly on the damp grass. He pulled a long withered stem from a tuft beside him and began to twist it in his fingers. 'Branwald,' he said, 'do you want to go back to your mother and sister?'

Branwald didn't reply. Into his mind flashed an image of the elegant, gentle woman who was his mother. He saw her eyes as they had looked at him on that cold morning that seemed so long ago and yet was only yesterday. He saw the sadness even more clearly than when he had stood before her — the sadness that would only go away if his father came back.

'No,' he conceded. 'We must go on. We will go by the Way of the White Ones.'

❧

They made their way down to the margin of the trees, and through them to where they had left the canoe. The first thing Branwald did was to unfold the leather map and lay it on the back of the upturned canoe.

'It does not say how long this way is, how many hours it will take us.'

Maloof, at his shoulder, stared at the map. 'Well,' he said, 'if it takes four days to go over the mountain on foot, surely it can be no more than a day and a half when one is travelling along a swiftly flowing river.'

'That is, if we meet no obstacles. What could this be?' Branwald asked, pointing to the words 'The Forest'. 'And "The Kanaka Sump"? And "Pogik"? And "Cathedral Lake"?'

'It could be that these words are here in order to warn us of the dangers,' Maloof replied. 'That is why the old man gave us this map. If we go carefully and watch the map, we will be ready for them before we come to them.'

'Let us go, then,' said Branwald, although his heart shivered within him at the thought.

They put their food and their spare clothing into the canvas satchels, which they slung around their shoulders, and tied the paddles across their backs. Then, carrying the empty canoe, they struggled through the trees and out onto the steep slope that overlooked the sink-hole. Soon they had hoisted the canoe onto the last ledge below the hanging ivy. Without speaking, they laid it down and turned to look northwards along the winding Rivelvan, each aware that this might be their last look at green growing things, their last few breaths of clear mountain air, their last moment ever in the daylight.

Then they bent, grasped the canoe and, Branwald leading, entered the dark passage of Bragan's Nostrils.

The descent to the riverside was not difficult, although Branwald again had to hold the Firebolt in his hand in order to light the way. They went boldly, speaking in calm and friendly tones to each other, knowing that there might be listeners and not wishing to startle them. By the froth-speckled river they laid the canoe down and placed their belongings in it, all the while watching the gloomy passage-ways and corners nearby. Branwald took one last look at the wrinkled map, noting that the first name, 'The Forest', was more than a quarter of the way along the winding route. He turned to speak to Maloof, but found him standing on the wet clay, his face turned towards the falls, his eyes closed, his lips moving.

'What are you doing?' Branwald shouted. His friend did not show any sign that he had heard. Branwald stared at him, frowning.

After some moments, Maloof opened his eyes. He did not speak because of the tumult of the falls, but his thought was clear and strong. 'The Forest People believe that the Mother Spirit looks over all living things. Everything is connected. We are connected with the birds and the creatures of the forest, just as we are connected with the Island People, with the White Ones, even with the Orelord and his minions. The Mother gives life and She takes it away. The Forest People say that to be ready is what matters. I was preparing myself.'

Branwald felt at a disadvantage. There was nothing in the grim doctrines of his own people that could help him now, he thought. All he was aware of was a determination to go on for his mother's sake, mingled with a deep-seated fear of the journey ahead.

When Maloof was ready, they seated themselves, anchoring the craft by digging the paddle-blades into the soft, shallow bottom. Branwald sat at the prow, the Firebolt in one hand, his paddle in the other.

Just before they pushed off, Branwald searched the dark places again with his eyes. Then, above the thunder of the falls, he heard the sound again: another long, plaintive, high-pitched cry which filled the roof of the cavern. It seemed to be coming from the passage by which they had entered.

As he stared at the place, Branwald saw something white against the blackness: a human figure, half-concealed by the angled opening. Motionless, it seemed to be watching them.

Branwald glanced at Maloof. He had seen it too, for he was reaching out his hand towards it. But Branwald did not wait. He pushed hard against the bottom, balancing as the canoe slid out into the current. In a moment the craft was away and picking up speed.

Branwald took one last glance. He saw the figure, framed in the opening, its hand reaching towards them. Branwald stroked powerfully forward, fearful of a missile. He had to adjust his aim as the river began to veer to the left. In a few moments, the light from the bottom of Bragan's Throat was gone, and they were drifting along in a moving pool of light that came from the shaft of the Firebolt.

CHAPTER FIFTEEN

'**W**e're going too fast! Slow down!' Branwald shouted.
A long spear of calcite, its tip almost touching the water, came rushing at them out of the darkness ahead. He shouted again and pushed it away with his paddle. The stalactite rasped along the side of the canoe. He felt the craft tipping and adjusted his weight to keep the balance.

'Back-paddle, Branwald!' Maloof called.

Another stalactite sped past them, too close for comfort. Branwald propped the Firebolt against the prow and back-paddled strongly. He ducked his head to avoid three smaller stalactites, welded together in a crusty mass. The canoe slowed down. The pale spears drifted past more slowly.

Branwald picked up the Firebolt again. The glow from the blade increased. He saw that the roof was higher on the left, so he pushed the prow in that direction.

'There is no need to paddle,' Maloof said. 'Let the stream carry us. As long as we can see what's before us, we can avoid the dangers.'

Branwald felt less fearful about the speed of the flow, now that he could see over thirty yards ahead by the Firebolt's light. The water was deep and there were no rapids. His fear, however, was of meeting an obstacle, such as a line of sta-lactites so low across the river that there would not be clearance for the canoe.

The danger from rushing water and lurking rocks might not be the worst, however, he thought. He knew now that the White Ones did exist, after all, and it was difficult for him to believe that he and Maloof would avoid contact with them. Thus, as each new corner approached, he steeled himself for he knew not what.

Soon afterwards, they were traversing a wide stretch of

water, sticking close to the left-hand wall as the course curved in that direction. Branwald casually swept with his eyes the inverted jungle of hanging shapes in the low-roofed spaces away to his right. There, behind a fence of pale pillars, he thought he saw a movement. The shape he saw was low and white. It could have been a person, seated close to the surface as if in a canoe, but it was too far away for him to be sure. As he focused on it, it merged with the still white formations that surrounded it.

Branwald opened his mouth to speak, but decided against it. Maybe it was his imagination .... Then the time for action was past: they had rounded the curve, and the shape was lost from view.

~

They had been drifting for many hours, by Branwald's reckoning, and the speed of flow seemed to have lessened. The river was widening, and by the light of the Firebolt the boys could see rounded green rocks just under the surface.

The roof was still festooned with great thickets of stalactites. This hanging forest began to drop closer and closer to the surface of the river. There were more pillars than stalactites. Soon they were so close together that there was no space for the canoe between them.

'We have reached the Forest,' remarked Maloof grimly, as they levered themselves back upstream.

'There must be a way through,' Branwald said, panting with effort. He aimed for a narrow gap between two fluted columns but misjudged the width. The canoe, wedged firmly, came to a stop. He felt the current piling up against the stern. There was a tense moment as they carefully prised the canoe backwards until it was clear of the gap. They turned it by holding onto the thin columns on either side. Then they drifted across the face of the forest, searching for a passage.

'Wait,' said Branwald, when they had almost reached the left-hand wall. 'There's a rope there.'

It was true. A ragged rope tied to a column led to another one further into the forest.

'The White Ones have done this,' breathed Maloof. 'This is their Way.'

They followed the zigzag rope, and always there was room for the canoe. Soon the dense stands of rocks began to thin out; scattered stalactites appeared among them, and in a few moments there was clear water ahead.

'Well,' said Maloof. 'The first obstacle over!'

'Yes,' Branwald grumbled. 'But what is the Kanaka Sump?'

'If the White Ones can get through it, then we can!' retorted Maloof.

Some time later they approached a formation that hung from the roof of the cave like a tied-back curtain. The Firebolt's glow caught streaks of colour in it, reds and yellows and creamy whites. 'Like a rainbow!' exclaimed Maloof.

As they passed under it, Branwald prepared for another bend in the channel, because he saw a blank wall of rock ahead. They emerged from under the hanging folds and he searched for a route. There was none. Yet the river continued to flow.

Then Branwald became aware of a sucking sound, the kind he remembered hearing when he had pulled the stopper out of the great stone trough outside the door of his home and watched the water swirling down and being swallowed by the round opening at the bottom. He lifted the Firebolt higher, looking towards where the sound was coming from.

'There's something there,' he said, pointing. The nose of the canoe swung to the right and dipped slightly. Then Branwald dropped the Firebolt and furiously back-paddled.

'Back! Get back!' he shouted. 'It's a whirlpool!'

The prow was dipping alarmingly. Branwald dug deep, trying to lever it away from the dark hole that lay ahead. He could not see it, but the sucking sound, louder than the thrashing of their paddles, was very close. He grunted with the effort. The canoe slowed, the stern drifted further to the right, but the nose dipped lower. Branwald dropped to his knees on the floor. Salty perspiration trickled into his eyes and mouth. He gritted his teeth and back-paddled faster. He heard Maloof straining with effort.

Slowly their forward movement came to a stop. Then they were moving backwards. The current was slacker, the sucking sound further away.

Branwald lifted the Firebolt again and saw a small beach

behind them and to their left. They swung the canoe and drove it onto the pebbles. They anchored their paddles, their breath coming in gasps, while the whirlpool of the Kanaka Sump seethed and sucked in the darkness a short distance away.

'We were lucky,' Maloof said, when he had regained his breath. The light of the Firebolt showed that twenty yards downstream, just before the solid wall, there seemed to be a hole in the river's surface. Branwald watched a small island of foam floating past. When it reached a point about ten yards from the wall, it dropped from view. In a moment he saw it flit across, in a curving sweep; it flashed past twice more, and then it was gone. Branwald followed its passage in his mind. He imagined the particle of foam swirling round faster and faster until it came to the centre of the vortex, the black compression point that closed it in and drove it circling down and down into an abyss that had no bottom, and he shivered.

'There is no way through there,' he said, his eyes searching the distorted landscape. His body felt weary and he wanted something to eat. 'Come on. Let us eat something. Then we can look at the map again.'

Maloof made no reply. He stood up and lifted his satchel from the canoe. His face was pale in the light of the Firebolt, and Branwald knew that his friend was shaken.

There on the beach, they ate venison and cakes and drank cool river water. Then Maloof produced two apples. When Branwald caught the sweet smell of the apple's skin, the memory of mellow autumn evenings under the tree behind his house came to him. He sank his teeth into its firm flesh, and the sweet juices brought him back to the sunlight under a puff-cloud sky on his island home. He felt better. He would be there again, he told himself. He and Maloof would win through.

They studied the map again. They found the place called 'The Kanaka Sump' and examined the markings. There was a kind of archway spanning the solid line of the river. Just north of the arch, however, a broken line curved away from the river, skirting the arch and a black dot a little south of it, then rejoining the line of the river.

'There is another way out of this place,' Branwald concluded, folding the map again.

'We should have some rest,' said Maloof. 'We have been paddling for many hours, and if we are tired, it is more difficult to see approaching dangers in time.'

Branwald did not disagree, although he didn't think he would be able to sleep. If both of them slept, they would be leaving themselves completely defenceless.

'I will keep watch, while you sleep,' he offered.

Maloof was already spreading his cloak on a bed of pebbles. 'Whatever you wish,' he said.

'Would it not be better to keep ourselves away from the river? We can drag the canoe behind those columns.' Branwald indicated a cluster of pillars under the low roof to his right. 'We would not be seen there.'

Maloof shrugged his shoulders. 'I think it does not matter what we do or where we go. If the White Ones want to find us, they will find us. They know already that we are somewhere on the Way.' He began to settle himself on the cloak. 'Do not fear them, Branwald. The one that we saw near the mouth of the cave — I believe it meant us no harm. The White Ones are not to be feared.'

Before settling himself on his own cloak beside Maloof, Branwald shifted the canoe until it formed a shield between themselves and the dark cave through which they had come. He wrapped the Firebolt in its covering and placed it on the stones between himself and Maloof, the handle close to his hand. Then, in a blackness such as he had never before experienced, he stretched himself on the sloping beach, feeling the weariness of his body. The incessant suck and gurgle of the whirlpool echoed through the recesses and grottos around him.

～

Branwald woke with a start. Something cold was moving across his face. He twisted his head away and struck out with his hand, but made no contact. There was a sudden cry from some creature that moved quickly away across the crunching pebbles. Branwald reached down for the Firebolt, but it was not where he had left it. In panic, he ran his hand across the smooth stones, but it was not there.

Maloof stirred beside him. 'What ...? What is it?' His speech was thick with sleep.

'Something's got the Firebolt!' cried Branwald, leaping to his feet. In the blackness where the footsteps sounded, he saw a faint glow, and against it the shape of a crouching human figure, moving quickly away from him.

'Hieeey!' he yelled, with all the power of his lungs. As he started to follow the retreating figure, a glowing object appeared on the ground at its feet. It was the Firebolt.

'Hieey!' Branwald shouted again. The running figure paused momentarily, glanced behind, then continued its flight. Branwald hurried over the uneven ground, ducked under a dark point of rock and recovered the Firebolt, still half-covered by its wrapping. The white figure was rounding a lattice of fine shards of rock on a higher level.

Branwald heard Maloof's hurrying feet close behind him.

'Come back!' shouted Maloof. 'Come back! Do not be afraid!'

Branwald gave chase. The figure glanced behind again and saw him. Desperately it scrambled over a dark mound and slid down the other side. Both boys were calling now. Momentarily they saw the white face turned towards them, the open mouth a dark blob, the eyes reflecting back the light from the Firebolt. Then the figure dropped out of sight.

'Come on!' said Maloof. They reached the mound and scrambled over, Branwald keeping the beam of the Firebolt pointed towards the roof. Through a gap in the columns he saw a pebbled slope to the river. The figure was dragging a squat canoe towards the water's edge. The boys raced.

'Wait!' Maloof called.

The figure, realising it would not escape, let go the canoe and straightened. It turned to face its pursuers, holding its white hands before its face in a defensive gesture.

The boys stopped several paces from it. In the enclosed space, the only sound was their quick breathing. When the full light of the Firebolt fell on it, the figure lifted the folds of its hooded cape across its face, turning its head away at the same time. Then it spoke.

'If you harm me, my people will know.' The words were clear, and the voice was unmistakably that of a young girl.

'Do not be frightened,' Maloof said. 'Please do not be

afraid. We mean you no harm. We are only two boys and we are on a journey.'

The girl was silent, her only movement the quick rise and fall of her shoulders.

'Do you understand what I say to you?' Maloof asked. She nodded. 'What is your name?'

The girl lifted her head a little and said, 'My name is Aiyan.' Branwald, not yet recovered from the alarm, scanned the place behind. Nothing moved but their shadows.

Maloof said, 'Where are your people? Where are the others?' No reply. 'Are they near here?'

The girl shook her head. 'Some live near the Fount, and others near the Lair of the Gretchin,' she said.

'Why do you not look at us?' Branwald asked, half afraid of seeing some terrible deformity in the girl's face.

The change of voice made her start. She made a gesture with her white hand. 'The firing,' she said. 'It hurts my eyes.'

There was a sudden scraping sound from above, where the beam of the Firebolt had been playing on the roof. An icicle of rock plunged straight down and buried its point in the pebbles of the beach, several yards to the girl's left. She uttered a cry and stepped away.

Branwald, realising the cause, moved the point of the Firebolt back until it pointed at the stones behind him. He eased his grip on the weapon, and the light dimmed.

'I am sorry,' he said. 'Do not be alarmed. It is safe now.'

The girl turned towards them, lowering her cloak. The boys saw a pale, oval face, regular in its features, except for the eyes. They were large and slightly protruding, but what startled Branwald was the fact that the pupils were huge. There was no sign of the normal whites, except in the very corners.

The girl stared for a long moment at the faces of the boys, her pupils tinted slightly pink where the reflected light from the Firebolt caught them.

'Why are you following us?' Maloof asked.

Aiyan shook her head. 'I do not follow you. You passed me on the way. I am on my way from the Fount to the Lair of the Gretchin. It is the beginning of the Cycle of Life. One from the

Fount must go to those at the Lair of the Gretchin, in order to bring the nuts and get the salt and the fruits. I am the one.'

'You? Alone?'

She shrugged her shoulders. 'I am not a baby.'

'But why you?' Branwald asked.

She shrugged again. 'The others are too old.' A pause. 'Where have you come from? Where is your home?'

'We come from the Islands,' Maloof explained. 'Beyond the mouth of the cave. We do not mean you or your people any harm. We are sorry we frightened you.'

'I was only a little frightened,' Aiyan replied. 'I do not believe everything they have taught me about the Dark Ones. But I did not think you would wake up when I touched you.' They saw a fleeting smile on her lips. 'We have not had any Dark Ones in our world in my lifetime. There is nothing here for your people.' The statement was almost a question.

'We are on our way to the other end, and beyond,' Branwald explained.

'But why this way? My father says that the Dark Ones go over the top of the world to reach that place.'

'It is a long story to tell,' said Branwald.

'I would like to hear it,' Aiyan said, and abruptly sat down cross-legged on the pebbles.

Branwald looked at Maloof. Maloof smiled. 'You tell it,' he said.

Branwald told Aiyan about their fathers' journey, about the Orelord, about Urkor, the Old Soldier and the strangers on the Pass of Feyan. He did not mention the Firebolt.

Aiyan looked at him in silence for a moment. 'Then my people are right. Evil ones still inhabit the world above.'

'Some are evil, yes,' Maloof interrupted. 'But there are many kind and good ones.'

Again she regarded them for a moment. 'And you?'

Half amused by the simplicity of the question, the boys exchanged glances. 'In all of us, the good struggles with the evil,' Maloof replied. 'We are for the good.'

'Can I touch your faces?' Aiyan asked abruptly.

Branwald nodded. She stepped close and lifted her hands hesitantly. Her cold fingers traversed his brow, descended to his eyes, his nose, his mouth and chin. Finally the hands went to his hair and moved down along both sides of his face until they met under his chin. It was a strange sensation. Then Aiyan turned to Maloof and repeated the procedure, all the while making no sound. When she had finished, she stepped back and looked from one to the other.

'Where is the Lair of the ...?' Maloof asked.

'Gretchin? It is at the other end of our world, where the waters' — Aiyan indicated the river beside her — 'drop away to the world of the Dark Ones, to your world.'

'How far is it?'

'No more than half a night.' She turned to look at her canoe. In the faint light, Branwald saw that the forward section of the craft was loaded to the gunwales with sacks. 'If you want to, you can come with me.'

The boys were happy to accept Aiyan's offer. They learnt that she had been ahead of them, some distance back, but she had heard the warning sound made by her people — the strange high-pitched wail that the boys had heard too. She had hidden herself behind the pillars, where Branwald had seen her. Curious, she had followed them in her small canoe, and had found them sleeping. Creeping closer, she had found that they didn't seem to be as repulsive as she had always believed Dark Ones to be. Then her sensitive fingers had woken Branwald.

They were making their way back towards the boys' canoe when Aiyan indicated the Firebolt in Branwald's hand. 'What is that?' she asked.

He was reluctant to reply. 'It is .... We do not really know what it is or where it first came from,' Branwald said finally. 'It was given to us by the Old Soldier. It has existed for a very long time. It has great power, but such a power as can destroy the one who carries it.'

Aiyan took a step away from the Firebolt, averting her eyes. 'My people have told me of a weapon such as this. It has been in our world once before. They still speak of it, and some of them fear it. You will see some of its doings before very long.'

Branwald pondered her words. Was it possible that the

Old Soldier had come through the Way of the White Ones on his journey to the Kadach Pit so many years before?

'But why did you take it?' Maloof asked, when they had returned to their canoe and Aiyan was examining it with restless fingers.

She was silent for a moment. 'I do not know why I took it,' she said slowly. 'If I had known that it is a firing thing, I would not have .... I did not think.' She shrugged her shoulders in the dim light. 'I just took it.' She shielded her eyes as she glanced towards where the Firebolt lay on the floor of the canoe, its tip still glowing. 'But now we must set out. My people are awaiting me. If you take your canoe round to where mine is, I will show you the way past Kanaka.'

When the boys paddled round, they found Aiyan lifting sacks out of her canoe, which was similar to the ones they had seen near Bragan's Throat. At the very bow, on a raised framework, rested some kind of metal receptacle in which a weak flame burned.

'This is the most difficult part of the journey for me,' Aiyan said. 'All who come on the Cycle journey must unload the canoe at this place, carry everything to the other side of Kanaka, and then come back for the canoe. Now you can help me, if it so pleases you.'

The boys lifted a heavy sack in each hand, gripping them by the cords that tied up their necks. By the light of the Firebolt they followed Aiyan upwards, through a petrified forest, until their way was blocked by a blank wall. Aiyan led the way along the base of it until she came to an opening. 'Be careful here,' she warned.

To Branwald's surprise, the opening was perfectly cylindrical in shape and sloped steeply downwards. He edged down it, body turned sideways, until he found himself standing on a circular plinth at the bottom. From it, a series of shallow semicircular steps led down into another dark chamber. Soon he heard the swish and gurgle of water to his left. Then they were treading their way through another thicket of rock, down and down, until they stopped on a muddy bank by the edge of the black river.

'This passage,' said Aiyan, as they climbed back through

the cylinder, 'is not a natural one, as you can tell. I said that you would find the work of a weapon such as yours on this journey. Here is one example of its power — a power that was once used to help my people.'

At the top, Branwald stopped. 'You mean that this passage was made by some implement?'

'It was made by a weapon that could cut a path through the solid rock, so that my people could pass the Kanaka and make their way to the Fount.'

'The man, the bearer of this weapon — what was he like?' Branwald asked.

'They say that he had been a warrior, a fighter against the evil ones. But when he came into our world, he had been wounded — not a wound to his body, the old ones say, but some other kind of wound, a kind that I do not know.'

'The Old Soldier!' breathed Maloof. 'He came this way.'

It took two further trips before Aiyan's canoe was empty and all the sacks were deposited on the other side of the Kanaka Sump. Then the boys placed her canoe on top of their own and carried them both through the twisting ways.

'Are there no boys among your people who could make this journey?' Maloof asked, when they had reached the riverside again. 'Or who could have come with you?'

Aiyan regarded him for a moment. 'You speak like the boys at the Lair, who think that only boys could make this journey.' She made an exasperated sound. 'Now I know that boys everywhere are the same. But to answer your question: my little brother is only five Cycles old. I will bring him with me when I am sure he will not be frightened. As for the others, my parents are old, and even they are young compared with the rest. There are no other young ones there.'

'And at the Lair?' Branwald asked.

'There are three there who are my age, two boys and a girl. There are some older ones who could make this journey, but it is a difficult one going against the stream. And we need the salt and fruits more than they need what we have to give them.'

They laid the canoes side by side on the wet slope, and began to load the sacks into Aiyan's — she had politely refused their offer to carry some in their canoe.

'My people are a dying race,' she said. 'There are some who say that we should return to the world of the Dark Ones, that the Dark Time has long passed. But the great light in the roof of the world hurts our eyes. Others say that we would become prey to animals and even to evil ones if we were to venture there. So the fear keeps us in our own world. And we will stay here, I think, until we fade away to nothing.' Her tone was matter-of-fact, with no trace of feeling, but Branwald felt a sadness for the girl and for her people.

'And you? What do you want?' Maloof asked.

Aiyan shrugged her shoulders. 'What I want is not important now. My parents and the old ones need me. I am the only one who is able to climb to the top of the Fount when the night comes there, to collect what we need from the forest. I must do this as long as they are there.' She started to slide her canoe down the slope towards the water. Then she paused and looked at Maloof. 'You are the first one ever to ask me that.' Then she continued with her task.

'The Gretchin? What is it?' questioned Maloof.

'When my people came there first, a great beast called the Gretchin had made his lair there. They used the firing to drive him and his brood out into the Blighted Lands. He never returned, although some say that they still hear him bellowing in the valley below.' Aiyan shrugged again. 'I have never heard him, though. The old ones use him to frighten the young ones. I think he is just another one of their stories.'

A short time later, they were once again drifting through the fantastic landscape of the Way of the White Ones. Aiyan led the way, her slight figure luminous in the darkness. Branwald occupied the stern seat of his canoe, with the Firebolt propped before him so that Maloof's body acted as a shield between its glow and the girl. The river flowed with hardly a ripple; the only sound was the regular dip and lift of the three paddles. The air was cool and still.

CHAPTER SIXTEEN

S ome time later, the roof over them began to lift, and the river to widen. The echoes took longer to come back to them.

'This is Cathedral Lake,' Aiyan called. 'Soon you will hear the Pogik. Perhaps he is hungry.' She glanced back at her companions.

'What is it?' Branwald asked in alarm.

Aiyan stopped paddling and allowed them to draw level. Her eyes were huge.

'The Pogik? He comes up from below. Sometimes he is angry. We must keep away from him.'

Soon they began to hear a sound — a faint gurgling and rushing of water, which gradually became louder. It seemed to be passing them on the right. The surface of the river became more disturbed, as if something in the darkness was agitating it. The boys hugged the left-hand wall, while Aiyan seemed unconcerned.

'The Pogik is quiet at this hour,' Aiyan said. 'Sometimes, when much water falls on the world above, the Pogik will not let you pass, because the chamber fills. But there is nothing to fear now. The Pogik is sleeping.'

'The Pogik is not a creature, then?' ventured Maloof.

Her laughter echoed through the great cavern. 'The Pogik is a river that flows in. But he makes a good story, don't you think?'

They looked at her with mild amusement on their faces. 'Yes,' said Maloof, ruefully. 'The old ones are not the only ones who can tell stories.'

'Soon, if you use your firing rod, you will see the Cathedral in the centre of the lake,' Aiyan said. 'When we were many, my people used to live even in this place. They called the shape on the island "the Cathedral".' The gurgle of the Pogik became fainter. 'No one comes here now, apart from me.'

'What is a cathedral?' Branwald enquired.

'It is a word from before the Dark Time, my father says. He says that the Olden People made many great buildings, which towered almost to the roof of the world. They had parts in the walls where light in many colours came in. But the cathedrals, too, were lost in the Dark Time.'

The structure that loomed out of the lake ahead was not unlike many of the formations which Branwald had already seen in the cave, except that it was much larger. As he drew nearer, however, and held the Firebolt aloft, he saw that, while the massive formation itself was a natural one, it had been carved and shaped in places by agents which were not natural. A flight of steps spiralled upwards from the water's edge, hedged by a banister of slim stalactites, precise and symmetrical. On the sides of the great mound, the natural benches had been levelled to form balconies. Higher up, he saw that many of the blunt stalagmites had elaborate carvings on them, spiralling upwards or encircling the rock.

The three were silent as the canoes drifted past the deserted pile. Branwald imagined that the ghosts of the lost, sad race which had once lived and walked in the Cathedral were standing there, silent and watching, on the lonely terraces and balconies, visited only occasionally by this one child on her solitary journey. He wondered how Aiyan felt as she looked at this abandoned monument to her race. When he glanced in her direction, however, her face was turned away.

'Could you not live with the others, at the Lair of the Gretchin?' Maloof asked.

'We could,' Aiyan replied quietly. 'They have often asked us to come. But my parents, and the others — they are old. They have lived all their lives near the Fount. It is the place they know. I think they wish to die there. So I cannot go yet.' The words were said without emotion, as if the subject was something that did not concern her at all. These should be the sentiments of one who is old and wise, Branwald thought.

'How old are you?' Maloof asked.

'I have lived fifteen Cycles of Life. This is my fourth journey to the Gretchin's Lair.'

133

'When we come back from the mouth of the Great River,' Maloof said, 'we will come to the Fount to see you.'

Aiyan turned her face towards them and smiled. 'I would like that.'

~

In the quietness that followed, Branwald thought again of the Old Soldier, and wondered if it had really been he who had come through the Way so many years before. He recalled the frail figure of the old man standing in the Kadach Pit; he could not imagine him as a young man.

And then, unaccountably, Branwald remembered Urkor. Where was he now? A pang of unease grew in Branwald's stomach. What if Urkor had gone back to Redwood Island in search of Branwald and the Firebolt? Of course he would not find him there; but what mischief he would stir up if he had guessed where Branwald had gone! What if Estel was implicated and hauled before the Elders? Or, worse still, what if Urkor were to go to her house? Branwald remembered the look — not just a look: the thought, the lust in the man's mind. Surely the people, his own people, would not allow any evil to befall her. Surely Vokt and Spen and the others would protect his mother and Eroona ....

Branwald felt strongly the need to know. He searched for an image of Eroona, but nothing would come. It was as if there was something between them, blocking it. The mountain, he thought. He would try again when he emerged from the cave.

Maloof cut across his thoughts. 'The stranger will not waste time by going back to the islands, I think,' he said quietly. 'If he guesses where we are going with the Firebolt, and if he wants it as much as we think, he will follow us. But he does not know of the Way of the White Ones, so he must ascend the mountain to the Pass of Feyan. You must not fear what may never happen, Branwald.'

They had left the Cathedral far behind when Aiyan spoke again. 'My people at the Gretchin's Lair will be alarmed if they see you with me. They have seen no one from the Upper World since the warrior came this way. I will have to warn them, so that they will be prepared. There is a special sound that we use, so do not be surprised when you hear it.'

'Are we near the end?' Branwald asked.

'We must travel for some distance still, but we are near enough for them to hear me. Usually, when they know I am near, they come to meet me. This time, I am not sure what they will do.'

She rested her paddle across her knees and put her hands around her mouth in the shape of a funnel. The sound she made was similar to the weird cries the boys had heard near Bragan's Throat, except that it came in regular waves. It made the hair stand up on the back of Branwald's neck. He listened as the long echo of the cry dwindled and dwindled in the far recesses of the cave.

Aiyan picked up her paddle again, but she did not dip it into the water. 'Shhh! We must listen,' she whispered.

For several minutes they listened to the quiet ripple of the river in the dark places. Then Branwald's skin tingled again: out of the blackness ahead of them came a faint answering cry, low at first, but gradually rising to a quivering ululation that held for a long moment and then faded away to nothing.

'They have heard,' Aiyan said. 'I do not think they will meet us on the way.'

'Do they know about us?' Branwald asked.

She nodded. 'They know that there are two Dark Ones with me. But in our signal calls, we do not have words to say what you are like.'

'What will they do?' Branwald continued.

'They will hide,' she said simply.

Some time later, Aiyan pointed to several structures by the riverside. 'That was Estepo's room,' she said. 'That was Thurlo's.' The 'rooms' seemed to have been constructed by using existing pillars of calcite as supports and filling the spaces between with regular blocks of rock. Branwald saw no sign of occupants.

The river swung to the left and Branwald saw, in the distance, a faint triangular patch of light.

'The Lair of the Gretchin?' Maloof queried. Aiyan nodded, but placed her fingers on her lips.

As they advanced, the boys saw more and more of the

buildings, some black and silent, others with a faint internal flicker of light. There was not a sound, apart from the thrusting of the paddles. The triangle of distant light was growing larger. Then Branwald became aware of pale shapes standing, motionless, in the doorways of the buildings. The White Ones were watching.

'I will speak to them,' Aiyan whispered, as the canoes drifted towards a sandy bank, near which stood a structure larger than the others. 'Put the Firebolt down.'

Branwald put the instrument on the floor of the canoe and half-covered it with the map.

'Ancient Tagel!' Aiyan called. 'Ancient Tagel, are you there?' At the door of the building there was a slight movement, as if someone had changed position. 'Do not be alarmed! The Dark Ones with me mean us no harm. They are travelling through and beyond our home, to the mouth of the Great River.' She paused and waited.

There was another movement near the door. A tall figure with rounded shoulders, dressed in a white hooded cape, stepped cautiously out onto the flagstones. When he spoke, his voice was deep and solemn and old.

'Aiyan, you are welcome here, as you always have been. But you know the ancient practice of our people. The Dark Ones, whose forefathers destroyed the Upper World, have never been invited to come among us. This has been the rule of our people for generations. Why have you broken it now?' The man's presence was impressive and full of authority. Branwald looked at Aiyan, trying to gauge her response.

'I know the practice of our people,' she replied in a steady voice. 'And I did not invite these Dark Ones into our home. I found them already here. They have been kind to me and helped me with provisions, and I have shown them the way so that they can continue their journey ....'

Tagel shook his head. 'Aiyan, child, you are young and do not know.' He turned to the two boys. 'Dark Ones, this is no place for such as you. I must ask you, on behalf of my people, to leave this place at once. The way to the world of your people is there.' He pointed with a thin white finger towards the patch of daylight. 'Now go!'

In a deeper part of the cave, to the old man's left, there was a movement; but as Branwald looked, it stilled.

'We will go,' Branwald replied. 'But we want you to know that we are not your enemies, and we mean you no harm. We thank you for our passage, and for Aiyan's help.'

Tagel regarded Branwald in silence. Behind him, in the darkness, definite shapes were moving towards the river. Branwald thought he saw long, thin objects in their hands. Warily, he glanced down at the Firebolt.

Aiyan spoke again. 'My people, you remember the warrior who came this way in the olden days, and who helped our fathers to find a way past Kanaka with the great weapon. Did he not say that one day it would return?'

The white figures stopped moving.

'Why are you speaking thus?' the old man demanded, and in his tone there was anger.

'Because,' retorted Aiyan in a ringing voice, 'one of these Dark Ones is the bearer of the weapon!'

The old man took a step backwards. There was a sound like a gasp, a sharp intake of breath, from the ghostly group behind him. Then came the sound of shuffling feet as they sagged back into the darkness from which they had come.

Tagel lifted his right arm, palm forward, as if to stop Aiyan from speaking. 'Enough!' he cried. 'The Dark Ones were ever deceivers and liars! They have suborned you, girl! They have contaminated you with their vicious trickery!' Yielding to an impulse, Branwald bent and picked up the Firebolt, shaking off the soft leather covering. 'They have not changed! They have —' The old man broke off as he saw the glow from the Firebolt.

Branwald, keeping the beam aimed at the water, lifted it high. The vault of the cave was suddenly filled with shrieks and yells, as the White Ones scattered in a jumbled mass. Tagel fell upon his knees on the flagstones, pulling the folds of his cape over his face. Then, leaning forward with his elbows on the ground, he spoke in a low tone.

'If this is truly the weapon of the warrior, then I ask your pardon, young brave, for doubting you. But the memory of my people is a long one. We cannot forget the deeds that caused the world to darken and the living things to decay. We cannot forget the deeds of the Dark Ones.' He lifted his head, but kept the cloak across his face. 'Forgive me. I cannot look at you. The weapon is too bright.'

Branwald felt a sneer rise to his lips as he looked at this pale man kneeling before him. He felt an urge to display the power of the Firebolt, which he still held triumphantly above his head. He looked around for a suitable target. But Maloof's voice cut across his thoughts. 'Branwald, that is enough. You have shown it. It is enough.'

Branwald stared at him as if he had just woken from sleep, or from a trance. Then he lowered the weapon, loosening his grip. Slightly embarrassed, he dropped the Firebolt into the canoe and covered it. 'Yes,' he muttered. 'I am sorry.'

Soon afterwards, Branwald, Maloof and Aiyan stood on the dusky beach, surrounded by a chattering crowd of White Ones. Branwald felt many hands running over his body and face, as they timidly examined him and Maloof. Others stooped to look at their canoe and at its contents. In the near-darkness, Branwald tried to watch the many hands traversing the craft, but Aiyan reassured him. 'Among our people, everything belongs to everybody. We do not own anything as individuals. Thus we do not fear that another will take what is ours, as some in the Upper World do.'

'The White Ones do not seem to have the same objections to taking from strangers,' Branwald gently reminded her.

She bowed her head, remembering, and for a moment she was confused. 'I am sorry,' she said. 'The Firebolt is not the same as other things.'

'You must take some refreshment with us,' Tagel said, 'before you continue on your journey.'

The refreshment, when it came soon afterwards, included many foodstuffs which Branwald had never tasted before — cakes of tiny compressed seeds; a small brown fruit which tasted vaguely like an apple that had been left until it was old and shrunken; a drink, sweet and fruity and slightly fermented, that heated the back of his throat as it slid down — as well as more familiar foods: smoked fish, slightly leathery, and crisp autumn-flavoured nuts from one of Aiyan's sacks.

Branwald, Maloof and Aiyan sat on raised stones around the glowing embers of a fire, in front of Tagel's room, with the old man and his wizened little wife. Other members of the small community stood a respectful distance away, watching with great round eyes.

When the meal was over, and the gathered White Ones had drawn into a closer circle around them, Branwald and Maloof told the story of their quest and of how they had come by the Firebolt. Branwald, remembering the strange proud exultation which had come over him when he first showed the instrument to the old man, felt slightly ashamed. He could not understand why he had acted so.

When their story was ended, a hush fell on the gathering. Tagel gazed into the crumbling embers of the fire; then he lifted his head and spoke. 'I believe there are many like us White Ones, who have survived the Time of Darkness. You will find others hidden in secret places, happy that they still live and breathe. Some may have turned their backs on the great Upper World, where we once lived amongst green and growing things, when the world was new and unspoiled. They have lost hope.' He paused for a long moment. 'Indeed, I sometimes think —' He seemed to be speaking only to himself. 'I sometimes think that we have made that mistake too.'

He turned his head to look at the boys. 'But you two brave ones will keep our hopes alive. When your task is completed, you must come back to us and recount your deeds. We had thought that the warrior who once came into our world was the last of those who stood against the evil forces. But now we see that there are others — others from the Upper World who are prepared to struggle with the evil ones. This gives us hope that someday — someday, my people may yet return to a world made new, where even the White Ones can live without fear.'

There was a murmur from the gathered circle, and Branwald sensed that the old man's words did not meet with the approval of everyone there.

Tagel stood up and addressed his people. 'My people, we live in a time of change. Maybe the old cycle is coming to an end.' He stilled several protests with a movement of his hand. 'Maybe the new one is coming upon us and we cannot yet see it. Be open to it, my people, and have courage, just as these two Dark Ones must have it. We wish them well in their quest.'

~

A little later, as the boys prepared to leave, Aiyan stood with them by their canoe.

'If the world were different, I would go with you,' she said. 'But it is not possible. I hope that I see you again.'

'I hope so too,' Maloof said.

'You cannot leave the Lair of the Gretchin by canoe; fifty paces from here, the river tumbles down into the world below. But you will find a path on the right-hand side, and this will take you down to the level ground. What there is further on, I do not know for certain. There are dangers, yes, but those that we are warned of when we are children may not be the real ones.' She raised her hand and touched them each on the cheek. 'It is morning in the Upper World. The light is strong and, until you have gained the shelter of the trees, you can be seen from afar. Be careful.'

The boys slid the canoe to the water's edge, stepped in and pushed off. The White Ones, gathered along the bank, stood in silence.

'Goodbye,' Aiyan called, and waved her hand. The others took up her action. 'Goodbye,' they called.

'We will meet again,' Branwald called back. Then, with strong thrusts of their paddles, the boys moved towards the light.

CHAPTER SEVENTEEN

After the darkness of the cave, the white intensity of the daylight was so strong that Branwald had to squint his eyes. Then, as they adjusted, he saw a patch of blue sky framed in the opening ahead. His nose sensed again the sweet freshness of the air. He was exhilarated. They had gone into the depths of the mountain and come out the other side!

When they came close to the place where the speeding river dropped abruptly from sight, the boys beached the canoe and hauled it out of the water. Then, without speaking, they walked out along the flat rock into the morning light and gazed at the scene before them.

They were looking down on a great valley that led away from them between ranges of mountains that stretched across the horizon as far as the eye could see. Beside them, the river, gushing out of the cave, began a headlong tumble to the valley floor far below. The brown sides of the valley were steep and scarred with gullies. They were bare of trees, except at the very bottom, where the river was; there, however, there was a rich carpet of trees and shrubs. The river wound between low spurs until it disappeared from view around the great shoulder of a mountain many miles distant. Over all the rumpled surface, the drifting cumulus clouds slid their clinging shadows.

'We should have asked,' said Maloof, after they had gazed at the scene for several minutes, 'if there are any people down there.'

Apart from several tracks that wound along the contours just above the shrub-line, there was no evidence of any human habitation. Branwald looked at the distant cloud-capped peaks, and wondered how far it was to the mouth of the Great River.

'These matters can not be known now,' Maloof said, startling him. 'We cannot traverse rapids until we come to them.'

Branwald, slightly irritated, turned to look at his friend. 'Do you always know what is in my mind?' he asked.

Maloof shrugged his shoulders. 'Not all the time. But when your thought is joined with your fear, sometimes I can feel it. But you can read my thoughts too.'

'I could before. I think I still can, when I am not thinking of something else.'

'When you are fearful or angry or ashamed, it is more difficult to hear another's thought,' Maloof said. 'But now that we have come this far, maybe there will be less for us to fear.'

Branwald stayed for a moment gazing at the scene. 'At least,' he said, 'now we will be able to see the dangers.' He stepped out into the sunlight and examined the slope below him. 'There is a track here,' he said. 'Let us begin.'

The morning sun was hot on the boys' shoulders as they struggled down the sloping track with the canoe. At the bottom, the path led through a stand of willows to a cool arbour by the water's edge. As they laid their load down, they noticed that there were many boulders projecting above the surface of the speeding waters.

They knelt and scooped handfuls of the cool liquid to quench their thirst. Then Branwald took the map again, and laid it across the bow of the canoe. He found the exit from the Way of the White Ones and followed the zigzag line of the Great River downwards.

Two tributaries joined the main channel from the right, and one from the left, before he found the word 'Biloh' written beside a small square by the riverside. Below this, where two roughly-drawn lines crossed the river, was written 'The Bridge of Shihara'. Several inches below, where a cluster of rectangles was drawn on the left bank of the river, he saw the words 'Bridge of the Ancients (Ruins)'. Not far below this, again on the left bank, were the words 'Land of the Galians'; below this again, the artist had attempted to draw the shapes of trees, clustering on both sides of the river all the way to the sea at the bottom. Before it reached there, however, the river was joined by another river, entering from the west. The

142

words 'Ochre Flood' were written there. Far to the left, near the source of the river, were drawn three buildings; beside these was written 'Monastery of the Sordiana'. Finally, near the mouth of the river was a cluster of irregular shapes and the words 'Tarquan Islands'.

'Let us deal with Biloh first — whatever it is,' said Maloof, wiping his mouth with his hand.

They readied the canoe and, having studied the flow of the water, decided on their route. Then, standing on the grassy bank, Maloof bent and scooped up some water in his cupped hands. He held it before him, facing the river. He closed his eyes and spoke in a quiet tone.

'Mother of all creation, this is the water that gives us life. Let it bear us in safety till the end of our journey, and let the power of the Light and the Good prevail.'

Maloof took his place in the front of the canoe, Branwald settled himself in the rear, and they pushed off into the turbulent stream.

The river was difficult to negotiate. It flowed fast, meandered in loops to left and right, and was studded with large, rounded granite rocks. The boys knelt on the floor, resting their buttocks against the seats, sometimes leaning out over the water, driving the paddles down, hauling great swirls of water this way and that as the current tossed them about. Their main concern was to prevent damage to the craft itself. If the canoe were holed, their journey would be at risk.

The danger posed by the boulders in the river's bed, however, did not last more than a couple of miles. The gradient soon became less steep and the flow less fast. Moreover, several small streams joining the river added to its volume, so that the rocks began to drop below the surface and the clear smooth stretches became more frequent. The noise of the tumbling water became quieter, and the boys became aware of the hum of insects in trees and bushes, as the heat of the day began to draw them out of their resting-places.

'Wait,' said Branwald, as they came to a wide, smooth stretch. 'Look back.'

They swung the canoe around and held it stationary against the current. On the mountain-face behind they saw the Lair of the Gretchin, the small black opening from which the river poured, its water falling in foamy streaks down the dark rocks. Above this loomed the brown mountain, rising in rugged steps to the distant peaks where pockets of winter snow still lay.

'Eagle Mountain!' breathed Branwald. 'I would know its shape anywhere.'

They gazed at it in silence, each of them struggling with thoughts and feelings beyond words. Branwald found his eyes drawn to the V-shaped cleft in the peaks which he knew was the Pass of Feyan. His thoughts swept over the crest and down to the islands, to his mother and sister. He resolved that, as soon as they stopped, he would speak to Eroona.

The river's course was becoming less arduous. The mountain slopes above were still bare; the riverside trees and bushes, however, were in the first bloom of spring, a spring which was earlier here than in the boys' home. There were trees and shrubs that they had never seen before. Maloof reached out to touch a broad-leafed, deep green plant festooned with large pink blossoms.

'This is for my true love,' he joked, resting his paddle across his knees and plucking the delicate silky petals.

Watching him, Branwald thought that his friend was different from the carefree boy he had known years before, before Maloof and his mother had been denounced and banished. There was, for instance, the praying that he had done several times. Maloof had never been what one might call religious. True, he, like all the other young ones on the islands, had observed the strict regulations of the Elders. He too had been imbued with a deep-rooted fear of being denounced in the Assembly, or even of less serious censure by those dour, ascetic men. But he had never, as far as Branwald could remember, voluntarily prayed to the Dread Spirit, as he had to this 'Mother' he had named.

There was something else, too. Maloof seemed not to know the feeling of fear. And he seemed to know when Branwald was afraid or anxious. As well as that, he did not always act like a sixteen-year-old boy. When Branwald had been tempted by the power of the Firebolt, Maloof had spoken more like an adult than like a boy, and had made him resist the dark urges. The question that had been lurking in the back of Branwald's mind became clear. Why had Maloof not been chosen to be the bearer of the Firebolt? He was stronger, braver, wiser — far more suited to the formidable task.

Maloof interrupted Branwald's thoughts. 'Do you think we will meet any more girls on this journey, Branwald?'

'The Great River is very long,' Branwald replied. 'We may come across others who live in its valley before we reach its mouth.'

'Yes. I hope they will all be as friendly as the White Ones,' Maloof said.

When the sun had reached its zenith, the boys stopped to eat. The day had become hot, and the air amongst the overhanging trees was heavy and humid. They pulled the canoe onto a spit bank and ate, sitting on the flattened grasses under a drooping willow, where the sunlight could not reach them. Around them, the sound of birds was sporadic in the intense heat. In the grass, the insects kept up their busy hum.

When they had eaten and slaked their thirst, Maloof took out his fishing line, cut a slender willow rod with his knife and baited the hook with a red berry. He found a deep hole under a shady bank, seated himself with his back to a tree and began to dip the berry slowly up and down in the water.

Branwald moved back from the river. Settling himself in the crotch of a low-growing tree, he began to take deep, slow breaths, letting the tension drain out of his body and his mind.

After a while he began to think of home. He saw in his mind's eye the dry limestone walls and weathered shingle roof of his home. He pictured Eroona, seated on her couch in her chamber. He saw her gazing out through the window in the direction of Eagle Mountain, and he called to her. 'Eroona.' He waited a moment and called again. 'Eroona, it is I, Branwald.'

He closed his eyes and waited, hoping for — willing — an answering call.

Then it came, a faint sensation deep in his brain. 'Branwald! Oh, Branwald! I have been so worried because you didn't speak to me. Are you all right? You seem very far away.'

'Yes,' he answered. 'We have been deep in the cave under Bragan's Throat, and have only this morning emerged at the other side of the mountain.'

Branwald spoke in thought for several minutes before the effort of sending his thoughts across that great distance drained his mind of energy and he had to stop. Eroona told him that another fire had appeared on Goron's Knoll in the evening of the day on which he had left. To everyone's surprise, it was the stranger, Urkor, who was waiting there. He was ferried back to the island and immediately prevailed upon Garel and Tregor, with offers of gold, to raft him and his two ponies back to Goron's Knoll without delay. He spoke little and gave no explanation for his sudden departure, and, when questioned, he said he did not know where Sildon's canoe was. Elder Kyran wagged his head and hinted that Urkor had gone to search for the mythical Firebolt and, having failed in his quest, was returning, in high bad humour, to where he had come from. Others were disappointed and upset, believing that now there was little hope that the men who had gone away could be rescued from the clutches of the Orelord.

Feeling his energy weaken, Branwald focused on a sensation of warmth and reassurance for his mother and sister. Then the image became too faint, and he lost contact.

Branwald was roused from half-sleep by an exclamation from Maloof. His friend was swinging a wriggling trout out of the water and onto the bank. Maloof caught the frantic fish and ran his hand under its belly, speaking quietly to it. His movements were slow and measured. When he had finished his incantation, he took careful aim with the heavy handle of his knife and broke the fish's neck with one deft blow.

'I am sorry, beautiful one,' he said quietly. 'But you must give your life so that we can live.'

~

The boys rested in the shade while the sun slanted westwards. From some nearby tree they heard the crooning lullaby of a dove, and further away there was a sound like a

146

heron's strident croak. There was one sound which Branwald did not recognise, however: a sharp, high-pitched bark in the distance, followed by another one closer at hand. He raised himself on his elbow and turned to listen. Maloof was already sitting upright, his face turned toward the sound, an arrow ready in his hand.

The sharp bark, now very close, came from high in the trees. Looking up, they saw a movement. A dark, hairy shape with long arms was swinging from one branch to another. They watched as it gradually came closer through the leaves. They heard the sharp bark again, and then an answering one from another tree.

'Come on,' said Branwald, dropping the canvas rucksacks into the canoe and sliding it towards the water's edge.

A short, hairy animal dropped from a drooping willow branch and began to lope towards Maloof, who was standing on the sand bar, facing it. Branwald, hurrying to position himself on the stern seat, glimpsed the creature's face. The eyes and forehead were human-like, but the nose was more like a snout and was completely covered in hair.

'Get in!' shouted Branwald. Maloof, who had been moving backwards towards the canoe, stopped in his tracks and lifted his bow. Another squat shape was advancing through the grass on his right. Maloof drew back the arrow and called out, 'Guard your life, creature!'

At this the first one suddenly stopped, and Branwald saw its face clearly. Its small eyes stared unblinking at Maloof, and its black lips curled back to reveal white teeth set between jagged canines. Then it lifted its head, and the sound that came from it was for all the world like wild, abandoned laughter. Maloof, still holding the shooting position, took a step back towards the canoe. Branwald saw other dark shapes advancing through the grass behind the first two.

'Come on, Maloof! Get in!' he called, pushing the stern out into the river.

The first creature started to advance again, but Maloof took one step in its direction and it stopped, as if uncertain what to do. Maloof spoke quietly, and the other creatures stopped also. They began to jabber, bobbing and shaking their heads.

'Stay, creatures!' Maloof called. He turned and walked slowly back to the canoe. He stepped in, and Branwald pushed off.

As if released from a spell, the creatures came leaping through the grass, uttering high-pitched, savage yelps. They raced onto the beach in a tumult of flying gravel and ravenous snarling. They pursued the canoe along the bank, flinging pebbles and leaping up and down, until a thicket of shrubs blocked their progress. When the boys last saw them, some of them were already swinging up into the trees again.

'Friendly little fellows,' remarked Maloof, as they sped along.

'I wouldn't want them to find me sleeping,' said Branwald.

'Yes! But they are not so brave when you face them. They are just bluffers.'

'Do you think they were once people like us?' Branwald asked, although the idea revolted him.

'Those, if I am not mistaken,' continued Maloof, 'are what the Forest People called "the Hairy Ones". They live in the trees and eat nuts and fruits, they say. They are not people, but animals, like dogs, except that they live together in groups. I have heard some of the Forest People say that they are only dangerous if you run from them, just as dogs are.'

'I will remember that,' Branwald said ironically.

～

Soon afterwards, Branwald told Maloof how he had spoken with Eroona. 'Eroona said that the stranger, Urkor, has left the islands, with his ponies, and has gone back up the mountain.'

Maloof nodded. 'Yes,' he said, as if he already knew. 'But he will be several days behind us. And I cannot imagine that, even here, horses could equal our speed for a full day. I think there will be no danger from that one for many days yet.'

～

The rest of that long afternoon was uneventful. The river continued to wind southwards through the brown mountains until, when the boys looked back along the valley, they could no longer see the Lair of the Gretchin or even the peak of Eagle Mountain above it: a great humped spur blocked their view. Occasionally they saw a dark figure moving high in the

148

trees nearby and heard the staccato bark of a Hairy One. Later in the evening, they saw a line of deer-like animals moving along a winding track high on the side of the mountain; soon after that, they surprised a large brown bear cavorting in the shallows by a forest clearing. The animal took one look at the canoe and then, with a surprised snort and a great amount of splashing, bolted for the bank. The sheen on its smooth fur rippled and quivered as it lolloped towards the trees.

'A Gretchin?' said Maloof, laughing.

Dusk was falling when they came to a small wooded island, separated from the right-hand bank by several yards of speeding water. Here they would spend the night.

The sun had dropped behind the western ridge, but there was still light in the azure sky. They tilted the canoe on its side, to form a barrier against the soft breeze, and began to gather twigs and sticks for a fire. They grilled Maloof's trout over the crackling blaze, toasted two wheaten cakes on a forked twig, and followed these with roasted nuts and the last of Maloof's apples. Then, their hunger satisfied, they sat cross-legged, their cloaks draped over their shoulders, hugging the fire as the cool night fell, talking about the events of the day and listening to the night sounds of the forest.

'Do you think the Hairy Ones can swim?' Branwald asked, eyeing the rushing channel which separated them from the bank.

'I would say they are like dogs and foxes: they swim only if they have to. I think if we keep a fire blazing, we will have no trouble from any of the forest creatures.'

When they had piled the remainder of the firewood onto the slumping embers and wrapped their cloaks around themselves, they prepared for sleep. But sleep would not come to Branwald. In spite of his efforts to free his mind, a strange shape kept forming there. There was a river, and a straight structure bridging it. There were men on this bridge, but he could not see them. They were watching for something or somebody approaching on the river. Something precious was coming. Branwald heard a voice in his mind. 'Stop them,' it said. 'Do not let them pass.'

Branwald sat up, frowning. This voice, these images were too clear. Maloof was awake too, raised on one elbow, watching Branwald in the red glow of the fire.

'Can you, too, hear it?' Branwald whispered, scanning the dark riverbank nearby. Maloof nodded. 'It is thought-speaking,' Branwald continued. 'Someone is giving warning that we are coming. That we have something ....' He broke off as the realisation came to him. Instinctively he reached for the Firebolt. 'It is Urkor.'

Maloof reached over and stayed his hand. 'You will not need that now, Branwald,' he said. 'If it is he, he is still far away, on the mountain. Yes, I heard him. He is warning those who are at a bridge somewhere ahead.'

Branwald stared into the glowing embers, the tension in his stomach easing a little.

'We should not be surprised,' Maloof went on. 'And now that we have heard it, we know what lies ahead. We can be prepared.'

At last Branwald lay down again. He wished he knew where Urkor was. As he drifted into sleep, he was faintly aware of a voice calling to him over the roof of the world, a distant plaint that seemed to carry in its tone the sadness of a people.

CHAPTER EIGHTEEN

Branwald woke to the sound of crackling firewood and the pungent smell of wood-smoke. It was early morning. Maloof sat on a low stone nearby, plucking the feathers from the limp body of a grouse. Branwald watched him in silence, seeing the deft hands, the serious face, sensing the deep calm in Maloof's mind.

In some way that Branwald did not understand, it had been ordained that Maloof should travel with him to the mouth of the Great River. Branwald did not think that, on his own, he would ever have had the courage to embark on such a venture. So Maloof was with him to give him courage. But he was more than that. He was a guide, a provider, a protector for Branwald on his journey. Maloof possessed such calm assurance in the face of unexpected obstacles. Branwald's initial response on seeing the Hairy Ones had been to turn tail and run; but Maloof had stood his ground and faced the danger.

Branwald found Maloof looking at him thoughtfully. He turned away, not wishing his friend to know his doubts. He wished he were strong. He wished he were brave and calm like Maloof. 'Mother,' he prayed, although he had no idea what kind of spiritual presence he was addressing, 'make me brave.'

Maloof's voice broke the stillness. 'Branwald, if we are meant to reach the mouth of the river, then we will reach it. The Forest People say that it is not the length of our lives, but how we use them, that matters. They say that to be ready is all. We must try to be ready. There are things that we cannot do; but there will be others to do them. We must believe that the Good will eventually overcome the Evil, because without this belief, there is no point in going on.'

Branwald rolled out of his cloak and crouched by the fire to warm himself. Downstream, a delicate veil of mist hung over the surface of the water. Somewhere nearby, a bird was swelling the air with his song.

'We will go on!' Branwald vowed. 'We must go on!'

To save time later, Maloof roasted the grouse on a make-shift spit over the fire before they took to the river again. At first light he had waded across the nearby channel and waited at the edge of a clearing for the early foraging birds to descend from their roosts in the trees. His first shot had been lucky, he said.

Before setting out, they did an inventory of their food stocks. Apart from the grouse, and Branwald's three wheaten cakes and Maloof's five oaten ones, all they had were several handfuls of nuts, the remains of those Aiyan had given them. They knew that they would soon have to rely on fish and any game they could kill. Branwald wanted to set two baited lines in the river each night, but Maloof quietly disagreed. 'We do not need to let our brothers and sisters, the fish, suffer more than is necessary. It will be enough for one of us to rise early each morning to fish or hunt for that day,' he said.

The boys made good progress, as the river was becoming wider and deeper. The valley sides were less steep and had receded some distance from the river, and the riverside trees and bushes were spreading upwards into the gullies that creased the lower slopes. The boys passed many small streams flowing in from each side, and one larger river, brown and muddy, that tumbled out of a steep-sided valley on their right.

Around mid-morning, Branwald noticed something among the riverside trees. There were two rectangular openings, at about head-height, in what looked like an ivy-covered rock-face.

'There's something there,' he said to Maloof. 'Pull over.'

Beaching the canoe and taking their weapons, they pushed through the tangled undergrowth till they came to a structure which had clearly been built by human hands. Branwald stretched to look in through one of the half-choked windows. There was no roof, but the inside walls still stood, although they were smothered in places by the invading forest growth. Here and there, through gaps in the ivy, what had once been a smooth plastered surface showed through, stained and weathered by years of exposure to the elements.

'There are others,' said Branwald, pointing through the bushes. 'There was a village here once.'

'Before the Dark Time,' Maloof replied.

They stood there in silence, while a dove cooed softly in the ivy overhead. Branwald wondered about the Dark Time. Had the light of the sun gradually darkened, over a day or a week or a month? Or had the darkness descended in an instant, a sudden cataclysm bringing terror and death to the people, whoever they were, who had been living in this large house? The Elders had always said that the Dark Time was a punishment for the transgressions of men, a tribulation sent by the Dread Spirit. Branwald imagined this avenging Spirit roaring down out of the heavens with a great cloud of blackness in His train, denouncing His errant people as He swept angrily across the face of the world.

Then Branwald asked a question that he would not have dared to ask a week before. 'Why do you think the Dark Time really happened?'

Maloof thought for a moment. 'The Forest People say that the Dark Time came because men caused it to happen, but no one has ever told me exactly how. They believe that some men had ceased to respect and love the earth and all the living things that the Mother has put there, that they treated the earth as if she were a slave, a thing to use and then throw away. When they began to treat people in the same way, the darkness came. The Forest People say that it was not the Mother who brought the Dark Time, but the selfishness in men's hearts.'

Branwald found himself thinking about the stranger, Urkor. There was an evil man, he thought. It was possible to understand how men like him could have brought a great curse upon the world.

'The evil is in each one of us,' Maloof went on. 'And this struggle will always be with each one, whether they cleave to the Evil or to the Good. This is what my people say.'

Branwald felt a twinge of irritation. 'Why do you call the Forest People your people?'

Maloof had that same calm look in his eyes. 'Because the Forest People received me and my mother when we escaped from the Island of the Banished. They did not ask what our crime was, or what our beliefs were, but they took us in and fed us and clothed us and gave us a home when they did not need to. The Forest People do not have lists of rules and observances which they use to control their people. Their people do not live in fear. They require only that you show respect to all the creatures that the Mother has put on the earth. I cannot forget what they have done for me and my mother, and I cannot change what I have become since I first came to live with them. They are my people now.'

He saw the hurt in Branwald's eyes, and his face softened. 'But that does not mean that I cannot love those who are not of the forest. Branwald, you are my friend. Part of me is still on the islands. When all this is over, maybe the Island People can learn from the Forest People. Then the two peoples can be as one.'

His smile was so winning that Branwald could not refuse to take the outstretched hand and grip it tightly. Then, a little embarrassed by the intimacy of the moment, he looked back towards the river. He was just in time to see a small hairy figure darting from the cover of a bush towards their canoe.

'Hi!' he shouted, releasing his grip on Maloof's hand and bounding towards the intruder. The creature — smaller than the Hairy Ones they had seen, with a flatter face and longer arms — looked up in fright, then grabbed a satchel from the floor of the canoe and darted back into the cover of the bushes. The two boys set up a cry and rushed towards the spot where it had disappeared, but they could not see it.

Then they heard a derisive laugh from above. The hairy intruder was prancing up and down on a high branch, its white teeth exposed in a grin. One hand gripped a higher branch; the other, Branwald's satchel. Realising that his bow was in the canoe, Branwald turned to get it.

'No,' called Maloof. 'Bring the Firebolt.'

In a moment, Branwald was back with the weapon. The

creature was rummaging through the contents of the satchel, seemingly unconcerned about the boys. Maloof's eyes glinted. Branwald, reading his thought, smiled. He uncovered the weapon and caught the handle.

'I will distract it,' Maloof said. He moved back to a sandy patch and began to leap wildly into the air, flinging his arms about and uttering sharp cries. The creature looked down, its yellow eyes wide with curiosity. It watched for several moments. Then it threw its head back and began to jabber, its long teeth again exposed.

By this time, Branwald had focused the beam on the section of the branch that lay between the animal and the trunk of the tree. The creature stared down again at Maloof, who was doing somersaults in the sand. It did not seem to have noticed the white beam that was cutting through the bough.

Without warning, the branch started to drop. The creature screamed as it fell, tumbling in the air. It landed with a solid thump in the soft soil under the tree, the satchel still gripped in its left hand. The boys charged, yelling. The creature released the satchel, bounced to its feet, took one wide-eyed look at them, gave a yelp and scampered away through the bushes, forgetting in its terror that it could climb.

'Hah!' yelled Maloof, slapping the bushes for effect.

'And tell your friends too!' Branwald shouted.

They watched until the hurrying form was lost to view. Branwald retrieved the satchel. It felt good to be able to laugh again. 'That one won't be so cheeky next time,' he remarked, as they pushed out onto the river again.

An hour before dusk they came to another, larger island, on which they set up camp. They were weary and hungry. While Branwald lit a fire, Maloof lay on the bank by a deep hole in the river and dipped for trout. When he returned with two glistening fish, the fire was glowing hot. After the meal, they gratefully wrapped themselves in their cloaks and slept by the spitting embers.

~

Early the next morning, before setting out, they studied the map again. There were no features there, however, by which they could tell how far they had travelled.

'Biloh may be the village where the ruins were,' Maloof said. Not far below 'Biloh' were the words 'Bridge of Shihara'. They would need to be watchful. Somewhere ahead, they knew, others were waiting for them.

A little later, as they were drifting around a bend in the river, the boys noticed a log lying on a sandbank ahead. They were only thirty yards from it when it suddenly moved, on thick stubby legs, down to the water's edge; with hardly a ripple, it submerged itself, pulling a long tapering tail after it, till only a small crust of skin remained above the surface.

'What is that?' Maloof said quietly, pausing in his paddling. They were drawing closer to the creature, and in the crust of skin they saw an eye staring at them, unblinking.

Maloof lifted his paddle and brought the flat of the blade down, hard, on the water. With a sudden swirl, the creature sank and was gone, leaving only a small disturbance on the surface. Alarmed, Branwald reached for the Firebolt, at the same time leaning over and searching the water below him for any threatening shape. Maloof fitted an arrow to his bow. They sat, tense and poised, for several minutes, while the canoe drifted and turned in the current.

'Look! There!' exclaimed Branwald. He pointed back at the sandbank, now well upstream of them, where the creature was emerging slowly from the water. It hauled out its long tail, shook its protruding snout from side to side once or twice, and then became quite still.

'It's like a huge lizard!' exclaimed Maloof.

Not long afterwards, they saw two more of the great lizards on the sloping bank. The creatures remained unmoving in the warm evening sun, apparently unconcerned, as the boys drifted past.

'These are big harmless idlers,' was Maloof's comment.

∿

The river was becoming slower, and deeper. It still swung from left to right in sweeping curves, but there were no longer any rapids or sudden drops in the level. It was wider, too — nearly a hundred and fifty yards in places, Branwald estimated — and there seemed to be a greater extent of flat, densely-forested land on either side. Low, tree-covered hills could be seen here and there between the river and the retreating mountains, whose lower slopes were clothed with a covering of green. The trees, too, were changing: the birches and alders were giving way to unfamiliar, broad-leaved varieties. The boys saw clusters of ruined buildings more frequently. Most of them were engulfed by riverside vegetation; here and there, however, some stood stark and lonely on the higher slopes above the tree-line. They saw several of the giant lizards resting on rocks or sandbanks, and an occasional dark shape in the high branches of trees, but no people.

~

Late in the afternoon, they saw the bridge ahead. Quickly they swung in behind a rocky outcrop and beached the canoe on a soft bank overhung with leafy boughs. Then, through a gap in the bushes, they examined the distant structure.

It contained no curves or rounded arches, as the stone bridge over Feyan's Stream did. Though stained by time and draped here and there with vegetation, the structure was straight as an arrow, as if some giant mason had hewn a mighty plank of rock from a mountain and rested it on three narrow uprights embedded in the river.

Among the trees near the east end of the bridge stood the familiar blocky shapes of derelict houses. These, however, were more numerous and densely packed than those the boys had seen before, and they stretched away from the riverside until they were swallowed by the trees.

'There is someone on the bridge,' Maloof said.

Branwald saw several dark figures moving at a leisurely pace near the centre of the span. From the surface of the bridge rose a trickle of smoke.

Branwald's eyes dropped to the two wide channels sheeting under the rectangular arches. There was little chance that they could pass in the evening light without being seen. He squinted at the sun, which was dipping towards the western horizon. It would be dark within a couple of hours.

Maloof nodded in agreement. They hauled the canoe out of sight of the river and settled themselves to rest. They would pass when darkness set in.

Lying in the cool shadows, Branwald thought of Eroona

and of his mother. He resisted the urge to try to speak with them, however. If he could intercept Urkor's thoughts, then it was likely that the man could intercept his. Then there were the people on the bridge .... Better to take no chances.

Daylight had shrunk to a faint glow when the boys rose. In the gloom, they readied the canoe. But, glancing in the direction of the bridge, Branwald noticed a strange light. Parting the bushes, he and Maloof were alarmed to see a line of lights strung across the river, hanging from the parapet, highlighting the bridge against the deep purple beyond. On the water's surface, the reflections shifted and danced. There would be no passing here.

In silence they pondered what to do. To portage round the obstacle ahead would require them to wait till daylight, a delay of nearly twelve hours. And there was no guarantee that the area inland from the bridge would not be guarded as well.

'You know the clumps of floating stuff that we saw?' Maloof said. Branwald nodded. 'Well, if we dress the canoe as one of them, and lie on the floor, we can pass even now.'

Branwald thought about that. 'And if they see us?' he said.

Maloof inclined his head. 'It will not happen. But if the worst comes, we must use the weapon to frighten those who would threaten us.'

~

A little later, the boys slid out onto the silent water. The canoe was covered with a pile of leafy boughs that drooped to the water's surface on each side. Sitting on the floor, the boys used their hands to paddle the canoe out to a point from which they guessed the flow would carry them through the right-hand opening of the bridge. They flattened themselves on the floor, pulled loose branches over their faces and waited.

Through the leaves, Branwald saw the lights drifting closer. Each one was capped by a kind of hood with a dirty white lining, which threw the light downwards.

The yellow flames were almost over him. He turned his face to the side, sure that its whiteness would show through the branches. A deep voice directly above him said, 'It is no matter.' The accent was not that of the Island People.

The canoe drifted under the span, and they were in welcome

shadow. There was no further sound from above.

The boys waited until the bridge was a distant silhouette before easing the branches over the side. The plan had worked perfectly. They paddled downriver for several miles, keeping to the open water, before striking for shore. By the Firebolt's light they found a sloping ledge near the base of a low cliff and settled themselves for the night. They were well satisfied. Their first contact with those who would try to defeat them had ended in victory.

In the morning they did not eat before setting off in the half-light. They were aware of the enemy behind them, and of the need to distance themselves from the bridge. They knew, too, that there was the possibility of further encounters, and they could not feel that these would be friendly.

The sun was high in the morning sky when they saw, on the side of the valley ahead of them, a flock of sheep moving slowly upstream, just above the tree-line. Soon they could hear the plaintive bleating of the animals and the insistent barking of a dog. Then they saw the grey-clad figure of a man, a little distance behind the flock. He was short, white-haired and slightly stooped, and he was swinging a staff back and forth in front of him as he walked.

'He looks harmless enough,' Branwald said quietly. At this, the man on the mountainside, although he was over a hundred yards away, turned to look towards them.

'He does not trust us, though,' Maloof said.

As they drifted past, the man turned his head slowly to follow their passage. He remained unmoving until they were out of sight.

'I would prefer to deal with the Hairy Ones,' Maloof joked. 'Old White-Hair did not feel any friendliness towards us at all.'

'It is hardly likely that he is alone,' observed Branwald soberly. 'There will surely be others.'

❧

They went on, watchful for any sign of other people. But the only creature they saw was a deer-like animal descending towards the river. They did notice, however, that the derelict buildings among the trees were becoming more numerous.

Soon afterwards, they saw the ruins of another bridge on the river ahead. And looming above the trees near the eastern end of this ruin, stark against the bare mountain behind, was a square tower. The mantle of clinging creepers and the bulging bushes on its roof and sides told the boys that it, too, was derelict and empty. There was no sign that any living person was near.

The boys were close to the ruined bridge and Branwald was selecting a smooth path for their passage when, from somewhere beyond, they heard the sound of children's voices. Unable to halt their movement in the increasing flow, the boys sped through the gap.

A group of children was approaching the river through the trees. The leading child, a boy of about twelve years, was just bursting through the low shrubs towards a pond of calm water by the base of the bridge. Black-haired and slightly plump, he wore only a sleeveless vest and knee-length breeches, which revealed the deep brown of his arms and legs.

Seeing the canoe, he halted, surprise and fear in his wide-eyed stare. He shouted something over his shoulder, and the clamour behind him was suddenly stilled. As they sped past, the boys saw several young faces, each crowned with straight black hair, staring at them from under the hanging willow boughs. The children's eyes had a curious upward slant at the corners.

'Let us speak with them,' Maloof said.

Branwald did not hesitate. They turned the craft and began to paddle back towards the children.

Seeing this, the leading boy gave a loud warning cry. Holding his arms out in a gathering motion, he herded the others quickly back into the trees. There were shouts and screams as the children stampeded away from the water.

'Come back!' Maloof called. 'Please come back! We mean you no harm!'

'We only want to talk!' Branwald shouted. But their shouting seemed only to act as a spur to the retreating group. By the time the boys had the canoe beached on the sand bar, there was no sign of the children. Branwald flung his paddle onto the floor of the canoe and prepared to give chase.

'No,' said Maloof. 'Wait.'

'What? Why?'

'We will only frighten them more. Then they will not trust us and will tell us nothing. I think if we wait here they will come back.'

They stepped out onto the sand and listened. Not far away, they heard snatches of subdued conversation.

'They are thinking about it,' Maloof said. 'Let us sing to them.'

'*Sing*?' Branwald frowned in disbelief, but his protest was cut short when Maloof began, in his strongest voice, to sing 'The Song of the Fishes', a lullaby which Branwald had learned on his mother's knee.

Branwald looked back through the trees, but no child was visible. When he saw the mischievous grin on Maloof's face, he shrugged his shoulders and began to sing the harmony line.

'We swim through the waters of lakes and of rills.

We swim where the water is clean in our gills.

We leap through the thundering falls and we sing,

As we tumble in torrents by Elderton Spring ....'

Branwald had to fight down a feeling that he was being silly, but the blend of the two voices was pleasant and he continued, all the while watching the shadowy glade where they had last seen the children. They were just finishing the third verse when he saw a movement deep in the under-growth. Then a small stone came flying through the high branches and struck the canoe, close to where Maloof was standing. Maloof gave a sudden loud groan, grabbed his stomach, staggered around in a circle several times in a most dramatic fashion, and collapsed on the ground. Branwald was startled, but Maloof winked at him from his prone position.

There was silence from the trees for a moment. Then Branwald heard a chuckle, followed by the musical sound of a child's laughter.

'I am Branwald,' Branwald called. 'And this one, whom you have just killed, is called Maloof. We have come from very far away, from over the great mountains to the north.'

There was a muffled response from the trees. 'We want your help,' Branwald continued, as Maloof slowly rose, grinning, from the ground beside him. 'We do not know this way, and we need you to tell us what lies ahead.'

There was a movement in the underbrush, and the first boy's face appeared. There was a guarded, suspicious expression on his face. 'You are from the Metal King!' he challenged, in an accent that was strange to Branwald's ears.

The boys exchanged glances. Then Maloof replied, 'No, we are not. We have never heard of the Metal King.' Other faces appeared in the hanging leaves, their expressions betraying more curiosity than suspicion. 'But what is your name?' Maloof continued.

The boy pushed forward, ahead of the others. 'My name is Meechin,' he said, his eyes darting from the boys to the canoe and back again. 'Where did you get that boat?'

'It is mine,' Branwald said. 'My father made it. Would you like to go on the river in it?'

The boy's eyes searched Branwald's face again. 'Alone?' he asked.

'No, with one of us. It would be too difficult for you alone.'

The eyes checked him again. 'You will not take me away to the Metal King?'

Branwald smiled. 'No. We will not take you away. And if your friends want to come on the river too, we will take them.'

In a moment, Branwald was surrounded by eight clamouring brown-skinned children, each of whom wanted to be the first to go in the canoe. He and Maloof took turns at paddling them slowly around the sheltered lagoon, their bright eyes and excited faces attesting to their enjoyment.

The children told the boys that they belonged to a tribe called the Galians, who spent their lives wandering the valley of the Great River with their flocks of sheep. The man whom the boys had seen earlier was one of their band; the children called him Fairchin the Shearer. They spent the winters on the lowland pastures on the outskirts of 'the Wild Lands' — a vast, marshy jungle, they said, which stretched all the way to the mouth of the river. In spring, before the summer rains turned the pastures into marshland, they set out northwards for 'the Bare Lands', as they called them, and lived among the ruins on the river's bank. Summer, for them, was a time of freedom — not only from the mosquitoes and the grass-roofed huts of the lowlands, but also from the marauding ships of the 'Metal King', which came upstream at intervals from the mouth of the river, searching for slaves to work in their master's mines.

'My uncle and his two cousins were taken by the Metal King,' Meechin explained sadly. 'After that, we moved our homes far back from the river.'

'We told you that we did not know the Metal King,' Branwald said. 'But now I think we do. Our people know him by another name. It is he whom we are seeking.'

Meechin and the others drew back in alarm. 'Then you *are* from the Metal King!' Meechin exclaimed.

'No,' Branwald insisted. 'We are not. The Metal King is our enemy!'

'But why do you seek him?' exclaimed a thin-faced girl. 'The Metal King is cruel. He will make you slaves!'

Branwald told the children about his father and Maloof's, and how he believed that they were slaves of the Orelord. He did not speak about the Firebolt, however. When he finished, there was sympathy and sadness in the eyes of the children.

'But what can you do?' the girl asked. 'The Metal King has great ships and a great army. What can two boys do against his power? It is foolish! I do not understand why you do this.'

'We have been sent on a mission,' Branwald replied, shrugging his shoulders. 'We have to go.'

Meechin, who had been looking at the boys thoughtfully for a few moments, spoke. 'Men of the Metal King went up the river. Did you not see them?' His eyes darted from one to the other, gauging their reactions.

'We may have,' Maloof answered. 'There were people on the bridge above here.'

'The Adamant Bridge! And they let you pass?'

'Not quite,' said Maloof. He gave the children a brief account of how he and Branwald had passed the bridge, while their eyes opened wide in wonder.

Another girl spoke, her face showing her concern. 'But if those men are on the bridge, then we will not be able to reach the willow pastures on the other side!' Anxiously, she looked back towards the trees. 'I must go and tell Fairchin the Shearer.' She rose and hurried away.

Before the children parted from the boys, they gave them several strips of dried meat which, to Branwald, looked exactly like wet leather. They would last for many months, the children said. They stood watching with amusement as the boys chewed stubbornly on thin strips which they sliced off with their daggers.

'It's like chewing an old moccasin,' Maloof remarked, to much laughter.

As they prepared to take their leave, Meechin warned the boys that to travel any further on the river would be danger-ous. In recent times, the boats of the Metal Soldiers had been patrolling further and further upstream. If the boys should meet one, a flimsy canoe such as theirs could not hope to outpace it. They would surely be captured and made to work as slaves in the mines.

'We are grateful to you for this knowledge,' Branwald said, when the boy had finished speaking. 'We will be care-ful. But why do you and your people stay so close to the river?'

'We stay away, except when we need water for our sheep and ourselves,' Meechin replied. 'Anyway, we can see the boats coming, from the higher places. The men of the Metal King do not like to leave the river and climb, so we are safe.'

'But Fairchin?'

'Fairchin would be of no use to them. The Shearer is blind. His dogs lead him and guard the sheep.'

Branwald sensed a kind of awe in the children's eyes when, a short time later, he and Maloof prepared to relaunch the canoe. The little ones stayed close to them, touching them in an absent-minded way and running their hands over the canoe.

'But are you still going on?' a ruddy-faced girl asked.

'Yes,' Branwald replied. 'We must go on.'

'Branwald!' called Meechin, as they pushed off once more. 'When you find your father, ask him about a man called Gorchin and his two cousins. My father would make a feast for many days if they came back to us.'

'I will do so,' Branwald called back.

A few moments later, when he looked back towards the ruined bridge, he saw the children still standing where they had left them. Their hands lifted in a final wave; then they were out of sight behind a copse of alders.

~

The two friends became more cautious. At each bend in the river they stayed near the inside of the curve, where the water was slower, so that they might inch carefully along and scan each new stretch before venturing out on it. Whenever they had to make a crossing, they went directly across the current from bank to bank, staying in the open for as little time as possible.

They were making a wide crossing when they came to another river-mouth, its banks wild and apparently deserted, opening from the east. In midstream, Branwald felt Maloof's startled thought and followed his friend's eyes back towards the bank of the tributary behind them.

There, moored in a small inlet, was a long, black boat, the biggest boat Branwald had ever seen. Over twice the length of his canoe and many times broader, it sat moored to the bank by several hawsers. The prow rose more than a man's height out of the water, and a curved deck extended back over a third of the boat's length. Protruding vertically from the centre of this deck was a thick cylindrical pipe, out of which billowed grey smoke. In front of this chimney, resting on a black frame, was another cylindrical pipe, but this one was horizontal, and there was a round black hole in its snout. Some instinct told Branwald that this was a weapon.

They heard a shout. A dark figure was climbing up out of the boat's hold, looking in their direction. As they watched him, three other figures appeared from the trees on the bank and stood staring.

'Paddle, Branwald!' Maloof urged. There were more shouts. Branwald needed no other spur. The right bank and safety were over a hundred yards away.

There was a sudden loud hissing from behind them, followed by a rhythmic throbbing. Glancing back, Branwald saw that all of the men were aboard the boat — except one, who was bending over the mooring-ropes on the bank. Branwald dropped to his knees and dug his paddle deeper.

A shrill blast of sound spread over the flat water, rousing a startled flock of birds from the trees. The black boat had pulled away from the bank and was coming after the canoe.

Branwald's eyes searched the bank ahead. They needed a space, an opening to the land. But the wall of greenery ahead was blank and impenetrable.

The men were shouting. It was the kind of sound that Branwald had heard men use when, with their dogs, they chased a frightened hare in the fields above Feyansdoon — a high, yipping cry. The black bow, pushing a bulging wave before it, was only thirty yards away and bearing down fast. Branwald knew they wouldn't reach the safety of the bank.

'Turn!' he shouted to Maloof. They twisted their paddles, and the stern swung round to face the pursuers.

'The Firebolt, Branwald!' Maloof called.

As Branwald searched with his free hand for the weapon, he saw the bearded face of a man standing on the deck, legs apart, one hand on the bow railing. He wore a black belted tunic, and a black cloak swirled in the breeze behind him. He shouted words that Branwald could not distinguish above the clamour of the boat. Maloof shouted again. Branwald found the Firebolt, and shook off the coverings.

The advancing prow came straight for the canoe. It seemed about to run them down, but at the last second it veered to the left. The bow wave swelled towards the canoe, and Branwald steeled himself to ride it. He heard the jeering of the men as they swept past, but he didn't dare take his eyes from the coming wave. He leaned into it, felt it lift and swing the canoe round, then leaned the other way as the craft dropped into the trough.

The boat crossed behind them and began to circle. Branwald saw a line of leering faces along the railing as it ploughed past, and he braced himself for another wave.

Maloof shouted again. Branwald lifted the Firebolt, his mind clear and resolute. He grasped the handle firmly and aimed at the curving hull of the boat, a little behind the bow and just below the surface of the streaming water. A beam shot forth, lifting and falling as the new wave washed under the canoe. The light grew brighter. Branwald focused his mind on the movement of his own craft, trying to counter it, to keep the beam fixed on a single point on the boat's hull.

Suddenly the clamour of the men changed. There was a momentary hush; then the yelling began again, but this time it was a confused din, the sound made by men who are frightened. Branwald saw a white wisp of steam drifting back from the place where the beam struck the hull. He tightened his grip, willing all his concentrated energy into the Firebolt.

The boat started to swing away from him. The light from the Firebolt was so white that it hurt his eyes. He traced a line along the hull, at the waterline, as the boat moved away at speed. Maloof was shouting, 'Be careful! Do not strike one of them!' Branwald lowered the Firebolt, tracing a sizzling line along the surface of the water.

The shouting on board the black boat continued. As it headed back towards the mooring, several of the men ducked down into the hold. Moments later, one of those still on deck lifted a container of some sort from below and emptied its contents into the river.

'We've holed them!' Maloof cried.

On board the boat, the baling action was being repeated, faster and faster. The helmsman changed course and swung the craft towards a low sand-spit which jutted from the bank. A frantic throbbing came from deep in the hull. The boat was labouring, as the river crept higher and higher along its hull.

When it was no more than five yards from the bank, one of the men, holding a coiled rope in his hand, leaped into the water. He landed with a splash, found his footing and began to wade waist-deep towards the spit, playing the rope out over his shoulder.

Suddenly, there was an cry from one of the men still on the prow. There was an abrupt swelling in the water beside the first man. As he screamed, a long brown shape surged up out of the river, two great jaws grabbed him around the waist, and in an instant he had disappeared under the surface.

Branwald saw the man at the prow leap cat-like to the tubular weapon beside him. He fumbled for a moment with its workings, and then swivelled it round and downwards. There was a flash of fire, a puff of smoke, an explosive report. At the same instant an oblique spout of water shot up from the surface of the river, near where the man had disappeared. The flocks of birds over the trees set up a new clamour.

The keel of the sinking boat had driven into the shallows. There was a loud crunching sound, the boat stopped, and two men who had been at the prow went tumbling forward into the water. Meanwhile, a man at the back of the boat had picked up a long, wide-muzzled tool and was pointing it at the water's surface. There was a sharp crack, and a flash of fire stabbed downwards from its lower end.

Branwald looked on with horrified fascination. He watched the patch of water where the man had gone down, seeing the ripples fading. Then, thirty yards nearer to the canoe, something broke the surface. The man's head and raised arm appeared, rotated slowly and sank beneath the surface again. Then the river smoothed out as if nothing had happened.

The sharp reports were still coming from the boat, however. Branwald saw a sudden streaking splash in the water beside him, and realised that he and Maloof had become the target of some kind of weapon.

'Come on!' he said. 'They are shooting something at us.'

Quickly they bent to the paddling. There was another explosive report from behind, a whizzing sound, and then the water to their right erupted into a great hollow spout.

'Faster!' shouted Maloof, swinging the prow to the left. They redoubled their efforts and the canoe sliced through the water. There was another report; seconds later, a missile struck the water behind them, drenching Branwald's back with spray.

They were soon out of danger, however. The reports from behind them ceased; when they looked back, they saw that the men were on the sand-spit, pulling on the mooring-ropes, trying to haul the stricken boat up onto the sand.

It was some moments before Branwald broke the silence. The unexpected attack on him and Maloof had shaken him, but the violence and ferocity of the assault by the great lizard had left him shocked. 'I didn't intend him to die,' he said.

'I know,' Maloof replied. 'But you mustn't blame yourself, Branwald. You had to use the Firebolt. They would have capsized the canoe or taken us captive. They were not just having fun, as men sometimes do. Another minute and we would have been in the water. So you had to use it.'

'They are Oremen.'

'There is little doubt of that. Their boat is made of metal. No simple farmers or fishermen could have made that.'

'Were they waiting for us?'

Maloof's shoulders rose and fell again. 'Maybe. Or maybe they were hunting, for food or for people. Who knows?'

'Or waiting for someone else to come down the valley.'

'You mean Urkor?'

'Yes.'

Maloof nodded. 'And if it is so, it will be good for us. I do not think that boat will travel much further, and it will be a difficult journey on foot or even on horseback from here to the mouth of the Great River. The further he is behind us, the better.'

Branwald scanned the wide river ahead. 'There may be others. Maybe we should get off the river.'

Maloof looked at the dense jungle on the riverbank. 'There is no way through there,' he said. 'I think if we are careful and watchful, we can deal with a boat.'

Branwald did not reply. He was thinking about the lizards. They were not 'harmless idlers', as Maloof had called them, but deadly predators that could strike without warning. What protection could their flimsy craft give him and Maloof in the event of an attack?

'Branwald, we have travelled many miles through the lizards' domain. They have shown no interest in us. We must not let what we have seen, terrible as it was, shake our resolve. Now is the time for courage. We must go on.'

Branwald knew that Maloof was right. But he did not speak. It still annoyed him that his friend could hear his secret thoughts. He continued the steady rhythm of the paddling, keeping the Firebolt uncovered and close to his hand, and he constantly scanned the water ahead for any sign that one of the creatures might be lurking there.

When the sun was low over the western hills, the friends turned into the mouth of a quiet creek. Such islands as they had recently seen were little more than long sandbanks, offering no protection from the great lizards. This creek, roofed with leafy waterside trees, wound deep into the forest. There was no wind, and even the creatures of the forest seemed hushed. The boys found a bank of dry sand and prepared to eat and rest. They lit a fire and picked clean the bones of the grouse which Maloof had cooked the previous day.

In preparation for sleeping, they cut down a number of branches; by lodging these horizontally high in the forks of adjacent trees and placing other branches across them, they constructed a raised platform. The work, however, took longer than they expected. The stars were already appearing when they finally stepped back and inspected their work.

It was rough, and not very comfortable, but it was over six feet above ground level. They lifted all their belongings onto the platform, tied the canoe securely to the trunk of one of the supporting trees and, climbing up, settled themselves by the glow of the Firebolt, which Branwald had tied to a branch just over their heads.

Branwald lay on his folded cloak, looking into the deep star-speckled void above, listening to the sounds of the surrounding forest. From near at hand came the throaty croak of a bullfrog and the cheeping of some night-bird. In the distance Branwald heard a sudden shrill scream, and he imagined that the life of some terror-stricken creature was at that moment ebbing away in the grip of some fierce predator. That was the way of life, he thought. That was the way it had been with that Oreman, when the lizard had pounced without warning. That was the way it might be with himself and Maloof, if the Dread Spirit wished it to be so.

Branwald's thoughts drifted into the future. What lay in store for them at the mouth of the river, if they ever reached it? It seemed to him that, by travelling on the open river, they were exposing themselves to increasing danger. Moreover, the Oremen had seen the Firebolt. If it was true that the Orelord wanted this weapon, then it might be only a short time before he knew where it was and who its carriers were.

Branwald thought of the Firebolt and of its frightening power. What use would it be to him if he came face to face with a determined enemy, since he must not use it against him? He wondered what would happen if he did use it thus — not to kill, but to injure an aggressor. To allow the beam to fall for a fraction of a moment on an enemy could not be so wrong, he told himself, especially if his cause was a just one.

Maloof's sudden voice beside him startled him. 'The Forest People say that, long ago, men walked upon the stars.'

Branwald smiled to himself. The Forest People did indeed have strange ideas. 'The stars are not big enough for a man to walk upon,' he replied.

'They say that some of them are many times greater than the earth, but that they look small because they are so far away.'

'And how would those men have travelled through the sky?' Branwald queried, his scepticism verging on sarcasm. 'Did men once flap their arms and fly through the air?'

'No,' replied his friend evenly. 'They had special boats that could leap up with a great noise and soar away from the earth.'

Branwald was silent. Several days before, Maloof's ideas would have seemed preposterous, even sacrilegious. In his mind's eye he could see the face of John the Scholar, expressing horror at such blasphemy. But now .... He had seen the black metal boat of the Orelord, a boat that could move at great speed without paddles. He had seen the stark silent ghosts of buildings, and the sleek single-span bridge across the whole width of the river — relics of the people who had lived before the Dark Time. Maybe it was possible. Maybe at some time in the past, before calamity fell on the world, men really had had boats that could traverse the emptiness of the sky and reach the distant stars.

'The Forest People say that there was a time when the moon was much brighter than it is now, and that those dark patches you see on its face are where people from the earth have made their homes,' Maloof went on.

Branwald let his eyes drift over to where the moon peered

171

through the branches. It was true: there were dark patches on its face. But the idea was incredible!

'They even say that the Firebolt came from one of those distant worlds.' Maloof spoke as if, this time, he did not expect to be believed.

Branwald did not respond. His eyes drifted to the faintly glowing tube above his head. He had no theory which might explain its origins. Its power was beyond the capacity of any craftsman on the islands to create. But maybe a people who, long ago, had made such bridges or such buildings as he had seen — who, even now, could make the black boats — could also have made the Firebolt.

'The Forest People believe that there is only one Firebolt,' Maloof went on. 'That is because there is no one who knows how to make another, because it was made by the creatures of that distant star. I think this is why the stranger, Urkor, wants it so much.'

As Branwald watched the pale blue blade above him, turning Maloof's words over in his mind, his former misgivings came back. If what Maloof said was true, why should he, Branwald, of all the people on the earth, have been chosen to be the possessor and guardian — even if only for a while — of such a formidable instrument? There was nothing in the events of his life which made him in any way different from the other boys he had known.

Maloof was different. He had suffered and changed and grown. Surely Maloof was the one who should have been chosen! Branwald wondered if the old man had made a mistake. Maybe he had intended Maloof to have the Firebolt and had become confused between the two of them ....

'Branwald,' came Maloof's quiet voice in the darkness, 'I do not understand it either. All I can say is that I feel that you are the chosen one. My task is a different one, although I do not know it fully yet. Remember that to be ready is all.'

CHAPTER NINETEEN

Branwald found himself standing on the edge of a high, dark cliff. He was frightened. In the darkness, a dizzying depth below, he saw the glint of restless water. The wind whispered and moaned around him and in the sky there were dark shapes, black against the moon. Far away, borne on the gusting wind, he heard voices, calling, crying, shrieking.

Then he was in a tunnel, black and wet, spiralling down and down. He felt the hot air, heavy with black dust that wafted up from below. Now there was only a single voice, clearer and less frantic. It was inquisitive, as if sensing a stranger approaching.

Then he was at the margin of a city, a city of broken dwellings. There were no paths, and he knew that he must search for someone, a young person. He began to climb over broken, ivy-covered walls, the roofless ruins of houses. He struggled over rubble-strewn floors, his need to find the person becoming more pressing. He scaled another wall and looked into the room beyond. A figure sat on a stool by a fire, its back turned towards him, its head hooded. He felt the need to speak with this figure, but the voice called again, and suddenly he found himself on a straight, flat roadway. He looked along it, searching the gloom, fearful of not finding the one he searched for. He heard the voice again. 'Who are you?' it asked. He was about to answer when the flat road suddenly turned into a precipitous descent, dropping down to a frightening chasm. He was falling, falling ....

Branwald woke with a start and found himself lying on his back, his hands gripping the boughs that he lay on. The moon blinked down at him through scudding clouds. He glanced at Maloof to see if he was startled too, but his friend was breathing quietly beside him, his head cradled in the crook of his arm. Branwald's heart pounded. He searched the moonlit branches around him, but there was nothing there except the leaves moving in the night breeze. He listened, but heard nothing above their rustling.

Then he sensed the voice in his mind again. 'Who are you?' it asked. 'And why are you coming?'

Branwald lay still, frowning. It was all part of his dream, he told himself. But the voice was there still. 'I know you are coming with another. Tell me who you are.'

Branwald was fully awake now. He focused his mind, concentrating its powers. 'I am Branwald,' he responded. 'Who are you?' He waited. Instantly, he sensed distrust.

'I am who I am. But we must know who you are. We have many enemies.'

Branwald sat up. 'I am only an enemy of those who have imprisoned my father.' He waited.

'Who is your father?'

'My father is Feowald the Protector, from Redwood Island.' He felt a surge of excitement from afar. Then the question, 'Where are you now?'

Branwald hesitated. A warning note sounded in his mind. The voice he heard seemed genuine enough. But what if others were listening? Into his mind flashed an image of Urkor's cold stare. He saw the man, at that very moment, lying under the same stars, in the mountains to the north, his mind brooding on the Firebolt and on the boy who was preventing him from having it. Maybe Urkor, too, was waiting to hear the answer to the question.

'I do not know who you are,' Branwald thought. 'Or where you are, or what you intend towards us.' He paused and waited, but there was no returning sensation. He went on, 'If you are a friend, I will speak with you again. If a foe ....' He abruptly cut off his thought. He had disclosed enough about himself — maybe too much. He had a strong sense that the one who had spoken with him was not an enemy. He was half aware of a silent plea, a cry for help, which had not been in the conscious mind of the sender. There was a gentleness, too ....

Branwald turned onto his side. Was he imagining all this? he asked himself. Who could be speaking to him thus? How

174

could they have known that he was 'coming', as they had said? 'Coming' — that meant that the other was ahead of him, somewhere downstream. He tried to visualise the terrain that lay ahead, the islands at the mouth of the Great River, the face of the one who had been speaking with him, but he could not. His mind was weary and sapped of energy. He drifted again into sleep.

~

It was bright morning when Branwald woke again. Yellow sunlight slanted down on him through the leaves. The air was warm.

He turned towards Maloof, but saw only his friend's cloak lying dishevelled beside him. He sat up and looked down. The canoe was still where he had tied it the evening before. He looked back along the still waters of the creek, towards the river, but the only movement was the sudden flit of a blue-winged bird.

Branwald swung himself down onto a lower branch and was on the point of dropping to the ground when he saw Maloof, barely fifteen feet from him. His friend was sitting cross-legged on a lichen-encrusted rock that lay, a miniature island, in the shallow water near the head of the creek. Opposite Maloof, across the narrow channel, a small stream trickled down from among the trees, rippling the still surface of the creek. Immobile as a statue, his arms folded on his chest, Maloof was gazing at the quiet water. Even from that distance, Branwald could clearly see the faint blue haze that enveloped his friend's body.

At first Branwald thought Maloof was fishing. He was on the point of calling when something about Maloof's demeanour, the calmness of his face in the sunlight, made him hesitate. A red-bodied dragonfly hovered near Maloof's face, but he did not appear to be aware of it. Curious and a little awed, Branwald eased himself into a sitting position on a lower branch, careful to make no sound. Maloof seemed hardly to be breathing, and Branwald sensed in him an inner stillness that he should not disturb.

He allowed his eyes to drift down to the broad lily pads which floated on the creek below him. On the smooth green surface of one of them lay a transparent pearl of water, sparkling when the sunlight caught it. On a nearby leaf, wider than the wooden platter in his mother's kitchen, rested a ladybird, bright red with ebony spots. A small white-throated bird glided across the creek and landed on a low speckled rock on the bank. Branwald watched as it dipped its head under the water, held it there for a long moment and then lifted it again. Beyond it, the dappled creekside trees stood upside-down on the surface of the water, so calmly did it flow.

Branwald became aware of sounds. The trees around him were aflood with birdsong. He recognised the shrill pipe of a throstle, but the others, sweet or raucous, were new to him. From somewhere in the trees came a sharp tapping, like urgent knocking on a door. Branwald stepped down onto the ferny ground, the better to see the source of the tapping, and smiled when he saw a rust-coloured bird clinging to the bark of a tree. He had seen woodpeckers in the trees of Woodfern Island.

When Branwald next looked at Maloof, he saw that his friend was leaning backwards, propped up by his out-stretched arms, regarding him with a quizzical smile. 'Want to swim?' Maloof said.

The water was clear and deep enough to swim in. Among the stones on the bottom Branwald spotted an ambling crayfish. 'Right!' he retorted. 'There's our next meal.'

There was a fevered race to see who could hit the water first. Branwald pulled shirt and tunic over his head in one movement and slid off his pants and moccasins. Maloof was still hopping on one foot, his brown body naked except for the pants wrapped round one ankle, when Branwald dived in. The cool shock was momentary. He searched the flickering bottom for the crayfish and was in time to see a sudden spurt of sand where it had been, then nothing.

He came to the surface, tasting the clean freshness of the water. Maloof's head appeared nearby, his face creased with laughter, his teeth white against the sun-browned skin. 'Warmer than the Elvan — the last time we swam,' he remarked. It was true. The water felt warm on Branwald's body. He stroked away towards the mouth of the creek, thrashing his legs, relishing the freedom and the exercise.

'It's the same water!' he called back, dropping his feet to the sandy bottom. 'It has travelled with us.'

Maloof caught up with him, treading water. 'Where's the breakfast?' he enquired, mischief in his eyes. They both sucked in air and dived down through the bubbling water, searching the gravel bed. Among the stones ahead of them, they saw a movement. Arms flailing, they raced towards the crayfish, bubbles streaming from noses and mouths. Neck and neck, arms outstretched, they were almost upon it when it felt their shadows. In a flash it was gone.

Back at the surface, they laughed, blowing spray from their faces, relieved to enjoy again the simple pleasure they had known before.

Then, from far away in the trees, came a sound that Branwald knew: a sharp, high-pitched bark. There was an answering bark from somewhere behind them, but nearer. 'The Hairy Ones!' he exclaimed, striking out for the bank.

Hurriedly they pulled on their clothes, watching the high branches around them. The barking was coming closer. Branwald climbed up to the makeshift platform, retrieved the Firebolt and his bow and, without a word, passed Maloof's bow and quiver down to him.

Moments later, they saw a dark shape leaping across a space between two trees a little to their left. They watched as it worked its way towards them. Farther left, another shape was moving through the high branches towards the creek. It gave a sudden loud bark, and Branwald felt the hair move on the nape of his neck.

'These are two more bluffers,' Maloof said quietly, but Branwald noticed that he had notched an arrow to the string of his bow.

The foremost animal advanced until only one broad-leaved tree separated it from the boys. It peered down at them through the crowding leaves. Its face, completely covered in hair, was longer than that of a human, and a ridge of bone protruded over each eye. Its upper lip was drawn back to expose a wide set of teeth, the canines long and pointed.

177

But there was little threat in its demeanour. Instead, it began to cackle, shaking its head from side to side and jabbing a hairy finger in their direction. When the second one came to rest on a nearby branch, gripping the bough above it with a long, snaky arm, the pair started such a jabbering and cackling that Branwald was reminded of two humpbacked old hags whose sole delight was to jeer at and slander anyone who passed.

'These are jokers,' said Maloof, stepping forward to gain a clear view of the noisy pair. He looked steadily at them, then lifted both hands until his fingers were pointing directly at them. The jabbering began to lessen. The two creatures regarded Maloof with increasing interest. They fell silent, their small eyes focused on his face.

Maloof stepped back towards Branwald. 'They are quiet now. Let us eat,' he said.

Branwald gazed at his friend. 'What did you do? How did you do that?' he asked. 'You did it with the dog of the Forest People, too.'

Maloof thought for a moment, frowning. 'I don't know,' he said. 'I never thought about it. I just look at them, and think myself into their minds. I have to see their eyes, though.'

Branwald looked up at the Hairy Ones. One of them was rummaging through the hair on its belly with careful fingers; the other was gazing placidly down at the boys.

Before sitting down to eat the last three oaten cakes, the boys baited two of Maloof's fish-hooks with small strips of the dried meat the children had given them and cast the lines into the deepest part of the creek, tying the ends securely to a young sapling on the bank. While they ate, they watched the lines. The Hairy Ones, still high in the trees and emitting sporadic grunts, had begun to move along the creek-side towards the river. They seemed to have lost interest in the boys.

Before their meal was finished, the boys caught three crayfish, which came dripping from the water, clutching the bait greedily in their claws. Maloof murmured soothing words over them before killing them with his knife and storing them in his satchel.

CHAPTER TWENTY

When the canoe was packed and ready, Branwald took out the map once more. He wanted to know how close they were to the mouth of the river. He found 'The Bridge of the Ancients (Ruins)' and, passing 'The Land of the Galians' below it, saw that the only feature that lay between them and the mouth of the river was 'The Ochre Flood'. He estimated that they had little more than a quarter of the river's course to traverse before they reached the Tarquan Islands.

The morning was bright and very warm, and the river sparkled in the sunlight as they swung out of the creek mouth and turned south, hugging the shadowy left bank. Downstream, the wide, flat expanse of water was walled in by densely packed trees on both sides.

The river travelled across a flat landscape in great swinging loops, which doubled back on themselves until it seemed to the boys that they were heading east one moment and west the next. On the inside banks of the curves, crescents of white sand lay invitingly in the warm sun, except where the sinister shapes of lizards sat unmoving. Narrow, forested islands split the river into channels; on some the boys saw dark creatures, smaller than the Hairy Ones, squatting on low branches or crouching by the water's edge, watching the canoe with wide expressionless eyes.

Soon the boys saw, to their right, the wide mouth of a tributary river. Not long afterwards they noticed that a yellow-brown stain was spreading slowly, from the right, across the clear waters.

'The Ochre Flood!' Branwald exclaimed. It was a relief to know that the feature which, on the map, had seemed so fraught with danger was merely a silt-laden tributary spreading its muddy tide across the clear waters of the Great River.

~

The boys heard the boat before they saw it. The distant chugging sound carried to them along the wall of greenery by the river's edge. When the black prow came sliding round the bend downstream, the boys were already hauling the canoe up into the foliage of a low, curving branch; with the added weight, it drooped almost to touch the water. They steadied themselves against the smaller branches, trusting to the deep shadows and the hanging leaves to keep them from being seen, and waited.

The boat came on, more slowly than they had expected. They could hear men's voices drifting over the smooth river. The tones were gruff and relaxed. One man guffawed aloud, the echoes dwindling through the trees. The black craft passed slowly upstream, grey smoke belching from its chimney. It seemed an age before it was out of sight.

Branwald did a quick calculation. It would take these men no more than three hours to reach the place where the boys had left the other Oremen stranded. This meant that by mid-afternoon, the black boat might return, searching for the two canoeists.

He was turning these possibilities over in his mind when Maloof spoke. 'If we fear that they may come upon us un-awares, then we can take to the shelter of the trees till night falls, and travel in the darkness.'

'Yes,' Branwald agreed. 'But we can keep our course until the sun begins to slope down to the west. If these men are going to meet the others, they will not return before that time.'

~

It was mid-afternoon when the boys turned the canoe onto a sandy beach nestling in the elbow of a long curving island, and dragged it into the shelter of a channel which had once sliced across the island, but which was now dry and weed-choked. High overhead, creamy wisps of cirrus cloud formed a delicate pattern; but in the west, the sky near the horizon was blocked by a dark bank of cloud.

The boys had not seen any lizards for some time, as the river here flowed between steep banks crowned with a dense wall of greenery, and there were few sandbanks. The wooded

180

island would give them cover, while allowing them to hear the boats of the Oremen if they should pass.

They found a part of the channel's bed which was shielded from the river by high tufts of fern-like growth. Here they prepared to eat.

The lighting of a fire became a problem straight away, however. If they lit one, and the black boat returned, the smoke would immediately give away their location. But the only food they had left was the strips of dried meat and the three uncooked crayfish.

'I am ravenous!' exclaimed Branwald.

Maloof was already preparing two baited hooks. 'We cannot take the risk of lighting a fire,' he said. 'We will have to wait till dark.'

'But the boats may travel in the dark also. Maybe they have lights,' Branwald argued.

Maloof, frowning as he sliced a strip of meat, was silent.

Then Branwald had an idea. In the smooth grey rock nearby was a small pebble-filled hollow, shaped like the inside of one of his mother's pots. He bent and scooped out the pebbles; then, using his wooden goblet, he half-filled the hollow with water. He took the crayfish from the canoe and dropped them into the water. Shaking the wrappings from the Firebolt, he took it to the hollow.

'What are you doing?' asked Maloof, in alarm.

'I am going to use this,' Branwald declared.

Branwald pointed the instrument at the surface of the water. Keeping the beam away from the crayfish, he tightened his grip and focused his thoughts.

The beam became white. A wisp of steam drifted upwards from the surface of the water. Then a line of bubbles winked up from the rock below. As Maloof came to stand beside him, Branwald moved the point of the beam from side to side, careful to avoid the rust-coloured fish. The bubbles spread and more steam drifted away. Moments later, the water was boiling merrily.

'It's working!' Branwald said.

A short time afterwards, they sat down to eat the steaming crayfish. They cracked open the brittle bodies and claws with stones. The meat was delicious.

After the meal, while Branwald kept lookout from atop a large boulder at the water's edge, Maloof crawled along a dead tree that had fallen out over the water, and tied the two baited fishing-lines to it. In both directions, the river was empty as far as the eye could see.

'Now,' said Branwald, when Maloof was back on solid ground, 'we will find a sleeping-place where the lizards cannot reach us.'

'Then we will go hunting,' Maloof promised.

They found an outcrop of rock, near their campsite, surrounded on three sides by broad-leaved trees whose branches almost met across the top. About five feet up the steep south side was a ledge, less than two paces wide, and slightly sloping. They cleared away the low scrub and tufts of grass and placed their robes, satchels and paddles on the ledge.

'It was our destiny to find this place,' said Maloof, picking up his bow. 'Now let us see what creature is destined to be our food.'

~

Branwald felt pleased to be walking again. The long hours crouched in the canoe had stiffened his lower back and buttocks, and he needed exercise to free them. The island, however, was very overgrown, and there were no passages through the dense vegetation. Branwald led the way, using the Firebolt to shear through the ferns and branches that blocked the way, while Maloof, bow poised, scanned the trees ahead.

The island was narrow, and it was not long before their course brought them to the river again. The bank sloped steeply down to the swirling, muddy water.

Suddenly Branwald stopped. Through a web of branches he saw three ducks on the water, only two or three yards from the shore. They were feeding on morsels that flowed to them on the water's surface.

Branwald looked questioningly at Maloof. The ducks were less than ten yards from them.

Maloof shook his head. 'They're too far out,' he whispered.

'Even if I shoot one, how will we get it?'

Branwald tried to assess the depth of the water. 'I will wade, or swim,' he whispered. 'It will be easy.'

Maloof frowned, his dark eyes surveying the scene. Then he nodded. 'All right. But if it drifts out, you must leave it. There will be other game.' He raised the bow and took aim. Branwald stepped aside to give him a clear view, at the same time stooping to leave the Firebolt on the ground. Stealthily he slipped off his jerkin.

The bowstring twanged, and there was a sudden alarmed squawk and the frantic flapping of wings. But only two birds rose from the water. The third, transfixed by an arrow, was floundering in a circle, flapping one wing in a vain attempt to follow its companions.

Branwald burst through the covering greenery and leapt from the crumbling bank, his hands outstretched to grab the floundering bird. He hit the water, steeling himself for the jar against the bottom, and his hands closed around the duck.

The next moment, the river closed over his head and his ears were filled with bubbling. Surprised at the depth, he kicked his feet to bring himself back to the surface, reluctant to let go of his prey. When he felt the current tugging at his legs, however, he held on to the bird with his left hand and used his right to stroke himself up. The bank should be close by, he thought.

As he broke surface, he heard a strange sound nearby. He looked for the bank; it was only four yards away.

But someone was screaming. Alarmed, Branwald realised it was Maloof. 'Branwald! Get out! Now! Get out!'

In the water to his left Branwald saw a movement, a brown bulge on the surface approaching fast. He released the duck and struck out desperately for the bank.

A great red throat opened beside him. He felt the fetid breath and saw the jagged yellow teeth. He struck out blindly, feeling his heel connect with a solid surface. The huge upper jaw towered over his head. He twisted away from its smashing descent.

It never came. A white streak of light shot from the bank. The beast roared, a great brassy bellow, and reared out of the water. Then, as if tethered to the bank by the beam of light, it twisted and writhed to escape. Branwald kicked hard, felt the stones under his feet, pushed himself backwards into the shallows, and scrambled up onto the bank.

Maloof was locked in a frozen stance, holding the Firebolt before him, aiming it at the beast, a strange and frightening expression on his face.

Branwald leaped to his feet, scrambled over mossy stones and tufts of fern, and flung himself at Maloof. He felt a sharp shock in his hands as they closed round his friend's wrist. Both of them crashed against the trunk of a tree and, glancing off it, fell among a cluster of ferns. Branwald felt Maloof's resistance, saw his twisted, distorted face and heard his snarl of rage.

'Maloof! Let go!' Branwald cried, gripping the Firebolt's handle and trying to tear it from his friend's grasp.

The contest was short: suddenly Maloof's resistance ebbed away. The Firebolt came loose from his hands and, with a groan, his body went limp.

Branwald tossed the instrument into the thicket beside him and stood up, breathing hard. A glance at the river told him that the lizard was gone. 'Maloof ....' he began.

Maloof lay unmoving, his face deathly pale, his eyes closed. He was scarcely breathing. Branwald knelt beside him, gripping him by the shoulders. 'Maloof! Are you all right?'

Maloof showed no sign of having heard. Only a barely audible moan showed that he was alive.

Branwald put his hand behind Maloof's head and shoulders and lifted them to rest on his knee. 'Maloof! Speak to me!' he pleaded. A cold terror was growing in his stomach. 'Maloof! Please!' There was no response, no sign of recognition.

Afterwards Branwald could not clearly remember how long he had remained in that crouched position, clutching Maloof, babbling entreaties to him and prayers to the Great Mother and even to the Dread Spirit. He remembered only the first feeble flutterings of his friend's eyelids, and the beginnings of hope and gratitude. It was a long time before Maloof finally looked into Branwald's face and whispered to him: 'I had to do it, Branwald. It was the only way ....'

'It's all right, Maloof. I know,' Branwald said, wiping the beads of perspiration from his friend's brow. 'You had to do it.'

'It's just that ... there was no time to see its eyes. And when the beam struck it, I couldn't let go. I wanted to let go, but it wouldn't let me. It seemed to be sucking all my strength out of me.' Maloof paused, gasping a little for breath. 'It had me in its power. If you hadn't broken the beam ....'

A shudder ran through his frame, and he closed his eyes again.

~

The evening had grown dull, and a leaden bank of cloud had drifted across the sun. Branwald helped Maloof back through the dense undergrowth to the rocky ledge. He dragged Maloof's inert weight to the top, laid him on the sloping rock and wrapped him in both their cloaks. Some sense told him that Maloof needed hot, nourishing food, so he cleared the water and blackened sand from the makeshift pot, put fresh water and the remains of the crayfish into it and went to examine the lines they had set.

Sure enough, one of them was stretched taut. Branwald hauled in the chunky, sharp-spined fish, dispatched it with the handle of his dagger, gutted and sliced it, and dropped the pieces into the hole with the rest. He shrank from using the Firebolt; but, because there was no other way, he took it gingerly and directed the beam at the water. In a few moments he was offering the warm, fishy brew to his prostrate friend.

'That was good,' Maloof said weakly, when he had emptied Branwald's beaker. 'I feel better.' He sat up, drew up his legs and tried to stand, but grabbed Branwald's shoulder as his legs crumpled under him. He lay back against the rock. 'Just give me a little time,' he said. 'Then my strength will come back.'

His strength did not return, however. The black clouds drifted over them and the day grew dark, and still Maloof could not stand unaided. His face remained pale and haggard.

Then, as if the day itself were an agent of some malicious power, it began to rain. The first drops splashed loudly on the rocks and the leaves; then the rain became a deluge.

Branwald rushed to the canoe and dragged it onto the ledge; turning it upside-down and propping one end in the fork of a nearby branch, he made a makeshift roof over Maloof.

By the time that he himself had crawled under its dripping gunwales, however, he was soaked to the skin, and the cloaks covering Maloof were stained dark with rain. Even when Branwald had settled into the cramped space under the canoe, the warm drops pelted the rock beside him and splashed against his legs. The canoe above him resounded with a continuous patter, and the water flowed down the sloping rock and soaked his buttocks.

Branwald was desperate. Maloof was ill and needed help. But where could that help come from? The Galians? But they were far upriver. Even if Branwald could struggle back against the current, in the blinding rain, there was no guarantee that he would find them. And then there was the danger from the Oremen ....

Branwald thought of his mother and Eroona. If only he could speak with them, they would tell him what to do. In desperation he closed his eyes and willed his thoughts to fly along the great valley and over the mountains, to his home. 'Please!' he whispered. 'Please, Dread Spirit, let them hear!'

He calmed himself and thought more slowly. 'Eroona! Mother! Can you hear me?' He waited tensely, keeping his mind open, waiting for an image, no matter how faint. But no image came. There was nothing except his own fear and his own despair.

He tried again, but even as he focused his mind, the sense of failure overwhelmed him. His anger sought a target. Why had he gone in search of the Old Soldier in the first place? Why had he set out on this crazy journey with that sinister weapon?

Branwald looked out into the rain. It was falling in a constant downpour that showed no sign of lessening, so heavy that the trees were vague shapes behind an opaque stream of water. He decided that he and Maloof would have to spend the night in this place, and that they would need better shelter.

He struggled out from his cramped quarters. He found a

cluster of shoulder-high ferns, dripping with rain, and sliced through the thick central stems with his dagger; then he collected armfuls of the fallen greenery and brought them back to the canoe. He selected those with twin branching stems and draped them upside-down across the upturned craft, so that one frond hung on each side. The single stems he laid thickly against the sides of the canoe, until a wall of dense vegetation hung on either side. With water streaming down into his eyes, he baited the fishing line again, having already checked the second one and found no fish there, and set two night-lines.

Then he crawled up into the narrow chamber where his friend lay, still swathed in the sodden cloaks. By the blue light of the Firebolt, Branwald inspected Maloof's face. He was sleeping, his breathing light but regular. His face, however, was still pale. Spreading the edges of the cloaks a little wider, Branwald stretched himself beside Maloof and tried to sleep.

But sleep would not come. Instead there came a sick feeling in his stomach as fear laid hold of him again. What if Maloof should be so ill that he could not go on? What if he should die?

Fear twisted and turned inside Branwald. And as it festered there, guilt, like a noxious weed, took root in the same place. It was his fault that this had happened. He hadn't thought before urging Maloof to shoot at the ducks. How could he have forgotten about the lizards, after the grim warning on the previous day? He had rashly leaped into the water, leaving Maloof with no option but to use the Firebolt to save him ....

And then he remembered something that the Old Soldier had told him: 'Do not ask another to bear the Firebolt in a struggle that is rightfully yours.' Remembering the pang of sorrow which he had felt from the old man, Branwald groaned aloud in anguish at the realisation that he had allowed that very thing to happen to Maloof.

'Mother!' he pleaded, as the hot tears came. 'Mother of the Forest People! Please do not let Maloof die! Please!' He put his free arm around the sleeping form of his friend, needing to share his own warmth and strength and life with him.

The night crawled along interminably. Several times, when Maloof moved weakly in his sleep, Branwald raised himself and spoke quietly to him, reluctant to disturb his rest, yet wanting Maloof to hear him and to respond. Each time, however, he was disappointed. Maloof merely muttered incoherently and lapsed again into sleep.

At last, the staccato patter of great drops on the canvas above Branwald's head began to fade into the distance. He fell into a troubled sleep.

CHAPTER TWENTY-ONE

Branwald heard a sound. He opened his eyes. The rain still pattered, as if it had been falling since the beginning of the world. The grey light of morning filtered through the wall of ferns. He felt wet and stiff. He could not remember what his dream had been about or who had been speaking in it.

Then he distinctly heard the voice of a young person saying, 'Somewhere near here.' He lifted his head in alarm, searching for the Firebolt. The voice was real and it was not far away. Branwald heard the guttural bass of a man replying, but could not distinguish the words.

He gripped the Firebolt and rolled over so that he was facing the sound. He was resolved. If he had to fight for himself and Maloof, he would do so. He would not fix the Firebolt's beam directly on his target, as Maloof had done with the lizard; he would make slashing strokes with it. He would do damage enough. He would rather die than allow himself and Maloof to fall into the hands of the Orelord.

The voices fell silent. Branwald listened intently, hardly breathing, cursing the rain that drowned other sounds. He stealthily parted the ferns and peered through the grey slit, but saw nothing except the straight streaks of rain. He was beginning to wonder if he had imagined the voices when he heard, above the drumming of the rain, the young voice saying, 'Is there anybody there — under the canoe?'

Branwald did not move. Indecision racked him. Then, sensing no threat in the young voice, he spoke out. 'Yes. There are two of us.'

There was a gasp of surprise and pleasure. 'It is them!' the young voice exclaimed.

A man's deep growl broke in. 'We have come to help you. But let us see you. Come out.'

Branwald took a deep breath. Holding the Firebolt so that the glowing beam pointed downwards, he parted the ferns and crawled out.

A short distance away, at the edge of the clearing, stood two people, dressed in long hooded cloaks made of a blue translucent material. Branwald could not see their faces for the driving rain and the hoods that shadowed them. One was tall, very bulky in the upper body; he carried a bow with a fitted arrow pointing at the ground. The other was shorter and slighter, and the slim white-bodiced shape beneath the cloak told Branwald it was a girl.

'Are you the son of Feowald the Protector?' the girl asked. Her voice was slightly husky.

Branwald's eyes widened. 'Yes,' he exclaimed. 'I am he. How do you know who I am? Where is he?' He dropped from the ledge and started forward, but the man stepped quickly in front of the girl and brought the bow to firing position. Branwald saw a long, thin face, with deep grooves on either side of the mouth. Beneath the transparent cloak, the naked shoulders were bunched with muscle.

'What is that bright thing you carry?' the man demanded.

Branwald stopped and looked down at the Firebolt. Its beam was making a fizzling pattern on the soaked rock at his feet. 'This is .... There is no danger for you in this. It is a thing that I have been given.'

'Espirit!' exclaimed the man, peering with half-closed eyes at the Firebolt. 'What is it?'

'This is a thing called the Firebolt,' Branwald said. A feeling of power was growing in him. His hand gripped the handle even more tightly. The man stepped back as the beam became whiter than the sun. The rock below began to crackle.

The slight one stepped forward quickly, pulling back her hood. The face of a young girl appeared. Her nose was wide at the bridge, and her eyes were wide-spaced. Her dark hair hung in two long plaits. Her chin was firmly set. 'You will not need that weapon here. We come in peace. This is my father, Morung, and I am Sula. We have been searching for you through the hours of darkness. We come to help you. Your friend is not well.'

Branwald stared at her. How could she have known? 'Yes. He is not well.' He frowned and stared down at the instrument in his hand. How could he have, even momentarily, forgotten about Maloof? Was it the Firebolt's doing?

With an effort he loosened his grip and dropped the weapon on the rock. He looked at the girl. 'He is ill. He needs — we need help ....' He could not continue.

The girl came closer. Her voice was gentle. 'We are the People of the Tarquan Islands — those of us who remain. We have travelled all night to come to you. Come with us, but hurry. We must be off the river before the rain stops.'

'We will come,' Branwald said huskily. He turned to the man. 'Can you help Maloof? He is very sick.'

Maloof stared at them with bleary eyes when Branwald flung the ferns away from the canoe and gently shook him awake. He lay pale and lethargic as Branwald introduced the two strangers and began to explain what was happening. Branwald placed his hand on his friend's brow and held it there, and, as he spoke, Maloof became more alert. He caught Branwald's hand in his and smiled weakly. 'We are near the end,' he whispered.

'Yes,' replied Branwald. 'We are with friends now. Soon you will be better.'

'What happened to him?' Morung asked, studying Maloof's face with serious eyes.

'He used this against a lizard from the river,' Branwald said, indicating the Firebolt. 'It took his strength away.'

Morung looked sceptically down at the Firebolt, whose glow was now a faint blue. He shook his head. 'I cannot help you. But there are old ones of my people who speak about an instrument such as this. Maybe they can help.'

'My father — do you know where he is?'

Morung hesitated. 'Your father ....' he said, searching Branwald's face with deep brown eyes. 'Your father is not with us now.'

'Is he —?' Branwald began.

'When last I saw him, he was strong and well. He was wounded in the defending of the islands, but he was well recovered when the men of the Orelord finally took him.'

Morung's expression was that of one who knows he brings bad news. 'He is now in the mine, with many others of our people.' He waited, his eyes still focused on Branwald's face.

'And Brugarh the Woodman, my father?' Maloof asked weakly.

'I am told that he is there too,' Morung replied gently. 'And he is also well.'

'Where is this mine?' Branwald asked.

Morung turned to look downstream. 'It is near the mouth of this river, one day's paddling from here, on the mainland west of the river's mouth.'

Branwald looked sharply at the man. 'How can you know all this?'

'I should have told you. Rafik, a man of our people, managed to escape from the Oremen during the storm. He has been with us for over two weeks. He has told us about many of our people who are in captivity.' Morung broke off to look up at the clouds, which had lost their grey pallor and were beginning to break. The rain had eased to a thin drizzle. 'But we must leave here. It will not be long before the rain stops.'

Morung helped Branwald to place the canoe on the ground and load the boys' meagre possessions into it. They carried it to the river's edge, where another, longer canoe lay upturned on the beach. It was made of the bark of trees; wide strips of bark had been stitched together and the joints sealed with a yellow, resin-like substance. Maloof, who was still unable to stand unaided, was laid on the broad floor of this craft and cocooned in animal skins.

The two Tarquans pushed off into the current, heading downstream. Branwald, alone in his own canoe, followed, paddling hard to keep up. The strangers hugged the left bank, sweeping in under the overhanging branches as often as possible, pausing in their paddling now and again to listen and to scan the misty expanse of water around them.

An hour passed; then another. The rain stopped, and a pale sun peered through a dense haze in the east. Branwald noticed the character of the river changing. There were more islands now, and many still channels opening back into the jungle. When Branwald reached down and scooped a handful of water to drink, it had a salty taste.

Branwald was grateful when the canoe in front finally swung left, into a narrow, tree-lined canal. Soon they were passing through a maze of similar channels. They crossed gravelly bars that rasped under the bottoms of the canoes, and struggled through gaps where the trees overhead almost met in mid-stream. Branwald noticed round wooden floats on the water, with fishing nets suspended from them. The channels became narrower and narrower. Branwald was certain that he would never be able to find his way back to the river.

At last, in the distance, he heard the warning barking of dogs. Through the drooping branches ahead, he saw a small lake. Along the shore, raised on a high scaffolding of stilts, stood four flimsy-looking huts. Their walls were made of straw-coloured wattle, and the steep roofs were thatched with a thick matting of reeds. In the shadows beneath the overhanging eaves Branwald saw window openings, at several of which stood people watching the canoes' approach. On a low wooden jetty below the huts, three speckled hounds were prancing excitedly, baying a warning. Several canoes, identical to the one carrying Maloof, lay moored on the water. A blue haze of wood-smoke drifted out from beneath the huts.

As the two canoes moved onto the lake, Branwald saw several people emerge from the high dwellings and clamber down rickety ladders to the jetty. In the dark window spaces, more faces appeared. There was a rising chatter of voices mingled with the baying of the hounds. Several brown-skinned children appeared on the jetty, some of them clad only in flimsy loincloths. At the edge of the jetty were three men, dressed in light sleeveless vests and loose pants tied in at the ankle.

'Summon Bengue,' Morung called to them, when the canoes had almost reached the jetty. 'We will need her.'

One of the men turned and stepped onto a gangway which ran under the nearest house, through the stilts. Branwald saw that there were a number of dwellings built among the trees, behind the fronting four, and that a system of gangways running between the stilts connected them with one another.

The two remaining men knelt and grabbed the gunwales of the canoes as they came alongside. Their brown eyes flickered over Maloof before turning to Branwald.

'These two boys are from the People of the Islands of the North,' Morung announced, in a voice so loud that the people at the windows above could hear him. 'This one' — jerking his thumb in Branwald's direction — 'says he is the son of Feowald. And this one is the son of Brugarh.'

A hum of talking swelled out from the houses above. The five children — two boys and three girls, none of them above twelve years of age — crowded at the edge of the jetty, gazing with serious, unselfconscious eyes at the two boys.

One of the men, who had high cheekbones above a clean-shaven jaw, knelt on the jetty and helped Branwald out of his canoe. 'You are welcome to the village of the People of the Swamp,' he said gruffly, and Branwald detected a note of irony in his tone.

Two women, dressed in brightly coloured sarongs, had descended the rickety ladders and were hovering over the larger canoe, clearly intent on ministering to Maloof.

'What happened to him?' the taller one asked Branwald. He hesitated.

'He has a strange sickness,' broke in Morung. 'He is very weak.' The women paused, eyeing Maloof uncertainly. 'No,' Morung went on, 'it is not catching. You may tend to him.'

Within a few minutes the men had removed a panel from the side of the nearest hut, Morung's, and a stout timber beam with a wooden pulley attached was fixed to the roof above this space so that the rope suspended from it almost touched the jetty. A makeshift stretcher was attached to the rope and, in a short time, Maloof was winched up and swung in under the roof. He was conscious, but Branwald thought he seemed weaker. He spoke briefly to Branwald before being hoisted. 'I will be stronger tomorrow. Just give me a few days and I will be ready to go with you.'

Branwald nodded his encouragement. 'Yes,' he said. 'Just a few days.'

Branwald was on the point of climbing up the ladder to the hut when Morung touched his arm. 'You had better not leave the weapon in the canoe,' he said. 'The young ones here are very curious.'

Amidst a group of whispering children, Branwald knelt on the jetty and picked up the Firebolt.

'Have you really come down the Great River from the Islands of the North?' a round-faced boy with mischief in his eyes asked him. The others crowded behind the speaker. Branwald nodded.

'Is this your canoe?' asked a smaller girl. He nodded again.

'Can we take it for a paddle?' burst out the boy again. 'Me first!' Branwald was instantly surrounded by the clamouring group. He looked towards Morung. The man shrugged his shoulders.

'Yes,' said Branwald. 'But first you must carry everything in it to the place where my friend is.'

There was a sudden outburst of pushing and squabbling, which was stilled by a sharp command from Morung. 'Hedin, you get into the canoe and pass the things up to the others. Everyone will get something. And be careful!' Satisfied that order had been restored, Branwald slung the Firebolt over his shoulder and followed Morung up the ladder.

There were two rooms in the hut. In the larger one, Branwald saw seats of woven reeds around a wide, raised wooden disc which he took to be a table. Maloof had been laid in the shaded corner of the smaller room, the floor of which was strewn with mats and rolls of fabric.

'Bengue will come soon,' said the tall dark-haired woman quietly, as she bathed Maloof's brow with a soft, perforated substance which Branwald had never seen before.

'Who is Bengue?' asked Branwald.

'She is the wise one and healer of our people. She will know what to do.'

Branwald was sceptical, but he kept silent. How could any ordinary person know about the Firebolt and its sinister power?

'You must be hungry,' the other woman said. 'Sula will bring you to the cooking-place and Wayana will give you food. There is nothing you can do here while we wait for Bengue.'

Maloof's quiet nod gave him permission, so Branwald, still carrying the Firebolt, followed Sula, who had been watching in silence from the corner.

They walked between the weathered stilts towards a clearing in the forest, some distance behind the houses. The familiar smell of wood-smoke scented the air.

Sula had discarded her translucent cloak. As she led the way along the swaying gangway, Branwald noticed the firm calves of her legs below the buff-coloured pantaloons, and the olive tint of her upper arms where they emerged from her sleeveless bodice. In the gloom under the huts he thought he saw a faint green glow around her.

Branwald was thinking about his father. 'This one, Rafik, who escaped from the Orelord — is he here? I would like to speak with him.'

Sula shook her head. 'He has gone with a scouting party towards the mouth of the river. He may not be back for several days.'

They emerged from under the huts, onto a succession of wooden planks laid end to end on the wet clay to form a path through the dense stands of trees.

'I thought that your people lived on islands — the Tarquan Islands?' Branwald said.

Sula glanced at him sharply. 'We did. Until the Orelord's men came. They took a great many of our people: my brother Ganden, my friends, many others .... We had to gather what was left and come here.'

Branwald knew that she was affected. 'I'm sorry,' he said. 'It seems that we have all lost someone to this Orelord.'

They passed onto a bare path worn on solid ground. 'How did you find us?' Branwald asked.

Sula turned her head and, although she did not smile, her teeth showed white against her olive skin. 'Do you not recall my mind-voice yesterday morning?' she asked. 'Was it not you who spoke with me?'

'So it was you!' Branwald exclaimed. 'I was not sure what I should say. I was afraid that enemies might be listening.'

Her eyebrows lifted, and her face grew serious. 'Do you think that the men of the Orelord can speak with the mind-voice?'

'There is a man who came to the islands in the last days before we left.' Branwald watched Sula's face. 'He said he was one of the Tarquan Island People, and that he was looking for help for my father and the others. He said his name was Urkor. Do you know him?'

'Urkor,' she repeated, frowning. 'No. There has never been anyone with that name among our people. And no one has gone from here on such a mission. What did he look like?'

'Tall and strong, with black hair and beard. But inside he is cruel and ruthless. He can understand my thoughts. He wants the Firebolt. He is following on the river.'

'Following you? Have you seen him?'

Branwald shook his head. 'I know that he is coming. He is angry because we have eluded him. He has revenge in his heart.'

'You can feel him in your mind?' Branwald nodded. 'But he cannot hear you? Surely the Oremen cannot speak in thought?'

'I do not know about the others. But I think this one can, when he is near me.'

'Do not fear,' Sula said. 'He will not find you here.'

Her words, however, did not take away the dark presentiment in Branwald's heart. Urkor's revenge seemed already to be taking place, he thought grimly.

Branwald and Sula were approaching a clearing. Branwald saw a number of people bustling around a stone-ringed fire-pit, over which a wooden tripod, blackened with smoke, had been erected. Set in the trees some distance to the right stood a thatch-roofed building, much bigger than any of the others Branwald had seen.

'That,' said Sula, pointing at the larger house, 'is the People's House, where we have meetings, and where the children are taught. But you asked me how we found you .... I knew that something had happened yesterday evening. It came suddenly, as a dark — a sort of blackness .... I searched and searched for your thought, and when I found it I knew there was something bad — something frightening. So I persuaded Father to come with me. Did you not feel that we were coming?'

Branwald shook his head. 'No. I do not hear well when I am troubled.'

At the smoke-blackened ring of stones, Wayana, a stout woman with enormous flabby forearms, was stirring a steaming brew in a large black metal pot suspended from the tripod by a soot-encrusted chain.

'Aha!' she chortled, in a voice that rasped in her chest. 'That is a fine young man you have found, Sula!' She chuckled mischievously, and her ample breasts quivered under her hessian bodice. 'He looks hungry, too.' Wayana dipped a wooden ladle into the brew and examined a dripping portion. 'Chat away for a while longer and it'll be ready,' she wheezed, her merry eyes peering out at the couple above fleshy cheeks.

'Come on,' said Sula. 'I'll show you the new smokehouse.'

Branwald followed, knowing the girl was trying to be kind, but feeling bad that he could not respond. They went along another path, this one winding and sticky with wetness, which climbed through the giant trees. Branwald looked back towards the houses, reluctant to distance himself from them.

'You are worried about Maloof,' Sula said.

'Yes,' Branwald admitted. Tears swelled in his eyes, and he blinked them back. Sula turned towards him. He looked into her green eyes and felt in his mind her great sympathy. 'Be of good heart, Branwald,' she said quietly. 'If anyone can cure him, Bengue can.'

The smokehouse was a long, low wooden structure standing amidst a grove of evergreens. Several men were perched on the roof, fixing the last yellow planks in place.

'Since we left our home on the islands,' Sula explained, 'we have eaten less fish than we are used to. The men hunt for animals in the forest, but our desire is for fish. That is what we have always eaten. Soon we will be able to preserve fish in this house, so in times of scarcity we will not go hungry, as we did when we first came here.'

'But the men of the Orelord — do they not know where you are?'

'They may know. But they cannot come close to us, because their boats cannot traverse the bars and narrow places. Anyway, we would hear them coming and escape into the forest. We have provided for that. We will not be caught again as we were on the islands.'

'What about Bengue?' Branwald asked, glancing back towards the settlement. 'Why must we wait for her to come? Where is she?'

Sula began to retrace her steps. 'Bengue spends much of her time in the forest. She knows about herbs and animals. She can talk to the spirits, and she can find a soul that is lost.'

Branwald frowned. What a curious expression! According to the Elders of his own people, a person could lose his soul if he transgressed any of the Sacred Precepts of the Dread Spirit. Only a public confession of the deed, and a submission to the punishment prescribed by the stern moral guardians of the community, could restore the guilty one to wholeness. He felt another twinge of guilt. He had been rash and foolish in his actions. Was he going to be held responsible for Maloof's illness?

His reverie was interrupted. In the trees near the huts, several children were running towards them.

'Sula! Sula!' they called. 'You both must come. Bengue is here.'

~

When Branwald climbed up into Morung's hut, he saw a frail, shrunken figure kneeling beside Maloof. Bengue's white hair, tied with a yellow band that encircled her head, hung below her shoulders, which were draped with strips of woven fabric. The rest of her garb consisted of a grey long-sleeved dress made of some rough cloth and girdled at the waist by a green sash. The dress covered her feet. Branwald could not see her face.

Morung, standing by the window, made a gesture for them to be silent. Branwald stepped to one side and settled himself to watch.

Bengue began to rock silently back and forth, with her

199

head bowed over Maloof, whose face was in shadow. Then she spoke, so quietly that the words were not clear. Maloof answered her in a throaty whisper. Branwald strained to hear. Maloof was telling her about the incident with the great lizard, when he had used the Firebolt to save Branwald's life.

When he had finished, the old woman was silent for a moment. Then she put her hands on the ground and nimbly rose to her feet. She turned to Morung, and Branwald saw her face for the first time. Her skin was dark, like leather, except for the grooves and wrinkles everywhere. From the way her lips puckered, he guessed she had no teeth. Her eyes, however, were sharp and bright as a bird's.

'I need to see this weapon,' she said, and her voice was full and gentle, the voice of a much younger woman. Morung looked at Branwald, who unwrapped the leathers from the blade and laid the Firebolt on the floor before Bengue.

He fancied that her eyes widened, just a little, when she looked at the Firebolt. She said nothing for several minutes; she simply stared down at it. Then, without changing her expression, she looked for a long moment at Branwald. There was curiosity there, and, when she smiled faintly, he felt a strong sympathy from the old woman. She nodded slowly, never taking her eyes from his face. Branwald began to feel embarrassed.

'Pardon me,' Bengue said. 'It is so long since I saw this' — she indicated the weapon — 'and one who bore it.'

She turned to Morung. 'I will have to search in the other worlds for the lost part,' she said. 'I will need the Kailas drums.'

CHAPTER TWENTY-TWO

The ceremony of searching for Maloof's soul would not begin until night had settled over the small community. The intervening period was a difficult time of waiting for Branwald. When Bengue returned to the forest to get what she called 'my crystal' and other things, Branwald sat for a long time beside Maloof, occasionally speaking quietly to him, or, when Maloof slept, just watching. Instinctively he felt that as long as he was there, Maloof's strength would not fail.

But Maloof was very weak. On two occasions, the vigilant women lifted him from his bed and tried to get him to walk unaided, but he could not do it. Instead they became his crutches: one on either side, they took him to the outer room, circled the dining-place several times and then brought him back. Branwald saw, from the sheer determination on Maloof's face, that he was trying, that he wanted to walk. But Maloof's gaunt face and lifeless eyes when he returned to his couch frightened him.

At last, when his friend sank into a fatigued slumber, Branwald got up and descended the ladder. Dusk was settling in, and in the west the sky was streaked with crimson. He stood on the jetty, looking at the dark trees on the other side of the lake, hearing the evening sounds of the forest creatures and, nearer, the subdued murmur of voices in the adjacent huts.

And then it struck him. There was an air of defeat, of pessimism about this place. Since he had arrived, he had seen no one smile except the woman at the cooking-place and the children. True, Bengue had almost smiled at him, but he could not say that there had been any mirth there. Branwald would not have blamed her if a certain irony had struck her while she looked at him. He, the guardian of the Firebolt, had

201

almost allowed it to kill his friend.

He thought about the coming ceremony. He was sceptical. He did not understand what the old woman meant when she said that Maloof had lost part of his soul, and he could not see how anything she might do would cure him.

He turned to find Morung beside him. 'The night is the worst time,' said Morung quietly. 'It is the time for memories.'

Branwald could find no suitable response. It was not the kind of remark which adults normally make to boys of sixteen. Anyway, he was trying not to remember the events of the previous day. They were too painful.

'The "Firebolt", as you call it,' went on Morung; 'how did you come by it?'

Branwald was not inclined to speak of that fated instrument, but another part of him needed to share the load with an adult. Maloof was very ill, the river downstream was fraught with danger, and he felt less ready than ever to continue with the task that he had undertaken.

'It was given to me by an old soldier,' he said.

'Was his name Bradach?'

Branwald was surprised. 'Yes. Did you know him?'

Morung nodded. 'I saw him once. And he gave you the weapon?'

'He gave it to me, but I ....' Branwald shook his head. He could not go on.

Morung was silent for a while. Then he said, 'Sometimes it is difficult to see the light. But we must struggle against despair. Remember, the only real mistake is the one we do not learn from. We, too, have had our struggle. We have had to live with the knowledge that our loved ones have been enslaved by the Orelord, while we must stand helplessly by, because, as yet, we lack the power to help them. But Bengue has told us many times that our help will come from higher places. Maybe this weapon is what we have been waiting for. Tomorrow, when Maloof is stronger, we will have a council, and we will consider how best we can help you in this undertaking. Till then, my young hero, be of good cheer. After the darkest time, there comes always the dawn.'

~

The ceremony of soul-retrieval was to take place beside the cooking-place. When Bengue gave the word, Maloof's litter was lowered carefully to the ground and carried to a space by the fire, which had already become the centre of a circle made by the small community. Here he was lifted off the litter and laid on a blanket spread on the bare earth. As Branwald took his place in the circle, close to Maloof, he saw two men seated cross-legged to one side, with twin bowl-shaped drums held between their knees.

Bengue, a black figure tinted red by the leaping flames, stood by Maloof until all present were seated and quiet. 'I need the power of the circle to help me in my search,' she said. She took Maloof's right hand in hers, motioning another woman to do likewise with his left. Then she seated herself on the ground beside Branwald and caught his hand with her free one. Without a word, each person in the circle took the hands of those beside them.

'Breathe deeply and slowly,' Bengue said quietly. There was not a sound except the crackling of the fire and the soft breathing of the people. 'We are part of the cycle of life,' the old woman intoned. 'We are connected with all things, with the trees and with the creatures of the forest and of the river, with the air and the soil, the clouds and the moon, the sun and the stars.'

Branwald felt a shiver run up his back. Something strange was happening in his hands. They were becoming warm. His whole body felt the heat. It throbbed through his veins, through his arms and legs. It was as if some powerful energy was swirling around the group, surging and pulsing through him into the old woman and, through her, into Maloof.

'Mother! Mother of all Creation!' Bengue called, her face upturned to the darkness above the encircling trees. 'Help me to find the damaged soul of this young boy. His task is not yet done.'

Bengue stood up, releasing the hands that she held. Her face was copper-bronze in the glow of the fire, but her frail body, to Branwald's eyes, was enveloped in a green-blue glow. From a string on her belt she took a sphere-shaped container, which she held aloft and shook vigorously. A hollow rattling sound filled the clearing and echoed through the trees beyond. The old woman knelt beside Maloof and began to sing, her voice now rising above the rattling, now being drowned by its frantic rhythm. To Branwald's ears, there was no melody in the song. It was a low moaning that rose and fell like the wind around his mother's house on a late-autumn day.

Slowly the noise diminished. Bengue crouched lower and lower over Maloof's still frame. She laid down her rattle and stretched herself full-length on the ground beside the boy, keeping her shoulder, hip and ankle in touch with his. The gathered people sat as still as statues, their eyes fixed on the old woman.

Then the drums began to beat, at first very quietly and slowly. The men playing them moved only their hands. Slowly the rhythm became quicker and the volume increased. Branwald felt his breathing becoming faster. The throbbing beat seemed to have entered his very bones. He closed his eyes. A great darkness beckoned, a darkness in which he could see no light, nor any shape at all. He was floating away, and he did not want to go ....

Abruptly he opened his eyes and stared at the fire. The flames leaped upwards from the white heat at the centre. Branwald shuddered involuntarily, fearful of what was happening to him. The drumming was drawing him into its insidious rhythm, urging him to close his eyes and yield to its frenetic beat. But he resisted it. He consciously slowed his breathing and looked around at the faces nearby. All eyes were on the old woman and Maloof, but even in the flickering firelight he could see that the people were calm, with an air of quiet expectation about them.

The drumming had gone on for a long time when Bengue finally moved. Her arms began to rise slowly, fingers outstretched as if about to grasp something. The drumming stopped.

In the deep silence that followed, Bengue cupped her hands together, as one would to catch a butterfly. She rose, keeping her hands together, and moved round until she was looking down at Maloof's face. Then she knelt, bent low over

204

his forehead, opened her hands slightly and seemed to blow through them onto Maloof's face. This done, she lifted her rattle again and shook it for a long moment over his body.

When at last she stopped, she gently put her hands under Maloof's shoulders and lifted. He sat up. He seemed stronger. Bengue rose to her feet, seeming to pull him with her hands, although they were no longer touching him.

Unsteadily, Maloof stood up. He took one step, then another. A sound like a sigh came from the encircling people. Bengue said aloud, 'Welcome home, Maloof,' and suddenly Branwald could not see for the tears that flooded his eyes.

'Branwald,' Maloof said in a strong voice. 'I am better.'

Blinded with tears, Branwald grabbed his friend in a silent embrace. When he released him, he found the whole community gathering around to touch the healed one with their hands. When Branwald saw that they were smiling, it was too much. Unable to contain his welling emotions, he broke down and wept openly.

The women came to him and engulfed him in motherly embraces; they petted him and crooned soothing words over him, so that he was even less able to stop the great sobs that shook his body. It was only when Sula stood before him, smiling, that he swabbed away the tears with his hand and gulped back the crying.

'Bengue has great power,' she said. She came close to Branwald and kissed him on the cheek. 'And she does not even require you to believe.'

He nodded, but by the time he had found something sensible to say, Sula had moved on.

～

That night Branwald slept on the floor of Morung's hut, beside Maloof. He slept well, waking only once; he stared for a moment in puzzlement at the dim roof-trusses overhead, before the memory of Maloof's recovery came back to him. He listened to Maloof's even breathing beside him and felt relief sweep over him again. A great weight had been lifted off him. He turned and slept once more.

Morning brought sunlight and the sound of children's voices in play. Branwald looked for Maloof but found his sleeping-mat vacant. Rising and looking down from the wide window opening, Branwald found his attention drawn to a small lagoon near the jetty, which had been cut off from the lake by a palisade of stakes driven into its shallow bed. There, amid shouts and squeals of pleasure, Maloof was swimming with a group of bronze-skinned children. He seemed strong and healthy.

Branwald allowed his eyes to wander across the scene before him, realising that he had not really seen it until that moment. The early sun threw long shadows of trees out onto the water, which he thought was not as deep as it had been on the previous day. Above the trees on the other side of the small lake, a few flimsy white clouds drifted across from the west. The rays of the sun held a heat that Branwald had not noticed before. He stayed at the window for a few moments, breathing out his relief. Then he went to join the swimmers.

Later, when the boys were seated on the ground near the cooking-place, eating breakfast — a bowl of bland-tasting mush offered to them by Wayana — Morung approached them with two other men, whom Branwald did not remember seeing before.

'This is Rafik,' said Morung, indicating the taller of his companions.

Branwald got quickly to his feet. He saw a broad-shouldered, straight-backed man, naked to the waist. His wide cheekbones made his chin seem narrow. His long black hair was tied behind his head.

'I am happy to meet you,' Branwald said. 'I wonder if you can tell me about my father, a man called Feowald who was taken by the Orelord's men.'

Rafik's eyes flickered over Maloof before returning to Branwald. His expression was stern.

'I know Feowald,' he said, nodding. 'He was well when I last saw him — as well as any man can be in that place.'

Morung completed the introductions. The man with Rafik, shorter and more fleshy, was called Tass. His forehead was furrowed with creases that gave him an anxious appearance.

'There will be a meeting of the people shortly,' Morung went on. 'We will see what help, if any, we can give to you young warriors. Now I must go and prepare.' He excused himself and went away with the man called Tass.

Rafik stayed, however. From the gridiron which Wayana had rested on a bed of embers, he carefully lifted a grilled fish onto a wooden platter. Then, seating himself, he began to eat the crumbling white flesh, picking it off the bones with his fingers. 'Sit,' he mumbled through a full mouth.

When the boys were seated, Rafik jabbed a piece of fish in Maloof's direction.

'Your father?'

'Brugarh,' Maloof said.

Rafik frowned in recollection. 'He is there. He is a strong one too.' Then he went on chewing.

'Tell us about the place where they are,' Branwald requested.

Rafik finished eating the fish and licked his fingers thoughtfully. 'The Orelord has a passion for metal, any kind of metal, mountains of it. That is why he tears the earth apart, why he strips the trees from her breast and gouges great holes in the hills. To do this, as you know, he needs many workers. So he takes them where he finds them. Your fathers and the others who came with them were unlucky: they were with us, on Oyster Island, on the night when the boats came the second time. Your people wanted to fight, but the men of the Orelord had muskets — long barrels which make a great sound and fling a metal ball no bigger than your thumb, at great speed, in any direction they wish.' The boys exchanged glances. They had met such a weapon already.

'Do you think that our fathers could escape, as you did?' Branwald asked.

Rafik stared into the heart of the fire and shook his head. 'I was lucky. I was brought out to the islands to gather fruits for the Orelord's table. Not many of the workers are allowed to do this.' The muscles in his brown arms rippled as he spread his hands. 'The reeve selected me because I knew the place. We were on the return crossing, at dusk, when the storm struck. It was just one wave.' He shrugged. 'When the boat keeled over, I just swam in the darkness. The others — I do not know what happened.'

'And how did you manage to reach your people here?'

Maloof asked. 'Did you even know where they were?'

'I knew that they had to be somewhere on the river. I searched until I found them. That is another story,' Rafik said. 'But you asked how it is with your fathers. Those who are left in the mine are strong. They have to be. The Orelord will not feed the mouths of those who cannot work any more.' He saw their mute stares and answered the unspoken question. 'He told us — he came into the mine once — that the weak and sick ones would be returned to their homes on the islands when they could work no longer.' His upper lip curled in an ironic sneer. 'But his men always seem to lose them overboard before they reach the islands. The great lizards have grown used to this.'

'How many hours to the mine?' Branwald interjected, peeling the hide covering from around the Firebolt and spreading the map of the Great River on the ground between himself and Rafik. The man examined the skin with curiosity.

'It is less than a day's paddling. You see the islands there?' Rafik pointed to the river's mouth. 'Well, just west of them, on the mainland, there are cliffs and a mountain which we call the Red Mount. Around here.' His finger jabbed at a point on the map. 'There is a great hole in that mountain, which is made mostly of iron; much of it has been carried away in the ships of the Orelord. Week after week they come, fill their holds and sail east to the Smoking Lands, far beyond where the sun rises.'

'And the workers, where do they live? *How* do they live?' Branwald asked.

'The workers used to live underground, in the old mine shafts. It was easier for the Orelord to guard them down there. But when he found the tunnel that the men were digging, he built long huts inside a stockade, and now the workers are crammed into them every night. The pit itself, the Bastion — that's the Orelord's tower, where the women are kept — and the stockade are surrounded by an iron palisade more than twice the height of a man. There are guards posted day and night.' Rafik glanced at Branwald through narrowed eyes. 'It would take an army to rescue anyone from there, and you know that we have no army.'

His eyes fell on the Firebolt lying on the ground beside him. Reaching over, he took it by the handle and pointed it at the trees overhead. 'Maybe with this thing,' Rafik said, more loudly, 'a man could —'

'Do not hold it like that,' Branwald told him, in alarm. The blade glowed white and the beam played among the high branches overhead. Rafik held the Firebolt away from Branwald, a half-smile playing on his lips.

'A man might do great things ....' Rafik repeated.

He was interrupted by a loud creaking from overhead. 'Watch out!' Maloof shouted, scrambling away. Branwald glanced up and saw a thick bough falling towards him. He leaped to one side, grabbing Rafik's arm. Pulled suddenly off balance, the man rolled onto his back — not a moment too soon. A nine-foot-long bough crashed onto the ground where he had been sitting.

With an exclamation, Rafik dropped the Firebolt onto the ground. Its light died immediately.

'Espirit!' exclaimed Rafik. 'What thing is that?'

Branwald did not respond. He picked up the Firebolt and returned it to its wrappings. Several people who had been passing stood in wonder. Branwald heard the whisperings. 'Come on,' he said to Maloof. 'It is time for the meeting.'

The meeting, attended by the adults of the community, was held in the large thatch-roofed building near the smoke-house. Many of the adults were already there, seated on low frame benches, when the boys entered. There was a hush as they took their seats. Branwald saw Sula seated on the opposite side, and waved to her. She smiled in reply.

Then Morung came in, followed by several men and women. His upper body was bare, except for a short cape made of different-coloured strips of furred hide. He wore the strangest head-dress that Branwald had ever seen. A long blue cloth had been wound around his head; over this had been placed what looked like the jawbones of some strange creature. However, where another animal would have had a single row of teeth, this one had many rows in each jaw, each row smaller than the one outside it. The teeth were pointed like the blades of a saw, and they sloped inwards, towards where the throat of the animal had once been.

When the others had taken their seats and quietness had descended, Morung addressed the attentive audience.

'People of the Tarquan Islands, and young men from the Islands of the North, when the history of our people is written, these days, I believe, will be memorable ones. And whether these will be named among the great or among the sorrowful days, I cannot yet tell.

'We all remember the joyous time, over two years ago, when our brothers from the far north came down the river to tell us that Feyan's people still lived, when we had for so many years given them up for dead. We all had been taught, too, the legend of Bradach, the great warrior of our race who took it upon himself to carry the Firebolt into the wilderness. For some of us, it was just that — a legend. But now we know that the legend is true. The Firebolt has come back, and its bearer is one of our own people. And we meet here today to decide what we must do.'

In silence Morung gazed around at the people; in silence they gazed back at him. 'We have suffered. Our people are still suffering. Some of you will say that we have suffered enough, that there is no need to bring further sorrow upon these last remains of the Tarquan People. But the Firebolt has been sent back to us. We cannot ignore that fact.'

Branwald looked at the faces of the people. He felt, as he had felt before, the great sadness among them, and he understood that their loss was as great as his.

A woman spoke from the centre of the room. 'I have lost a husband, a son and a daughter to the Orelord. I know my children still live. Rafik has said so. And Emix may still be ....' Her voice faltered, but quickly recovered. 'What I want to say is this. If anything could be done to bring them back — to bring all the others back — I am prepared to suffer more. I know that I cannot fight against the metal boats and the muskets, but maybe the Firebolt ... maybe now something can be done.'

A murmur of support swept through the gathering.

Another woman's voice, shrill and petulant. 'We have lost enough, I say. We saw what those muskets can do to our men.

We have no protection against those. We would only lose more.'

The first woman spoke again. 'You have not lost a husband or a son, Sister Onida. Your husband and children escaped on that black night. It is easy for you to talk.'

Then Rafik spoke. 'I know the Firebolt has come back, but what has that to do with us? What good is it to have an instrument that will destroy the bearer if he tries to defeat his enemies with it? It would be better simply to give it to the Orelord and let him destroy himself with it. Then, if he is gone, his men will not continue this rabid quest for metals. They will go back to where they came from.'

'Yes!' another woman called stridently. 'And before they leave they will feed the rest of our men and women to the lizards, and go home laughing at the sport they have had!' Another murmur of approval.

'Do not misunderstand me,' Rafik responded. 'As you all know, my Leah is still in the Bastion of the Orelord. I say that we cannot leave those whom we love in his hands any longer. All I say is that we must not rely completely on this weapon. The boy who carries it is brave, but he is also young and he has little experience of such a powerful thing as the Firebolt.'

Branwald rose to his feet, not sure what he was going to say, but needing to speak. All eyes turned towards him. 'I know that the Orelord wants the Firebolt. That is why he sent Urkor and his men to our islands. But I fear what he would do if we were to give him this weapon. In the hands of such a man, the Firebolt would only increase its power for destruction.' The eyes of the people bored into him. Their faces were grave.

'And what evidence is there that in your hands it will be any better?' Rafik's voice was surprisingly harsh.

Branwald took a deep breath. 'I do not yet know the Firebolt well. And I have not always used it, or allowed it to be used, well. It is a very powerful weapon and can do great harm, it is true. But I believe that it can do great good, too, and I am determined to learn to use it properly.' He sat down, surprised at what he had said.

Rafik spoke again, and his tone was mocking. 'And does this

mean that we must wait until such time as young Branwald has learned how to use the thing? How long will that be? By that time all our people could be dead ....'

Maloof stood up. His voice was strong and vibrant. 'The Firebolt was given to Branwald for a reason. I was sent with him for a reason. That reason is not clear to us yet, but the Mother Spirit knows. I believe that our destiny, whatever it may be, lies waiting for us at the end of the river. I feel certain that it involves our fathers, and another one also. That is why Branwald and I must and will continue our journey. If you can help us, that will be good. If not, then let it be so.'

In the silence that followed, Branwald listened with his mind to the people around him. He felt a wave of admiration and sympathy directed towards himself and Maloof.

Morung spoke again. 'There are many of us who want these brave lads to succeed.' Another murmur of approval. 'Therefore, I propose that we form a band of volunteers to travel with them as far as the Arms of Kiura and the Citadel. There will be little danger if we are careful. From the high Citadel we will be able to see the Red Mount and the movement of the ships in the Strait. After that, we can decide what should be done. But we must act now. The task must be attempted before the man Urkor returns, and before he, or others, can tell the Orelord that the Firebolt is approaching. Is there anybody who opposes this course of action?' There was a long silence, with much exchanging of glances. Rafik sat in silence, looking at the floor.

'It is decided,' said Morung. 'We will prepare immediately.'

~

It was agreed that the expedition would set out before first light on the following morning. If the rains came, the party would take the direct route and follow the river. If not, they would keep to the sheltered, winding channels which would allow them to make ground towards the river's mouth. Then, when dusk fell, they would take to the river.

Three men and — to Branwald's surprise — one woman were selected for the journey. In his canoe, Morung would take Atula, a lean young woman whose eyesight and hearing were known to be above the ordinary, and who, according to

Morung, could endure hardship as well as or better than most men. In the second canoe would be Rafik, who, despite his doubts about the mission's success, was anxious to go. His offer was accepted by the assembly because of his experiences in the mine. With him would be Targye, the man who had helped Branwald out of his canoe when they first arrived. Maloof and Branwald would travel in their own canoe.

The remainder of the day would be spent in making preparations: in gathering the necessary supplies and in readying the canoes, spare paddles and weapons.

CHAPTER TWENTY-THREE

'**I** must go into the forest to gather fruits,' Sula said to the two boys, when they emerged from the meeting-house. 'Would you like to come?'

Before they could answer, however, Maloof was surrounded by a waiting crowd of children who clamoured for him to go with them to Dusky Stream, where the crayfish were 'thick', as Hedin put it. He protested only mildly as they dragged him away. Branwald shrugged his shoulders. 'I will go to gather fruits with you,' he said.

The two young people put the Firebolt and Sula's bow and arrows on the floor of Branwald's canoe and set off along the winding creek that led back towards the river. After a short time, Branwald noticed something that puzzled him.

'Why is the water flowing towards us from the river?' he asked.

'That is the tide,' Sula said.

Branwald disliked displaying his ignorance, but he wanted to know. 'Tide?'

She glanced back at him, as if to see if he was joking. 'The ocean. It rises and falls twice every day, and the flood comes up the river each time. It is nothing,' she said dismissively. 'My father says that it is caused by the moon, but he has some strange beliefs. Come. We must turn here.' She indicated a narrow creek, and Branwald guided the canoe into its mouth. Here the water was shallower and the trees formed a continuous canopy overhead.

'I am going to ask Father if I can go with you tomorrow,' Sula announced, as the canoe drifted along a darkening pool.

'He will not allow you,' Branwald said. 'It would be too dangerous.'

'You think that girls cannot be brave,' she scoffed.

'No,' he said, remembering Aiyan, the frail daughter of the White Ones. 'But I think that fathers love their daughters too much to allow them to be in danger.'

'I think it is necessary,' Sula stated. 'What you are trying to do is important for us. There are many whom we love in the Orelord's mines, and we would sacrifice much to gain their safe return. But I feel frustrated that there is so little we can do to help you. We have no army of fighting men. Yes, maybe it is your destiny to go to the end, as Maloof said; but maybe your destiny depends upon others, on people like my father and me. We must do what we can, even if there is some danger.'

'But there is nothing that you can do that your father —'

'But there is, you see.' She turned to regard him with bright eyes. 'You can talk to me in the mind-voice, and I can talk to you. Think what that could mean. Even if I or my father cannot be with you in your danger, you could speak your thoughts to me, you could tell us what is happening, and if there is anything that we can do to help you.'

Branwald thought about that. In his mind a voice was saying that he would not need the help of others in the ordeal that lay ahead. He, Branwald, bearer of the Firebolt, would sweep away all obstacles in his path until he came face to face with the Orelord, that cruel tyrant who had enslaved his people. When that moment came, he would force this despot to cower before him, to send out orders that all the prisoners were to be set free ....

But another voice was impinging. What about Urkor? He was the only Oreman Branwald had met. And he was only a messenger. How much more formidable would his lord be? Yes, Branwald would need help, as much help as he could get. And even if he and Maloof were alone and isolated somewhere in the domain of the Orelord, it would be a great comfort to hear the voice of a friend and to speak to that friend, even if only to ask what Morung, an adult, would advise.

'I will be with you when you ask your father,' Branwald said. 'I think you should come.'

They had arrived at a place where the trees parted to allow

215

in the daylight. Branwald saw round green fruits hanging low, near the water's surface; he guided the canoe close to the heavy branches, and Sula started to pick the fruits and drop them onto the floor of the canoe. Curious, Branwald pulled a fruit from a nearby branch. There was no aroma from the deep green skin, and when he pressed it with his fingers, they made a small indentation in the solid flesh.

'We call these greenfruit,' Sula said. 'They do not taste sweet, but they give energy on long journeys.'

On the way back, Branwald asked a question that had been bothering him. 'Do the women and girls who have been taken by the Orelord also work in the mines?'

'Some of them do, Rafik says. And others prepare the food for the soldiers and the workers.' Sula paused for a moment. 'They live in the Bastion which the Orelord has built. Rafik said that some are forced to bear the Orelord's children.'

Into Branwald's mind came an image of Urkor. He remembered the way that the man's cold eyes had looked upon Estel's body, and he felt again in his mind the carnal violence of the thought.

'I would rather die than be one of those,' Sula said quietly.

The rain started before they reached the settlement. It came down in heavy straight lines, and in no time the young people were saturated. There was no discomfort in the deluge, however. Branwald lifted his face to the huge warm drops and allowed his body to soak in the refreshing torrent.

'On the islands,' remarked Sula, sweeping wet strands of hair from her face, 'my people used to say, "The raindrops are the tears of the Earth Mother".'

Back at the jetty, Branwald held the canoe while Sula placed the wet green fruit on the wooden planks. Bending over her, he saw the clear olive skin of her neck and shoulders, and the way her soaked bodice clung to her firm round breasts. He watched her slender fingers purposefully lifting the wet fruit. Glancing up at him, Sula caught his unguarded look. Her eyes held his for a moment and they smiled, although her mouth remained serious.

Then, with a start, Branwald remembered that she could read his mind, and he was embarrassed.

'I am sorry,' he mumbled. Sula's eyebrows arched in query. 'I was staring,' he explained.

Her teeth flashed in a smile. 'Do you not have girls on the Islands of the North?' she said.

After they had delivered the greenfruit to the store hut, they found Morung and Targye in the communal house, applying steaming pitch to the hull of a canoe. The rain drummed faintly against the thick thatch overhead.

Sula waited until Targye had gone to get some new mooring-rope before she spoke to her father.

'Father, I want to go with you tomorrow.'

Morung looked at her, then at Branwald, and then back at her. He dabbed at the congealing pitch with a piece of flat bone. 'You cannot come, Sula. You know that. It would be too —'

'No, Father. Please listen to me.'

Morung put down his spatula and turned calmly to look at Sula. She argued as she had with Branwald, her eyes flashing and her hands gesticulating. Her father listened without interruption, watching her placidly. When she had finished, he stared at the damp clay underfoot for several moments.

'If your mother were alive,' he began, shaking his head slowly, 'she would lash me with her tongue for even considering taking you.' He looked at Branwald. 'What do you think, young man?'

'I ... I do not know what she would have said ....' Branwald stammered.

'No. I mean about taking Sula.'

Branwald chose his words. 'I think that Sula should not be put into any danger' — he heard her gasp of disbelief — 'unless there is a very good reason for doing so. But I also think that if the Orelord is to be defeated, it will not be by Maloof and me alone. We will need help. And it would help if there were someone with whom we might speak in thought. But I do not know about the place where you intend to go — how safe it is. If there is a risk that Sula could be taken by the Orelord's men, then she should not go.'

Morung nodded in agreement. He heaved a long sigh. 'You speak wisely,' he said. 'There are many things that I would risk for the sake of defeating the Orelord. But you, my little flower, you are not one of them. I will speak with Rafik, and then we will talk again.'

～

'Well, at least he did not refuse outright,' Branwald remarked, as the two picked their way through rivulets of rain on the earthen path that led back to the cooking-place.

Sula shook her head. 'I know him,' she said. 'He will not let me go.'

～

The afternoon was a busy one for the boys. First they had to carry their canoe into the large hut, where it was inspected by Targye. He coated the lower part of its hull with fresh pitch, pared off the feathery perished wood from the blades of the paddles, and replaced the mooring-ropes. Then he set the three young ones to work — Sula could not be excluded from the preparations — gathering the supplies for the journey. There were dried fish to be wrapped, salt and dried fruit to be measured out and tied in small leather pouches, and greenfruit to be wiped and stored in larger sacks.

While this work was in progress, the men worked on their weapons. Morung's deft hands fashioned several dozen new arrows from straight rods; he filed the metal heads until the points scored the skin of his thumb when he ran it lightly over them. Then there were fish-hooks and lines to be sorted and rolled so that they could be readied in seconds.

Atula brought in a large roll of a blue transparent material similar to that from which Morung's and Sula's capes were made. She measured Branwald and Maloof for size and carefully cut out two capes from the roll. 'It is not very comfortable being wet all the time,' she said in explanation.

Branwald was curious. 'How did you make this?' he asked.

'We did not make it,' she replied. 'It was made by the Old People, before the Dark Time. We found it in the ruins.'

Maloof's eyes widened. 'There was nothing like this in the ruins that we saw.'

'Eastwards from our islands, along the coasts, there are many ruined cities of the Old People.'

'Did you find other things as well?' Maloof asked.

Atula shrugged her shoulders. 'There were other things, but we have no use for them. Our fathers took only what they could use.'

$\sim$

Dusk fell early, but the rain did not stop. Before the people retired to their huts, Morung called them together in the meeting-house. Bengue was there, with her rattles and her crystal. When all were assembled, Morung called the six venturers to stand in the space in the centre. At Bengue's request, the seated ones joined hands, and the six in the centre joined hands with one another; then the old woman became the link connecting the outer circle with the six in the middle. Immediately Branwald, who was holding Targye's hand on one side and Maloof's on the other, felt a tingling surge of energy sweeping in through one arm and out through the other.

'The Life-Force of your people go with you,' the old woman intoned. 'And may the Great Mother Spirit guard you until it is time for you to return to Her.'

She continued to speak, but her words were unintelligible to Branwald. The sounds became a chant, rising and falling in a weird cadence that gave him a strange feeling. He became aware of the warmth in his stomach, in his limbs. He felt that he was a small part of a greater whole. He felt strength and support and love coming from the people around him.

Silence fell, but still nobody moved. Branwald closed his eyes, listening to his own regular breathing, hearing the patter of rain on the roof. When he opened them, he found Bengue's eyes fixed upon him. Her expression was kindly, but her gaze was so fixed that he could not look away.

He felt the grip on each of his hands tighten. The old woman began to speak softly, looking at him, addressing him as if there were no one else in the room.

'Remember,' she whispered, 'evil can only hurt those who yield to their dark side. Even if we fail, we only fail if we have yielded to the Dark. Remember the Good, Branwald. Remember the Light. Remember the Love, the Love, the Love.'

Bengue's voice faded away to nothing.

Then, in the silence, there came the rustle of people rising to their feet. In silence, they came to Branwald and touched him with their hands, as they had touched Maloof. He had never in his life felt so alive, so full of strength, so valued by others.

~

A short while later, when Sula and the boys had climbed up into Morung's hut to prepare for the night, Branwald asked Sula if her father had said anything.

'He said that I cannot come,' she said. In the dim light of the candle, Branwald saw her face and felt her disappointment.

'With luck, we will not be away for many days,' he consoled her. 'What is to be done should not take long.'

Sula smiled at him in the gloom. 'Be careful, Branwald,' she whispered. Her fingers gripped his hand. 'And come back to us.' She stood unmoving before him, her hand gripping his, her head bowed. Instinctively Branwald put his arms around her. She rested her head against his shoulder.

'Maybe even from the mouth of the river I will be able to speak with you in thought,' he said.

'But you will be so far,' she whispered. 'And I will be so helpless!'

There was nothing left to say, so he held her till, after several minutes, she pulled back from him. 'I'm sorry,' she said. 'I shouldn't be .... It will be hard enough for you.'

'I will come back soon,' Branwald promised, touching her cheek with his hand.

~

It was that still, grey time just before dawn when the boys were shaken awake by Morung.

'It is time to go,' he whispered.

They dressed in silence and followed Morung towards the place of the fire. Before descending from the hut, Branwald glanced at Sula's still form on the floor of the living area, but there was no sign that she was aware of his leaving. It was just as well, he thought.

The rain had stopped, but the trees were still dripping as the boys neared the fire. Targye, Rafik, Atula and several other adults were already seated, eating a savoury broth that Wayana had prepared. As they ate, other people appeared out of the dimness under the huts and gathered quietly round the ones who were leaving. There was little said.

It was the work of a few minutes for the helpers to ready the three canoes and stock them with the cargo, which had been stored under Morung's hut. The first canoe was being lowered into the water when Branwald saw Sula descending by the ladder. She was wearing her transparent cape and carrying a bulging satchel.

Morung stopped what he was doing to watch her drop to the wharf and turn towards him. Her face was pale and set.

'Father,' she said, and there was a ringing quality about her voice. 'I want to go with you. I must go with you.'

Morung looked at her standing defiantly before him. 'Sula,' he said. 'This is the first time you have gone against my wishes.'

'Father,' she challenged again, 'will I be in more danger with you than I would be if the men of the Orelord come to this place when you are gone?'

'Sula —'

'You cannot stop me from following you!' she declared, her eyes sparking with determination.

Morung looked around at the sober faces of his people and sighed. 'You remind me of your mother,' he said. 'Come on. Sit in the centre of my canoe, and may the Mother who has given you life protect you.'

～

The party set off amidst a chorus of farewells. Branwald waited till the others had pulled away before pushing in behind Rafik's long canoe. He waved at the still figures on the wharf, wondering when he would see them again. Then the crowding trees slid across his view and they were gone.

It was good to be paddling again, Branwald thought. And it was different now, too. Before, he and Maloof had been alone in this vast wilderness of trees and waterways. Now they were paddling in the company of people who, though virtual strangers, seemed close to him in the way that his own family were close. There was comfort in that knowledge.

No matter what lay ahead at the mouth of the Great River, at least he and Maloof would face it knowing that there were friends close by.

Now, however, there were more pressing concerns. The adults in front were paddling at a furious pace, and the boys had to buckle to it to keep up. The 'tide', however, was flowing with them, so that they moved past the grey water-side trees at remarkable speed.

The dawn came quickly. In the east, fluffy clouds showed soft gold underbellies as the first rays of sunlight caught them. There would be no rain this morning. It seemed that they would not be able to take the open river route.

Their route took them through a maze of channels towards the south-west. Several times they had to portage across marshy flats and over low forested ridges.

At last, as they wound westwards along a tree-walled creek, Branwald saw the twin black arches of a bridge crossing the channel ahead. Though smothered in places by plants and creepers, the mottled stonework still showed through.

'This is the Bridge of Kraga,' Morung said quietly. 'Here is the road of the Old Ones that the Galians used to use.'

When they reached the bridge, the others waited while Morung hacked with his machete to clear a passage for the canoes to the muddy bank. A short time later the canoes lay on the layer of matted grass that was the surface of the roadway.

Branwald examined the bridge and the raised causeway that led away from it in both directions. The roadway, bounded on either side by a low moss-draped wall, was about twenty paces wide. Along its grassy covering ran a track such as animals of the forest might make. Southwards, this path was overhung by bushes and trees; not far from the bridge, it disappeared into the dense growth.

'We will eat now,' said Morung. 'Then we will portage.'

The meal of dried fish and fruit, washed down with musty-tasting draughts from the animal-skin bottles, was quickly over. Then it was time to move. Morung was anxious that by nightfall they should have reached a point near the left bank of the Great River, opposite their destination, the Arms of Kiura, which lay on the distant right bank. Then, in the late dusk or early dawn, they would make the crossing.

As he and Maloof struggled through the undergrowth with the laden canoe, Branwald could not but recall the fateful day — such a long time before, it seemed — when they had set out on their search for the mouth of the Great River. The portage through the pine woods of the Forest People had seemed much easier. Now Branwald's tunic, soaked with perspiration, clung to his back, and the slapping branches stung his arms and legs.

'Where does this road lead to?' he asked Sula.

'The Old People made them to go from one of their great villages to the next,' she said. 'They had great machines, Father says, that could move without horses along these roads, just as the boats of the Oremen can travel along the water without paddles or paddlers.'

'How do the boats do this?'

'Father says that they have a fire in the boats, which makes steam out of water, and in some way this can make the boats move across the water.'

'I wish we had one of them now,' Branwald said. 'Then we wouldn't have to labour in this way.'

'Father would not travel in one. He says that the Orelord is just like the Old People. He is continuing where the Old People left off, plundering the earth, with no care for the future. Father says that in the Orelord's land the sky is black with choking clouds of smoke, the rivers are poisoned beyond recovery, the trees stand withered on the hillsides.'

'Is this why he has left his homeland and come to the mouth of the Great River?'

Sula shook her head. 'They say that when he has taken what he wants from here, he will return again to his homeland. His mastery of metal gives him power in his own land, Father says, and now he cannot do without it. He has to have more and more of it.'

'But what does he do with it?' Branwald asked.

She shrugged her shoulders. 'You must ask Father this. I do not know. He makes boats, of course, and Rafik says that the Bastion is made of metal which is so strong that even the bolts from the Oremen's muskets would not be able to pierce it. It is big enough to house hundreds of people, and in it the Orelord is said to have everything that he wants, living a life of ease, doing no work.'

'We know that there is one other thing that he wants,' said Maloof. 'He thinks it will give him all the power he needs.'

Branwald was silent. He tried to imagine the Orelord. What did he look like? What kind of man was he? Did he talk and eat and sleep and love like other men? Or was he hard and cold and unyielding, like the metal that he so coveted?

'We do not know what the Orelord is like,' Sula said, answering his unspoken question. 'Rafik is the only one of our people who has seen him.'

'What is his face like?' Maloof asked.

'Rafik says that none of the captives is allowed to look upon his face, on pain of death. But he also says that the Orelord's eyes are black. So he must have looked at him.'

In the tangled growth on both sides of the roadway, they began once again to see the overgrown ruins of buildings. Branwald was consumed with curiosity about these dark relics of the Old People, but he knew from Morung's purposeful gait that he would have no time to explore them.

In the late afternoon, the little party stopped by a trickling stream to eat. All were tired, Sula having taken over the paddling from Atula several times. They had been travelling along a straight track for hours, and the land around and below them had become more marshy. The animal track along the top of the causeway had made the going easier, however.

While they were resting by the stream, a plump bird, slightly larger than the doves of Feyansdoon, fluttered down to land on the sandy bottom of the stream near them. Targye, the silent one, picked up his bow with slow fluid movements, slipped in an arrow and, while the others remained as still as statues, shot the bird clean through the breast. Branwald heard the man muttering some words as he dispatched the creature with a twist of his hand, and he thought of the two Foresters, Mitko and Chenk, on the slopes of Eagle Mountain.

Soon after that, they came to a wider body of water, over which another bridge, half-smothered in greenery, carried the ancient roadway. Shading their eyes against the sun, Morung and the other adults studied the new channel winding away westwards towards the river.

'This is the one,' Rafik said. 'This is the way I came.' He pointed at the water below the parapet of the bridge. 'Down there you will find the old canoe.' Branwald looked down, but he could see only black water. 'Just round yonder point,' Rafik went on, 'you will see the ocean. The Arms of Kiura are directly across.'

They decided to go no further on that day, the sun being directly in their eyes. They would make camp, retire early and set off before sunrise on the morrow.

They found a patch of ground below the causeway where a large tree had toppled during a recent storm, leaving a wide bare patch where the roots had lifted the soil as it fell. Here they made a fire and cooked the bird which Targye had shot.

Later, in the soft light of dusk, the three young ones strolled back across the bridge while the adults prepared the sleeping-places. Branwald's mood was sombre. His curiosity about the ruins of the Old People, so pressing earlier, was blunted. Thoughts of the morrow filled his mind.

'What are the Arms of Kiura?' he asked Sula, when they had seated themselves at the top of a steep slope that fell down to the water's edge.

'It is a place where the ships of the Old Ones used to come. Father says that those ships were many times bigger than even the Orelord's ships. A large number of the Old People must have lived there, because there are many of the old houses there. The Citadel is a great fortress on the highest part of Kiura. From it you can see the islands and the Veyan Straits, and the Red Mount where the Orelord has his mines.' Sula reached towards a yellow-barked shrub to touch a delicate bud with her fingers. 'When I was young, before the Dark One came, we often went to the Arms to look at the Old People's places.'

Maloof spoke. 'Is there a way from there to the Red Mount?'

'My people have always travelled by sea. But they say

225

there is another way like this one, a road of the Old People.' Sula turned to Branwald. 'I wish I could come with you, but I know Father will not let me go beyond Kiura ....'

'You will be able to help by speaking with us when we have left you. And we will tell you what is happening, and you can tell your father.'

'I have only known you for a few short days,' she said. 'And now I am fearful that I will not see you again for a long time. Maybe never. Promise me that you will be careful, that you will come back soon.'

Branwald looked into her wide, dark eyes, not wanting to disappoint her, yet unable to deceive her. 'We cannot promise,' he said. 'We do not know what the future holds. But ....'

'We will come back,' said Maloof, 'if the Mother Spirit wishes it to be so.'

Sula did not reply. She sat beside Branwald, looking towards a sunset sky that spread its pink and orange and gold along the surface of the water.

Maloof rose to his feet. 'I will walk in the forest for a while,' he said, excusing himself.

Watching him go, Branwald frowned. There was something about Maloof that was different. It was a quietness, an aloofness, as if part of him was away in some distant place and did not want to come back.

'What has happened to him?' Sula asked. Again she had read Branwald's thoughts.

'I do not know,' Branwald said.

'He has been to a place that we have not been to,' she said quietly. 'What was he like before?'

Branwald frowned again. He had never had to answer such a question before. 'Maloof,' he said, 'is like a brother to me. He was lost to me for a long time, but he came back.'

He saw the question in Sula's eyes, so he told her about Maloof's banishment from Feyansdoon, about the loneliness he had felt after that loss, and about their reunion above the Karn Gorge. 'Maloof is stronger than I am. He has learned something from the Forest People that I have yet to learn. Maloof has less fear than I have. I could not have come this far without him. But now, there is something there .... I do not know whether to fear it or befriend it.'

'You must take great care, Branwald. Maloof may need you yet.'

Branwald sensed Sula's warm caring and admiration, and he felt strongly the connection that had grown between them in those short few days.

'With Maloof and you near me, I will be stronger,' he said. 'And I will come back.'

CHAPTER TWENTY-FOUR

It was still dark when Branwald was shaken out of his sleep by Targye. 'Come on, young warrior,' whispered the man. 'It is time to cross the Great River.'

Even in the light of the hazy half-moon, Branwald could see the still blanket of fog hanging over the water. He rose, keeping his cloak around him, and stood by the newly-roused fire until the cold of the hard ground had melted out of his body. In silence he ate the leathery fish and the tart fruit that Rafik gave him. In a short time they were ready to set out.

They hugged the left-hand margin of the inlet as they paddled westwards into the ghostly fog. There was no sound save the dipping of the paddles and the occasional knock where a blade touched the side of a canoe. Slowly the left-hand shore swung southwards, and before them lay a sinister grey emptiness, the wide estuary of the Great River.

The canoes halted. 'Keep close together,' Morung warned. 'The river will flow from right to left as we cross. Remember, sound carries a great distance over open water, so watch your paddles.'

In the grey light of dawn, they turned away from the sheltering trees and set off into the silent mist. The enveloping grey-white cloud closed in behind them, cutting them off from the sight of any object except for the other canoes. They paddled with long, silent strokes, dipping and lifting the blades carefully, so that the only sound was the rhythmic swish of the prows with each forward thrust. Everything beyond the margins of the fog was muffled into silence.

When they had been proceeding for what seemed a long while, Branwald became uneasy. The far bank should surely have appeared by now, he thought. He checked the direction of the current beneath him, thinking that maybe they had become disorientated in the fog and veered off course. The flow still moved from right to left, however; they were still on the crossing. Yet Branwald's unease did not lessen. Frowning, he scanned the greyness to his right.

Maloof turned in his seat. 'What is it?' he asked.

'I don't know,' Branwald whispered. 'Just something ... coming.'

The canoes ahead were slowing. Morung had his hand up in a signal for silence. Then Atula, her canoe facing upstream, cupped her hands behind her ears and became perfectly still. Branwald listened too, but could hear no sound. He watched Atula's face. Her eyes were wide, her mouth tense.

Suddenly she dropped her hands and grasped her paddle. 'Get off the river!' she said. 'The Oremen are coming!'

The next half-minute seemed to last for hours. Branwald's whole existence shrank to a single-minded, frantic effort to keep in touch with Rafik and Atula's canoe. He was aware of nothing but this and the fear — fear of the threat that lay in the fog upstream.

Then, to his relief, he saw a shape looming out of the river — something like a low ridge topped by bushes. As Branwald drew closer, he saw that it was a high wall. Morung abruptly changed course, and Branwald followed. In the mist ahead, a gap appeared in the massive barrier. Moments later the three canoes were powering through it.

They were in a calm place where the water, cut off from the sweep of the current, was smooth and still. Morung altered his course to follow the base of the wall, along which grew clumps of stunted trees and bushes. Branwald became aware of the thought, 'The Arms of Kiura', and in his relief he replied, 'Thanks to the Spirit!'

Morung again held up his hand, and the others stopped paddling and listened. In the distance they heard a muffled, continuous throbbing sound from somewhere upstream. It was coming closer.

Morung bent to his paddling again. Branwald, last in line, felt his scalp tingle as he searched the mist ahead for the end of the wall, where the land should be. Not far away, a clump of trees bulged out from the stonework, their fronds touching the water's surface; Morung swung his craft in behind them, and the others followed.

They listened again. The throbbing was coming closer. Branwald clearly heard men's voices on the still air. Although he could not see, he followed them towards where he thought the gap in the enclosing wall should be, waiting for them to pass the still space, listening for the sudden muffling that would tell him they had gone on downriver.

But the sound was not fading. The throbbing of the boat became faster. It was growing louder.

Morung began to drive the nose of his canoe into the foliage beside him. 'Quick! In here!' he growled. Rafik was aiming a little to his left. Branwald picked a spot closer to the wall and drove the canoe into the trees. There was a brushing and slapping of wet leaves against his face and a rasping of the prow against branches. Then a wall of greenery closed behind him. He came to a stop in a low, leafy cavern crisscrossed with heavy branches. He readied himself to climb out of the canoe and along the branches towards the wall, but when he glanced at the others, they were sitting motionless, their heads turned, listening.

Branwald reached down and slipped the wrappings off the Firebolt. The throbbing became louder still. Branwald was certain that the boat was coming in through the gap.

Then the harsh coughing was right beside them, moving slowly past. There was a strange pungent smell, as of burning pitch. Branwald felt the canoe rise and fall as the bow wave from the boat slid under it. He crouched low, fearful that at any moment the weapon on the prow of the craft would spit fire into the trees. He looked again at the Firebolt, a part of him wanting to take it in his hand, but Maloof was watching him, shaking his head and thinking, 'No, Branwald. Wait!'

The seconds crawled by, and the boat drifted away from them. It circled slowly within the Arms; then it started to move towards the left. 'They are going,' thought Maloof, his face calm and serious. A man's guttural laugh drifted across to the listeners, and Branwald looked again at the Firebolt.

Then, suddenly, the sound of the boat was muffled. The travellers held their breath. The throbbing faded away, until at last they could hear it no more.

For a long time no one spoke. Then Morung carefully moved aside the curtain of leaves and peered out. 'They are gone,' he said. 'Come on. Make for the ruins.'

Out in the open again, Branwald saw that the fog had lifted enough to show part of the river's surface outside the gap in the wall. He was in a wide triangular space enclosed on two sides by the huge, curving Arms of Kiura. On the third side, less than a hundred paces away, he saw a jumble of trees along a walled shore. Even the blanket of greenery could not disguise the ruined buildings which stood, square and silent, along the water's edge. Behind them the land, littered with further ruins amongst the invading jungle, rose steeply into the rising fog.

Branwald was silent. He was trying to hide the thought that had remained in his mind after the fear had gone. He watched Maloof's back for any sign that his friend knew what was there.

'Yes, Branwald,' the thought came back. 'I felt him too.' Beyond all shadow of a doubt, Urkor had been on the boat of the Orelord.

Branwald caught Sula, close by in her father's canoe, watching him intently, and he was certain that she knew. 'Do not say anything yet,' he pleaded in his mind. 'If they know that he has been here, they will want to return to the village.'

Sula nodded. 'I will not tell,' she thought.

The Islanders located a set of stone steps, hidden among the trees along the waterfront, and drew the canoes up them onto a cleared space in the shelter of a crumbling wall. Leaving them there, Morung led the way up another set of leaf-littered steps to an elevated terrace bounded on three sides by a low parapet; the fourth side, furthest from the river, was the wall of a roofless ruin. The floor of this area had once been tiled, but the joints between the tiles were tufted with a chequered pattern of grasses. Looking out over the eastern parapet, Branwald saw the silver surface of the river at the mouth of the harbour and, in the distance, the faint dark line of the eastern shore.

Sula came to stand beside him. 'He was on the boat,

wasn't he?' she said quietly.

He could not lie to her. 'Yes. How did you know?'

'I felt something — something dark and cold.' She paused, and her eyes read his face. 'Do you think he knows we are here?'

'That was the thought I had. But maybe it is just ....' He did not want to admit that it might have been his fear.

She gripped his arm. 'But if he knew, Branwald, why did he go away?'

He shook his head. 'I do not know. He is a devious one.'

'We should tell my father and the others.'

'No, Sula. Not yet. Just give me a little time. If he is still near, I will know — soon.'

'I do not like it, Branwald. We may be in danger. I must say something ....'

'Just wait till I return, will you? I will go and look.'

Sula made to go with him, but her father's voice came from below: 'Come on, Sula. There are things to carry and food to prepare!'

With the Firebolt and his bow and quiver slung at his back, Branwald slipped away. He climbed upwards on a narrow path that showed signs of having been cleared within the past few years. There were algae-stained tree-stumps jutting from the cracked pavement, and here and there piles of rotting branches had been pushed to one side. He turned left along a wider way, crowded with young saplings and low-hanging boughs and flanked on both sides by roofless ruins. This way would take him towards the southern arm of the harbour, behind which the Oremen's boat had disappeared.

When a fallen tree blocked his way, Branwald climbed into the dusky interior of a house and picked his way through piles of crumbling debris till he came to a high opening looking south. He saw the great southern arm jutting into the river on his left; beyond it, the empty expanse of water grew wider and wider until, far away, it seemed to merge with the sky. And there in the distance, as if suspended between water and air, were several low oblong shapes.

Branwald sucked in his breath. 'By the Mother,' he breathed. 'The Tarquan Islands.'

His eye followed the right bank of the river as it curved

232

westwards, and came to rest on a tall structure silhouetted against the silver ocean beyond. It was located at the eastern end of a long ridge that rose from the forested plain and ran away towards the west. Although its base was hidden below the trees, the walls of the building rose sheer and black above them, like a thick torso. Where the shoulders should be, the walls angled inwards for a distance until they came to the neck, then rose sheer again to form a square head. The roof, sloping up on two sides to a point at the top, overhung the head slightly, giving the impression of protective headgear. On the east side, however, the shape was different. Starting from the neck, the wall dropped backwards, like the slope of a pyramid, until it reached the trees some distance behind the main structure. To Branwald, it looked like a great cloak sweeping down and back from the black shoulders.

'The Bastion of the Orelord!' he whispered. 'I have seen this in my dreams.'

To the right of the Bastion, the mine was clearly visible. A great pit had been delved into the eastern flank of the mountain. Three sides of this pit, as far as Branwald could see, were rust-stained and precipitous. The fourth side opened towards the east, where, like a huge sentry, the Bastion stood, facing into it.

'Father! Oh, Father!' Branwald said softly. A surge of feeling rose in his stomach, and he groaned aloud.

He forced his eyes away from the distant structure and scanned the stretch of water close to the nearer bank of the river, outside the Arm. It was empty.

Branwald frowned. Surely the Oremen's boat could not have been fast enough to gain the distant curve where the coastal forest would hide it from view. He searched the trees that lined the nearer bank, but saw no black shape moving under them. He looked along the rough coat of bushes and trees that cloaked the harbour wall, but nothing moved in the shadowy places.

Something stirred in his mind again, and with it a fear. He descended to the path and found a narrow, tangled passage that led downward towards the harbour wall. He stopped by the corner of another ruin and listened. There was no sound, not even birdsong. The feeling was stronger.

Branwald unslung his bow and fitted an arrow to the string. He was about to move forward through a low thicket of shrubs when a movement in a gap between two houses caused him to duck back. Framed clearly in the space were the head and shoulders of a black-haired, bearded man moving stealthily upwards from the harbour.

Branwald did not think the man had seen him. His first thought was to run; but, looking up along the long cluttered passageway by which he had just descended, he decided it was too risky. Instead he climbed the grass-carpeted steps which led through the doorway of a large three-storied ruin. He sheathed the arrow and unslung the Firebolt from his back. Then, his heart thumping, he stepped into the gloom to the left of the doorway and listened.

From somewhere near the harbour side of the building he heard low voices, then silence. Then, from near the bottom of the steps, he heard a rustle, as of someone pushing through bushes. He waited for them to pass, his hand hovering over the handle of the Firebolt. But there was no further sound.

'Branwald!' The sudden call made him jump. 'Branwald, I know you are here!' The voice came from just outside the doorway. There was no mistaking Urkor's deep, guttural tone.

Branwald made himself stone, not even breathing. How had Urkor known he was there?

A footstep sounded, closer now. Branwald looked into the darkness of the building for better cover, aware of the sickening feeling that he should have run when he had the chance. His hand hovered over the Firebolt's handle. If need be, he thought, he would make sweeping slashes with it, so that the beam would not linger on his adversary for more than a fraction of a second ....

'It is time to talk again, young one.' Urkor's tone seemed placatory. 'It is time to stop this, before you and the one who is with you are both killed.'

Branwald saw a black opening deep in the building. Lifting his feet carefully, he moved towards it, watching the entrance behind him. Somewhere outside the wall, there was a scrabbling sound, as if someone was climbing. He reached the doorway and slid around it, brushing a mass of clinging cobwebs from his hair and face.

'It is no use, young one.' The voice came again. Branwald saw a shadow moving on the step outside the door. 'There are many of us. You are only two. We must have the weapon. We *will* have the weapon.'

Branwald closed his eyes and tried to calm his mind. He tried to force a picture of Sula into the blankness there, but he could not. In desperation he thought, 'Maloof, come! Come now! I need you!'

A sound came from the floor above his head. Somebody had climbed up from outside. The trap was closing.

Urkor's voice came again. 'There is no need to call the other one. What can he do against the muskets of my men? Better to tell him to stay away. Then he will not be killed.' A pause. 'You do not want to be the cause of his death, do you?'

Another pause. 'Branwald, do not destroy yourself with the weapon. Don't be a fool. What you must decide is this: will you give it to us, and have a chance to see your father again, or would you prefer to wait till we come to get it?'

The mention of his father loosened something in Branwald. He could not let himself and the Firebolt be taken. He had to get out of this place. Directly in front of him was another doorway. Through it he saw a small, distant rectangle of daylight. He steeled himself to run.

'Don't be a fool, Branwald. You cannot escape from here. Give the Firebolt up now, and live. Surely you do not want your father to learn that you came all this distance only to waste your life here.'

There was a sudden flash and a loud blast from the darkness to Branwald's left. In the same instant something smashed into the wall near his head. He dropped to one knee, gripped the Firebolt's handle tightly and turned it towards the place. It blazed a shaft of light into the gloom. He saw a shadow move in through a doorway; in anger he aimed the beam at the protecting wall, but the sound of scattering masonry told him that his target had moved away.

With the Firebolt held before him to show the way, Branwald raced for the distant opening. The beam sheared through hanging curtains of cobwebs. He stumbled over heaps of mouldering material. From behind him came a shout.

The opening, as he neared it, became a narrow window space about five feet from ground level. He took off his bow and quiver and tossed them through, stretched to leave the Firebolt on the outside ledge of the window, and then hauled himself up, aware that he would be silhouetted for anyone in the building behind him. The mossy pathway outside was just below window level. As Branwald got his shoulders through, he reached for the Firebolt, which had rolled off the ledge.

A booted foot kicked the Firebolt out of his reach. When Branwald looked up, he saw the round black bore of a musket only inches from his face; above it, the hard eyes of a bearded man stared down at him.

Branwald closed his eyes. He waited for the explosive final moment. He could think of nothing except that black hole at the end of the musket.

There was a swish and a thud, and the man grunted. Branwald opened his eyes. The man's face showed surprise. He grunted again and started to reach his hand round towards his back, but before he could do so, his knees buckled under him. As he fell, the musket fired in a blast of flame and smoke, but the muzzle had wavered to one side and the shot did not strike Branwald. The musket clattered onto the hard path, and as the man pitched forward Branwald saw the shaft of an arrow protruding from his back.

Then he heard his name being called. Rafik was framed in the opening of a passageway, across a flat place that had once been a street. He was fitting an arrow to his bow.

'Come on, young one!' he urged. 'Run!'

Branwald scrambled to his feet, snatched up his bow and arrows and the Firebolt, and ran. He reached the passageway and leaped into the shelter of its walls.

'Go on! That way!' Rafik said curtly, indicating the steps that led upwards.

Branwald had gone only a short way when he realised that Rafik was not following. He turned. Rafik was crouching, raising his bow, steadying himself. He fired. Branwald heard a cry of pain from beyond. He looked up along the steps again, unsure of what to do. He wanted to run, but his pride would not let him. He, the bearer of the Firebolt, could not run away and leave Rafik to fight alone.

The tall islander was running towards him. 'Quick! There are two!' he called. 'In there!' He indicated an opening in the wall, ten yards away. Branwald dashed, taking giant leaps. When he gained the doorway, Rafik was close behind. 'Ready your bow!' he panted. 'We will need it.'

Branwald searched for an exit deeper in the dark building, but saw only blank walls. Rafik grabbed his arm and pushed him towards the darkest corner. 'Go there! I will take the first one. You must take the other, if he comes. You *must!*'

Branwald stepped towards the shadowy corner and crouched behind a low mound. Dropping the Firebolt on the ground, he unslung his bow and began to fit an arrow. His hands were shaking. The string found the notch and he drew it back. Rafik was by the doorway. Branwald saw the glint of metal in his hand.

The doorway darkened, and the barrel of an Oreman's musket poked gingerly through. Rafik waited. The Oreman peered into the room.

Rafik leaped like a cat. He grabbed the musket and pulled. As its owner staggered forward, Rafik's left arm found the man's neck and pulled back. His right swung and drove the knife into the man's ribs.

But even as Branwald watched in horror, the second Oreman's shadow fell on the doorway. Branwald drew back the bowstring and tried to steady his arm. Half of the man's body came into view. The man peered in and located the sounds of struggle. His musket came up.

Branwald drew back the string another inch and released. The arrow lodged in the man's breast, beside his right armpit. He cried out and slumped to the right, but did not fall. Instead his eyes searched the darkness, seeking his assailant. Branwald drew another arrow from his quiver and started to fit it, but his hands failed him when he saw the muzzle swing towards him. He crouched lower.

A figure rushed through the doorway and leaped at the

237

man from behind. It was Targye. The musket exploded with a deafening blast of smoke and fire. Then Morung was there, and Maloof. The Oreman put up a desperate struggle, but his musket was useless to him and the odds were too great. In a moment the terrible deed was completed, and he and his companion lay quivering in their death agony on the floor.

'How many were there?' Rafik asked, sheathing his dagger.

'Five, I think,' said Targye.

'Then there is one left,' Rafik said, picking up his bow. He looked at Morung. 'He must not get away.'

Morung nodded. 'We must get to the boat. Come on.'

The three men hurried down the steps and onto the ancient street. Branwald, following behind with Maloof, looked at the still bodies of two other Oremen, but Urkor was not one of them.

'Stay with me, boys,' Morung said, as Rafik and Targye loped away, their bows at the ready. 'And remember, if the one we seek fires his musket, he must be killed before he can reload.'

Branwald hurried down the twisting path, his eyes alert for any movement ahead of Morung. He saw the sheen of water between two buildings and knew the harbour was not far away.

'You heard my call?' Branwald said to Maloof.

'Yes,' replied his friend. 'I was almost asleep. It came like a kick from a horse. I knew you were in trouble.'

'I am glad you weren't asleep.'

The boys had reached the steps that led down to the massive harbour wall when they first spotted Urkor, nearly a hundred yards out on the pier. He was running, head down, arm forward to clear a way through the bushes. Forty yards behind him, Rafik's head and shoulders appeared momentarily in a clearing and then vanished.

Branwald gave chase, taking huge leaps down the steps, heedless of the slapping branches. Now he was the hunter, Urkor the hunted. He reached the level surface of the pier, found a gap and dashed into it. He heard Morung calling him, but he did not pause.

He heard the boat before he saw it. A throbbing blast of

sound came from behind a cluster of trees ahead, and a cloud of blue smoke ballooned upwards. However, when Branwald cleared the bushes and reached the edge of the wall where Rafik stood, the black craft was already thirty yards away and picking up speed.

Rafik glanced at Branwald and then at the Firebolt. 'Use the weapon!' he commanded. 'Use it against the boat! Quickly! If he escapes, we may as well go back to the swamp!'

Branwald caught the Firebolt's handle and dropped face-downwards to the ground, as Maloof arrived beside him. He saw the crouching figure of Urkor in the mid-section of the boat. He pointed the weapon, and the white beam traced a steaming path along the water. The light touched the stern, wavered and then locked onto the target. Branwald saw Urkor turn to look, and saw his sudden movement as he swung the boat in an attempt to evade the beam. Branwald gripped more tightly and followed its track.

Urkor leapt onto the forward deck and crouched over the black horizontal tube that stood there. It swung round. Branwald instinctively flattened himself, but he did not release the Firebolt.

There was a flash, a belch of smoke, and something heavy smashed into the wall six feet below Branwald. A cloud of dusty smoke swirled up and momentarily blinded him. The beam wavered, but Branwald gritted his teeth and again found the target. The craft was slowing, he thought. He raked the stern with the beam, trying to keep its point just at the water-line.

The boat had almost reached a slight bulge in the riverside trees when Branwald lowered the Firebolt and relaxed his hold. His eyes were watering and he could not see clearly. But there was no doubt that the rhythm of the throbbing was slower. The craft slid behind the trees and out of sight. The throbbing became a stuttering. Then the sound ceased completely.

'He is sinking,' Rafik muttered.

'We must make sure,' Targye said. 'Come. The canoe!' He and Rafik turned and hurried back towards the ruins.

'You did well, young one,' Morung said, helping Branwald to his feet. 'But it is not finished yet. Come on.'

They met Sula and Atula near the top of the steps by the pier. Each carried a bow and arrows. 'They came back,' Branwald said. 'One is getting away!'

When Branwald reached the terrace, Rafik and Targye — each carrying one of the muskets of the Oremen — were already launching their canoe. As they paddled away, Morung and Atula were busy gathering the belongings together. 'We must leave as soon as they return,' Morung said grimly.

When the preparations were finished, the three young ones stood together by the wall of the terrace, watching the mouth of the harbour, while Branwald spoke quietly about what had happened. He said little about the killing of the Oremen, but he knew that Sula could sense his disturbance whenever the memory came back to him. Moreover, he was worried that Morung would advise abandoning the venture and returning home. The others were silent when he finished his account, and he felt that they shared his fears.

'We cannot go back now,' Sula said. 'We cannot leave Ganden in that place.'

Soon afterwards, they saw the two men in the canoe returning. They were at the water's edge when the men stepped onto the wharf.

'The black boat is sunk,' Rafik said tersely. 'Only the nose remains above the surface. It is about twenty paces from the bank. We saw no sign of the man.'

'Do you think he ...?' Branwald asked Targye.

The tall man shrugged his shoulders. 'The lizards probably got him, but we cannot be sure.'

～

They held a council at the bottom of the steps, out of the glare of the sun. Morung spoke first. 'We have been lucky to survive this attack uninjured,' he said slowly. 'It could have been different.' He looked at Branwald. 'We could have lost, not only lives, but also the weapon. And if that had happened ....' He shook his head. 'But now we have to decide what is best to do. It seems to me that —'

'There is one question,' Rafik's harsh voice interrupted. 'How did these men know that we were here? They could not have heard us, and they didn't see us or they would have

240

closed in on us earlier.' His hard eyes rested on Branwald's face. 'So how did they find us?'

Branwald stared at the man, sensing the accusation in his tone. Anger rose in him.

'What are you saying?' he said.

'I am saying, boy, that they knew we were here. I ask how this can be.'

'I do not know,' Branwald lied.

'I say you do, boy! Maybe you would like to explain!'

Maloof spoke quietly. 'There was someone on the boat who can follow another's thought.'

There was a quick exchange of glances among the adults. Then Morung looked at Branwald.

'Is this true? Can the Oreman Urkor speak in thought?'

Branwald blushed. 'Yes, I think he can.'

Rafik's eyes flashed. 'But why did you not tell us this before we ventured on this journey with you?'

'I ... I thought Urkor was a long way from here. I didn't think —'

'If this is so,' Morung broke in, 'then there will be other Oremen who also can do this. That means that those at the Bastion may already know about our presence here.' He paused, his expression grave as he scanned their faces. 'If that is the case, we have lost the element of surprise. We would be foolish to go on.'

Rafik cleared his throat. 'That may be, Morung. But we do not know these things for sure. Maybe Urkor is dead. Maybe only those who were with him knew about us. The risk is greater now, true. But as for me, I have set out. I must go on.'

Maloof spoke again. 'You will not be alone. We will go with you. We have come too far to turn back now.'

Branwald caught the look in Rafik's eyes. It was scathing, but the big man said nothing.

Their eyes drifted to Targye. 'I will go further than here,' he said quietly. 'It is not yet time for me to return.'

Atula spoke. 'Wherever Morung and Sula go, I will go also.'

As the others waited for Morung to speak, Branwald read what was in his mind before he spoke it. He was thinking about Sula. He would not put her at risk.

'I cannot go as far as the Bastion with you,' Morung said. 'But if you are determined to go on, I will go a little further.' The others nodded in understanding.

'But, Father,' Sula exclaimed, 'do not forget that Ganden is in that place! We cannot return while there is a chance of freeing him!'

Morung looked at her with kindly eyes. 'I know, my little dove. That grief is a heavy one for me also. Ganden may soon have a chance to escape. But if I were to lose you too, I could not bear it.'

Rafik rose to his feet. 'I am going now,' he stated, turning towards the canoe.

Targye said, 'You travel by water? Is this wise?'

Rafik shrugged. 'It is the fastest way. The sooner we get there, the better.'

'But we will be exposed on the sea,' said Atula. 'If they know about us, we will be seen from afar as we near the Bastion. This is not the way.'

Rafik sighed. 'If we walk from here, it will take a day. It is too long.'

Morung spoke. 'There is an inlet about five miles from here. You know it. It leads to the Bridge of the Cormorants. We can take the canoes as far as this inlet. There is an old road from there to the Red Mount.'

They waited for Rafik, who was standing with his back to the group, gazing towards the south. He nodded his head.

'I will go along with this,' he muttered.

~

The sun had climbed only halfway into the eastern sky when the group set out again. To Branwald it seemed as if it should be close to setting, so much had happened since they had set off into the fog that morning. He remembered to leave the Firebolt on the floor of the canoe at his feet, where the blade could catch the rays of the sun.

The canoes slid out of the harbour, keeping close to the pier and aiming for the shelter of the wall of trees on the bank. In silence they passed the sinister snout of the black boat protruding from the water. Branwald scanned the dense foliage nearby for any sign that a swimmer might have reached it and hauled himself to safety. There was no sign, however.

Rafik and Targye set a gruelling pace. They slowed only when another slight curve in the bank approached, inching cautiously around it before picking up the pace again. The river was so wide that Branwald could only vaguely make out the detail on the hazy eastern shore. He had never seen such an expanse of water.

Just before noon, the travellers reached the mouth of the inlet that led westwards to the Bridge of the Cormorants. Their journey had been uneventful. There was no sign of any Oremen. The canoes slid into another narrow, winding waterway, where the high boughs of the trees provided welcome patches of cooling shade.

They had been travelling thus for some time when Atula, seated at the prow of Morung's canoe, said something. The adults immediately stopped paddling, Rafik and Targye turning in their seats to watch her. She stood up in the narrow craft, her face lifted, listening.

'Smoke,' she said quietly. 'Wood-smoke, coming on the air.'

Branwald sniffed. It was true: he caught the faint but familiar smell on the light breeze wafting from the west.

'Someone is at the bridge,' Morung said. 'Targye, go and see.'

It took only moments for Rafik to manoeuvre his canoe close to the south bank and for Targye to climb out, his bow and quiver in hand, and disappear among the trees.

'Get the canoes off the water,' was Morung's next command. Branwald knew why. It was possible for an Oreman boat to have reached the bridge by this very route.

Soon the party was gathered beside the canoes in a clearing. They watched and listened, all eyes focused on the direction in which Targye had gone.

He returned sooner than they expected, sliding noiselessly into the clearing from the south.

'Oremen, four of them, with a boat,' he whispered. 'They have a fire on the bridge and a tent nearby. At least four muskets, as far as I can see.' He looked at Rafik. 'They would not be hard to take.'

'They should not be here,' Rafik said, his eyes staring in the gloom. 'I do not like it.'

'They laugh and joke and do not see what is happening around them,' Targye replied. 'They do not expect anything.'

Rafik reached for his bow. 'Whatever their purpose, they are in our way.'

'But we do not need to kill them,' Maloof said. 'We can simply avoid them and leave them there.'

There was contempt in the curl of Rafik's lips. 'You want to leave four of these blocking our way back? What if we need to return this way?'

'If we leave them there, the Oremen at the Bastion will not expect us to come from this direction.' Maloof spoke slowly and calmly. 'Even if they return to the Bastion, these men will report that they have seen nothing.'

Morung looked at Targye and Atula. The woman spoke. 'The boy argues well. These men do not need to know we are here. But if we attack them and one of them fires his musket, it will be heard over a great distance. And there is always the danger of injury or worse.'

'What about you and the girl?' Targye's question was directed towards Morung. 'Are you coming with us?'

Morung shook his head. 'We are already too near for my liking. I had hoped to wait for you at the bridge, but that is not possible now. We will move deep into the trees and wait for your message.'

And so it was decided. Rafik, Targye, Branwald and Maloof would strike overland away from the river, in a south-westerly direction, until they found the old road which Morung had spoken of. They would follow it till they were close to the Red Mount. Then, having made a reconnaissance, they would decide what to do.

CHAPTER TWENTY-FIVE

In a short time the small party was ready to set out. All four had knapsacks slung over their shoulders, holding food and kindling for several days. Each carried a bow, a dagger and a quiver of arrows. Targye and Rafik each carried a musket, and the Firebolt hung down Branwald's back.

They whispered their goodbyes in the shadows, as the sun drifted towards the south-west. When Sula came to Branwald, he felt what was in her heart: fear that this might be their last chance to speak together, hope and belief that he would succeed in his task.

She gripped his hand tightly. 'I will pray that our Mother keeps you safe.' Morung nodded his approval.

Then, with Targye and Rafik leading, they set out.

At first, their progress was slow. They stopped frequently to listen, and then moved on again. Rafik's route towards the south-west took them through crowded stands of thin trees. When they came to open spaces, they skirted round them. The mass of the Red Mount rose ahead, and they were wary of watchers on the heights.

At last they came to a raised embankment, clearly another lost roadway of the Old Ones, that ran southwards. Wider than any they had seen before, it carried the imprint of many animals on the thin track that wandered along its surface. Targye examined it carefully, but found no sign that men had been there.

'Now we must be watchful,' Rafik said. 'A little further on is a path that leads to the heights. Remember that it may be used by the Oremen, so at the first sign of anything, get off the path and into the trees. Keep your weapons ready, but do not use them unless we are fired upon.' He looked up at the scarred mountain-top, which seemed very close. 'If we can get to where the trees stop, and see where the outposts on the rim are stationed, then one of us should be able to creep to the lip and look down into the mine. All right?' The others nodded. Then, having unslung the Oremen's muskets from their backs, the two men set off.

Branwald, behind Targye, examined the weapon he carried. It had a long blue-black pipe, even longer than the Firebolt, at the forward end. At the rear was a polished wooden stock, which became wider as it neared the end. Halfway along were several protruding levers. Branwald wondered how such a flimsy-looking weapon could send a missile through the body of a person.

Soon afterwards, Rafik veered to the right and halted where a narrow path branched downward off the embankment. Branwald traced its course and saw that it soon began to rise and wind upwards through the trees. The mountain loomed over them.

Rafik turned to regard the boys. 'This is where the real danger begins. Four of us is a large number. For two it would be easier.'

'What do you mean?' Branwald asked.

'I mean that this is work for men who know the place. You have your lives before you. There is no need for you to come to the mountain-top with us.'

'But what would we do?'

Rafik looked into the nearby trees. 'You can wait for us in the forest.'

Branwald glanced at Maloof, who was staring at the two men.

'It will be safer,' Rafik went on. 'All right? We will return when we have seen what we need to see.'

In the pause that followed, Branwald heard Maloof's clear thought. 'He wants the Firebolt, Branwald. He is going to ask you for it.'

'But we need the weapon,' said Rafik.

'No!' retorted Branwald. 'Not the Firebolt!'

A sudden flush swept into Rafik's neck and cheeks. 'But we will return immediately. It is only a precaution. There would be no harm —'

246

'No!' exclaimed Branwald. 'It cannot be! It was given to me! It is my responsibility.'

As Rafik turned abruptly away, he did not hide the flash of anger in his eyes. 'If that is how you want it,' he said, 'on your own head be it!'

The tall Tarquan stalked away down the path, his long-bow ready in one hand, a musket in the other. The others followed. Soon they had climbed high enough to look out across the forested plain that they had been traversing. Far away to the north-east, the red-tipped mass of Citadel Mount shimmered in the heat.

The sun slanted westwards and the air became warmer, and still the travellers pushed upwards. After an hour, they paused to rest by a trailside stream whose bed was stained with rust.

Branwald looked north again. Citadel Mount seemed higher now, but his attention was caught by what lay behind it, to its right. There, hazy with distance, lay the Great River, winding in great loops across the forested plain. And there, far away, a faint blue outline above the northern skyline, lay the mountains; and beyond them, somewhere, was Feyansdoon.

The longing in Branwald's heart for that place, and for the two people there whom he loved so much, was scarcely bearable. He felt a hand grip his arm, and Maloof was there, his eyes, too, riveted on the distant peaks.

'Branwald, if anything should — should happen at the Red Mount, I would be happier if I knew my mother would have someone to look after her.'

Branwald looked sharply at his friend. 'Nothing is going to happen.'

'No, Branwald. Do not say that. We do not know what lies in the future. We do not know what will be required of us in the hours ahead.'

Branwald was silent. This sombre talk from Maloof made him uneasy. This was not like the Maloof he had come to know, the one who had countered Branwald's own doubts and fears when they had seemed about to overwhelm him. Could it be, Branwald wondered, that Maloof's encounter with the Firebolt and his subsequent healing by Bengue had wounded his spirit, so that his courage was failing him? Certainly he had changed. He was quieter than he had been before. He seemed to prefer the solitude of the forest to the company of his friends and of his own people.

Maybe, Branwald thought, he would have to face the task ahead without relying on Maloof. And maybe — although a part of him felt that the thought was unworthy, even as he considered it — maybe Maloof was not part of the great design after all ....

'Branwald, we all have our parts to play. I am certain of that. But now is the time to remember the words of the Old Soldier. The Firebolt must serve only the bright side. It would be better to cast it away for ever than to put it at the service of the dark side.'

'Dark side!' Branwald felt irritation. 'Who is to say which is which? I must use it to free my father — our fathers — and to teach the Orelord a lesson.'

Maloof was thoughtful, his eyes lost in the distance. 'Maybe all things have their place, Branwald. Even the Orelord. When people do wrong, maybe it is because they cannot yet see ....'

Branwald frowned. 'You are beginning to sound like the Old Soldier,' he said sarcastically. 'You do not have to lecture me.'

'I was sent with you to help you with your task, remember? And I have already endured much, Branwald.'

Branwald felt a pang in his heart, a bitter remorse for the barrier which he had erected in his own mind and which had blinded him to Maloof's pain. 'I am sorry,' he said. 'You have suffered more than I have.' He swallowed hard. 'I do not know why I could not see it. I should have known it, but something inside me blocks me ....' He was distraught, disgusted with himself.

'But this is how the Firebolt must work, Branwald. You must learn to know yourself, and I have learned that this knowledge does not come without pain. But you are learning. You have learned something already, and you will learn more.'

'But what about the Orelord?' Branwald's heart was gripped by the icy hand of fear. 'How can I face him if I am like this? One moment I feel brave and ready to face any danger, while the next I am filled with fears.'

248

Maloof was silent, and Branwald's heart sank lower.

'Branwald,' Maloof said at last, 'we must prepare. There is help and strength available to us: the wisdom of the Old Soldier, of the White Ones, of Bengue, and of the people — our people — who have already shared their strength with us. That energy can still be ours, but we must find a way to call it up. We must go together to the forest before we meet the Dark One.'

Afterwards, as he toiled upwards along the mountain track, Branwald revolved these thoughts in his heart. He wished he could see his dark side so that he might guard against it. But everything seemed muddled. Did his fear come from the dark side or from the fair? Was it not this waiting, this delay among the remnants of a defeated people, which was at fault? If he could only come to grips with the Orelord, the Dark One who was the cause of all the suffering, then his people would know what it was to strike back at the powerful oppressor. They would regain their spirit and their courage. They could become a great people.

~

In the early evening, the travellers came to a widening in the trail. Branwald saw a rock-face, to his left, against the base of which lay a pile of great boulders. It was evident that the rocks had been used to block off an opening in the rock-face: above the highest rock, the top of a rough archway could be seen.

Rafik halted, wiping his brow. 'The ancestors of the Old People knew something about taking the iron from the earth,' he said. 'They made these passageways into the mountain. Indeed, some of them can be seen on the face of the pit, for the Orelord's machines have gone deeper even than these. When he found out they were there, he ordered the mouths to be caged in with an iron fence and the exits to be closed off. He did not want his precious workers escaping through a mine of the Old People.'

'But does this one open into the pit itself?' Branwald asked.

Rafik turned to look at him, an ironic smile playing on his lips. 'And if it did, what help would that be? We are not worms, we are men. And it would take more men than we have here to shift that pile.' He waved his hand carelessly towards the blocked entrance.

'I can find a way,' Branwald said. In his mind was a clear picture of the cylindrical tunnel through the rock at the Kanaka Sump. 'With this.' He lifted the Firebolt.

'Ha! We are talking about solid rock, boy!' said Rafik. 'Not branches of trees!'

But Branwald was sure of his ground. 'It has the power,' he said. 'If I can do it, and if this passage opens into the pit, then we may not need to face the dangers that are above.'

He clambered up the rocks. Reaching the top, he crouched, examining the blockage. He imagined he could feel a draught of cool air wafting out from the spaces between the rocks. He studied the massive topmost rock and gripped the handle of the Firebolt with his two hands. He planted his feet firmly on two lower rocks, aimed the nozzle at the rock and willed all his strength and power into the instrument.

The beam materialised, glowed blue, then white. There was a crackling, sizzling sound, and powdery smoke drifted upwards. The beam sheared downwards through the rock. When it reached a little over halfway, there was a sudden sharp crack, and the rock split in two. Branwald jumped aside as one half began to slide to the right, coming to rest against the rock-face. The other half remained in place, but already the opening was big enough for a small boy to slip through.

'I will split this other half,' Branwald said. 'Then we will be able to get in.' He sheared the remaining half into three blocks. Then Targye and Maloof climbed up and slid them crashing down onto the lower rocks.

'Espirit!' exclaimed Targye. 'There is cold air coming out of this.' He clambered down and disappeared into the opening. In a few moments his head reappeared. 'Come,' he said. 'I think the boy has found us a way into the very den of the Orelord!'

'But first,' warned Rafik, indicating the shattered pieces of rock, 'we must hide these. They must not be seen by anyone who passes.'

It was the work of a few moments for them to hide the

pieces in the undergrowth nearby, and for Targye to lop a thick shrub, which they pulled into the opening after they had entered the shaft.

Branwald, holding the glowing Firebolt aloft, led the way. He carved through a rustling curtain of spiderwebs and shook the clinging substance from the instrument. He felt the cool breeze on his face as he ducked around dripping red stalactites, which hung from a roof that was barely above head-height.

Behind him he heard Rafik curse. 'Give us more light there, boy!' he growled. Branwald gripped the handle tighter, and the beam intensified.

They came to a fork in the passageway. Feeling the draught from the right-hand shaft, Branwald chose it. Twice more they came upon junctions in the dark tunnel, and each time Branwald followed the cool wind, only pausing long enough for Targye, at the back, to memorise the route by which they had come.

Then, after many minutes, they saw a pinpoint of daylight in the distance. 'Take care, Branwald!' whispered Targye. 'The light!' Stealthily they advanced. And then Branwald saw a mesh of bars criss-crossing the oblong opening.

'It is the fence,' he said quietly. His eyes, adjusting to the brightness of the daylight ahead, began to see beyond the opening. But there were no features to be seen, only a distant, rust-stained wall of rock in shadow.

The fence had been erected, not at the very edge of the opening, but several paces into the shaft; so the travellers, when they reached it, could still see only the rugged far wall of the pit.

'Boy,' growled Rafik, 'you must use that weapon again.'

Maloof spoke. 'But what if there are watchers on the rim beyond?'

'Wait, then,' said Rafik. He pulled his cloak from his rucksack, shoved it through the mesh of the fence and, with his arms protruding on the other side, let it hang down to make a screen. 'Cut!' he ordered.

Holding the Firebolt so that it was aimed at the tunnel floor beyond the fence, Branwald carefully cut through the bars. In a short time he had cleared a space big enough for a man to crawl through.

'Wait here,' said Rafik, dropping to his hands and knees. He crept to the opening, staying close to the shadow that fell along the right-hand wall. He scanned the high lip of the mine; satisfied, he moved forward, parted the yellow grasses at the edge and looked down. The others waited. After a few moments he beckoned them forward. 'Keep low!' he growled.

Branwald gazed down into the pit of the Orelord's mine. From where he lay, a stepped wall dropped more than two hundred feet to the floor below. He saw men working, many stripped to the waist, their brown backs glistening with sweat. Some were using long-handled hammers to drive spikes into the cracks in the bedrock, their thin ringing blows echoing round the great cauldron. Others were using levers to pry slabs loose from shelves of rock. Others, whom Branwald took to be guards, were dressed in dark cloaks and metal headpieces; they were located on high points around the floor, either standing or slouching against rocks. Each had a long-barrelled musket close at hand.

Then Branwald saw a black machine, with steam belching from its chimney, sitting motionless on twin rails of iron held together by wooden cross-pieces. In a line behind this machine and connected to it stood about ten long carts, which men were filling with lumps of shattered rock. Branwald followed the track to a narrow cutting which was the entrance to the pit. It exited through an archway in a high mesh fence, which was guarded by two other dark-garbed figures, and swung out of sight to the right past the towering black Bastion of the Orelord.

Branwald gasped. Now that he could see its base, rising from the bare rock not fifty paces from the gates of the mine, the building seemed huge. Several hundred feet high, it looked more than ever like a giant sentinel standing guard: on the flat wall of the head, where the face should be, there were two recessed window openings, making two square, staring eyes on the blank visage.

'Over there,' Rafik said, pointing at a wooden stockade to

the right of the Bastion. 'That is where the men sleep. When they finish their work they are herded there to eat their slop.'

'And the women?' Targye asked.

Rafik turned his eyes to the black mass of the Bastion. 'They live in the depths of the Bastion.'

'Is there another barrier beyond the Bastion?' Maloof asked.

'Yes, boy. There is a great iron wall which encloses the Bastion, the stockade and the tracks, from the very edge of the pit down to the harbour.' He pointed again. 'You can just see part of the wall to the left of the Bastion. And those huts raised above the wall — that is where the guards keep watch. Even if you were to escape from the compound where the huts of the workers are, you would only get as far as that wall before the guards drilled your body full of holes with their muskets. There was one who tried it once. They left his body there until it stank.'

'And is there a gate at the harbour?' Branwald asked.

'There is a gate where the guards are billeted. The track goes through their quarters. Sometimes, when they are drunk, they pour oil on the ore in the wagons and set it alight, in case any of the workers might be trying to escape in the ore.'

'And that building?' Maloof asked, pointing to a round-roofed structure in the trees some distance beyond the compound.

'That is just the gas tank,' Rafik said dismissively.

'What is this gas tank?' Maloof asked.

'Gas is a fuel. It is like air, except that it burns. The Oremen use it to light the lamps that are fixed high on the fence all around, so that even on the darkest night, the place is lit up as if the noonday sun were blazing down on it.'

Branwald looked down again at the brown-backed men in the pit below. There must have been several hundred, scattered across the uneven floor. Which one was his father? His eyes darted from one figure to another, but he could see no distinguishing feature. All had long unkempt hair; all were bearded.

'Come back,' said Targye. 'We have seen enough for now. We must make a plan, if there is any plan that can avail against the power that is here.'

They crawled back to the rusting fence and sat on the hard floor. Branwald waited for one of the men to speak.

Targye cleared his throat. 'It will be difficult. Even with two muskets, we would not have a chance if we confronted the Oremen.'

'No,' agreed Rafik, glaring at Branwald. 'With only three to fight, we would be overwhelmed. It would be certain death.'

Branwald felt the jibe, but he ignored it. 'We will have to get a message to our fathers and the others, so that they can prepare. And they will need weapons.'

The two men stared at him in surprise, but he went on. 'Do they bring their tools into the compound with them?' Rafik shook his head, a sneer on his lips. 'And are the gates to the mine closed at night?' Again the bearded islander shook his head, his face growing serious. 'Then one of us will have to climb down, gather the tools and bring them as close to the compound as possible. With the Firebolt, it will not be difficult to cut a passage through the compound wall and the iron wall beyond. But if the workers are to escape and not be shot by the guards, we will need to extinguish the lights. Do you think this is possible?'

Rafik looked at Targye, as if gauging his reaction to Branwald's speech, but Targye simply waited for his answer. 'The gas comes from the great tank in a single pipe,' Rafik said, 'which feeds many smaller ones. If someone could shut off the valve where the pipe begins, the lights would go out.'

'How many Oremen are there altogether in this place?' Branwald asked.

Rafik shrugged his shoulders. 'Seventy — eighty .... They come and go. The ships always bring fresh ones and take others away.'

'And are they all on duty at night?'

Rafik shook his head. 'There are eight lookout posts around the perimeter wall, with two men in each. Two at the gates of the mine, usually, and maybe ten at the harbour, guarding the gates and the ships.'

'So,' went on Branwald, 'if we were to cut the gas pipe and then the compound wall, and if the men were ready, there would be a chance that they could escape into the forest. It would be morning before the Orelord could begin pursuit, and we might be able to slow him down.' Targye was showing interest.

'But there is one thing you have forgotten,' growled Rafik. 'Our women are inside the Bastion. Are we going to free the men and leave our women to be slaves?'

'I am sorry, Rafik,' Branwald said. 'I had forgotten. We cannot do that.'

Rafik leaned back against the rock. 'What we do not know is what the Dark One in the Bastion is thinking. He may not yet know about the boy and the weapon. But if he does ....' He looked round at them in the half-light. They waited. 'What would you do, if you knew that the sons of two of your slaves were coming to free them with a weapon such as this?'

The boys were silent for a moment. 'I would try to kill them,' Maloof said.

'But if you were afraid of the weapon?'

'I would use the boys' fathers as hostages, to trade for the thing I wanted,' Maloof answered.

'Very good, boy,' Rafik growled. 'But what trade could there be? Your fathers' lives for the Firebolt? Even if you were to hand it over, do you think that he would let you and your fathers leave here, once he had in his hands the very weapon which he has longed for?'

'If he were a man of his word, he would,' Branwald said.

'Hah! A man of his word!' Rafik scoffed. 'Boy, you have so much to learn!' He glared at Branwald. 'This is what the Orelord is like, simple boy! He would prefer that his slaves were dead than that they should escape his clutches. Do you understand? That is why, when we strike, it must be with all the power that we have. There must be no time for them to recover.'

Another pause. 'So,' said Targye finally. 'When the lights go out, we will need to free the men and penetrate the Bastion at the same time.'

Branwald nodded. 'And it cannot be done without the help of the men below. They must be prepared.'

They were silent again. Then Targye spoke. 'A man could climb down into the pit from here, under cover of darkness.'

'True,' Rafik replied. 'But the workers will be in the huts at that time. So he would have to get out through the gateway and into the compound without being detected.'

'If he were to leave a message in the pit, where the men would find it in the morning ....' Maloof said.

Rafik frowned. 'This would require us to remain here another day,' he said. 'Every hour we delay increases the danger. We do not know if the one called Urkor still lives, or what messages he has sent. We cannot risk another day. Whatever we do must be done tonight. And if the men are to know, they must be told before they return to the compound. Once inside there they are segregated into huts, and it is forbidden for them to communicate with one another.'

There was another long silence. Branwald rose and crept back to the edge of the opening. Maloof came to join him.

'If only I knew which one was Father,' Branwald whispered, peering down at the activity below, his eyes darting from one toiling figure to another. 'Then I could try to speak to him.'

'Try it anyway,' Maloof encouraged. 'I will watch the guards. Three of them are talking. The others seem asleep.'

'Take care, young ones,' Targye warned.

Closing his eyes, Branwald began to compose his mind. He had never spoken in thought with his father — nor, indeed, with anyone else, before his father had gone away. He focused all his energies on his thought. 'Father,' he called. 'It is I, Branwald. I can see you.' He waited, his eyes running across the busy scene. There was no sign that anyone had heard.

'Father,' he called again. 'Listen to me!' The three guards were still talking; the others had not moved. 'I am here! I am looking down on you. It is the time. Tonight. Tell the others to be ready.'

'Look, Branwald! There!' Maloof was pointing. One of the figures, who had been loading rocks into one of the wagons, had stopped his work, and his bearded face was turned upwards towards the rim of the pit.

Branwald felt a great surge of feeling in his chest. 'Father!' he thought. 'I am here. Look!' On an impulse, he reached out his arm over the edge and waved it three times. The figure below stood stock-still, as if frozen to the spot. Branwald waved again.

Maloof nudged him. 'Beware!' he warned. 'The guard!' One of the guards who had been talking was moving away from his companions, towards the worker, who, seeing him approaching, bent to his task again. The guard strode over to him and struck him in the ribs with the butt of his musket. The worker staggered, but did not fall. He took hold of a rock and resumed his work. The guard watched him for several moments; then, satisfied, he returned at a leisurely pace to his companions.

Branwald fixed his eyes on the worker. He felt certain that this was his father. He shook his head to quell the sorrow in his heart, but the tears spilled over. He wept silently for the man below, for the father whom he had longed to see for so long. He wept for the kind strong man whom he remembered, for the humiliating blow he had just received, for the injustice that had brought him to this helpless state. He felt Maloof's hand gripping his arm, and knew that he was weeping too.

'Speak to him again,' Maloof whispered. 'Tell him to give us a sign.'

Branwald composed himself. 'Dear Father,' he thought, 'we have come to free you. But you and your companions must help us. If you can hear me, let us see you throwing a rock into the empty wagon behind you.'

They watched, hardly breathing. The man looked round at the guards. Then he lifted a rock, hefting it against his chest. He turned, walked back to the empty wagon and flung it in. The hollow clang resounded around the wide walls.

Maloof scuttled back to the two men. 'Feowald has given us a signal!' he told them. 'Branwald spoke to him in thought, and he has given a sign that he has heard.'

Rafik was sceptical. He crawled to the edge and peered down. Branwald pointed out the solitary rock in the wagon below.

'So,' Rafik growled. 'You spoke to him, you say. What did he say to you?'

257

'I did not hear anything,' Branwald answered. 'But I am certain —'

'Speak again, then. Ask him to point out this one's father' — he indicated Maloof — 'if he is here.'

'I will try.' Branwald focused his mind again on the toiling figure below. 'Father, Maloof, son of Brugarh, is with me. If Brugarh is near you, show him to us if you can.' They waited. They saw the man below glancing around, as if searching for someone. Branwald listened, trying to keep his mind still and blank, but the knowledge that he was so close to his father was too disturbing. What if something should go wrong now? A terrible thought gripped him. Perhaps he would make a mistake at this crucial time — perhaps, even though he was so close to his father, he would never have a chance to speak with him ....

But the man below was moving. He picked up an implement and climbed towards a shelf where three others were labouring to split a large slab of rock. As he passed one of them, he paused and placed his hand momentarily on the man's shoulder. Then he set to work beside him.

'My father,' Maloof whispered hoarsely. 'That is he, surely.'

'All right,' Rafik said. 'This is what you tell him ....'

~

When Branwald had finished conveying Rafik's instructions to his father, he was exhausted. Once or twice, as he laboured to send clear messages, he had fancied that a faint image was registering in his own mind, but there was nothing clear or definite.

He told his father that all the other men must be prepared for escape during the coming night; that an assault was planned on the Bastion, to free the women, before the escape; that their tools and implements would be placed beside the gates of the mine after dark; and that the element of surprise was crucial. He said that there were men with him — he did not say how many — and that they were armed. He did not mention the Firebolt.

'If you have heard and understood, Father,' Branwald thought, 'give me another sign. Strike the rock three times with your hammer.' The man below climbed to a higher shelf, stood poised for a moment, and then struck the rock-face three clear blows. 'Thank you, Father,' Branwald thought. 'Thank you!'

Then, remembering something important, he thought, 'My mother and Eroona are well and long for your return.'

The response came in a wave of sorrow and longing that broke against the shores of Branwald's heart and almost swamped him. His chest tightened and a broken sob escaped him. He could not bear to look down any more. Swallowing hard, he crept back into the shadow of the mine shaft and sat, unable to look at the men.

'I told him,' he said, when he had composed himself. 'He showed that he understood.'

'Good,' said Targye in a kindly tone. 'It was well to keep the message short. We cannot tell when one of the Oremen may intercept your thought, or whether there are any of them on the high rim of the mine.'

The sun had dropped out of sight behind the west wall of the pit. It would be dark in little over an hour.

In the darkening shaft, they held a council. It was agreed that at dusk Rafik and Branwald would go out onto the mountainside and work their way back along the ridge till they came to the high perimeter wall. When darkness fell, they would penetrate the wall close to the gas tank and cut off the supply. Targye and Maloof, meanwhile, would climb down into the pit as soon as the workers and guards had returned to their quarters for the night. There, in the dark-ness, they would collect the tools from under the wagons — where, according to Rafik, they were placed every evening, to protect them from the weather — and bring them to the gates of the mine. Then they would wait until the lights went out, break through the gates, and ensure that the men had access to the tools.

'And now, young ones,' said Rafik, 'since Targye and I may have to use these muskets tonight, I will show you how to load the charge into them. I have seen the Oremen do it often.' He showed the boys how to pour the powder from the metal boxes into the muzzle of the musket, how to follow this with a lead ball, and how to pack the charge tightly in the base of the barrel with a long rod. 'You may need to do this many times before this night is over,' he explained.

Branwald got to his feet. 'Maloof and I must return to the forest,' he said.

'No!' Rafik replied. 'It is too risky for any of us to go outside now. We are safe in here.'

Branwald stood his ground. 'We will keep within the shelter of the trees. Never fear.' Maloof nodded and rose to his feet.

Rafik was surly. 'It is your decision,' he grumbled. 'But do not stay on the path. And leave the Firebolt in the shaft. And if any of the Oremen should come upon you, do not lead them to this place.'

CHAPTER TWENTY-SIX

By the light of the Firebolt, Branwald found the way to the end of the shaft by retracing the footprints which they had left earlier. They crawled cautiously out of the shaft and, disregarding Rafik's instruction, hid the Firebolt in a nook among the rocks. The sun was hovering over the horizon. They stood a while listening, but heard only the lethargic calls of birds. A faint pink haze blurred the shape of the distant Citadel. The air was still and heavy. Branwald thought of Sula. He wished she and Morung were with him and Maloof. He longed to tell them what was happening. However, he did not risk speaking to her.

'Listen,' said Maloof quietly. 'There is a stream.'

They followed the sound of trickling water to a line of willows and aspens that wound uphill through the forest. From a short distance upstream came the subdued thrashing of water falling from a height. Through a gap in the quivering aspens, they entered a sheltered grotto where moss and green plants formed a soft blanket on the angular rock-face over which the stream tumbled. A fine spray of mist from the falls cooled their faces.

Without speaking, the boys found places to rest: Maloof on a fallen tree-trunk by the falls, Branwald on a moss-covered rock nearby. The stream tumbled over sleek, mossy boulders that could have been there since the beginning of the world, so rooted and solid they seemed. The soft plash of the water smothered all other sound.

Branwald did not feel the need to speak. They both knew that this was a time for silence, a time to recollect what was past and to prepare for the task that was almost upon them.

Branwald recalled his home. In his mind's eye he saw again the weathered roofs of Feyansdoon and the stony surface of Watcher's Path. He saw his mother's dear face framed in the doorway of his home, her eyes scanning the high places on Eagle Mountain. He saw Eroona walking sadly down Fisherway, seeing the empty place where his canoe had once lain. He tried to remember the face of the Old Soldier and what he had said about the Firebolt and about himself, its bearer, and he wondered if there was something important which he had forgotten. He recalled his and Maloof's meeting with the Foresters, their killing of the stag and their words of advice. He remembered Aiyan, the sad waif of the White Ones, condemned by the limitations of her own people to remain in her gloomy subterranean world. He thought of the cheerful young Galian nomads who had befriended him and Maloof and given them food. He considered the healing and strength which Maloof and he had gained from the Tarquan Islanders. He thought of Sula, waiting with her father in the forest for news of her brother. And it seemed to him that the hopes of nearly all these people rested upon him, and upon what he could achieve in the coming night; and this thought made him quail with fear. Even with the Firebolt, he thought, the odds against him were great.

In his distress he turned his thoughts and his eyes towards Maloof. His friend sat still as a statue on the tree-trunk, his hands resting on his knees. His eyes were set as if he were looking at an object miles away. In the filtered light, the blue aura surrounding his body seemed more clearly defined than Branwald had ever seen it.

What disturbed him was that he did not find any answering thought in Maloof's mind. Maloof was in a place which Branwald did not know. It was as if Maloof's thoughts had slowed down until they were a part of the slow rhythm of the water, of the green growing things, of the wind and the sky, of the earth itself.

Branwald had sensed this before in Maloof. It was something which Maloof had learned from the Forest People, something to do with their sense of everything being connected, their belief in the Mother Spirit that dwelt in everything that existed — unlike the Dread Spirit of the Island

Elders, a remote Absence that dwelt in some grim and distant place.

Because he had a strong sense that Maloof needed to be in that place, Branwald did not disturb him. Instead he closed his eyes and began to breathe slowly and deeply. He tried to look past the fear in his heart, not granting it the privilege of occupancy. When it could not hold his attention, it began to weaken.

He became aware of another energy, faint though it was, reaching him through the sound of the water, the breath of the air, the feel of the cool spray of mist on his skin. And this energy was saying to him that his strength was not Branwald's strength alone. It was Maloof's, Sula's, the Old Soldier's, his mother's, Eroona's, Aiyan's, his father's — the strength of all those who willed him to succeed in his quest. He was not alone. The power of the Good and of the Light was with him. He was merely its instrument. He must do what he had to do, and if the task required him to suffer, even to die, then so be it. He was Branwald, bearer of the Firebolt. He would not shirk his duty.

~

Branwald did not know how long he had sat on the mossy rock when he sensed a change within him. He felt a sudden stab of pain — not a physical sensation, but a deep sadness in his heart. He wanted to cry out, and had to tighten his throat to avoid doing so.

He opened his eyes and glanced at Maloof. He had unfolded his arms and, spreading them wide, was lifting them, palms upward, towards the green canopy above. Branwald saw his face. He read a sorrow greater than the world in Maloof's eyes and heard his friend cry out, 'No! Mother! Not that!'

Branwald clambered across the slippery boulders towards his friend. 'What, Maloof? What is it?'

Maloof started, as if from sleep. He stared in Branwald's direction. When Branwald saw the tears welling in his eyes, he leaped towards him, wanting to protect his friend from the monstrous thing that was in his mind, shutting his own mind to keep it from entering. Knee-deep in a pool, he grabbed

Maloof in his arms and held him. He felt his friend's body shaking.

'What? What is it? What did you see?' He did not know if he himself was frightened; but, in a way that he only understood much later, he felt an overwhelming need to take away Maloof's fear. He desperately needed him not to be afraid. Maloof had always been the strong one. When their task had seemed impossible, he had given Branwald the courage to go on. It was intolerable to Branwald that now, as they were nearing their journey's end, Maloof should be stricken with fear.

'Tell me!' Branwald insisted.

Maloof did not answer. His hands clung tightly to the back of Branwald's tunic, his head resting on Branwald's shoulder. His breaths were long and laboured.

After what seemed a long time, he relaxed his grip and drew back. He wiped a tear from his pale cheek. 'It was just a ... just a dream that came to me,' he said simply, looking down at his hands. 'It frightened me. I'm all right now.'

'But you felt something — saw something. What was it?'

Maloof avoided Branwald's eyes. 'As I told you, it was only a dream — a nightmare. It signified nothing.'

Branwald's need to know was stronger than his dread of the answer. 'A dream of your father? My father?' Maloof shook his head. 'Of the future? Of what will happen to us?'

Maloof shrugged his shoulders and lifted his eyes to Branwald's. 'It was a dream of death,' he said. 'But what of that? Anything that we dream can be interpreted in any way. We should not allow a dream to change our plans.'

A sense of foreboding had descended on Branwald. 'Someone is going to die,' he said quietly.

Maloof was silent for a moment. 'Branwald, there is no way of knowing what the future will bring. The future lies in our hands.'

'Do you think we should go on?' Branwald asked, although he feared the response.

There was a long pause.

'Yes, we should go on,' Maloof said, very slowly.

Branwald sat down on the tree-trunk. His concern was

less for himself than for Maloof. He did not want his friend to suffer again. It was good, he thought, that Maloof would stay in the pit of the mine with Targye, while he and Rafik tried to breach the defences of the Oremen. It would be safer there.

'Branwald, do you remember the promise you made to me?' Maloof asked.

'Yes, Maloof. If anything happens — your mother ....' He reached out and gripped Maloof's hand. 'I promise this again.'

Maloof's grip tightened on his hand. 'And I will do the same for your mother, Branwald.' A pause. 'We have come a long distance together.'

'And we will travel further,' Branwald answered hoarsely.

CHAPTER TWENTY-SEVEN

The face of the mountain was in shadow when the two friends approached the entrance of the shaft. When Branwald had recovered the Firebolt, they went in. The two men were waiting inside, Rafik's scowl betraying his displeasure.

'We have been searching for you,' he said. 'You should not have stayed away so long.'

'We were just sitting ....'

'It matters not, so long as you were not seen,' Rafik growled. 'Now, we must get to work.' He bent down and began to draw lines on the damp clay of the floor with his dagger. 'Some light here,' he ordered.

The others crouched around and, by the light of the Firebolt, Rafik drew a plan of the Orelord's stockade and showed them the exact locations of the gas tank, the compound which enclosed the workers' huts, the Bastion, the guards' quarters and the harbour.

'The men who guard the gas tank usually shelter in a hut they have built here,' he said, marking a spot by the perimeter wall which lay between the gas tank and the Bastion. 'Sometimes they walk around, but mostly they play games of chance in this hut. Now, whenever we use the Firebolt, especially after the lights go out, we must try to keep its light from being seen. By that time, the Oremen in the lookout boxes will be looking for any target for their muskets. We must not let them have one. We will cut through the wall here on our approach to the tank. There were bushes growing on the inside when I was here. When the lights go out, we will go to the western corner of the compound, here, and cut our way in. We may have to deal with guards inside, although they do not stay there all through the night, and we will have to open the metal bolts on the doors of the huts where the men sleep.

'There are three dangers. The main one will come from the guards in the lookout boxes. They will not be able to see without light, but if they think the men are escaping they may begin to shoot at anything or nothing. This one' — indicating Branwald — 'and I must deal with them. The other two threats will come from the Bastion itself and from the Oremen's quarters near the harbour. Targye, you and the young one and the men in the compound will have to try to keep the Oremen from the quarters pinned back there, although it will be difficult in the darkness.'

Rafik paused for a moment.

'We may have to cut our way into the Bastion. It is likely that the guards inside — there are always four at the entrance — will close the gates if the lights go out and if they hear anything unusual. But they will not expect intruders so close to them. To get into the basement of the Bastion and free the women, we will have to deal with some of the Oremen. In the darkness, this may not be too difficult. To deal with the Dark One himself, however, if he is within ....' Rafik stopped and looked pointedly at Branwald. 'This is a task for no mere child.'

Branwald looked steadily into Rafik's eyes. 'I will do all that is required to be done, and more!' he announced boldly.

'Your wife does not lie within that place,' Rafik retorted, a harsh edge to his voice. 'I am the one who has been wronged. It is fitting that I should be the one to right that wrong. I know the place and I know the Orelord. I should carry the Firebolt.'

'No, Rafik,' Branwald said. 'I cannot hand it over to another. It would be wrong.'

'This wrong would be small compared to the wrong that I and mine and yours have suffered, boy!' Rafik retorted. 'There cannot be a failure here. To fail here would be ....' He broke off and stood up. In the quiet of the passage the others could hear his breathing, heavy with emotion. Branwald said nothing. He sensed the thought in Maloof's mind, and he shared it: how much this man felt the loss of his wife.

Maloof spoke. 'If the Firebolt is to do its work tonight, it must be carried by Branwald alone. This is what the Old Soldier said.'

There was a long pause. Branwald could not see Rafik's face, but he was preparing to argue further when the tall islander spoke again. 'It is time for us to go. We must be near the wall before the darkness closes in.'

There in the gloomy passage they parted. Branwald and Maloof gripped hands, aware that in their hour of greatest danger they would be apart. There was no other way, they knew.

'May the Mother Spirit protect you,' Maloof said.

'And you too,' replied Branwald. Then, turning, he followed Rafik out into the dusk.

∼

The route which Rafik took led eastwards across the face of the mountain, dropping only slightly as it went. He and Branwald made good speed. They each carried a bow and quiver. Rafik gripped a loaded musket, and across Branwald's back hung the Firebolt, its blade covered with skins. An almost-full moon shone from low in the east, a thin veil of wispy cloud across its face. They travelled in silence.

When they saw the dark wall through the trees ahead, Rafik veered to the left and began to descend more steeply. They kept well into the trees as they passed the first lookout box. Then they could see the upper half of the Bastion, its black sides tinted by the lights glowing within the walls.

As darkness fell, Rafik worked his way closer to the perimeter wall, keeping within the cover of the last belt of trees, which was separated from the wall by a narrow space clear of vegetation. As they passed the lookout boxes, they heard gruff voices drifting on the night air, and once Branwald saw dark shapes moving in the high window spaces.

Soon afterwards, Rafik stopped and pointed. 'There,' he said. 'The gas tank.' Branwald saw the square outline looming inside the wall. They waited till an opaque cloud dimmed the moonlight a little, then crept into the deep shadow under the wall. The nearest lookout box was thirty paces behind them.

Rafik padded stealthily along the wall, and Branwald heard him sniffing. After a short distance he stopped. There was a strange smell in the air. 'This is the spot,' he whispered. 'Cut low down. Keep the instrument pointing towards the ground. The bushes will hide the light from anyone within.'

Branwald unslung the Firebolt. His heart beating rapidly, he gripped it by the handle and stepped close to the wall. The blade began to glow. Rafik moved round so that his body formed a screen between the instrument and the lookout box. 'Now! Do it!' he commanded.

It took only seconds for the Firebolt to shear a semicircular cut through the rusting sheet. Rafik bent and caught the edge of the piece of metal to keep it from toppling out onto the ground. Leaving it to one side, he dropped to his knees. 'Come on,' he whispered.

They crawled through and found themselves in the middle of a low thicket of conifers, small but sufficiently dense to give them shelter from the lights that were fixed at intervals just below the top of the wall. They moved the prickly boughs aside carefully, pushing the weapons before them along the ground, until they came to the edge.

They listened. In the distance, they heard men's voices. Branwald saw, almost directly above him, the dark mass of the gas tank, held aloft by a criss-cross pattern of metal beams which formed a kind of circular fence beneath the tank; within this fence, the weeds and grasses had grown unchecked. His eyes sought out the source of the voices. The area around the tank was enclosed by another, lower fence, this one made of vertical bars of iron with small spaces between. In this, about twenty paces to his right, there was a gateway. Outside the gateway stood a shelter with solid walls and a sloping roof. Branwald knew from the sound of their voices that the men were inside.

Rafik touched his arm and pointed at the lattice of girders under the tank. 'The pipe comes directly down from the bottom of the tank to be sunk into the ground,' he whispered. 'Quietly, now. Under the tank and lie among the weeds.'

Branwald eased himself out of the bushes and, crouching, crept into the shelter of the girders, dropping onto his belly when he reached the centre, where the weeds were highest.

Rafik landed beside him. 'There is a valve here,' he whispered. 'If we can close it and take the key, it will give us some time before they find another. Wait here. Do not move.'

He crawled a short distance to the base of a thick pipe which dropped from the black floor of the tank overhead. Branwald watched Rafik's dark head moving and bobbing as he toiled with something. The strange smell was stronger, and Branwald knew it was the gas.

After a few moments Rafik returned. 'There is no key,' he said tersely. 'There is only one thing we can do, and that may be dangerous. The Firebolt must cut through the pipe. I do not know if we can do this without setting the gas alight, but it is a risk we must take. When it is done, get out quickly by the way we got in. Will you do this?' Branwald nodded. Rafik took off his quiver and removed his cloak. 'Now, be quick. Cut clean across the pipe, and if it fires, run for your life!'

Crouching at the base of the pipe, Rafik held the cloak while Branwald prepared the Firebolt. He aimed at a point just below where the pipe entered the ground, gripped the handle tightly and concentrated.

The beam became white. There was a crackling sound and then a hissing. A sudden spout of flame sprang from the ground, swallowing Rafik's cloak in one greedy gulp.

Branwald leaped back, almost dropping the weapon in his fright. The flame leaped upwards, towards the base of the tank. Then Rafik was saying, 'Run, boy! Run!'

Branwald picked up his bow, ducked under a girder and leaped for the thicket. He dropped gratefully into the slapping branches, feeling Rafik's weight crashing in behind him. He crawled for the opening and got through.

In the distance he heard a shout, then another. He stood up, leaning back against the outside of the wall, looking along it to the nearest sentry box. Another shout came from that direction and Branwald froze, fearing that he had been seen. A glow was flickering inside the box, so he could faintly discern the faces of the men leaning from the windows. They were pointing and shouting, but not at him. They were looking at the gas tank.

'Quietly, now,' whispered Rafik. 'Back along the wall till we are directly behind the Bastion. Then we cut our way in again. Quick! Stay close to the wall!'

Branwald started back along the wall, lifting his feet high to avoid being entangled in the briars that crowded there. He could hear a hubbub of voices above and inside the wall, and his urgency increased. Now that the defenders were alerted, the element of surprise was gone. Every second was vital.

At last Rafik called a halt, again at a point halfway between sentry boxes. 'I do not know what lies on the other side,' he whispered. 'There is danger if the lights inside are still burning, but we must make an entry. Try to aim the beam vertically, so that it stays close to the inside of the wall. And do it quickly!'

With growing tension, Branwald did as he was bidden. The smell of burning metal rose to his nostrils as he held the Firebolt steady and cut a triangular shape in the wall. He grabbed the cut piece to keep it from falling out; the edge was hot to touch.

He ducked his head and looked inside. All was in shadow. The lamps were flickering and gave little light. About thirty yards from him was what he took to be the wall of the Bastion, its surface faintly illuminated by the flames below the gas tank.

There was a shout from the lookout box to his right. There was a flash, a sudden loud report, and something hard and metallic struck the inside of the wall close by. Branwald ducked back out.

'They have seen the beam!' exclaimed Rafik. 'Go on! We must gain the shelter of the other side of the Bastion. Cover the instrument or they will see you when you run.'

Quickly Branwald wrapped the Firebolt in its covering.

'I will go first,' Rafik said. 'You wait a few moments. Then run after me. Ready?'

'Yes.'

Gripping the musket, Rafik ducked into the opening and loped towards the Bastion. When he had almost reached it, there was a double report from the direction of the sentry box, but he did not falter.

Branwald ducked through and raced across the space. He heard another loud report just before he reached the wall. The shouts of men came from his left, near where the leaping flames were lighting up the sky. He hurried on, crouching low, searching for the shadow ahead that would be Rafik. Rounding a jutting buttress, he was grabbed by a strong arm and pulled into shelter.

'Keep low!' Rafik hissed. 'They will not come for a few moments. That' — he pointed at a long, high-walled structure, part of which stood between them and the flaming gas tank — 'is the compound where the workers are. They will have heard the shots and seen the flames. They will be ready, but there may be guards. You must go round that corner farthest from the sentry boxes, and make an entrance. I will give you protection.' Leaning the musket against the wall, Rafik unslung his bow from his back and took a handful of arrows from his quiver. 'Now run!'

Branwald took a deep breath and raced for the dark compound. From behind, he heard a shot. He gained the shelter of the compound wall and rounded the corner.

He shook the wrappings off the Firebolt and gripped the handle. A strange excitement was coursing through him. Again keeping the beam almost vertical, he sheared through the rusty metal. This time he had to cut along the bottom as well, for the sheet was sunk into the ground. He had almost finished when a dark figure came rushing round the corner.

'Good boy!' It was Rafik's voice. 'Get inside quickly! They are coming.'

The piece fell away, and Branwald ducked in, searching the shadows for any sign of danger. Rafik pushed in after him, and Branwald saw that he was pulling the cutaway piece into place behind him. 'Shhh!' Rafik whispered. Moments later, they heard the sound of heavy footsteps hurrying past outside. 'Not a sound. Watch for guards.'

From the gloom at the other end of the long house they heard a sound. Branwald stood still, shielding the Firebolt with his body. Out of the corner of his eye he saw that Rafik had dropped the musket and was fitting an arrow to his bow.

A dark figure came round the far corner of the building,

walking slowly. Rafik aimed. There was a sudden oath from the man, and he stood still. Rafik fired. The man gasped, staggered back and fell heavily. A low moan came from him.

'Quickly! Cut the wall there!' Rafik ordered, indicating the house.

Branwald went to the corner of the building and aimed the Firebolt downwards. From within he heard the low rumble of voices. The Firebolt began to shear off the corner. There was the sound of a sudden movement inside, as of someone moving away. Then the corner piece came loose. Branwald pulled it away and it fell with a thud in the dust.

From the darkness where the man had fallen came the sound of heavy footsteps. Branwald heard again the sound of Rafik's bow, and a strangled cry. Another body fell.

Inside the building there was silence. Rafik knelt near the opening and called in a low voice, 'Men of the islands, this is Rafik. The time for your liberation has come. Who is within?'

There was a low murmur of voices, and then a bearded face looked cautiously out at them. 'It is I, Ethem. What is there to be done?'

Rafik caught the man's arm. 'Ethem! It is good to see you. But we have no time to lose. The gas tank is on fire. There is an opening here in the wall. You have no weapons except the tools you use by day. They have been brought to the gates of the mine. There are two of our people there who will show you how to get out of the pit. But if there are any whose women are inside the Bastion, let them know that we are going to attack it too. We will need the help of a dozen. Tell them, Ethem.'

The man was about to turn back into the darkness, but Branwald stopped him. 'Wait. Is Feowald in this building?'

'Feowald is in the one behind this one,' the man said. Then he was gone.

Rafik was watching the two men who had fallen. One of them was getting to his feet. Rafik dropped his bow and lifted the musket to his shoulder. There was a blast and a flash of flame from the muzzle, and the dark figure flopped backwards and lay still.

Inside the building, men were speaking quietly. From the

direction of the gas tank came a volley of shots.

'Now, follow me,' whispered Rafik. He led the way round the end of the building, stopping when the wide passage between it and the building behind came into view.

Nothing moved in the long space. Beyond, silhouetted against the flames from the burning tank, was the black wall of the compound and, rising out of it, the sinister shape of another sentry box, in the window of which were two bulky figures.

'They are watching,' Rafik said. 'Be quick, and keep out of their view.'

Branwald gathered himself and dashed across. He picked a spot on the end wall of the hut and began again to cut. He had almost finished when a shot rang out and the metal wall behind him rang with the impact of a bullet. He heard Rafik call, 'Quick, boy! Quick!' From the direction of the sentry box came several shouts and another shot.

Branwald sheared downwards and across with the beam. The cut piece fell outwards and he pushed it away. Then, bending low, he crawled into the dark building.

The fading light from the blade showed him a ring of bearded faces along narrow aisles between shelved structures which he took to be bunks. The air was fetid with the stench of sweat.

'Do not fear,' he said. 'I am Branwald, son of Feowald, of the Island People. We have come to set you free. Is my father, Feowald, here?'

There was a momentary silence. Then the men in one of the aisles began to make way for someone behind. In the dimming light, a tall figure came slowly forward.

'Branwald,' he said. 'My son, Branwald! So it really was you!'

'Father!' Through the rancid smock, his father's body felt thin and hard.

'Branwald, how did you get here? I cannot believe ....' Feowald began.

'I will explain later, Father,' Branwald said. 'Now there is no time to lose. This is what must be done.' He briefly explained the plan to them, while he unslung his bow and quiver of arrows from his back and handed them to his father. 'You will need these. The guards outside will try to prevent our escape.'

'But this thing — this weapon that you have — what is it?' his father asked.

'This is the Firebolt,' Branwald said. A hush fell on the men. 'I must go. Rafik needs my help.'

Outside, he saw Rafik's shape still at the opposing corner. Beyond him, other dark shapes were moving in a line from the building towards the hole in the compound wall. 'Tell those with you not to cross here yet,' Rafik called. 'We will have to dislodge the guards in the box.'

Branwald peered round the corner. The box was too far away for arrows, and even for a musket the narrow window space would be difficult to hit. He was aware of men coming out through the hole behind him. 'Wait,' he warned.

He gripped the Firebolt and focused the strengthening beam on the metal girders which supported the sentry box. There was a flurry of movement there, and then two flashing reports. Branwald gritted his teeth, trying to keep the weapon steady and his body hidden. He made light sweeping movements across the supporting girders. There was another shot, and something plucked at his sleeve.

But the beam was having an effect. The box shifted slightly. Branwald heard alarmed shouts. Then, as the beam cut through the last girder, the box lurched suddenly to one side. Amid frantic shouts from its occupants, it toppled out of sight outside the compound wall.

'Now,' Branwald told the men behind him. 'There, by the corner.' The men began to move quickly across the space, some of them pausing to greet Rafik with quiet words. A tall figure stopped by Branwald's side.

'I will help you open the other houses,' said Feowald.

They were joined by Rafik, and stealthily the three moved along the passage.

'Branwald, you cut the wall.' Branwald was aware that Rafik had called him by name for the first time. Quickly he carved an entrance into the third house. Then, while Feowald went in to speak to the occupants, Branwald and Rafik penetrated the fourth and last house. Within a few moments the remaining captives were streaming out.

'Here,' said Branwald. 'This way.' He went to the side of the compound wall that faced the mine and began to cut another opening in it. The beam came full circle and the piece fell out. 'At the mine gates,' he reminded them.

He stepped out through the hole and stood for a moment, his eyes adjusting to the dull glow. The gas tank was not visible, being hidden by the wall at his back.

Then he saw, fifty yards away, in the space to the right of the tank, the shapes of men running. For a moment Branwald thought they were the escaping captives; but then, with alarm, he saw that they were running towards him and that they were carrying weapons.

He turned to call for Rafik, but he was already there, levelling his musket. He fired. Branwald saw one of the figures fall, but the others — there must have been twenty or thirty of them — immediately veered to right or left, taking cover behind tree-stumps or piles of rubble.

'Get down!' Rafik called, crouching against the wall and pulling Branwald down with him. 'It is the fire! It lets them see.' There was a flash from behind a pile of stumps, followed by a volley of shots. Branwald heard bullets ricocheting off the wall above him. One of the escapees, who had just passed out through the gap, gasped, crumpled and fell to the ground.

Feowald, crouched beside Branwald, spoke to a man who was emerging through the gap. 'Modoc, bring him.' Without a word, the man and a companion picked up the wounded one and hurried away into the darkness.

Rafik began to crawl back towards the hole in the compound wall. 'Come with me.'

'Protect yourself, Father,' Branwald called, as he followed Rafik back into the compound. They went along the side of the fourth building, towards the point where the sentry box had been. Rounding the corner, they saw for the first time a long vertical slit of light in the wall. Gates, partly open.

'Now,' said Rafik, 'you must stand in the gap and, with all the power of the weapon, pierce the burning tank through the centre. The gas must be released, or it will burn for hours and our plan will fail.'

Branwald stood in the gap between the gates, set his feet firmly and aimed the Firebolt. He knew that the advancing guards were to his right, and he hoped that the right-hand gate would protect him from their muskets.

The white beam shot like an arrow from the nozzle. He brought it up to centre on the swirling flames that were engulfing the tank, then held it steady.

For several seconds nothing happened. Then, with a rising whoosh, a great column of fiery incandescence shot out from the side of the tank. It lit up the ground and the wall beside it as brightly as if it were the sun. Then, with an almighty blast, the gas tank exploded.

Branwald found himself lying on the ground. Through the open gates of the compound he saw a great balloon of fire swelling and swelling, as if it were about to swallow him up. Feeling the fierce heat on his face and neck, he raised his free arm to protect himself and rolled onto his face.

Then he was aware of hands pulling him to his feet, of someone supporting him towards the gap in the wall.

'Come on, Branwald.' It was his father's voice. Behind him, a great mushroom of fire swelled into the night sky.

Branwald's head began to clear. 'Where is Rafik?' he mumbled.

'I am with you,' growled Rafik, from behind. 'You did well, young one.'

Outside, Branwald leaned against the wall for a moment. His father said, 'Those guards will trouble us no more.'

'Now,' said Rafik. 'The Bastion.'

All three looked up at the black hulk that loomed into the star-speckled sky. Branwald fancied that there was light coming from several high windows near the blocky shoulder. No, he told himself. It must be the reflected light from the fire. The lights around the perimeter wall had gone out.

'Feowald,' Rafik asked, 'do the women still live below the ground level?'

'I have not heard any different. But there is little contact between the women and the men now.'

'All right,' said Rafik. 'We will get round to the dark side, away from the fire. Then we will go in.'

Branwald looked at his father. Feowald nodded. 'I will go with you,' he said.

'Be careful,' Rafik said. 'We will have to pass across the front, where the entrance is. There are always guards inside. Even when the doors are closed, they can see out through the slits. But if we stay close by the wall and move fast, they will have little time to see us. Now, the nearer corner. One at a time, and quickly. The sentries may be in the boxes still.'

Rafik went first. Branwald waited until he had gained the jutting buttress at the base of the Bastion before he raced after him. Having reached the shelter, he turned and watched tensely as his father ran across the open space. Branwald looked back towards the perimeter wall, where two sentry boxes stood illuminated by the fire, but he could not tell if there were men still in them. He was surprised that there were not more Oremen on the ground.

He and the others looked along the deserted area in front of the Bastion. On the ground near the doorway, two bright strips were visible. 'There are lights inside the building,' Branwald whispered.

Rafik nodded grimly. 'A separate gas supply. But we must go on,' he said. 'Now, as fast as you can.'

Branwald sped over the hard-packed earth after Rafik. He raced past the doorway, through the patches of light. As he neared the further corner, he heard a shout from within the building, but then he was round and into the deep shadow.

Feowald arrived in a rush of footsteps. 'The door is opening,' he said urgently. 'Someone is coming!' Quickly he fitted an arrow to his bow and peered back round the corner. Branwald saw him raise the bow, draw back the shaft and release. Deftly he fitted another and fired again. 'There are two who will not beat the workers again,' he said tersely. He handed the bow and several arrows to Branwald. 'Protect me while I get their weapons.'

Branwald put down the Firebolt and quickly fitted an arrow to the string. He watched as his father rounded the corner again and stealthily approached two dark mounds on the ground. He saw Feowald fumble for a moment, saw the dagger outlined against the brightness behind, and saw it plunge downwards twice.

Then another Oreman stepped out of the gate of the Bastion. Branwald brought the bow up, aimed and released. The man gasped, clutched his chest, staggered backwards and fell. Feowald, hearing the thud, quickly gathered the weapons and raced for the corner again.

'You did well, my son,' he panted. 'I have two muskets and two daggers. Now we will talk to them in their own language!'

Rafik was already crouching, his ear close to the wall, listening. He moved along several yards and listened again. 'Now, here!' he told Branwald. 'And keep the beam pointing down.' There was a note of excitement in his voice which Branwald had not heard before. 'Cut, boy! Cut!'

'What about the boxes behind?' Branwald said. Two sentry boxes were visible from where he stood, but in the darkness he could not tell if they were manned.

'They are gone, boy! Use the Firebolt. Cut! Cut!'

Branwald did as he was bidden. In a few moments, the heavy piece of metal toppled outwards. Rafik laid it on the ground. Then he crawled into the darkness within. 'Come on,' he said.

Inside, there was the smell of musty air and gas. In the Firebolt's glow, Branwald saw that he was crawling, just below ceiling height, into some kind of storeroom. He had to clamber downwards, across a pile of barrels, to the floor. Rafik was tugging at the metal door, but it was bolted from the outside. From not far away came the sound of women's voices, talking quietly.

Rafik stepped aside, and Branwald sheared downwards through the slit between the door and the jamb. The door popped out slightly. He pushed it and it swung open, the hinges squealing loudly.

The corridor outside was dark, and a yellow light glowed from around a corner at the end. Branwald listened. The talking had ceased. Across the corridor stood another door. Rafik nudged Branwald forward and he padded across, hardly breathing. There was the sound of rustling inside, and a woman's cough.

Branwald found the bolt on the door, and the big oil-stained lock that kept it in place. 'Cut, boy!' Rafik whispered.

The Firebolt sheared downwards through the narrow bar. The lock slid out, and Rafik eased the bolt back out of its socket.

The door opened inwards. There was the smell of sweat and of warm, stale air. Then, in the gloom beyond, they saw the white faces of women staring at them.

'Do not be afraid,' said Rafik. 'And do not speak. It is I, Rafik. I have come back to set you free.'

There was a silent moment before his words sank home. Then a wave of excited whispering swept back through the long chamber, followed by a rush of bare feet towards the visitors. Rafik greeted several of the women by name, but it was clear that he was searching for another face.

'Leah,' he said, when he could not find the one he sought. 'Where is my Leah?'

The women fell silent. Branwald saw the uneasy glances from one to another.

'She is not here,' a thin-faced woman said quietly.

Rafik searched her face in the gloom. 'Where is she, Peshta? Is she ... is she in the upper part?'

Peshta shook her head and, moving closer to Rafik, caught his arm. His eyes widened. 'Is something wrong, Peshta? Did something happen?' In growing desperation he searched the faces of the women. 'She was here before I left.'

'Rafik, she was taken back to the islands.'

'Taken back? But why? Why would she be —'

'She became ill,' Peshta went on. 'They took her and some others, ten days ago.'

'Why, then, she is on the island. I will see her there, when all this is finished.'

Peshta's glance at the faces of the nearby women was a plea for help. They stared back at her in silence. 'Rafik,' she said gently, 'I am sorry. You will not find her there.'

In the gloom, Branwald could see the whites of Rafik's eyes. 'No!' he whispered. 'No! Not that! Don't tell me that!'

With his free hand he caught Peshta by the shoulder, his voice rising. 'Not now! Not when I'm this close!' His voice cracked under the power of his grief. The pain in the man cut like a knife through Branwald's heart.

Rafik let the musket fall with a clatter onto the floor and pressed his fingertips to his forehead, as if trying to blot out the inescapable knowledge. A low moan of anguish escaped him. 'Don't tell me I came too late,' he whispered.

Helpless in the face of the immensity of the man's grief, Branwald could do nothing but stand beside him as his body shook with sobs. The others, too, stood hushed and silent.

'Rafik,' said Peshta at last. 'We feel your sorrow, too. She was a sister to us. But there will be time for sorrow later. Now, if we are to be freed, there is work to be done. This is what she would have wanted. She spoke of you before she went.'

From outside the Bastion they heard more musket-fire. Feowald said, 'I will go and see.' The others waited in silence, their eyes on Rafik, who stood still, head bowed.

'What must we do, Rafik?' a round-faced woman asked. 'You must tell us what to do.'

Rafik started, as if waking from sleep. Then, without a word, he picked up the musket and turned back towards the corridor.

Branwald, sensing the man's incapacity and the growing tension in the women, spoke. 'We have broken through the outer wall. The gas tank is ablaze and the men have already been freed.' There were several suppressed cries. 'They have gone to the mine gates to obtain tools with which to fight. Some are returning to help us here. But there is danger outside, and above us. Now listen. There is an opening in the outer wall close to here. As soon as you are given the word, you must run for it. Do not stay to gather possessions. And make no noise.' He caught Peshta's arm as she turned back into the gloom. 'Peshta, are there guards in the building?'

'They come down several times during the night. But mostly they stay on the next level, where they play at dice and drink their swill. But take care. They can come without warning.'

'How many of you are here?'

'Thirty-five remain.'

Branwald found Rafik in the corridor, staring towards the lighted area at the end. 'I am sorry, Rafik,' he whispered.

Rafik stared at him as if he were a stranger. Then he nodded slowly and looked again along the corridor.

Uncomfortable with the man's grief, Branwald went into the storeroom. His father was perched by the opening, listening. Branwald climbed up beside him and pointed out the place, no more than thirty paces away, where he and Rafik had penetrated the outer wall.

'The women can get out through there. There is too much risk in getting to the mine. If they get to the trees, they will be safe for the moment. We will find them later.'

'We must do it now, Branwald. Those two sentry boxes are empty.'

'I will send them up,' Branwald said.

CHAPTER TWENTY-EIGHT

Branwald found Rafik at the door of the storeroom, still watching the corridor. The women were crowded together at the door of their quarters, their faces tense and expectant. A child began to sob, but it was hushed into silence.

'You must leave now, through here,' Branwald said. 'My father will tell you where to go.'

He ushered the first women into the storeroom. They had difficulty in climbing up to the opening, for the barrels were loose and unstable. Then, just as the sixth woman reached the top, a barrel slipped and started to topple. Branwald grabbed it, but the dull clatter it made seemed like thunder. The sound jolted Rafik out of the trance that he was in, however, and he started to reload his musket.

Branwald could not understand why there were no Oremen around. Surely they must have guessed what was happening by now. He wondered where Targye and Maloof were, and what was happening to the men who had escaped.

There was an urgent call from Feowald. 'Branwald, they've opened a window above us,' he hissed. Branwald clambered up to the opening and looked up along the black wall of the Bastion. In an opening near the top, he saw a window lit from the inside, and two dark shapes leaning out. He heard men's voices. Branwald flattened himself against the wall, catching the arm of the next woman as she came out.

'Wait,' he whispered. 'They are watching from above.'

In the darkness, he felt his father's hand reaching for his. The strong fingers gripped and held. 'Branwald,' Feowald whispered, 'you may need to use the Firebolt now. If the men stay there, they will see the women and they will use their muskets against them.'

Branwald waited, holding the Firebolt by the blade behind

283

his back. But there was no sense of urgency in the tone of the speakers above. Then, from the direction of the mine, came shouts. The shadows at the window went away, although the sash remained open.

Branwald waited several moments longer. 'Go on, quickly!' he told the woman. She ducked out and ran for the opening. Another followed, and another. The fourth was halfway across the space when there was a shout from above. Branwald saw the muzzle of a musket being pushed out; it was followed by a man's head and shoulders. He swung the Firebolt out and up, gripping it by the handle. The beam shot up along the wall. The musket flashed once and abruptly withdrew. A woman fell to the ground, only feet from the safety of the opening.

Branwald stepped out from the wall and focused the beam in through the window above. He heard a muttered exclamation, but the rectangle of light remained clear.

'Help her!' he told the following women.

He kept the beam playing on the high window while the line of women scrambled past. There was no further sound from above. 'They are descending,' Branwald told himself. He stepped quickly away as the window sash, sheared from its hinges, suddenly began to plummet to the ground. It landed with a metallic crash beside him.

Several men came rushing around the corner of the building and, halting, took up firing positions. When Branwald swung the beam of the Firebolt along the ground towards them, however, they scattered and darted back around the corner.

'Run! Run!' Branwald urged the women. He focused the beam on the corner, from where he knew that musket-fire would come. He was beginning to feel hemmed in, on the defensive for the first time. He heard shots, but saw no flashes at the corner. Then there was a sudden surge of fighting yells from the front of the Bastion.

'Run, Father! Run for the wall!' Branwald urged.

There was the muffled report of a shot from the store-room, followed immediately by another. Branwald heard Rafik shouting. A woman cried, 'The guards are coming!' He lowered the Firebolt and pushed back through the opening into the dark storeroom, but the frantic scrambling of the women to get out over the barrels impeded him.

He found Rafik fitting an arrow to his bow, his musket thrown to one side. The last few women were leaving. There was a loud blast from the end of the corridor, and Rafik drew back from the doorway.

'Come on, Rafik. It is time to go,' Branwald said.

But Rafik did not move. Branwald found the big man staring at him. 'Your work is done here now, young one,' he said, his voice curiously strained. 'But I ... I have something left to do.' In the faint glow from the Firebolt, Rafik's eyes dropped to the weapon in Branwald's hand. 'I cannot keep these guards at bay with only a bow and arrow.'

Branwald moved to the doorway, gripping the Firebolt. He looked cautiously along the corridor. He saw a crouched figure at the corner. There was another flashing blast, and a lead ball struck the wall to his right. He started to raise the Firebolt. Suddenly something heavy crashed against the back of his head.

Then he was lying on the floor, his brain numbed and clouded. He shook his head and opened his eyes wide. He tried to call for Rafik, but the sound he made was thick and incoherent. He felt an urgency, but he could not remember what it was he had to do.

Then he remembered the Firebolt. He scrambled to his knees and looked about him for its pale glow, but he could not see it. His hand touched something, but it was only the cold barrel of a musket.

Branwald's head cleared, and he got to his feet. Where was Rafik? He glanced towards the end of the corridor, but it was clear. From beyond it came confused shouting.

And then he knew what had happened. Rafik had struck him, taken the Firebolt and gone down the corridor into the depths of the Bastion.

Branwald picked up the musket. His first impulse was to climb out and run for safety, but he could not do it. He knew that he had to go after Rafik, that he had to recover the Firebolt before it fell into the hands of the Oremen. And so, gripping the musket in both hands and with a terrible dread in his heart, he hurried towards the yellow light at the end of the corridor.

When he came to the corner, he knew for certain that Rafik had taken the Firebolt. A tracery of black scorch-marks was etched on the grey wall. Rounding the corner, he found himself at the bottom of a deserted staircase. He went up. The stairs opened onto a wide hall, lit with yellow lights.

Branwald paused near the top of the steps, crouching so that the floor of the hall was level with his eyes. Knowing that the musket in his hand had already been fired, he primed himself for flight. But the high-roofed hall was silent and empty. Along three walls a high balcony projected out over the floor, supported by cylindrical columns. In the fourth wall was set a wide flight of stairs, with dull grey banisters. Branwald could not see where they led.

He climbed the remaining steps and darted into the shadow of the balcony, uncertain of his route. From a distance came the sound of shots and of men yelling. Branwald saw that there were arched openings in the shadows under the balcony opposite, but he could see no movement there. He started to move towards the stairs, but drew back into the shadows again when he heard footsteps, running, coming closer. Three men, each carrying a musket, emerged from one of the archways and rushed down the steps by which Branwald had come.

Then he heard a man's voice, speaking stridently — Rafik's. He thought the sound came from above.

Branwald sprinted for the stairs, taking the steps three at a time. At the top he found a wide corridor. The weak yellow lights showed it was empty. The curving banisters rose to flank another flight of steps rising into darkness above. Then, somewhere along the corridor, he heard metallic rattling, as if a bolt was being drawn back. He ran for the next flight of stairs, taking great noiseless leaps till he was hidden in the shadows at the top. A black-garbed figure strode into view below and turned down the first flight, hard heels rapping on the metal. A curved helmet hid his face.

Branwald felt trapped. He should have stayed with his

father, he thought. He was angry with himself, too. He should have known that Rafik would try to get his hands on the Firebolt. He hadn't been watchful.

He stepped back from the stairs and tried to think. What if his father came looking for him? Then he too would be in great danger ....

The stillness was strange, eerie. In the gloom Branwald saw another rising flight of stairs. He listened. There was a sound from high above him, as if someone was dragging a heavy object across a floor. Noiselessly he climbed the steps.

At the top was another wide hall, but this time there were furnishings: three long wooden tables, flanked by rows of wooden chairs. Wrought metal designs hung on the walls. Branwald slid into the shadows of a doorway and listened. There was silence, as if the building was deserted. Could it be possible? he asked himself.

And then, as if in answer, came the thought in his mind, clear and strong and very close. 'So you have come at last.'

Branwald started. He looked around, but nobody was visible.

Another thought struck. 'Do not be afraid, young one. I have ordered my men not to shoot you. You are safe here.'

Branwald broke for the stairs, but as he reached the top he saw several Oremen at the bottom, their muskets at the ready.

Behind him there was a click. The door where he had been sheltering began to open, revealing a lighted area beyond. A deep male voice called out, 'Come in. Branwald, isn't it?'

Branwald did not move. Fear gripped his stomach. He was caught. The worst had happened.

He found his voice. 'Yes, I am Branwald.'

The man spoke again, his tone even and confident. 'You have no choice. Come in.'

With pounding heart, and with the musket pointing ahead, Branwald walked through the doorway.

There were three lights in the apartment: one on the high deep-red ceiling and one positioned on each of the side walls, overlooking projecting balconies. The lights were shaded and tilted in such a way that their full glow fell on the half of the room where Branwald stood. To his right stood a solid wooden chair with a red fabric-covered seat. Beside it was a low wooden table. He could see nothing in the darkness beyond. The door closed behind him.

'Sit down, Branwald,' the voice from the darkness said. The tone was not unfriendly.

Branwald held his ground. He felt he should speak. 'Who are you?' he demanded, trying to sound brave and confident. He lifted the musket, tilting the barrel forward. Immediately there was the sound of a movement to his left.

'No. Wait,' the voice said. A pause. 'I am Monkan, son of Caviston. Some people call me the Orelord. You have heard of me, I believe.'

'Yes. I know of you. You have imprisoned our fathers, and many of our people.'

'Your fathers? Who is your father, boy?'

'My father is Feowald the Protector.'

'And the other one's?'

'He is Brugarh.'

Branwald heard low muttering, as if the speaker was consulting with someone. Then the voice came again. 'It would be an easy matter to let you have your fathers back, Branwald. It is simply a question of exchange.' Another pause. 'Where is the weapon?'

Branwald tried not to think of Rafik. 'It is safe,' he said. 'It is in a safe place.'

There was a movement in the darkness where the voice came from, a glint of reflected light. Branwald half-closed his eyes to see better. A faint glow, an aura of dull yellow light, was there, but it seemed to come from behind some tall rectangular shape.

The voice came again, closer now. 'Don't you know that I do not need you, boy?' There was a hardness to the tone. 'I can have you killed with a click of my fingers.' A tall, shiny, cylindrical object was moving slowly towards Branwald. He could see his own image, thin and elongated, reflected there. 'And the reason why I do not do so is merely that I am curious. I want to look at the one who brought the Firebolt back to its rightful owner, and to find out where it has been all these years that I have searched for it.'

The cylindrical mirrored surface was almost in the light. It was nearly six feet high, and Branwald could see the face of a man behind its upper edge — a dark, bearded face, with long black hair framing broad cheeks and wide-spaced eyes. The aura was fainter now.

'Where have you hidden it?'

'My friend has it,' Branwald lied.

'And where is your friend?' The tone sharpened. 'Do not lie to me, boy!'

The mirrored shield rested on the floor, and the face moved out from behind it into the light. Branwald saw narrow shoulders under a grey-belted tunic. He saw deeply etched lines on both sides of the nose, and the glint of white teeth between the lips.

'My friend is safe. You will never get the Firebolt!'

The man sighed. 'Branwald, you are a brave boy, but so foolish. And you know so little. Tell me: who gave you the Firebolt?'

Branwald did not answer. A picture of the Old Soldier hovered at the edges of his mind.

'An old man? In the northern mountains?' the Orelord said.

Branwald could not banish the face of the Old Soldier from his mind. The Orelord nodded, his black eyes half-closed.

'So Bradach still lives.' His eyes drifted away to look into the distance. He shook his head slowly, and the teeth glinted as he laughed. 'After all these years of hiding, he has sent a boy back with the weapon. He is in his second childhood, or else he is a bigger fool than I took him for!'

'He is not a fool,' Branwald retorted, surprised at the strength of his own feelings. His fear had lessened. There was still hope. Rafik had the Firebolt. Maybe he had escaped with it. Maybe Feowald and the men would come.

The black eyes turned on him again. 'He and my father were brothers. Did you know that? Did he tell you that? But he did not act like a brother. He betrayed my father. He wanted the power for himself! And my mother ....' The Orelord waved a dismissive hand. 'But enough of that. In the end he was foolish. He made it easy for me. He sent back the Firebolt. Did he tell you that it belonged to my father?' The

289

dark eyes searched Branwald's face. 'No, I suppose not. Then you do not know that I am its rightful owner.' He nodded slowly with the conviction of his argument. 'Maybe later I will tell you the story, but there is no time now. Branwald, I must know where it is. You will tell me, but it will be easier on you if you tell me here.'

'And if I tell you, what happens?'

'All I want is what is rightfully mine.' The eyes were frank, honest. 'My bargain is this. The Firebolt for your fathers.'

Branwald was silent. He was remembering Rafik's words. How could he trust this man?

'Why do you distrust me? Why do you thwart me? I have befriended you. I have spared you. I can spare your friend, your fathers.'

'Our fathers are safe now,' Branwald retorted. 'Maloof is safe. They do not need your mercy.'

The Orelord lifted his head. He was silent, as if listening. Then he made a motion with his hand, and immediately several Oremen materialised from the darkness and went to stand on either side of the closed door.

The Orelord lifted his eyebrows. 'Your friend is coming,' he said. Abruptly he turned and went behind the shield again, lifting it slightly so that his eyes looked over the top. 'I want you to stand here in front of me, Branwald. If you do not do so, my men will have to kill you.'

Branwald stayed where he was. The Orelord clicked his fingers once, and Branwald heard a movement behind him.

'All right. I will stand there,' he said. He went and stood in the shadows where the Orelord had indicated, his back to the shield, his face towards the door. 'What are you going to do?' he asked.

'That depends on your friend. I do not have to kill him either. Maybe you could explain to him what the bargain is to be. He may find it easier to believe you.'

Branwald frowned. How could the Orelord know if Maloof was nearby?

The Orelord barked a sudden order. 'Bring him in!'

The door opened and two Oremen entered, half dragging, half carrying Maloof. His face was pale and drawn, and there was blood on his cheek. He seemed unable to walk without support.

When Maloof saw Branwald, he did not speak, but his thought was clear and strong. 'Branwald, you are all right!' In his mind, Branwald willed an answer, but something was blocking it.

When the Orelord spoke from the shadows, Maloof started.

'So, you came looking for your friend. How admirable. Well, he is here, untouched. But I see that he has been lying to me. He said you had the Firebolt.'

Maloof straightened and stared boldly into the darkness. He did not speak.

'Where is the weapon?'

'I do not know.'

The Orelord sighed a long-suffering sigh and came out from behind the shield again. 'You disappoint me,' he said. 'I would have expected a little more subtlety from those who have carried the Firebolt. Now it seems that I shall have to extract the information in a less pleasant way. Which is a pity. Bravery I can use; stupidity, no.' His tone seemed weary. 'Now, while we are preparing the fire, you and your friend here will have time to exchange greetings, and to concoct a good story. Those who have not experienced the hot gridiron always do. Then one of you can watch while we extract the truth from the other. I must tell you that the truth always comes out in the end.' He turned to Branwald. 'It would be so much easier if you told me where it is. Then I can keep my part of the bargain.'

'Tell me again what happens if I do,' Branwald said. He was distressed at Maloof's condition. He wondered where the others were. Had they all escaped and abandoned him?

'It is simple. You and both your fathers will be set free. You can go where you wish. Do what you wish.'

'But how do we know that you will do this?'

A flash of impatience crossed the Orelord's face. 'You do not know. You will have to trust me. Why do you not trust me? I can do great things for you.'

Branwald teetered. It would allow him and Maloof to walk free ....

291

'Do not do this, Branwald!' Maloof cried. The Oreman on his right lifted the stock of his musket as if to strike, but the Orelord raised his hand. 'No, no. Do not strike the boy,' he said.

'He lies, Branwald! Do not trust him.'

The Orelord took a step in Maloof's direction, but checked himself. 'Be quiet, you foolish boy!' he commanded. 'You do not understand!' He turned back to Branwald. 'The boy is distressed. He does not know what he is saying. But you, Branwald — you understand me. You know that I only want the thing that was stolen from my father, the thing that right-fully belongs to me.' His eyes were earnest as he gazed at Branwald. 'I know you have hidden it, or given it to someone else. I can understand why you have done so. It is a very powerful weapon, a frightening one.' His tone was almost sympathetic. 'It is too much for a young boy to carry. But now, Branwald, you do not have to bear the responsibility any more. Just tell me where the weapon is.'

'No, Branwald —!' Maloof's cry was cut short as the Oreman on his right jerked him backwards in mid-sentence. The Orelord raised a calming hand again.

'Your friend is ... upset. My men have had to subdue him and he has not yet recovered. But ....' He waited till he had Branwald's attention again. 'He too can share in the reward when this is over. He and your fathers.'

Branwald saw Maloof's blood-streaked face, his pleading eyes. He couldn't decide. He felt Maloof's anguished thought in his mind. 'No, Branwald! Resist this! You must be strong!'

'Branwald,' the Orelord broke in, 'I will find the Firebolt. Even if you do not tell me where it is, I will search it out. You know this. Why, then, do you resist me?'

He caught the sleeve of Branwald's tunic and pulled him to one side. He spoke quietly. 'I am giving you a chance. You must tell me all about the weapon, and about old Bradach, my uncle, whom I thought was dead.' Branwald looked back at Maloof, and then at the face of the man beside him. He could not read the Orelord's thought. 'Where is the weapon? Branwald, you must ....'

Abruptly the Orelord stopped. He turned his head to look towards the door.

292

Suddenly the apartment was illuminated by the brilliant beam of the Firebolt. Branwald saw Rafik framed in the doorway behind Maloof and his captors. Rafik held the Firebolt with both hands, and the beam scorched a crackling line across the ceiling.

'The weapon is here! Murderer! Hell-hound!' he cried.

The light in the centre of the ceiling went out and fell. Branwald leaped to one side to avoid the splintering debris. He was aware of Maloof breaking free and darting into the shadows to his right. Rafik dropped the beam and fixed it over the head of an Oreman who was in the act of raising his musket. 'Put it down!' he screamed. He swept the beam high across the width of the room. 'All of you. Put your weapons down!'

Branwald heard the clatter of muskets dropping to the floor. Rafik stepped into the room, pushing the door until it was fully open and his back rested against it. 'Come, boys!' he called. The boys hurried to his side. 'Go! Run! Get out!'

'Rafik —' Branwald started.

'Get out!' Rafik shouted.

Maloof grabbed Branwald's arm and pulled him towards the doorway. But Branwald could not go. He heard the Orelord shouting and saw that he was standing behind the metal shield again, with only his eyes and the top of his head visible.

'Your time has come, Orelord!' Rafik rasped. 'You killed my Leah. I loved her!' His voice cracked. 'I lived through all this so that someday I could be with her again. But now it cannot be, because you killed her!'

With terrible fascination, Branwald saw the beam descending. The Orelord ducked below the edge of the shield. The beam dropped to the surface where the Orelord's head should have been; but when it met the curved metal, a sudden fan of blinding light flashed across the room. There was a quick stir of bodies as everyone twisted down and away from it. Even Rafik flinched from the intensity.

The Orelord's shouts became intelligible. 'Kill them!' he was screaming. 'Kill them all!'

There was a flash and the roar of a musket from an Oreman to Rafik's right. Rafik staggered back against the door, but he did not fall. His eyes sought out his assailant. Slowly, and with great effort, he changed the aim of the Firebolt.

The Oreman started to run, but the beam was quicker. It found the Oreman's body and steadied. In horror, Branwald saw Rafik's face contort with pain. His arms were extended as if drawn out by some invisible force. The Oreman, trans-fixed by the beam, stood with his musket drooping at a crazy angle, his body frozen into a stance from which he could not free himself. No sound came from either man, but the beam glowed brighter.

Branwald, remembering Maloof's encounter with the great lizard, ran and hurled himself against Rafik's body from the side, hoping to dislodge the beam. The jarring shock sent Rafik staggering. As he toppled to the floor, the Firebolt flew out of his hands and skidded away. It slid into the shadows, collided with the wall and came to rest, its glow dimmed to a faint blue.

Branwald dashed to retrieve it, but the Orelord, darting from his shelter, was quicker. He grabbed it by the handle and lifted it high, leaping away from Branwald.

Crouched on the floor, Branwald looked up at the man's hard eyes. In that terrible moment, he read there that he had lost and that this was the end.

But it was clear that the Orelord feared the weapon. He held it at arm's length, the blade pointing upwards. The beam grew white. Tiny wisps of smoke drifted from the ceiling as it etched a crazy pattern there. Then, without warning, a piece of metal detached itself from above and dropped with a clang onto the floor. The Orelord jumped backwards, stared at the weapon in his hands and abruptly laid it on the floor. He stepped away from it as one would step away from a snake.

'Take them!' he shouted to his men. 'But do not kill them — yet!'

There was a rush of feet, and Branwald felt strong arms hauling him to his feet. Maloof, too, was pinned fast. In the shadows, Rafik lay where he had fallen.

The Orelord bent and gingerly grasped the Firebolt by the blade, lifting it carefully. When the blue glow did not change, he began to examine it. Branwald saw the expression on his face change. A look of satisfaction grew there. The bearded lips parted, and the Orelord smiled. He gingerly gripped the handle, watching the beam beginning to glow and the grey-white lines it traced on the ceiling. Then he took it again by the blade.

His voice took on a musing tone, as if he were speaking to himself. 'There was a time when I had almost grown tired of trying to find this. If my last effort had not succeeded, I should have given it up.' He lifted his head and laughed. 'And now here it is. It came to me without my lifting a finger.' He looked at Branwald, and his eyes grew colder. 'I might have let you go, if you had played fair with me. But now ....' He waved his free hand in a dismissive gesture. 'Take them away!' His tone seemed weary.

The guards began to haul Branwald away, but he struggled against their strong grip. He knew that his father and Targye and the freed prisoners outside would not be able to help him. But he could not finish like this.

'Wait!' he called. 'Hear me! The Firebolt will be of no use to you. It does not obey those who are evil!'

The Orelord's dark eyes turned to fix him with their stare. The guards paused in their efforts to drag him away.

Branwald searched for the grossest words he knew and spat them out. 'It will not obey you, for you are cruel and ignorant and such a coward that you take defenceless women and shut them in this hovel of yours!' The Orelord's eyes widened so that the whites stood out in his face. 'You are no warrior! You are a vile coward! You are a pig!' Branwald shouted.

The Orelord smiled and shook his head. 'Let him go!' he said quietly. He gripped the handle of the Firebolt with both hands, and the beam played on the ceiling. He began to lower it.

The guards hurriedly stepped away, but Branwald did not move. Instead he steeled himself. 'Mother of the earth and of all creatures, give me the strength to do what I must do,' he prayed.

The beam dropped lower, till it was close to his head. He

shouted, 'You think you are a great leader, but you are not! You are scum!'

The Orelord lifted the Firebolt as one would lift a hammer, and swung it downwards. Branwald closed his eyes and braced himself for the searing impact.

The terrible blow never came. Branwald half-opened his eyes and saw that the beam had gone to his left and its white point had become fixed on the floor beside his left foot. He made a sudden leap to intercept it, but the Orelord was quicker and moved it away.

'Hah!' the Orelord exclaimed, holding the Firebolt aloft. 'I am not a fool, boy. Do you think I do not know how to use this weapon?' He stepped out into the full beam of the lights. 'I have been preparing for this moment for years. There is no one who knows more about this weapon than I do. Except one, perhaps. But it will not be long before I am the only one, because you will tell me where to find him.'

'Never!' shouted Branwald. 'I will never tell you that!'

The patient tone again. 'It would serve you better, boy, to take thought for your own survival, than to be spitting out insults. But you are young, and spirited. This means that it will take a little longer to extract the truth from you. But only a little. Take them away!' the Orelord said to the guards. 'But do not start on them till I come. There is another little matter to be dealt with first.'

Branwald made one final, desperate play. His own fate he was prepared for, but he could not tolerate the thought that Maloof would suffer again because of his, Branwald's, mistake.

The two Oremen were closing in on him once more. Just as the strong hands touched his arms, Branwald pulled away and made a headlong rush towards the two guards who held Maloof. There were shouts. The guard on Maloof's left released him and began to lift his musket, but Branwald crashed into him, knocking him backwards. 'Run, Maloof!' he shouted.

Turning away from the staggering guard, he hurled himself at the other, who was grappling with Maloof. Branwald grabbed the man round the neck and pulled him backwards. Maloof broke free. 'Run, Maloof!' Branwald urged. Another man grabbed him from behind. Then a heavy weight crashed into both of them and knocked them forward onto the floor. A man's knee jarred down onto Branwald's back; something hard thumped into his ribs. He tried to rise, but the weight was too much. He was powerless.

The guards roughly hauled Branwald to his feet and began to drag him towards the door. Then one of the guards behind them gave a warning shout.

Looking back into the darkness behind the Orelord, Branwald saw that Rafik had risen from the floor. He saw Rafik's eyes, white and terrible, as he staggered towards his enemy. At the last second the Orelord sensed him there and turned, holding the Firebolt protectively in front of himself.

The beam dropped close to Rafik's shoulder. Rafik lurched towards it, his arm raised, stretching. His fingers reached it, intercepted it, seemed to pull it down across his chest.

There was a moment of complete silence. All eyes were fixed on the two men, frozen in a silent and terrible tableau. The beam entered Rafik's chest near his right shoulder, but he did not fall or move. His mouth was fixed in a horrible grin, and his eyes glared fixedly at his adversary.

The Orelord screamed. Branwald saw him try to lift the Firebolt, but he could not do it. His body had become rigid. He began to tremble. The trembling increased till his whole frame was racked by violent spasms.

A shot rang out. Rafik lurched to the left, a sudden red splash appearing on the side of his face. He fell on his side on the floor, but the terrible beam still held him transfixed. He tried to rise, but his arm crumpled under him. He tried again and again failed. Then, as the intensity of the Firebolt's light began to fade, his body sank slowly to the floor and lay still.

At that same moment, the Orelord dropped to his knees. The Firebolt fell with a clatter from his grasp. His body seemed like rubber. He wobbled to one side, then to the other. He would have collapsed if a guard had not rushed over and caught his arm.

There were sounds from the hall outside. Through the doorway Branwald saw men moving. He recognised Targye, a musket at his shoulder. The weapon blasted, and one of the

Oremen toppled to the floor like a sack of corn. The other guards scattered for the cover of the archways by the walls.

Branwald scrambled to a pillar and dropped to the floor. He searched for Maloof but could not find him. He saw two guards half carrying, half dragging the Orelord through a doorway at the back of the hall. Other Oremen were running after them. Branwald looked for the Firebolt and saw it lying on the floor, near the still form of Rafik.

Some of the Oremen sheltering in the archways began returning fire, in deafening explosions of enclosed sound. Branwald crouched low, knowing that he too would be a target. He heard shouting and recognised his father's voice, coming from outside the doorway. 'Come on, Branwald! Run!'

Branwald dashed for the Firebolt. He caught the blade, swivelled and raced for the doorway. Then he was hurtling down the steps, taking giant leaps between two lines of crouching men. Coming to rest on the first landing, he turned back towards the top. His father was there, an arrow ready in his bow. 'Branwald! I thought we had lost you!' Then Maloof came running, leaping down into the shelter of the steps. Branwald saw that he had caught up the great mirrored shield which the Orelord had let fall, and that he was using it to deflect the shooting which followed him from the hall. The men on the stairs carried picks and square metal shovels. Several, near the top, had muskets.

In the hall, the shooting had stopped. 'They are reloading,' Feowald said. 'Now that you are safe, there is no need to stay.' He spoke to the men. 'Those with the muskets, guard the rear. The others, leave, quickly!'

'No, wait,' cried Branwald. 'Rafik is there!'

He crept to the top of the stairs again. On the wall outside the Orelord's apartment hung two lights. Branwald lifted the Firebolt and aimed. The lights fell, and the stair-top was in darkness.

Branwald peered into the hall. Rafik still lay where he had fallen. Several dark figures were hurrying away through the doorway through which the Orelord had been carried. Branwald waited. There was no further movement. He heard an echoing clang in the distance. From the walls where the lights had been came a low hissing sound. When Branwald swung the beam of the Firebolt high into the hall, he found it deserted.

'They are gone,' he said.

Cautiously he entered the apartment, aiming the beam low around the walls, alert for any movement. There was none. A cold breeze blew from the doorway beyond.

Targye was already kneeling beside Rafik, his hand on his neck where the pulse should be. The others were silent.

Targye shook his head. 'He is dead,' he said.

Rafik's eyes stared at the floor. There was a red, bleeding hole in his right temple. A dark patch showed in his tunic near his shoulder.

Feowald was speaking to the men. 'The Oremen have gone to the harbour. They may be manning their quarters there, or they may be escaping. Are you still agreed that we should finish the job?' There was an answering shout from the men. 'All right. You three with muskets, lead on. That doorway leads down the long steps. From the bottom there is a tunnel to the harbour. Be careful. We will follow when we have seen to this one.'

The men crowded through the doorway, shouting encouragement to one another.

'Rafik saved us,' Maloof said, in the silence that followed. 'He saved us with his own life.'

'That is how I expected him to go,' Targye said. 'There are few men like Rafik. He is with his Leah now.'

Maloof, pale-faced, turned to Branwald. 'I saw this in my dream,' he whispered. 'But I could not see the face of the dead one. I thought it would be you or me.'

Branwald looked down at Rafik, remorse sweeping over him.

'I should have trusted him more,' he said. 'I didn't know .... I hope he has forgiven me.'

～

They carried Rafik's limp body down the dark, silent stairs to the storeroom where they had first entered. They lifted it up across the barrels and out into the clear night air. There were distant shots and shouting from somewhere on the other side of the Bastion.

From close by the wall there came a low call. It was three of the escaping workers, who had been left to keep watch. Briefly Feowald explained what had happened.

'To the harbour, then, is it?' one of the men asked. He was showing the others how to reload an Oreman's musket.

'To the harbour!' Feowald said. 'This night's work is not yet done!' He turned to Branwald. 'I must go now, Branwald. Take Rafik's body to where the women are, outside the walls. Then follow us, and be careful.'

'I will go with you,' said Maloof. 'I must find my father.'

'We will follow immediately,' promised Branwald.

When the others had hurried away, Branwald and Targye carried Rafik's body out through the opening in the perimeter wall and in amongst the trees beyond. From the shadows several women materialised.

'What is the news? What is happening?' one asked.

'The Oremen are flying to the harbour,' Targye answered.

'Oh, thank the Mother!' she cried. 'Our day of liberation has come!'

'You owe thanks to this brave man,' Targye said. 'Look after his body till we return.'

CHAPTER TWENTY-NINE

When Targye had reloaded his musket, he and Branwald set off for the harbour. The Bastion was silent. The flames from the gas tank were sinking, and the empty huts stood black against their flickering glow. The two skirted the open area near the fire, keeping to the shadows. Branwald saw several bodies on the ground, but he did not pause to see if they were Oremen or not.

The ground began to slope downwards and the perimeter walls to funnel in, narrowing the space. Low in the air ahead, Branwald saw billows of smoke, lit up from below, and he knew there was another fire. Then came the sound of shouting and cheering, punctuated by occasional shots. In the semi-darkness, Branwald stumbled across metal tracks; remembering that they led to the harbour, he followed them, quickening his pace.

He saw flames ahead and, soon afterwards, dark figures moving against them. Some of them had their hands raised and were cheering.

Crouching low, Branwald crept towards them, stopping by the thick trunk of a felled tree.

'These are our people,' Targye breathed, after observing the figures ahead for a few moments. 'By the Mother, they are!' He rose to his feet. 'Come on!' he called.

Moments later, Branwald and Targye were surrounded by a crowd of excited workers, eager for news and loudly proclaiming their exploits. 'They're running away!' one stocky man shouted. 'We've driven them into the sea in their boats!' 'We're burning their quarters!' another exulted.

Branwald searched the crowd for Maloof and Feowald, but could not see them. 'Where are the others?' he asked a sweating worker.

'They're at the harbour, trying to sink the ships!' the man said, pointing through an archway in the building before them, a section of which was burning fiercely. He looked at the Firebolt. 'You are Branwald, Feowald's son, who came to save us?'

'Yes, I am he. Is anyone hurt?'

The man's face became serious. 'Fifteen or sixteen dead, I'd guess. Others badly wounded. I couldn't rightly say how many.'

'There were five who came a short while ago. Where are they?'

'Feowald and the others? They got through while we were firing this.' The man pointed at the flaming building.

Branwald hurried through the archway, past the crackling fire. As he left the smoke behind, there was a new scent on the air — not quite the smell of fish, but close to it. Some distance below him he saw a long, glimmering swath of reflected moonlight stretching away towards the horizon, and he realised it was the sea.

He found a wide path that rang hollow as he descended. From lower down came the sound of sporadic firing. Then Branwald saw flaming torches ahead and heard the loud talking of men, coming in his direction. He and Targye took to the shadows and watched. Some of the men had shovels and picks slung on their shoulders. Others were carrying or supporting men who appeared to be wounded.

'What is happening?' Targye asked.

'They are going! Running away!' a man shouted. 'We're driving them into the sea!'

Branwald searched through the group, but neither his father nor Maloof was there. He heard the men calling his name, but he continued his descent.

He came to a low parapet, flanking the path, over which he could see the harbour below. He saw lights moving far out on the water, and, closer, another cluster of lights. There were flashes and the reports of shots. Then Branwald recognised another sound. It was the chugging of the Oremen's boats across the still water.

Three men were coming slowly up the path, the one in the middle being supported by the others.

'You're too late,' one said. 'They're gone. But we got a few of them. Get the ships with the Firebolt, young Branwald!'

Below, on the quay, Branwald could see another cluster of men. Far out on the water there was another volley of shots.

He hurried down. Something was wrong. There was distress coming from below.

When he reached the level place by the water's edge, he ran. Someone was lying on the ground where the men were gathered.

'Father!' Branwald called. Several men stepped back to let him through.

Maloof came towards him, still carrying the Orelord's shield. 'Branwald, it is your father.'

'Oh, no! What happened?'

'A stray musket-ball. In the thigh. I'm sorry, Branwald. I could not reach him to protect him with this. We are stanching the flow of blood.'

Branwald knelt beside his father. The thought of his mother was strong in his mind. Feowald was conscious, his eyes white against the dark skin of his face. A cloth was bound around his left thigh. Their hands gripped. 'Father!'

'Branwald.' There was pain in the voice. 'I will be all right, my son. This is nothing.'

Branwald glanced at the faces around. In the moonlight, they were serious, but several of them nodded. 'I have seen worse than this, young hero,' one man said. 'But we must get him to the women. They will know what to do.'

Branwald felt a kind of relief. It was as if he had been expecting that either Maloof or his father would be killed, and now that the worst had happened, Feowald was only wounded. He was alive. He would live.

As Branwald stood up, he felt Maloof's hand on his shoulder.

'The Mother does not need us for a while yet, it seems,' Maloof said. He turned to a tall man on his right. 'Branwald, you remember my father, Brugarh?'

Branwald took the proffered hand. His heart was suddenly full. He could not speak.

❧

Four men, one of them Branwald, carried Feowald to the space near the huts where the workers were gathered. Some of the women had already come back through the fence to share in the rejoicing, to greet the menfolk and to tend to the wounded, who had been left lying beside the stockade wall, where several small fires were being lit. Feowald was placed beside these while Brugarh sought out some women to attend to him.

The fires were slow to blaze, and the light cast by the moon was weak. 'Use the Firebolt,' a woman suggested. 'We need its light to see what we must do.'

Branwald gripped the Firebolt's handle and lifted the blade. The beam shot out into the night sky and the light cast a white glow on the ground and walls around. He moved the beam until it met the side of the Bastion and held it there, a grim sense of satisfaction gripping him. Why not show the fleeing Oremen the power of the Firebolt? Why not make the Orelord, if he still lived on board the fleeing ships, aware of what he had lost?

Deliberately he aimed at the upper corner of the building and cut diagonally across it. He heard encouraging calls from some of the men. To a chorus of shouts, and in a shower of sparks, the corner piece began to fall. It caught on an edge, hung momentarily, then plunged. People who were near the Bastion surged away as the piece dropped. It struck the ground with a noise like thunder, rolled over once and lay still, a cloud of dust swirling round it.

'Go on, Branwald!' a man shouted. Encouraged by this and exulting in his power, Branwald made a horizontal cut across the two windows, the great 'eyes', which were now dark and empty. The crowd moved further away as they realised what would happen. Branwald had to retrace the line several times before the great 'forehead' gave a sudden lurch forward. Men were yelling. Branwald heard his father's voice, but could not distinguish the words. He felt elated.

Slowly the great crown of the Bastion slid forward. Then, suddenly, the forward section dipped and the whole piece dropped in a tumult of shrieking and clanging. The sound of its collision with the ground was like nothing Branwald had ever heard. The rumbling echo rolled round the mine and out across the sea, and he exulted because he knew that the Oremen could hear it.

Then Maloof was beside him. 'Branwald, this is not the time for this. There are many wounded here who must be tended to ....'

'Let them be tended to, Maloof. This is what the people want, and I am the one who must do it.'

He was interrupted by another gasp from the crowd. A sudden burst of flame came from deep in the Bastion. They saw its leaping pattern on the windows and in the gaping hole in the 'head'. The people cheered.

Branwald aimed at the side of the building. He cut a long dagger-shaped piece off the corner; it plunged and embedded itself in the ground below. A spurt of flame shot out through the gash.

Branwald was resolved. He would destroy the Bastion of the Orelord. He would carve this great structure up until all that remained was a crumpled, crazy ruin.

But something was wrong. The light from the Firebolt was weakening; the beam was becoming less bright. Branwald gripped the handle more tightly, willing his power into the instrument, but to no avail. Gradually, the white light weakened, grew less and less intense, until at last all that remained was a deep blue glow.

Branwald stared at the Firebolt. How could this be? Why was the weapon not responding? He noticed that the people around him had gone quiet, and for some reason he was irritated with them.

Then Maloof was beside him, his arm around Branwald's shoulders. 'Even the Firebolt grows weary,' he said. 'You will have to wait for the sun, Branwald. You are weary too, after your great deeds. You need some rest.'

~

The Island People spent the remaining hours of darkness in counting their dead, tending to their wounded, telling and retelling the deeds of that glorious night, and making plans for the morrow. Some, who could not tolerate being still enclosed, went out amongst the dark trees — some wandering through the scattered groves, some just standing, touching the trunks of the trees as they would the face of a long-lost, intimate friend. Others, who were guarding the harbour approaches for fear of the Oremen's return, went on board the three remaining boats and learned how the black, smoky engines were able to propel them through the water.

Twenty-four of the imprisoned people had died, two of them women. Eighteen men lay wounded, five critically. The bodies of eleven Oremen lay near the entrance to the mine; thirteen more lay scattered about. There was joy, tempered with sadness. And there was praise from all sides for the two boys and two men who had carried out the daring rescue.

'This day will never be forgotten in the legends of our people!' exclaimed Peshta, the thin-faced woman who had told Rafik the news about his wife.

～

A little before daybreak, Branwald and Maloof were sitting outside the walls, on a rocky outcrop that looked out across the great sweep of the ocean to the south. The wound on Maloof's head, caused by the butt of an Oreman's musket when he had been caught entering the Bastion in search of Branwald, had been stanched. Maloof had his bow and the Orelord's shield with him, and the Firebolt lay on the rock beside Branwald. Below them, black smoke was billowing from the chimneys of two of the boats, as workers prepared them to depart with the seriously wounded.

The boys were quiet after talking themselves into weariness. Behind them the woods were beginning to swell with birdsong. Low in the eastern sky, the purple of the night was giving way to faint slashes of gold.

Branwald tried to clear his mind and focus on Sula, but he could not get a clear image of her. Something was blocking his energies. He gave up trying, hoping that she had felt something of what had happened. He wondered where she and Morung were.

Then they became aware of a new sound, floating up from the direction of the ocean, like a continuous repeated sighing.

'It is the waves,' Branwald said.

'Come on,' said Maloof. 'We will look.'

Branwald followed his friend. He was restless and tense, as if there was something he had left undone, but he could not bring it to mind. Perhaps, he thought, he was simply on edge because he still did not know what the Orelord's fate had been. It was likely, he knew, that even if the Orelord's men had dragged him to the safety of the boats, he was too weakened by his encounter with the Firebolt to be any real threat. Yet the thought that the man was out there somewhere made Branwald uneasy.

Maybe he should go back to his father, he thought. But he knew there was nothing he could do. The women had seen to Feowald's wound and made him comfortable. They had said that he would be ill, but that he would live.

The boys walked towards a roofless stone building silhouetted against the brightening sky. Beyond it was the sea. A slash of light was lengthening along the horizon.

By the east side of the building, they stopped. A cliff dropped sheer to the water. The surface of the ocean was restless, as Branwald had often seen Eagle Lake after the autumn gales, but the waves here were bigger and slower. They washed in against the base of the cliff with a sucking, hollow sound.

The boys cautiously peered over the edge. All along the bottom of the cliff, where the waves struck, the water was a churning, frothy white. Further to the left, where the cliff curved inwards, the boys glimpsed the white sand of a beach.

'This would be perfect for swimming,' said Maloof.

'You forget about the lizards,' Branwald replied, irritated that Maloof could think of swimming at such a time.

'There are none here. Lizards live only where many trees lie near the water's edge,' Maloof said, starting to move along the cliff-top towards the beach.

Branwald hesitated. He was still uneasy. He glanced around through the trees behind. The birds still sang their throaty anthems. It was foolish, he told himself. The Oremen were gone.

Branwald started to follow, but found that Maloof had stopped. When he came to where his friend stood, he saw why. Below them, drawn up on the nearer end of the beach,

307

lay a black shape, a wisp of grey smoke drifting from its centre. It was an Oreman boat.

Branwald stared at it in silence, his mind flooded with questions. Had some of the fleeing Oremen turned into this cove and circled back towards the mine? Were they even now waiting to ambush the unsuspecting workers?

Then he noticed something else. The birds were no longer singing.

Branwald plucked Maloof by the sleeve and started back towards the ruins. Then, in the trees to his right, he saw a dark figure running. Another appeared, and a third behind them. All carried muskets.

Then Branwald and Maloof were sprinting for the ruins. They spotted a jagged opening and burst through to a debris-laden, stony floor. Ahead, through gaps in walls, they saw the distant perimeter fence. But there was too much open ground between it and them.

'They have surrounded us,' Maloof whispered, holding the Orelord's shield in front of Branwald, his eyes searching the crumbling walls. 'Come, Branwald! This way!'

Maloof picked his way through scattered stones to the ivy-smothered opening in the south wall. When Branwald reached it, he recoiled. There was no ground outside, only the vertical drop to the churning sea far below. But Maloof was tugging at his tunic and pointing around the right-hand side of the opening, where the clinging ivy was dense. 'Climb round there,' he said. 'I will follow with the shield. They may not see us there. Be quick!'

Branwald slung the Firebolt over his shoulder and gripped the ivy. His foot found a niche. Maloof, his bow and quiver over his shoulder and his right arm hooked through the handle of the shield, followed. Below them, the sea rumbled and seethed.

Branwald worked his way along the creepers until he was shielded by the bushy foliage. His left arm was looped around a stout stem, his feet firmly lodged in a cleft. Maloof, beside him, lifted the shield to form a barrier between them and the opening through which they had come, angling it so that the edge did not protrude. Branwald heard Maloof's thought in his mind. 'Be silent, Branwald. Do not even think!'

They waited. In the east, the far mountain-tops were edged with gold and the sky was filling with light, but Branwald wished for the covering darkness to stay. He strained to listen, but the waves below drowned all sound.

He remembered the Firebolt, and unslung it by the blade. Then, with a sick feeling, he remembered that the power was gone from it. He had allowed his desire for acclaim and for revenge to carry him away, and he had wasted all the Firebolt's energy in his attempt to destroy the Bastion. And now, when he had most need of it, the Firebolt could not help him.

The minutes crawled by. The thought came to Branwald that maybe the men had given up the search. Maybe someone in the Bastion would see what was going on and send help ....

And then, with a blow that shook his being, the knowledge that Urkor was close by struck him.

He had no time for another thought. There was a movement at the opening, beyond Maloof. Branwald pressed against the creepers. Then a musket exploded. The shield in Maloof's hand jerked backwards against him, as if it had been struck by a sledgehammer. Branwald grabbed Maloof's tunic to steady him. 'I'm all right, Branwald!' Maloof cried.

A man shouted. Again a musket blasted; again the shield slammed back. Branwald tightened his grip as Maloof struggled to hold the creeper with his left hand. 'Hold me!' Maloof gasped.

Branwald knew that his friend could not withstand this assault for much longer. He released his hold on Maloof's tunic and gripped the Firebolt by the handle. There was a momentary pulse of light, but it did not last. Branwald pointed the blade over the top of the shield, in the direction of the opening, but the beam was blue and weak.

He heard men speaking. There was a pause, then Urkor's voice, very near.

'There is nothing you can do now, boy. The power is gone from the Firebolt. We saw it from the boat as we came closer.'

Branwald looked around the shield and saw Urkor's face at the opening. He was leaning out, warily holding out his hand towards Maloof. 'Give me the weapon, boy. That is all I need. Then you and the other one can go on your way. We will not harm you.'

Branwald felt Maloof's alarmed response. He looked down. The frothing water was very far away. He twirled his arm to wrap the Firebolt's cord around his wrist.

But Urkor read his thoughts. 'If you jump, you will certainly die,' he said. 'And the weapon will be lost forever.'

'Better that it should be lost forever than that you should have it,' Branwald said.

'You will die!' Urkor shouted hoarsely, bringing up the point of his musket. Maloof steadied the shield again.

'You still will not have the Firebolt!' Branwald shouted, glancing below again.

The musket blasted. As the shield came slamming back again, Branwald felt the creeper that Maloof was holding rip away from the wall.

Branwald shouted and grabbed for Maloof's hand. Their fingers touched and held, momentarily. Maloof's eyes caught his. His mind heard, 'Branwald.'

Then, as Branwald screamed Maloof's name, his fingers slipped and Maloof dropped away from him. The shield glinted as it spiralled around Maloof's body. Then the foaming water swallowed boy and shield together.

With rage in his heart, Branwald looked for Urkor. He saw the teeth bared in a grin, the hand stretched towards him.

At that moment, the sun peeped over the eastern mountains. It dazzled Branwald's eyes. He felt a sudden electric tingle in his right hand. The blade of the Firebolt was losing its blueness.

Branwald lifted the Firebolt and swung the pale beam across Urkor's face. He felt the shock in his arm. Urkor screamed. His hands flew to his face, and he fell backwards.

But the strength was suddenly gone from Branwald's arms. He felt the muscles of his left arm slowly relaxing. He tried to grab the creeper with his right hand, but it would not respond. Then he was falling, falling, down and down. As he dropped towards the swirling water, he felt a pain as if his heart was being torn in two.

He struck, plunged, was swallowed by cold, his breath

knocked out of him. There was a muffled roaring in his ears. He tried to breathe, but water choked him. Around him, the light was a translucent green. He tried to swim, but his arms did not respond. He kicked feebly, and his head came through to the air. He took one gulp and went under again. The Firebolt was no longer in his hand, but he thought the string was still attached to his wrist.

A cold draught was filling his lungs and he knew that he was drowning. Unaccountably, his mother's face swam into his mind. She was smiling. But she could not know, he thought.

He struck out weakly with his left arm. Something dark was in the water above him, a shadow drawing closer. A lizard, he thought ironically, coming to finish him off. He turned to face it.

A slim, straight shape plunged through the water towards him, but there were no jaws. He felt himself being caught by the tunic and lifted. An arm, slight but strong, gripped him around the neck. He felt legs thrashing against his back. He was being pulled upwards.

His head broke the surface, and he heard voices. He knew that he was dreaming, because the voice he heard was Morung's, and he knew that couldn't be. Then strong hands were holding him and he was being lifted, dragged across a hard surface ....

Branwald lay for what seemed a long time in the wet hold of the swaying canoe. Someone was pulling and turning him, twisting his head — a girl, speaking urgently. He had the wretched sensation of choking, of coughing, of vomiting salt water. He wanted to die. A dreadful weight lay across his chest. As in a dream, he heard distant musket-fire and shouts.

Then he found himself lying face down on hard, flat rock. There were people around. A man was crouched beside him, speaking earnestly. Branwald heard what he thought was Sula's voice, and he tried to sit up.

'Branwald?' She was there, white-faced, her bodice wet and clinging.

'Maloof? Where is Maloof?' he gasped.

Sula's eyes were wet. 'They have gone back for him, Branwald.'

'Is he all right? Where is he?'

'He is in the water. We couldn't take two. He told us to leave him and take you. Father has gone back for him.'

Branwald stared around him. He was on the wall of the harbour. People were standing, their backs to him, looking seawards. He heard the murmur of their voices, growing louder. Something was happening at the harbour mouth. As Morung's canoe came gliding in, Branwald struggled to his feet, holding Sula's arm to support himself.

Men knelt to grip the sides of the canoe. They were lifting a limp figure from the floor and placing him on the wall.

Branwald lurched towards them. 'Maloof!' he called hoarsely, his tears blinding him. 'Maloof!'

A man broke from the group around Maloof and stopped him. 'Let them be, boy. They are trying!'

Branwald pushed the man away. 'I want to see!' he shouted.

Several men caught and held him. Sula started to speak, but Branwald shouted, 'Maloof! Don't die! Please, Maloof. Please don't die!'

The men held him back. Sula put her arms around him, her head against his chest. Branwald lifted his head and shouted to the Great Mother, 'Don't let him die, Mother. Don't take him! Not yet!'

The activity in the huddled group was frantic. Morung was breathing into Maloof's mouth. The men were silent.

Again he breathed. The men leaned closer. Another breath.

Then a man shouted, 'He lives! The boy lives!'

CHAPTER THIRTY

A little later, while all the people except the lookouts at the harbour were gathering near the huts where the men had lived, Sula came to Branwald and Maloof. She was holding the hand of a tall, bearded youth whose forehead was wound with a strip of bloodstained cloth.

'This is my brother, Ganden,' she told them. 'He is safe and well, apart from that.' She pointed at the bandage. Ganden smiled down at her, and Branwald saw that he had the same wide-spaced eyes as his sister.

'This is a great day for my people,' Ganden told them. 'And we are grateful to you for making it possible. I and many of those you have freed look forward to hearing your story.' He offered his hand, and Branwald felt his lean strength.

When the people were ready, a council was held in the open air. The sun had risen above the horizon, but there was as yet little heat in the clear air. Morung and Feowald presided, Feowald lying on a raised bunk that the men had ripped out of a hut. It was decided that the most seriously wounded would be transported, with all possible speed, to Morung and Sula's village; the three boats of the Oremen were already stoked and ready to embark. The rest of the people would set out immediately on foot in the direction of the Citadel of Kiura. They would carry the dead on makeshift stretchers as far as the Bridge of the Cormorants. There they would be collected by the returning boats. The people had been unanimous that none of their dead should be cremated on the Red Mount.

When the men were satisfied that the ocean as far as the eye could see was clear of any craft, and when the boats carrying the wounded had left, the people gathered their few belongings and the litters holding the dead and filed out through the opening which Branwald had cut. The sun was high, and from the trees came the hum of busy insects; but the people were quiet, their joy at being free tainted by the deaths and injuries of their friends.

Branwald had resisted attempts by Morung and the others to persuade him to take a place in one of the boats. He had recovered almost completely from his ordeal, although his right arm felt weak and his legs tired. 'Let the boats carry my father and the badly wounded,' he said. 'I will walk.'

Maloof, Sula and Ganden walked with him; Morung had decided that Sula would be in less danger on land. She told them how she, Morung and Atula had happened to be near the harbour of the Oremen when Maloof and Branwald fell from the cliff.

They had been watching through the night. Having seen the beams of the Firebolt in the sky and the explosion of the gas tank, they had set out by moonlight in the canoe, intending to land on the coast near the Bastion. They had just reached the mouth of the inlet and were turning downriver when, behind them, they heard the Oremen's boat following from the Bridge of the Cormorants. Well hidden, they allowed it to pass; and as it did so, Sula knew that Urkor was on board. They followed with all speed.

Later, when Branwald was attempting to destroy the Bastion, they saw the beams of the Firebolt criss-crossing the sky, but did not understand what was happening. They were concerned, however, when the beam dimmed and went out.

When they saw the Oremen's boats speeding away from the harbour, they were elated; but as morning approached and they neared the beach, they were alarmed to see a single boat drawn up there, with smoke issuing from its chimney. Sula had wanted to try to reach Branwald, but, because of her sense of Urkor's nearness, Morung had forbidden it.

They had been resting in a small cove near the harbour when they heard shooting on the cliff-top, and they emerged just in time to see someone plummet into the water. Sula guessed it was Maloof. Risking being fired on from above, they hastened to his rescue. They had almost reached Maloof when Branwald fell.

While Sula was struggling to bring Branwald to the surface, Atula was in the water helping Maloof. Maloof, who had let go of the Orelord's shield in his efforts to stay afloat, had rejected all attempts to get him into the canoe until Branwald was safe. Then Morung, judging that the canoe would founder if they tried to get both Maloof and Atula into it, had tried to drag them, using the stern rope, but had made little progress. Atula had urged him to leave her and Maloof, to get Branwald — who still had the Firebolt tied to his wrist — to safety and then return with all haste to their rescue.

Having done so, Morung had found Atula in an exhausted condition, struggling to keep a semi-conscious Maloof afloat. With great difficulty he had managed to haul first Maloof and then Atula into the canoe. He had almost reached the harbour when the Oremen, driven off by the workers who had been alerted by their shooting, had sped away southwards in their boat.

'They were too fast for our men,' Sula added, reading the boys' minds. 'All of them got away.'

'There have been times,' Branwald said, when he was able to speak, 'when I thought that I and the Firebolt would be able to do all this, with no help from anyone. Now I know it could not have been. We owe so much to you and to the others.'

'We did only a little,' she said. 'None of this could have happened if you had not come.'

'It is ironic,' mused Maloof, 'that the shield of the Orelord was to protect us in the end.'

'It would have been a fine trophy to bring home,' said Branwald.

'Maybe it is better where it is now,' Sula said. 'The sea will guard it well.'

~

'When I saw you coming through the water for me,' Branwald joked later, 'I thought you were a lizard coming to eat me.'

Sula smiled. 'You would be too tough and salty for my liking, Branwald.'

Maloof, on the other side of her, was smiling too. 'You remind me of another girl whom we met on the way,' he

315

said quietly. 'Someday maybe you will meet her.'

Sula nodded. 'I would like to meet her, Maloof. All of us together.'

'The Great Mother must have had this in mind last night,' Branwald said.

Maloof's serene eyes looked at the other two. 'Perhaps She did,' he said.

CHAPTER THIRTY-ONE

It was morning in the Tarquan village, eight days later. Feowald, gripping a makeshift crutch, and the remaining men from the northern islands were ready to set out on their journey home. It had been agreed that they would be transported in the Oremen's boats as far upstream as the river would allow. From there they would continue on foot, unless they had the luck to meet some of the Hittion people from the western mountains, who might sell them horses. Feowald had insisted that he was fit to travel; in spite of his protests, the other islanders had constructed a litter in which they would carry him if his strength failed.

The whole community lined the wharf as the islanders made their farewells.

'Remember that there is a place for you and your people amongst us,' Feowald said to Morung, 'if you should ever need it.'

'We will remember. My people are not yet ready for such a move, but who can tell what the future holds? May the Mother Spirit be with you.'

Feowald turned to Branwald, whose empty canoe was still resting upside-down on the wharf. 'Are you still sure you want to do this, Branwald?' he asked.

Branwald nodded. 'You know I must, Father. We told Bradach we would. Maybe when you are healthy again, you will search for him in the Kadach Pit and tell him what has happened.'

His father nodded. 'I will do that, Branwald.'

Brugarh, Maloof's father, looked at his son. 'Your mother and I will look for your return every day, son. You know that.'

'I hope it will not be long, Father. I will return as soon as the task is finished.'

The canoes taking the travellers set off in convoy — the boats of the Oremen were unable to negotiate the shallow waters near the village — and soon they had passed out of sight behind the trees. Then Branwald and Maloof launched their canoe and began to load it with the provisions which they had prepared, surrounded by children fighting among themselves to carry the packs to the canoe.

'Can I come with you, Maloof?' Hedin asked for the hundredth time. 'Please!'

Maloof smiled. 'I'm sorry, Hedin. You know the answer to that question.'

'But I can fight, and paddle,' the youngster insisted. 'And I'm a great fisherman, and —'

'When you are older,' Maloof promised. 'Maybe you can come to see where my people live.'

The boy's eyes widened. 'Can I? When? Next year?'

Maloof laughed again. 'Maybe,' he said, ruffling the boy's hair. 'And now you can help me load the canoe.'

Branwald found Sula beside him.

'I know the answer, too,' she said sadly.

'You know how much I would like you to come,' he said. 'But there are the dangers, and the great distance to the Monastery. And there is also your father.'

'Do not forget your promise,' she said seriously. She kissed him.

'Yes,' Branwald said. 'I will come here before I return to my home. Do not doubt that.'

The boys climbed into the canoe, which was bulging in the middle with supplies. Branwald adjusted the buckskin map which was fixed to the thwart.

There was a clamour on the wharf as the gathered people called out their farewells. Then the boys pushed away from the weathered timber, turned the prow towards the west and stroked hard with their paddles.

As they came to the trees, Branwald looked behind. His eyes sought out Sula. He could feel her sadness in his mind. He waved once.

'I will come back,' he thought.

Then the Tarquan People were left behind, and Branwald and Maloof were alone.

~

In the annals of the People of the Tarquan Islands there is a new legend. It tells of how, after he and his friend Maloof had travelled along the Great River from beyond the northern mountains, Branwald, the bearer of the Firebolt, penetrated the Bastion of the Orelord, defeated him and his soldiers, and destroyed his great black fortress. It tells, too, of Rafik, the Tarquan Islander whose beloved Leah had died a prisoner of the Orelord, who gave his life so that his people could be free. It tells of many who fought in that great escape, some still living, others who died. And lastly, it tells of how Branwald and Maloof, after their fathers and the rest of their people had started on their journey towards their homes beyond the mountains, set out together, with the Firebolt, to deliver it to the Monastery of the Sordiana, far to the west. The story of that journey has not yet been written.

More Outstanding New Fiction from

WOLFHOUND PRESS

Celtic Fury

Seán Kenny

Jack Amonson was once a successful thriller writer. Now he
lives in Guadalajara, Mexico, tormented by memories and
dreams of the past. Seventeen years have gone by,
but each day he must live through those events again ....

At the height of his success, Jack and his actress wife, Maeve,
move to her home village of Rathbrack in the west of Ireland.
Very much in love, expecting their first child, and planning
their dream home — their future happiness seems assured.
But the land on which they lay the foundations is not really
theirs to build on, and bizarre and sinister events begin to
occur in the village .... Who are the old beggar Fortycoats and
the incredibly beautiful Áine?

The author of *The Hungry Earth* once again blends
supernatural occurrences and sexual intrigue in a story that
searches out the heart of the Irish condition —
a tale that will linger in your mind long after the last line ....

PB   £6.99   ISBN 0 86327 607 5

WOLFHOUND PRESS
68 Mountjoy Square
Dublin 1
Tel: (+353 1) 874 0354   Fax: (+353 1) 872 0207